D1450517

WARD KENDALL

Read What Others Are Saying About Ward Kendall's

Hold Back This Day

"Kendall is adept at maintaining a suspenseful narrative. As the novel progresses and the stakes rise, it becomes ever more difficult to put the novel down."

Alex Kurtagic, UK writer — Occidental Observer Magazine

"White men may have been rendered completely powerless in this society, but as long as they can still write first-rate fiction they have a voice, and Kendall is such a voice."

H.A. Covington — author of the Northwest Quartet

"I just read your book from cover to cover in only two sit-tings. It was absolutely excellent and incredibly profound; without a doubt, it is in the same league as The Camp of the Saints. As I read your book, I could not but help but think how the the nightmare of World Gov is coming to fruition in our time. You have scared the hell out of me."

Kyle Bristow — attorney and author of *White Apocalypse*

"Hold Back This Day" is surprisingly well written science fiction -- the characters actually act how real people in such a situation would act. This is unlike the typical science fiction story where the characters are often flat and/or unbelievable. Ward Kendall has a good insight into human nature, and it is a welcome change."

Amazon Reader — USA

"I have a particular affinity for the sci-fi books. One of the most popular is Ward Kendall's 2001 "Hold Back This Day," which imagines a future in which the evil all-powerful "World Gov" has forcibly united the population of Earth under one religion and, by way of enforced race-mixing, one uniformly brown-skinned population."

Ian Allen — *The New York Times* – July 30, 2018

Read What Others Are Saying About Ward Kendall's

Eternity Beach

"Eternity Beach tells an incredibly profound and powerfully compelling story of conflict between good and evil—and authentic love and abhorrent hate—which transcends time and space. The complex character development is excellent, and the incredibly adventurous and suspenseful plot is spellbinding. I cannot recommend the book enough. The captivating story is definitely one that stays with the reader long after they set the book down—which is admittedly very hard to do. Between Hold Back This Day and Eternity Beach—and hopefully more to come—Ward Kendall has provided much needed clarity to the present existential threats plaguing the West and has given voice to what must be done because of it in order for the destiny of the Occident to be fulfilled."

Kyle Bristow — attorney and author of *White Apocalypse*

"Abraham, Martin and John—and Adolf—are reincarnated in this epic novel of racial strife and revolution. Like Farmer's *To Your Scattered Bodies Go*, a nebulous alien power has revived humans on a distant planet. Shortly before his death and resurrection, the protagonist wrote a fiery masterpiece which became the spark to set off the White Revolution. This is the latest tour de force by Ward Kendall..."

William M. Knapp — Amazon

"Look out Nobel prize for literature aspirants—the MVP has arrived! If you read only one book this year—by which I mean EVER, let it be Eternity Beach."

Gregory A. Gaston — Amazon

"The story blasts off from page one -- and doesn't let up till the very end!"

George Carver — Amazon

Read What Others Are Saying About Ward Kendall's

The Towers of Eden

"A surprisingly complex novel about race/social class devolution and the ending-of-civilization in 2056. Similar in some ways to another excellent book, Serpent's Walk: the White Resistance leadership are not pure of heart and will sometimes kill simply out of megalomania; the reluctant hero is not at all convinced by the brutal logic of the necessity to take such harsh measures to save western civilization from the unwashed hordes."

William M. Knapp — Amazon

"Thoroughly enjoyed this book. Ward Kendall has a vision, that shows through in his writings. It may be a work of fiction, however it could very well be the future if things don't change."

Deplorable K — Amazon

"Loved the book and when i see something about the advancement of robotics i have wonders about the future even know we have problems of people that could work but refuse to and choose to live off welfare what are we suppose to do we we have all of them plus the one that like to work but there jobs are replaced by robots."

David C. Hill — Amazon

Read What Others Are Saying About Ward Kendall's

BEYOND THIS HORIZON
A WHITE NATIONALIST BLUEPRINT FOR TOMORROW

"I have a particular affinity for the sci-fi books. One of the most popular is Ward Kendall's 2001 "Hold Back This Day," which imagines a future in which the evil all-powerful "World Gov" has forcibly united the population of Earth under one religion and, by way of enforced race-mixing, one uniformly brown-skinned population." - Ian Allen – The New York Times – July 30, 2018

FAST TIMES AT CULTURAL MARXIST HIGH is a work of fiction. Names, characters, places, and incidents are the product of the author's imagination. Any resemblance to actual persons, living or dead, is entirely coincidental.

ISBN-10: 0692193693
ISBN-13: 978-0692193693

Printed in the United States of America
LMP-TX-9-15-18

ALTERNATE
FUTURE
PUBLISHING
2018

WARD KENDALL

"They used to say if man could fly, he'd have wings. But he did fly. He discovered he had to." - Captain James T. Kirk

Fast Times At Cultural Marxist High

WARD KENDALL

CHAPTER 1

"Hey, Hupp! I'm on my way down the hallway so you'd better have the money ya owe me, bitch!"

Andy Hupp ignored the voice and the coarse laughter echoing from down the corridor as he dug through his locker for his English Lit book, along with his homework assignment, due at third period class. Two weeks ago, Mrs. Kump had given her students a choice of reading one of four books: Aldous Huxley's *Brave New World*, Ray Bradbury's *Fahrenheit 451*, William Golding's *Lord of the Flies*, or George Orwell's *1984*. Since Andy had already read all four sometime back around the sixth grade, he did the unexpected: he wrote essays on each one, then sandwiched them neatly into the obligatory folder, per Mrs. Kump's primly executed instructions, ready to turn in.

He did that a lot, much to his teachers' consternation, relentlessly exceeding their expectations when most students did the opposite. He had begun the practice way back around the first grade, just because it came naturally to him, doing more than the teacher required, then quietly sitting back and observing their reaction. And why not? he told himself. He had no trouble doing it, giving more than the teacher expected, preempting any reason to ever turn a woeful eye upon him, as they so often did with other students. Like that time his third grade class was tasked with constructing frontier forts, with the suggestion that a simple cardboard box, a pair of scissors, and some poster paint and marker pens would do the trick. The following week, every student brought in just

13

that—except for him. Instead, his frontier fort was made from carefully selected tree twigs, each one cut and shaped like miniature pine logs and fashioned into fort walls surrounding a collection of interior cabins, replete with people, carts, animals, surrounding scenery, and a detailed report. The other kids were, by turns, astonished by his meticulous handiwork. Then, embarrassed by their own pathetic efforts, they became sullen with accusations that he had not actually made the fort himself, but instead accused him of being a dirty little liar if he insisted otherwise.

Which he did.

Ultimately, it took a signed note from his parents to set the record straight, stating that Andy had indeed made the fort, piece by careful piece. In fact, the note went on, Andy had refused to allow his father or mother to assist him, threatening not to do the class assignment at all, "if we so much as laid one finger on it," the Hupps explained. "And he meant it too," his mother elaborated, "You see, our Andy's a very serious little boy. With very serious intelligence and abilities. And with him you can count on one thing: if there's a way to overcome an obstacle, our Andy will find a way..."

And though Mr. and Mrs. Hupp had not meant it as a warning, somehow Andy felt it had come out that way. But then, perhaps, it was simply a sign of his parents' resignation, having learned early on that their son was a very self-reliant little boy. Thereafter, every new school year his teachers learned that as well: Andy Hupp was *indeed* a very serious boy...

"Hey Hupp, did ya hear me ya pussy! Ya better have that fucking money ya owe me!" came another bellowed warning, this time much closer, followed by more bouts of raucous, snickering laughter.

Andy Hupp calmly shut his locker door and turned to join the flow of students headed for class just as Tony Scarletti and three other seniors ambled up, rocking and jostling against each other like certain high school boys are wont to do, the kind all thick in the shoulders and neck and cocksure of themselves, much like the burly herds of beef cattle that roamed not far beyond the walls of Titanis High, out there across a million rolling acres of Texas Hill Country.

"Hey, Hupp. Ya hard a hearing?" Tony said, blocking his path. "I said, where the fuck's my money, bitch?"

Andy Hupp took in a thoughtful breath then slowly released it, even as he eyed the big white youth with the lumpy reddish dreadlocks dangling down the sides of his head like moldy, unburied dog turds. He might have been a handsome kid, except for the Rastafarian hair and the pronounced slouch of his mouth, which seemed unable to hold a horizontal line across the lower half of his face, listing instead to one side in a permanent leer. On a senior citizen it might have been evidence of a recent stroke; but on Tony Scarletti, Andy realized, it was nothing more than a sign of his being a dumb fuck. His eyes were his worst feature, however: like two small, coppery BB's shot into the thick dough of his face, dull and stupid looking.

Andy Hupp held Tony Scarletti's vapid stare for a moment, then shifted an eye to his three leering companions; like Scarletti, all played on the high school football team. He knew each of them, alright, at least by name. Most kids at Titanis High did. First there was Brodie Henshaw, the other white kid comprising this four-pack of trouble, perhaps the smartest one of the bunch, though that wasn't saying much. Same thick neck, same loutish face. The kind high school football coaches adored. And to Scarletti's left stood Jamal Perkins, the biggest of the four, built like a 300 pound sack of dog shit except this sack had a Chevy engine block stuffed into the middle of the shit.

Rock hard, Perkins was Titanis High's star linebacker. Eyes as black as his skin, they had a peculiarly sweet cast to them, almost a twinkle, thus earning him the campus nickname of Twinkle Toes Perkins. One could imagine him playing the role of black cupid in some ghetto stage production in Harlem. And next to him lurked Carlos "T-Bone"

Ramirez, a thick chunk of a Mexican much bigger than his kind usually got. Wearing a greasy smile, his mestizo face would have looked more appropriate carved into an Aztec sacrificial alter in 14th century Tenochtitlán rather than strutting about an upscale American high school. But between him and Jamal, Andy Hupp's creep-o-meter was going off the scale, even as he made an attempt to pass.

"Not without payin' up, dickhead," Scarletti said, shoving the flat of his hand against Hupp's chest and pushing him up against the lockers.

Andy decided to try reason: "You're mistaken. I never borrowed any money from you so I don't owe you a thing."

"Ya just don't seem to get it, ya little fuck. You're my flavor of the week, see? It works like this. I look around. I choose some pussy like you. Then you pay up. Now do ya get it, fuckwad? So dig out some bingo money for me and my bros and maybe we'll let ya pass." He leaned in close and whispered, his breath foul as a locker room floor. "I mean, a pussy like you don't want to be late for class, does he?"

"Bingo money? Sure," Andy said, clutching his books under one arm as he reached down and unzipped his pants. "But first you got to earn it."

"Oh, *monnnn*," T-Bone chortled. "Looks like the punk wants you to suck for your buck, Tony."

Jamal Perkins laughed too. High and shrill, like a hyena. "Suck for his buck? Hot damn, nigga! Gotta remember that one, homie! Suck for his buck! Sheeeeit! That was low, Ramirez, even for a wetback." They high-fived each other, hysterical with laughter.

Tony Scarletti's eyes flared and his face grew red as he focused on Hupp again. "You're dead now, motherfucker."

From somewhere down the corridor a shrill voice sounded: Mrs. Kump, standing outside the doorway of her classroom, hands folded neatly below her waist. She had observed the attempted shake-down of Andy Hupp, having noticed the gang surrounding him. "Boys! *BOYS!*" she shouted.

Ignoring the dried up bitch, as most of her students thought of her, Tony continued to glare at Andy. Besides, ignoring teachers was SOP—standard operating procedure—in today's modern high school.

"Hear me, Hupp? You're dead. If not today, soon. Got it, fuckface?" He turned to leave.

"Wait a minute," Andy called out. "Where do you think you're going?"

"Huh?" the big football player said, unable to believe Hupp still dared to address him even as he turned back around, only to see a dollar bill held up in front of his eyes, with Andy Hupp casually nodding downward at his unzipped pants.

"You forgot to earn your buck," Andy reminded.

Jamal and T-Bone exploded with laughter, punching each other's shoulders again as they executed another high-five. Only Brodie Henshaw remained neutral, eyeing Andy like he was a being from another planet. The kid had guts, no doubt about it. But Tony was sure to mess him up for that crack. A lot of kids, Brodie knew, regretted lipping off to him; the parking lot was littered with their teeth. And Hupp had not only crossed the line, he'd even set up a toll booth.

Tony Scarletti leaned in and cracked his knuckles one inch from Andy's face. "Ya must be hungry ya little pussy. Hungry for a piece of knuckle baloney sandwiched between two slices of knock-your-fuckin-face-against-that-locker. Because it's smartass motherfuckers like you always get beat up real bad after school. It's like...like—" he started to say, struggling to find the right expression.

"A tradition?" Andy offered, in the tone a teacher to a mentally defective student. As he knew it would, sudden derision cut the air like a rusty buzz saw—only it wasn't directed at him.

"Oh, Holy Mother of Jeeesus!" Ramirez gurgled with mirth. "Didja hear that, Jamal? First he's telling Tony to suck for his buck and now the punk is teaching him how to speak English! Oh, *monnnn*! I'm Mexican and even I speak better

English than you, Tony."

Tony Scarletti whipped his dreadlocked head around and snarled: "Shut your fucking trap, wetback! You speak best when you're down on your greasy knees picking lettuce in my daddy's fields or with Jamal's big black nigger cock shoved down your throat!"

T-Bone lunged toward Titanis High's star quarterback and shoved him hard across the aisle and up against the lockers on the opposite wall. "I don't take no shit from no dago homo like you, gringo motherfucker! You're just mad cuz the punk made you out a faggot–*faggot!*"

Andy Hupp didn't laugh.

He didn't even grin.

He just straightened the collar of his two hundred dollar leather jacket and proceeded on down the hallway, even as Tony Scarletti and T-Bone Ramirez tussled against the lockers, with Brodie and Jamal beating it out of there at Warp 9 headed in opposite directions.

No wonder, Andy thought: Principal Meevers was coming down the hallway. Earlier, Mrs. Kump must have summoned him on the classroom intercom system the instant she spotted trouble brewing. "Hurry, Andy!" she urged, ushering him through the doorway into the classroom. "You had nothing to do with that! I'll let Principal Meevers know, don't you worry."

Nothing to do with it?

Oh yeah I did, Andy thought, not worried one bit. He had rather enjoyed tangling with someone of Tony Scarletti's stature. Sure, he was an asshole. But a well-known Titanis High asshole. A celebrity, even, if a small town star quarterback from Bumfuck, Texas, thirty two miles northwest of Austin, could be considered such.

Once inside Mrs. Kump's class, Andy Hupp headed for his seat, third row over, sixth desk back, next to his best friend, TJ Sully. As he did, TJ motioned abruptly toward a spot below Andy's belt line.

Puzzled, Andy glanced down.

Uh-oh.

His zipper.

Still wide open—with a conspicuous patch of black-striped, gray-colored Mann Hunt briefs showing through. Without breaking stride, Andy deftly reached down and rezipped, even as he slid skillfully into his seat in one fluid motion. As he did, he caught a split-second glimpse of Lyla Van der Velden averting her bewitching emerald green eyes, her long mane of deep reddish-orange hair undulating down her back as she quickly turned front and center again, evidence that she had been observing him with interest.

Lyla Van der Velden...

Truth be told, she took his breath away.

All in all, certainly an interesting start for the day, Andy Hupp mused, settling comfortably into his seat. No more had third period come around than he'd offered Titanis High's hunky quarterback a buck for a suck, then got caught with his zipper down, black-striped underwear and all, by no less than Lyla Van der Velden two rows over, one of the prettiest girls in school.

"Class," Mrs. Kump said, holding her chin high, "time to turn in your essays on the author of your choice. And that means you too, Charlie Spitzmeier."

As several groans went up around the room, coming from several students who had failed to remember that today was the deadline, Andy Hupp, aged seventeen, passed his gray-foldered report forward, in the manner of a top-flight executive presenting a business proposal.

To his left, in row four, TJ Sully whispered: "Don't tell me, Hupp—you wrote essays on all four books."

"How'd you guess?"

"That folder you just passed forward looked a little thick, amigo."

Hupp casually shrugged, as if to dismiss the notion.

"What was that all about out in the hallway?"

"Oh, that. Just Tony Scarletti asking to borrow some money."

"Yeah, right," TJ smirked. "He borrows money like Jack the Ripper gives neck massages."

"I offered him a buck."

"A buck?"

"For a suck."

TJ leaned back in his seat and stifled a groan. "Don't tell me you actually said that to him."

"More or less."

"Jesus Christ, Hupp. He'll kill you for certain."

"Yeah, I did get that impression."

"What are you going to do?"

"Not sure. But I've got between now and lunchtime to figure it out."

"Class!" Mrs. Kump said, holding up a gray folder.

"That's yours!" TJ hissed.

"Just my lucky day, I guess."

"Class," Mrs. Kump reiterated, "this student's homework assignment just came to my attention. What can I say? I hold in my hands a compilation of not one, but four essays. And after a cursory glance, I must say they're all stunningly written."

"Oh, Lord, please spare me," T.J whispered from across the aisle, "Don't tell me I just heard her say 'stunningly'."

"Yes, I think you did," Andy Hupp whispered back.

"Then it's true. You did it again, Hupp."

"I'm afraid so."

"Star student strikes again."

"Just my fate, I guess."

"And what is so interesting down your way, Mr. Sully?"

"Oh. Oh...uhhhh....nothing, Mrs. Kump."

"Very well. Then perhaps you won't mind coming forward and reading Mr. Hupp's essay on William Golding's *Lord of the Flies* to the class."

This time, Andy Hupp could barely contain his laughter.

CHAPTER 2

For some reason the sound of the school bell marking the end of a class period always reminded Andy Hupp of the harsh trill of a prison bell, with he and his fellow students just a mob of sweaty convicts trapped inside some imaginary 1940's prison movie.

He had watched plenty of them, to be sure, there on his 30" computer monitor while surfing old movies on YouTube. And what he viewed often served as a sort of Rosetta Stone for translating the everyday happenings in his teenage life. Like right now—because there in the cavernous main corridor that ran the length of Titanis High stood Principal Budd Meevers, whom Andy thought of as both prison warden (like now) and at other times as the captain of a German U-boat prowling stormy seas in search of enemy students to torpedo.

"Andy, over here," Principal Meevers summoned.

Sensing his best friend TJ Sully slinking away, Andy reached out an arm and snagged him by the jacket before he'd taken half a step.

"What are best friends for but times like these," Andy whispered out of the corner of his mouth as they went forward to meet Principal Meevers.

"Remind me again sometime," TJ whispered back. "In the meantime let's just say I'm allergic to principals."

Obediently, they walked over to where their principal stood, on the opposite side of the wide corridor, all smiles and scholarly warmth, his arms neatly folded across his chest. Andy had to give it to old Meevers, though. He really did do his best to be Mr. Sunshine at times. Sure, he was also the school's designated, state-appointed prison warden and ever-prowling U-boat captain—with Andy and his best friend just two more hardened lifers (or so it seemed) under his jurisdiction. Even so, Budd 'Eager Meevers' Meevers also did a fair job of making their sentences as bearable as possible.

Actually, Andy Hupp kinda liked Budd Meevers.

In a tight squeeze he had been known for cutting him some serious slack, even though little escaped his 'Father Knows Best' eyes. For one thing, he let a lot of things slide that your average high school principal would have drooled over, seeking good cause to expel you.

And not because he was a wimp, either.

At six foot three, Budd Meevers was a fairly big man, athletic in a Saturday-afternoon-game-of-tennis sort of way, and bigger than even Tony Scarletti, small town football hero, resident star jock, borderline rapist (according to half a dozen girls) and all-around champion asshole.

"How you boys doing?" Principal Meevers greeted in that disarming way he had, one shoulder propped nonchalantly against the colorful bank of student lockers; all new, pure 21st century high-tech lockers, made from hardened polyethylene plastic and molded in sleek lines, then colored in an alternating mix of gay-boy lime, queer purple, and banana faggot yellow (as some students described them) befitting of the madhouse atmosphere of a modern stab-your-teacher-in-the-hallway, shoot-up-the-cafeteria with a Mac-10, American high school, Andy thought.

"We're doing fine," TJ cautiously offered.

"Good. Good," Meevers drawled, in a smooth, down home Texas accent, although he was not native born. Reflectively, he shifted his eyes to the taller of the two boys—Andy Hupp. A good-looking kid, Meevers thought; hair thick and golden-brown, although a bit unruly, befitting his character as one of the school's more notable iconoclasts. Girls certainly found him quite attractive, Meevers knew—except, perhaps, for his somewhat brainy persona, which seemed to radiate from his self-assured forest-green eyes. Odd combination: good-looks, brains, and rebelliousness–which caused cognitive dissonance in some.

Then again, Budd Meevers well remembered his own long ago school days, having fit the same mold. For in some ways Andy Hupp reminded him of himself. Maybe that's why he'd gone easy on him last year, when he and his sidekick TJ (Thomas Jefferson) Sully were caught red-handed running across the high school gymnasium roof with a Remington 12 gauge shotgun and a 9 mm Glock, in broad daylight, half the student body watching gape-mouthed from their classroom windows. Fortunately the guns hadn't been loaded, although Ms Pickering, one of the school's social studies teachers, had demanded a Swat team from nearby Austin be called in–a request that Meevers' had wisely chosen to ignore.

As it turned out, Andy Hupp, TJ Sully, and several other students were involved in making another 'Hupp Film Productions' movie, using the school as one of their locales. A serious production too, by student standards, judging by the ten thousand dollar AJA Cion 4K/UHD Camera (where the hell did students get that kind of money nowadays, anyway?) far more expensive than owned by the school's film department. And just like his straight-A school work, Andy Hupp was into some serious student filmmaking, honing his skills with each passing day, if in a troublesome sort of way. Along with TJ Sully, himself a talented writer, they were a pair not to be taken lightly, Meevers concluded.

And they were damn lucky for that, he concluded, or else he would've brought them up on criminal charges for having brought real firearms onto school property. Instead, he took them to his office after ordering them down from the rooftop using a bullhorn; probably the most dramatic day the school had seen in years. And the one kid most responsible for that day of drama now stood before him–once again.

"Heard you had some trouble with Tony Scarletti earlier,"

Principal Meevers began, as students continued to rush to and fro down the hallway past them.

"Yes, sir," Andy answered. He found that respectful behavior always worked best in situations like this. No sullen teenage rebellion for him. No brooding looks. He knew how to work the system.

"What was it all about?"

"Just a discussion," Andy offered, vaguely.

Budd Meevers smiled, his face full of patience. "Over what, Andy?"

"He just wanted to borrow some money."

Meevers cocked an eyebrow. "Borrow?"

Andy grew quiet, as if mentally dissecting all the permutations of the word.

"Or extort?" Meevers gently suggested, still with a friendly smile on his face.

Andy remained silent. Other students, standing nearby as they fiddled in their lockers, as if searching for the lost city of *El Dorado* or maybe a missing bag of potato chips leftover from yesterday's lunch—when Andy knew very well they were actually hoping to hear him rat out Tony Scarletti, which would get back to the high school jock at somewhere approximating four times the speed of light.

Sensing the reason for Andy's hesitation, Budd Meevers glanced over at TJ Sully. Same age, a few inches shorter, nice looking too, but in a more impish way. Maybe it was the spattering of freckles across the bridge of his nose, or those guileless gray eyes, which only served to conceal a cunning and perceptive mind. No doubt about it. He was dealing with two sharp cookies here. All innocent looking, but more was at play. Innocent enough when the heat was on. But turn your back for an instant and they could morph into gun-toting teenagers darting across high school rooftops, given half a chance.

"I offered him a buck," Andy finally said, truthfully, hoping that would be the end of it.

Yeah, right, TJ thought. A buck—for a suck.

"Did he take it?" Meevers asked.

"He decided not to."

"That's a first," Titanis High's principal said, well aware of Scarletti's reputation for randomly shaking down students to sustain his cash flow.

"Okay," Meevers said, "just wanted to get the facts straight. Better hurry along now. Wouldn't want to keep you boys from your next class."

"Anytime, Mr. Meevers," Andy said.

Meevers smile brightened a few watts, telling the boys he knew all about bullshitting and that nobody ever bullshitted him.

"Oh, one other thing..."

There it was, Andy thought.

A favorite tactic of certain high school U-boat captains. First let the enemy student go, then pull him back at the last instant. The old 'one other thing' tactic of high school submarine warfare, he knew.

Simple, but effective.

Andy paused and turned. As he did, Principal Meevers pushed away from the row of lockers, exposing Tony Scarletti's lime green locker door. "Know anything about this, Andy?" Across it, in thick black marker pen, somebody had scrawled:

Tony Scarletti will suck for a buck.
Just ask Andy Hupp.

Andy Hupp glanced at his best friend, one eyebrow raised in puzzlement. Sully returned the raised eyebrow, then both looked innocently at Budd Meevers.

"No, sir," Andy said.

"No, sir," TJ echoed.

"Tell me again how much money you offered to loan Scarletti?"

"A dollar," Andy said.

Meevers tapped the knuckle of a hand against the scrawl. "I thought you said earlier it was a 'buck'."

This time, Andy couldn't help but grin.

Torpedo number one had struck.

"Did I?"

Meevers gave both boys a once-over with his eyes. "You're both playing with fire when it comes to Tony Scarletti and his bunch. Other students have already seen this, and though I know you didn't write it, Andy, Tony Scarletti won't believe otherwise." He glanced pointedly at TJ. "As Andy's friend, you'll be a target too. And though I might be able to protect you while you're on campus, I won't be able to once you leave the premises. Do you both understand?"

Both boys looked at each other, then back to Meevers.

"We'll watch our backs, sir."

"Best you do."

And with that, Principal Meevers squeezed Andy's shoulder in friendly departure, then passed on down the corridor. A moment later, swallowed in a churning stream of students, he was gone.

At twelve o'clock lunch bell, Andy Hupp rose out of his History 101 seat as if suddenly summoned to the underground slaughterhouse of the Morlocks, along with all the other hapless Eloi of Titanis High. Filing out like Weena and her fellow drones, he was immersed in a tide of students seconds later, all anxious to stuff their faces inside the cavernous high school cafeteria, or roar off in muscle cars to nearby fast food hangouts located in the central part of Titanisville, population eight thousand three hundred and twenty-five, give or take.

Andy usually ate in the cafeteria, however.

And not for lack of a vehicle or money, either.

For what nobody in Titanis High knew, except for TJ Sully, was that he made some pretty decent pocket change working as a part-time commercial fashion model, selling his photogenic face in magazine ads via an Austin modeling agency with serious New York and London contacts. Starting at age sixteen, his face had since appeared in dozens of magazines as far away as Japan, with stops along the way in Paris, Johannesburg, and Sydney, not to mention all across the USA. For that, he had his mother to thank, having maneuvered him into the lucrative business via contacts she had made as a former model herself, and later on as head of the cosmetic department of Austin's most prestigious upscale department store, where she continued to network with many of the agencies she had once worked for.

At first, Andy had ignored his mother's hints suggesting he should try his hand at modeling, considering it just one step away from dropping his pants inside one of San Francisco's gay bathhouses. But he had dreams of working as an independent filmmaker one day, and eventually saw his mother's contacts in the lucrative modeling industry as a golden opportunity to finance those dreams...

Not to mention quit his fast-food job.

So when opportunity knocked...

He took a very deep breath—and answered.

So he was certainly one teen flush with ample cash, and could have easily offered more than a buck for a suck to that asshole Scarletti. Instead, he had invested some of his modeling earnings into a late model vehicle, although it sure as hell wasn't a muscle car or any other kind of babe magnet, much to the regret of three different girls he had dated. Still, his late model Mercedes-Benz cargo van was sleek and silver and totally cool, with the words Hupp Film Productions enameled in black along both sides. For truth be told, the town of Titanisville, Texas had never seen any teenager quite like Andy.

"Hey, Hupp!" someone called out as Andy rounded a corner and proceeded down another corridor, "Heard you got a new nick name around school!"

Whoever the voice belonged to, it was just one of many who knew his name, but whom in return he knew not a fucking thing.

The price of fame, he guessed.

"One Buck Andy!" someone else shouted. "That's what they're calling you now! Wait 'til Tony Scarletti hears!"

Like he hadn't already? Andy thought, cutting left and heading down another corridor toward the high school cafeteria.

"Hi, Andy!" some girl cried out. A smile, a flash of teeth, and then gone. Cute, too. Oh Lord, give me strength. Still, nice to know you're wanted, he mused, moving along at a swift clip.

"There he goes! One Buck Andy!" another kid cried out.

Oh boy. It was worse than he thought.

Especially in a high school with over a thousand kids, half bussed in from surrounding towns, it was lining up fast to be another Charlton Heston, "It's a madhouse! A madhouse!" kinda day.

In some parts of Titanis High the penitentiary/submarine vibe morphed into the surface of an alien planet, especially when entering the massive cafeteria, with its skylight-illuminated ceilings, indoor palms, and futuristically-painted walls interspersed with abstract chrome designs. He could well imagine Captain Kirk sitting at one of the dozens of round tables, with Spock and McCoy faithfully at his side. And so whenever he wanted to let TJ know where to meet him if others were listening in, he'd simply say the agreed upon euphemism: 'Talos IV'.

Yeah, kinda quirky.

Definitely geeky.

But then, Andy Hupp was kinda both.

Good-looking, smart, but definitely a bit weird.

"There he is! 'One Buck For A Suck' Hupp!" came another jeering cry.

Jesus, Andy thought. Who needed Samuel Morse and his telegraph when you had these morons around?

"Hey, dude!" a popular kid named Wade Muhlhauser called out as Andy passed his table, where he was holding court with his own loyal fans. "That was pretty cool what you wrote across Scarletti's locker door, bro! Suicidal—but totally cool!"

"I didn't write it," Andy called out in passing.

"Ain't what Scarletti believes!"

Well, there you have it, he thought.

More reason for the Italian Stallion to beat the shit out of him after school.

A moment later Andy Hupp melted into the lunch line. Already, dozens of students were ahead of him, but it was moving along at a pretty good clip so he had no worries. Nothing hick town about this cafeteria, however, considering it had been designed by one of Houston's top architectural firms. In both manner and style it mimicked a modern food court, much like one would see in any upscale suburban mall in Dallas or Los Angeles—with glass displays offering a surprising array of menu items, all dished up à la carte by smartly-uniformed kitchen staff. As such, the sleek modernity created a stylish atmosphere any hipster would've felt proud setting his metrosexual ass down.

Just one of the benefits of living in a small town populated mostly by affluent professionals, Andy Hupp realized; professionals who worked at many of the high-tech firms, insurance companies, computer manufacturers, and academic institutions located in nearby Austin, thirty-five miles away. They commuted for the money, but claimed it was 'the country air' and 'good schools' that made them choose Titanisville to live.

But Andy Hupp knew better.

And they did too.

Because even though Titanisville was largely crime free, offering a variety of amenities, a nearby lake, rolling, oak-studded countryside, and an exclusive country club, none of these facts were the primary reason most chose to live here. The real reason was simply not mentioned, but nonetheless hung in the air like a bit of dandelion fluff: the fact that Titanisville was 98% *white*.

Proof of that existed just by a quick glance around the cafeteria, Andy could see. He figured no more than 2% of the kids he saw were non-white. And those few were only here because of the low-income housing development that had gone up on the edge of town a year and a half ago. 'Unity Gardens', it was called, a government-funded project that Austin social reformer Dr. Rothman Adler had been instrumental in getting built. The town council had largely opposed his self-proclaimed 'enrichment' proposal, but after Adler made clear the Feds would likely cut off federal funding to maintain the nice lake and park surrounding the town if they did not accede, the council immediately became more agreeable. As a result, rumor had it that Dr. Adler had high-level contacts in Washington DC; however, nothing was ever proven...

So the council gave in.

As it stood, both Jamal Perkins and T-Bone Ramirez lived in Unity Gardens, which apparently had very little in the way of either. So far, there had already been three stabbings and one shooting at the complex. Discussing it one night at the dinner table, Andy's father had simply shrugged.

Of late he did that a lot.

Shrugged.

Like he had other things on his mind.

Troubling things...

"It's just a few incidents, Cynthia," he had remarked to Andy's mother, dismissively.

On her part, she did not shrug.

She just looked off in silence.

In recent months, Andy seldom knew anymore what she was thinking.

As for 'incidents' that too was a euphemism, just like 'country air' meant no blacks or Mexicans—or as close to that ideal that money could buy...

"Hey, hey, hey! It's the Hupp, Hupp, Huppster!" the nasal voice of Lawrence Micklethwaite called out. "Word's going around school that you told The Great Scarletti to suck you off! And yet—here you are, still walking around!"

Andy had just paid for his lunch and was en route to his usual table when Micklethwaite's obnoxious voice cut through the background chatter of the cafeteria like a rusty chainsaw. Tall, thin, with wiry, pale-blond hair, it was widely accepted that he had the richest parents in town. The emaciated youth seemed to find anything and everything amusing, even last year's terror attack in Houston, where eighteen people were butchered by three recent Somalian 'refugees'. "At least they weren't on welfare!" Lawrence had blurted out in Social Studies class, much to Ms Pickering's consternation. And then he had burst out in that annoying hack that few would have mistaken for laughter, even though that's exactly what it was.

"That wasn't me," Andy glibly shot back, "Don't tell anyone, but it was Jamal Perkins who said it."

"No shit? Ol' Twinkle Toes Muh Dick?"

And then Lawrence Micklethwaite forgot all about Andy Hupp as he busied himself relaying this latest bit of high school gossip, "Didja hear that, everyone? Hupp just let it slip that it was actually Jamal Perkins who offered Tony Scarletti a buck for a suck! Kick me before I puke!"

Vicious laughter rippled behind Andy as he made for his table. Well, well, he thought. Titanis High's telegraph was in full overload. And because of his insinuation about Jamal Perkins, he was now probably dead twice over. Still, it had been worth it.

With that new twist added to his hallway encounter with Tony Scarletti, Andy Hupp steered toward his table with his tray of food, where his faithful pal and fellow teenage movie mogul TJ Sully awaited.

Right there.
Sitting next to a pretty girl he didn't know...

CHAPTER 3

"Hey, Andy," TJ nonchalantly greeted, as Andy swung into a chair at the large round table they typically commandeered.

"Hey, TJ," Andy returned, darting a quick eye at the girl next to him, his way of asking who she was.

"This is my new friend Jeena," TJ introduced. "Remember? The one I told you about from drama class." He shot a shy glance in her direction, one that Andy didn't fail to notice. "I sort of asked her to have lunch with us."

"Finally got up the courage, eh? " Andy jibed, knowing his friend's shyness with girls.

As he settled in and proceeded to arrange his lunch items in preparation for the attack, he took in the new addition to their table. Not with a full blown, check-her-titties-out look, like Tony Scarletti might have done. Just with his peripheral vision, of which he was a master; non-intrusive, he liked to call it. Like a reconnaissance mission behind enemy lines, cruising over hilly terrain.

"Hi," Jeena said, her girl vibes turned on full as she in turn checked out Andy Hupp. "And that's Jeena with a 'J' by the way. And double 'e's."

Andy nodded.

He liked that.

Most girls would've left you believing their name was spelled 'Gina', as in Lollobrigida. An imprecise conveyance of information, he chose to call it. Something his well-ordered mind wouldn't have liked.

As such, her response might be a potential sign of logical thought processes. Amazing, considering she was female. If so, there might be order in the universe after all.

Plus one for Jeena.

That established, *now* he could check out her titties.

"Unusual spelling," Andy casually murmured, cracking open his bottle of Texsun brand orange juice as he casually swept his eyes over the targeted area. Not bad, he thought. Not bad at all. TJ certainly knew how to pick the ripe ones.

"Like, my mother's into really weird spellings."

"Oh?"

"Take my little brother. She spells his name 'K-r-i-s-t-o-f-e-r. Kristofer.'"

"Phonetic spelling," Andy remarked. "Not so weird, since English is a fluid language, and there is a gradual trend toward such spellings. For instance, last time I checked, Spee-D-Burger had a little sign out front just as you enter that says, 'Drive Thru' with an 'ru' rather than 'Drive Through' with an 'ough'. That's just one example that is used everywhere nowadays."

Jeena turned toward TJ. "You were right."

"I told you so," the freckled-faced boy acknowledged.

They both turned toward Andy, all smiles, as if they had just received A-pluses on their term papers.

"What?" Andy said, taking a long swig of juice.

"TJ said you were a college professor trapped inside a seventeen year old's body."

Andy Hupp considered that as he reached for his Tequila Lime grilled chicken club sandwich with guacamole and roasted green peppers and took a contemplative bite. "TJ's right," he said over a mouthful, "and that's why I chose him for a friend and business partner."

They both laughed.

"And arrogant too!" Jeena piped.

"Just like I told you," TJ confirmed. "Hupp's intolerable at times. Just ask any of his teachers, going all the way back to kindergarten. But just the kind of personality we need to make Hupp Film Productions a success."

"You two really are serious, aren't you?" Jeena said, looking from one boy to the other.

"Dead," Andy confirmed, as he looked at her from over the top of his upraised sandwich.

"Take George Lucas, for instance," Sully pointed out, getting a little excited as he took a bite out of his own sandwich, a bacon cheeseburger topped with an onion ring; he hardly ever bought anything else. "He was a college student only a few years older than us when he made a student film that helped launch his career."

"You mean the *Star Wars* guy?" Jeena queried.

Good sign, Andy thought. She knew who Lucas was.

"The same," Andy acknowledged, "although the student film that launched his career was a piece of shit. He called it *Electronic Labyrinth: THX 1138 4EB* if you can believe it. Check it out on YouTube."

"Wow. He cusses too!" Jeena said, teasingly.

"Yeah, sometimes," Andy admitted. "But generally I don't use scatological words." He picked up another seasoned fry followed by another bite of chicken sandwich. "Especially when I'm eating."

"Scatta-*what?*" Jeena echoed.

"Words that mean 'shit'," TJ offered matter-of-factly, munching down a potato chip.

"You guys talk like this all the time?" Jeena asked, reaching for the other half of her tuna sandwich. "Like you're big shot movie execs or something?'

"Only when we like to mess with girls," Andy said, grinning.

"I figured as much!"

They all laughed.

Which went unnoticed in the great cavernous room, now brimming with several hundred chattering high school students seated around dozens of identical round tables, all suffused in shimmering pools of purple, green, blue, and orange radiance filtering down through randomly scattered, multi-colored skylights. The Houston architects had wanted to create a festive atmosphere during lunchtime, and they had certainly succeeded. Titanis High's cafeteria was a textbook example of cutting-edge, 'teenage rad', replete with eye-catching neon-tubing running along the walls and other strategic places—an added decorative expense indicative of the town's overall commitment of offering their students the very best.

Considering the median household income was somewhere around fifty thousand, well above the national average, the tax base could easily support such frivolous touches, Andy knew. As it stood, Titanisville today was what America as a whole had once been: mostly white, middle class, and prosperous. There weren't many places left like it, but this was a fact lost on Titanis High's students, most of whom were too busy chasing self-centered pursuits to contemplate the troubled rumblings of social decay growing just beyond their town's borders.

For another ten minutes Andy, TJ, and Jeena chattered on amicably about nothing in particular while Andy scribbled cryptically in his tan folder, interspersed with cryptic jottings and arcane sketches that neither of his two lunch partners could discern. Then out of the blue Andy Hupp looked up and asked the girl her last name, his pen poised.

"Kirtland," Jeena replied, a little suspiciously. "First name, Jeena. Middle name, Nancy. Last name, Kirtland. Jeena Nancy Kirtland. Okay? And just for the record my mom still calls me Jinky."

Both boys looked at her, then at each other.

"*Jinky?*" TJ echoed.

"Well, just in case you're planning on writing my life story down in that notebook," she said, looking pointedly at Andy. "Just so you know, it was my mom's pet name for me when I was little. And she kept it ever since. You see, she took the 'J' of my first name and the 'N' of my middle name and the 'K' of my last name, then added a 'Y' on the end and respelled it 'Jinky' just to make it sound cute."

Both boys stared at her, as if at a never before seen phenomenon.

"Well! I told you my mom was into weird spellings!"

"I like it," Andy finally said, after a moment of stunned silence. "It's straight out of an F. Scott Fitzgerald novel. Or better yet Charles Dickens."

"Or maybe even *Gilligan's Island*," TJ quipped, which earned him a quick reprimand on the arm.

"Ouch," he said.

"You deserved it," she said primly. "For being a smart ass."

Andy looked down and scribbled something else in his notebook.

"Now what are you doing?" Jeena asked, eyeing him suspiciously.

"Adding you to our production list."

"Production *what?*"

"You're in drama, right? And Hupp Film Productions is looking for acting talent. So I added you to our production roster," he explained, adding: "Jinky." And from that point on that's what the boys decided to call her.

"Hold on a minute you two. I don't know anything about acting in front of a camera," she countered, now resigned to being called by her childhood nickname.

"Don't worry, Jink. It's not too much different from stage acting," Andy assured. "And with the right director–me–you'll do just fine."

She turned to TJ: "So that's why you invited me to lunch."

"That...and two other reasons," Andy mumbled under his breath, scribbling more notes.

"What two other rea–?"

Involuntarily both boys glanced in the direction of Jinky Kirtland's ample breasts then quickly averted their eyes, except that TJ was a split second too slow.

"Oh! Now I get it! *These* two other reasons! I should have known TJ!" And then she laughed, in quite an attractive way, causing Andy Hupp to once again scribble something down in his production notebook.

Then he looked up: "I can usually spot acting talent when I talk to someone, Jink. And I think you'll do just fine in front of a camera. You've a nice quirky touch that I like."

"She's the best actress in Mr. Whippendell's fifth period drama class," TJ confirmed.

"Thank you, TJ. That remark just earned you a second date."

"Way to go, dude," Andy said.

"You mean this was a first date?" TJ said, looking around stupidly.

"You betcha," she answered. "And you passed."

On hearing that TJ leaned back in his chair, hands clasped behind his head, beaming like Mr. Stud.

And Andy Hupp, smiling, made yet another note, this time regarding his best friend.

"Oh, wait!" Jinky cried. "We've got try outs after school today. You know, for *The Crucible.* And I've absolutely got to play the part of 'Abigail Williams'. It's just what I need to add to my résumé before I start my theater arts major at Texas State University next year."

"Don't worry," TJ assured. "It's a cinch you'll get the role. I mean, there's no way Mr. Whippendell could choose anyone else."

"Maybe," Jinky said, a little uncertainly, for there was a note of concern in her voice. "After all, this is the only play of the school year, and it's going to be a really big production. And Mr. Whippendell said there's going to be open try outs, remember? That means anybody in school can audition for the play, not just students in Mr. Whippendell's first, third, and fifth period drama classes."

"Shit," TJ said, "everybody knows you're the most talented actress in school, Jinky. I mean, didn't you tell me you've already had starring roles in five or six plays? You know, before transferring to Titanis High last year?"

"Well, if you count middle school it's been eight. Let's see now...I played 'Abby Brewster' in *Arsenic & Old Lace* in seventh grade, then 'Viola' in *Twelfth Night* and Bunny Flingus in *House of Blue Leaves* in eighth, and then there was 'Laurey' in *Oklahoma* in ninth, where I got to sing. That was back when I lived in Tulsa, by the way. They really love that play there as you can probably guess. And then a student-written play called *Body Parts* in tenth, in which I played 'Tammy', a dead student who comes back to life, which bombed pretty badly, by the way. So I really shouldn't mention it. And then last year's production of *Who's Afraid of Virginia Woolf?* in which I got to play 'Martha', a middle-aged hag that's totally unlike me."

"I tried out for that play," TJ recalled. "But only because you were in it, Jink."

"I remember! Although I hardly knew you then. Didn't you try out for the role of 'Nick'?"

"Yeah, I think that was it."

"Well, you should've gotten it, because you're a much better actor than the jerk who did. And he only got it because of two reasons: one, because everybody knows Mr. Whippendell's gay and two, because the student he gave it too had more muscles than you."

"Gee, thanks," TJ said, looking glum. "Guess I better go home and start lifting some weights before I collapse like a wet noodle."

"Muscles aren't everything," Andy Hupp remarked. "Brains are your territory, amigo."

"So you're calling me an anemic loser too?" TJ said, but there was a big, self-mocking grin on his face, and they all laughed.

"A very cute, freckled-face loser," Jinky said, her eyes sparkling.

Oh boy, Andy thought. Given any more looks like that,

and TJ's gonna fall for this girl big time.

"Well, guys," Andy interjected, tapping his pen against his notebook, "this meeting of Hupp Film Productions is officially underway, just so you know."

Jinky Kirtland leaned forward. "Before we go any further didn't you two get in serious trouble last year making some kinda movie right here at school?"

Andy leaned forward in turn, a lock of thick, unruly hair falling over one eye. Jinky thought it made him look like a pirate—a way cute kind of pirate.

"What makes you say that?"

"Don't play Mr. Innocent Little Boy with me, Andy Hupp. I've heard more about you than you might think. Girls talk you know."

Andy chuckled. This was getting interesting. "Okay, we kind of broke a rule or two when shooting *Bust Out* last year."

"Oh, that sounds wonderful. A movie called 'Bust Out'. That tells me a lot right there." She leveled two beautiful but accusing eyes on him. "So what were the rules you two broke?"

Andy shrugged as he looked off idly at the crowded cafeteria, searching for Tony Scarletti and the rest of his brawny gang. Thankfully, they usually ate lunch off campus, screeching out of school in Tony's red Trans Am. "Nothing much," he nonchalantly answered, looking back again at Jeena Kirtland. "Caught a little flak for bringing a couple of firearms onto school grounds, that's all."

"You mean, as in *guns*? *Real* guns? Oh my god," Jinky said. "What have I gotten myself into? I'm starting to think I'm sitting here talking to Dylan Kembold and Eric Hanson."

"Dylan Klebold," Andy corrected, "and Eric Harris."

"Whatever, Mr. Know-It-All!" Jinky fired back.

Andy looked at TJ and he looked at Andy.

"Girls," Andy mumbled.

"They can be difficult," TJ agreed.

"Look, Jink," Andy continued reasonably. "We're offering you a chance to work on a full blown independent movie. Imagine putting that on your resume. Besides, it'll be a kick. For starters, we plan to shoot in and around the Texas Hill Country, then market it as a direct-to-DVD movie via every film outlet we can muster. What's more, we have a shooting budget of twenty-five thousand dollars. That's right—twenty-five G's. Mucho dinero for an independent student-made film, let me tell you."

Jinky looked from Andy to TJ then back again. "If this is such a great big movie project you two are cooking up, then how come nobody from your 'Bust Out' movie is sitting around this table?"

Andy sighed.

He knew this question was coming, sure as daylight.

Girls could sure be nosy.

"Well, for one thing," Andy patiently explained, "several of the actors we used in that previous film weren't high school students."

"That's right," TJ interjected, hoping to bolster his friend's shaky position. "For instance, we used a real police officer to play a police officer in our last movie, uniform and all. Pretty cool, huh? A dude named Jim Piker. Looks a little like William Holden, if you know who that guy was. And then—"

"I know who William Holden was, you ninny! He won an Oscar for *Stalag 17*!"

"Very good," Andy said. "You know your movie history. Still, Holden was better in *Sunset Boulevard*."

"Yes he was!" Jinky fired back. "But how come you and TJ are the only members of your movie production? You haven't answered me that. What happened? Did you piss everyone else off?"

"Let's just say we have new requirements for this project and leave it at that, okay? As for *Bust Out*, TJ put in a fine performance in the lead role, playing a psychotic teen on the run after slashing his teacher to death."

"Oh, boy! Bet that went over well!"

"Listen, Jink, if you have any doubts about our abilities, wait 'til you see *Bust Out*. Not bragging, but TJ pulled off a real James Dean performance. Brooding, troubled, stuffed with angst."

"*Stuffed...?*"

"Like a Thanksgiving turkey."

Jinky rolled her eyes then looked skeptically at both boys. "You two really are something, know that? I'm not sure if you're just a couple of scam artists or pulling my leg or what. But if this new project is so great why isn't this whole table filled up instead of just us three?"

"We've already got a few others on board..."

"Well, kinda," TJ added, somewhat furtively.

"Oh, really? So where are they, TJ?"

Both boys looked at each other.

"Uhhh....around."

"I see..." Jinky slowly said, as if she were a school teacher who had just caught two students cheating. " Could it be they bailed on your latest project because they didn't want to get expelled or arrested next time you two bring a machine gun on campus? Or maybe even a live nuclear bomb?"

"We always aim for authenticity whenever we shoot," Andy remarked, tapping his pen thoughtfully against his notebook.

"I'm sure that impressed Principal Meevers," Jinky said, "especially after catching you two running around school with real guns."

"As a matter of fact," Andy explained, "Principal Meevers requested we give him a private screening of *Bust Out* right there in his office. Didn't he, TJ?"

"Oh, yeah, yeah," TJ confirmed, rapidly shaking his head. "Right there, Jinky. Right there in his office." He coughed. "Right there. For sure."

Jinky rolled her eyes at the sky-lighted ceiling.

"And after viewing it," TJ went on, "Principal Meevers

turned to Andy and said, "You boys have some real talent. Can't wait to see your next movie."

Jinky wasn't sure what to think, even as she looked again at Andy. To be sure, TJ was cute. But god help her this friend of his was drop-dead gorgeous. "Which is?" she queried.

"Which is what?" Andy asked.

"Your next movie. What is it about?"

Andy looked across at TJ. "Oh, that. Well, that's what we're still trying to nail down. Which is why TJ invited you to lunch."

"That and 'two other reasons'," Jinky reminded, her eyes narrowed accusingly.

"Uhhh....yeah."

TJ looked embarrassed.

Andy sighed.

And Jinky kept a close eye on them, like a cornered mouse watching two hungry cats.

"What we're trying to do at the moment is bring on board a few key people. I'll be directing again and TJ and I will co-write the script. We haven't got much yet. Just a vague idea. But what we are sure about is that we're going to need a young female lead with sex appeal. And I think you're exactly what we've been looking for."

Jinky's eyes widened. "Don't tell me. You're doing a porn film down in your parents basement and you want me to star."

"You'd be a natural," TJ said, unable to control his flippant mouth. Which only earned him another punch.

"You're about to kill off date number three, buster."

"Nothing like that," Andy assured, taking a look at his wristwatch. "But we're just about to reach the end of lunch period so we'll have to wait until our next meeting when TJ and I will have more of a script idea."

As they took the last few minutes of lunch period finishing up their drinks Jinky said in a low voice: "Who is that guy over there? He keeps glancing over at us, like he's been listening in."

"Like what guy?" TJ wondered, holding alight a last pota-to chip, as if he were Hamlet contemplating the skull of poor Yorick.

"Two tables over, sitting alone."

"Oh, him," TJ said, following her glance. "That's Rotten Crotch Crutchley."

Jinky half spit out her drink.

"Rotten Who Whatzit?"

"Rotten Crotch Crutchley. AKA Rodney Crutchley."

"That's terrible, TJ!"

"Hey, I didn't give him the nickname."

"Then who did?"

"It's a long story," Andy interjected, closing his film pro-duction notebook in preparation for leaving.

"Let's hear it," she said.

"You tell it, TJ," Andy murmured, stuffing his notebook back inside his backpack.

TJ shrugged, crunched down his last chip, then, with the practiced squint of an eye and a cocked finger, flicked an errant crumb away.

"Okay. But it's gross," he warned.

"I'm finished eating."

"You have. But maybe your stomach hasn't gotten the message yet."

"Go ahead," she urged, excited now as she pushed her tray aside in eager anticipation of satisfying her female instinct for gossip. Especially since there was only three minutes left of lunch period.

"Well, it all goes back to the day when Rotten dropped his pants in gym class last year and Jamal Perkins happened to notice he had some serious skidmarks."

"Serious...*skid....?*"

Andy looked up and performed a slow-motion face-palm.

"Don't tell me," he said.

"Don't tell you what?" Jinky inquired, puzzled.

"Don't tell me you don't know what skidmarks are."

She looked from one boy to the other, her puzzlement growing.

"Okay," Andy advised. "Give it to her slowly, son."

"Uhhh...you know," TJ stumbled, trying to find the right words. "Like—skidmarks. It's when..." But his explanation fizzled out as he looked over helplessly at Andy. But Andy just grinned back, as if saying, 'Life's a bitch, ain't it?"

"Ohhhhhh!" Jinky suddenly blurted. "You mean—?"

Andy chuckled. "By Jove, Watson, I think she's got it."

Then full realization struck. "*Ewwwwww!*" she said.

"Now you know."

"Were they that bad?" she timidly asked, furtively looking again at the hulking form of Rodney Crutchley. "You know... the skidmarks, I mean?"

"Let's just say that Jamal went around school the next day," Andy explained, "saying it looked like a semi-truck with bad rubber had been doing ninety down the freeway when it suddenly hit the brakes in the back end of Rotten's underwear."

"*Ewwwwww!*" Jinky repeated.

"And that's why he sits alone," Andy concluded. "Every school has its pariah. Rodney Crutchley is ours."

For a long moment Jinky Kirtland just sat there, thinking. Maybe it had been something in Andy Hupp's voice; something that had jarred lose a memory. Then she looked again at Rodney Crutchley two tables over, head down, seemingly oblivious to the vast crowd of people surrounding him. Or was it the other way around?

"I shouldn't have acted the way I did, guys," Jinky said, apologetically. "Reminds me too much of a kid I once knew. At the elementary school I attended back in Oklahoma. The kids there used to call him Booger Nose Bailey because he always had a chunk of crusty snot around his left nostril. You know, like he had some kind of permanent nasal problem or something. Anyway, when he turned thirteen he went out back of his house and blew his head off with his dad's shotgun."

TJ whistled. "Jesus Christ. No shit?"

Ruefully, Jinky nodded. "The story is still on the Internet. Once in a while I force myself to look at it...and hate myself."

"Why?" both boys asked at the same time.

"Because," she softly admitted, "I was one of the kids who called him Booger Nose..."

Andy and TJ glanced at each other, then lowered their eyes. Neither said anything. Then all three, one by one, slowly turned their heads around and looked across the room at Rodney Crutchley.

Sitting there.

Alone.

It was then, out of the corner of his eye, that Andy Hupp saw four guys suddenly enter the far end of the cafeteria—one of them Tony Scarletti.

Staring straight at him.

CHAPTER 4

"Okay," Andy said, gathering up his backpack in a rush. "We'll meet again tomorrow. Same time, same channel."

As Jinky and TJ gathered up their backpacks as well, Sully turned and noticed his friend glancing off through the milling throngs of students, an intense expression on his face. It was then that he too spied Tony Scarletti and his gang of football thugs shoving their way swiftly through the labyrinth of tables and students.

"Oh, shit," TJ blurted.

"Oh, shit what?" Jinky said, perplexed.

"You and Jink better split," Andy warned. "And fast. Forget the trays. There's no time to return them."

"Evasive maneuver 7 Captain Kirk?"

"Fuck yeah," Hupp said, meaning they were to take off in different directions.

And with that Andy Hupp spun around and bolted toward a side exit just as TJ Sully grabbed hold of Jeena Kirtland's arm and shot away by a different route, disappearing into a knot of students.

"What the hell's going on TJ!" she protested, swinging her head around just in time to catch Andy Hupp barreling through a side exit with four students in hot pursuit.

As for Andy, he had no time to glance back as his leg muscles kicked into warp drive. Even so, he caught a fleeting snatch of Jinky's voice yelling above the hubbub of the cafeteria: "And you two expect *me* to make a movie with a couple of crazies like you!" just as he reached the corridor and began sprinting like Jesse Owens at the 1936 Olympics, but this time with the added impetus of the Gestapo and Ku Klux Klan in hot pursuit. "Look out everyone!" someone in the corridor shouted, as he whizzed past, "Here comes One Buck For A Suck Hupp!"

For if nothing else, Andy Hupp could run like a mother-fucker.

"Now class," Ms Janelle Pickering pontificated, indicating the white board at the front of her Social Studies classroom, "if you remember from last time we outlined three important reasons why America is undergoing an inevitable and radical shift in its national character. So let's take a moment to review."

Andy Hupp, slouched lazily near the back of the room, looked up with disinterest at what Ms Pickering had written in neat colors with her Expo-brand dry erase marker pens:

> (1) Because America is a land of immigrants
> (2) Because diversity is our strength
> (3) Because Race is only skin deep

Yeah, yeah, yeah, he thought.

And turned away, other things crowding his mind.

Like Tony Scarletti, for one thing.

Sure, he'd outrun the bastards, half the student body a hootin' and a hollerin' at the spectacle as he tore down the hallway. Since morning, he had earned a new nickname too: 'One Buck For A Suck Hupp' which had spread faster than the Great Chicago Fire of 1871.

Scarletti wouldn't forget it, either.

Not by a long shot.

His enemies, and Scarletti had many, were certainly de-lighting in the knowledge that somebody had offered him a dollar for a blow job—a rare affront to the bully. Sure, they wouldn't say it to his face, unless they wanted theirs smashed. But he must be getting all kinds of sly glances around school right about now.

Girls giggling behind his back.

Voices gossiping.

Fingers pointing.

The works.

Hupp couldn't help but grin.

Briefly, he glanced up at Ms Pickering.

Since he wasn't listening to a word she was saying (he seldom did) he amused himself by studying her face. Sorta young, he guessed; that is, if someone in their mid-thirties could be called that. But what caught his attention was the fact that she had one of those oversized mouths he sometimes saw on people, especially in television sitcoms of the more obnoxious variety, the news media, and politics. Why was that? he wondered. Mouths that always seemed too big for their faces, like some sort of birth defect. But what could you do? You were stuck with what God gave you, for better or worse.

And Ms Pickering's mouth was big.

Wide.

Exaggerated.

Like a cartoonist's caricature.

Not ugly, really. Some might even call it sexy. But still kind of creepy in a way. Like something out of a carnival nightmare, he thought. Rimmed in red lipstick. Brimming with teeth. Nice teeth; but seemingly too many, like her mouth was overstuffed. All incisors and bicuspids and gleaming white enamel.

Carnivorous.

And all of them stuck on smile-mode.

Because every word she spoke seemed wrapped around a gratuitous smile. Lathered, soaked and drenched in one. And maybe that's why he found it hard to pay attention in Social

Studies, as if that smile were telling him things that just might not be true, so she had to sugarcoat them. As if every word she spoke was best taken sight unseen, unquestioned and unexamined.

Then again, maybe he over-analyzed things too much.

Maybe...

After another minute or two his eyes drifted away, like his attention. Even so, he somehow managed to maintain an 'A' in the class, acing all the homework assignments, quizzes, and tests she could throw at him. He suspected that bothered Ms Pickering, she of the perpetual smile, since she knew he was one of her best students, yet he treated both her and everything she blathered on about with such casual indifference. She had tried to engage him on a more personal level on several occasions, calling him over after class to comment about a clever paper he had written, her eyes all aglow with scholarly praise. And perhaps to show off her smooth legs as well, as she swiveled in her desk chair toward him, rather seductively it seemed, her thighs all firm and nyloned as they strained against the tight band of gray woolen skirt that she typically wore.

"You really should join our school's exciting Youth For Social Justice Club, Andy. It meets every Friday after school in the high school theater. There's always plenty of munchies provided. Plenty of girls too, which most boys don't seem to mind... And since I'm serving as student adviser I'm giving extra credit to every student who participates. Oh yes, none other than Dr. Rothman Adler of the Center For Human Understanding in Austin is involved. Yes, the very same Dr. Adler you may have seen on CNN news from time to time.

"Furthermore, every other Friday he makes it a point to drive up to tell us about all kinds of exciting new projects, such as the new refugee facility he was instrumental in getting built right her in Titanisville. As it stands, they're always looking for smart young volunteers to help out. In fact, I've been asked by Dr. Adler to seek out students just like you for that very purpose. And I don't mind telling you that it pays wonderful dividends to add that kind of experience to your résumé once you graduate from college, especially with the name Rothman Adler, PhD, attached as a reference. Potential employers like to see that kind of thing, Andy. They really, really do."

He remembered the abrasive sound of her nylons swishing against her skirt as she leaned forward, her eyes on his. "It shows them that you have a social conscience and can work in a team. So I'm sure a bright student like yourself can see the benefit in participating in such a wonderful after school activity, can't you...?" And then came the ever so subtle parting of her thighs, no more than an inch, but enough to tell him that it had been intentional.

That had been over a month ago, at the beginning of the new school year; now it was late October, and the new refugee facility was up and running and packed tight with Syrians, Somalians, and Guatemalans. What's more, it was now staffed with a dozen of Ms Pickering's students, volunteering after school and on weekends: mopping floors, working in the kitchens, and aiding the paid staff anyway they could as proud members of the Royal Order of Social Justice Warriors.

Funny thing, though.

After politely declining to join Ms Pickering's Youth For Social Justice Club and volunteer at the new, county administered refugee facility, that eternal smile had not faded with disappointment as he'd expected, but strangely intensified. Brightened, in the most fucked up sort of way, like a star going supernova, or maybe like lips pulling back from a mouthful of glistening fangs. And for sometime afterward he had been bothered by the incident, telling himself that no seventeen year old boy could be expected to fully understand how the adult world worked. But then, his dad had always said he had an overactive imagination.

Maybe so...

Whatever the case, ever after Ms Pickering had changed toward him. In a subtle, difficult to define way.

Hardened.

Now here he was, just after lunch, unable to decide which was worse: waiting for Social Studies to hurry up and end, or wishing for it to go on as long as possible, knowing that Tony Scarletti and his football teammates would be somewhere on campus waiting to ambush him, as they had many other students.

All things considered, he decided another half hour of excruciating boredom might be preferable to a fist in the gut, so he did what he usually did at times like these: he reached in and withdrew his tan-colored Hupp Film Productions folder, making sure Ms Pickering's attention was directed elsewhere. Once on his desk, he disguised his impromptu movie mogul office with a mess of papers and his two-inch-thick Social Studies textbook, then flipped open to the page of notes he had taken while at lunch:

"Cute girl! Way to go dude!"

His first impression of Jeena Nancy Kirtland.

Let's see...

"Nice voice," he'd added, *"but in bitch-mode would be formidable."*

Andy smiled, scrolling downward with two eyes the color of deep Canadian woods glimpsed through hazy winter mist:

"This chick doesn't push around easily. Goes after what she wants. Oh, boy. TJ better watch out!"

Andy read further:

"Eyes hungry looking. Predatory? Shit! Eyes like a tigress! But if TJ ever gets the courage to get her in the back seat of his car watch out! (Sexist, I know. Forgive me, Lord) But this is the look I want in my next female lead. And Jinky has a kind of innocent-sexy-hungry look that I like. Perfect for lots of close-ups. And those eyes. Blue. Pure fucking Nazi blue! (Oh, shit! Not that word! What am I thinking!) But this girl will do!"

Andy raised his eyes and looked off, thinking.

Last year's movie, *Bust Out*, a 30-minute short his best friend TJ had written, had helped move Hupp Film Productions beyond his earlier rinky-dink efforts shot throughout his junior high, freshman and sophomore years, using a three hundred dollar video camera picked up at Walmart. But last year, equipped with a new ten thousand dollar Cion Ultra High Definition camera, he and TJ Sully had coordinated nine students and seven adults during the production of *Bust Out*, most serving in multiple capacities, from actor to crew—but par for the course for many an indie film.

Now Andy Hupp was ready to tackle a full-length, 90 minute movie project. Equipped with forty thousand in savings earned from his part-time modeling job, he was ready to risk twenty-five on a low-budget film. His parents were aware of his plans, but knew better than to try to discourage him, lest he go full-retard and blow the whole wad on some serious partying and morph into a full-blown, irresponsible, meth-snorting teenager.

Only one problem.

And it was a big one.

He had no idea yet what his next movie project would be.

Sure, he and TJ had bandied about tons of ideas, in the high school cafeteria, over at each others houses, at a local burger joint in Titanisville–getting drunk on chocolate shakes and their own intoxicating dreams.

Sci-fi ideas were some of the earliest they'd considered.

Sitting down, they'd hashed out possible story-lines, interspersed with their extensive knowledge of the genre. They'd talked of movies like 1956's *Forbidden Planet*, the film Gene Roddenberry acknowledged had largely fathered *Star Trek*. They explored the rich vein of the 1960's, from *Robinson Crusoe On Mars* to *2001: A Space Odyssey*, then onward through the decades, from *Star Wars* to *Alien* to everything else in between, describing the story arcs, the sets, the actors, the directors, and the budgets, all with impressive detail and accuracy. Had their parents, their fellow students, or their teachers been privileged to listen in on these hours-long exchanges, they would have been stunned by the vast knowledge of American filmmaking these two seventeen year olds had accumulated. By the end of it all, however, Andy Hupp and TJ Sully came to the realization that twenty-five grand didn't amount to jack squat when it came to making a sci-fi film that wouldn't be laughed off the screen.

So they turned next to horror, another love they both shared. And repeated the process. Over the ensuing days and weeks, they dissected hundreds of movies, from pure schlock to such enduring black-&-white classics as *The Haunting* and *The Innocents*, then onward to well-known box-office blockbusters as *The Exorcist*. Finally, they narrowed their discussion down to *The Blair Witch Project*, a relatively recent movie that neither had been impressed with, except for the fact that it was ultra low budget and went on to gross almost a quarter of a billion dollars worldwide.

With that incentive to go on, both played around with several horror story ideas in a similar low-budget vein, some not half bad. Still, they couldn't quite come up with a satisfying script.

Next came monster movies, then Westerns (hell, they were living in Texas after all) and finally, after swallowing their pride, tossing around several sappy love story ideas, all of which turned out to be real pieces of shit which ended up as two half-finished screenplays that, upon rereading sometime later (to their absolute horror) almost made them puke.

At the end of it all they decided to revisit one of the easiest genres even Hollywood filmmakers often settle upon: crime. *Bust Out* was Hupp Film Productions best and most slickly-executed effort by far, and it was a crime story. As such, crime movies of the low-budget variety needed little in the way of expensive sets. And props mostly consisted of fast cars, fast guns, and fast women, which all three could be had easily enough.

So they were back to crime...

But what kind of crime?

What.

Fucking.

Kind?

"Don't you agree, Andy?"

Shaken from his reverie, Andy Hupp glanced up.

"Uhhh....sure."

"Sure what, Andy?"

The Mouth was talking to him.

Huge.

Glistening.

Full of teeth.

"What you said."

"Which was?"

Shit.

Busted.

Still, he could try evasive maneuver number 4, as per Captain Kirk, and maybe deceive this Romulan vessel approaching off the starboard bow.

"Well..." Andy tentatively began, "while I was sitting here listening (to not a fucking word you were saying) I had time to look over those three points up on the board more carefully..."

All eyes in the classroom were now on Andy, their bullshit detecto-meters turned up high. Had Andy Hupp been caught red-handed not paying attention, a big no-no in Ms Pickering's class?

With him it was hard to tell.

"And?" Ms Pickering prodded, maneuvering over to her desk and pressing her nicely-shaped ass against it, stretching the evocative material of her tight woolen skirt even tighter.

Nonchalantly, Andy Hupp picked up his pen and tapped it lazily against his Hupp Film Production notebook, releasing one of his characteristic sighs—as if he were reflecting carefully over the matter. In actuality, he had no ready answer, since he had no fucking idea what Ms Pickering had been talking about for the past twenty minutes while he had phased out into fourth dimensional Tholian space.

But when in doubt (he told himself) fire all photon torpedoes. "And I think they're flawed..."

"Oh, really? In what way, Andy?"

Andy looked up at the three points written across the board:

    (1) Because America is a land of immigrants
    (2) Because diversity is our strength
    (3) Because Race is only skin deep

"Take number one, for instance. Restaurants all serve food, right? But number one is like saying food is food, so it doesn't matter what's brought to your table."

Ms Pickering's mouth widened. A definite warning sign.

"Explain to the class what you mean, Andy."

"Not all food tastes alike, right? Most people prefer a steak dinner to a plate of grits or a bowl of beans, if given the choice. So I'm just saying that the immigrants of today can't be compared to those of earlier centuries. Like those of the 18th, 19th, and early 20th. Back then, what was being brought to our table isn't the same as what we're being dished up today."

"A nice metaphor, Andy. Steak, grits, and beans. But it might be lost on some of the students in the class, don't you think? Just what do you mean that what we're being "dished up today" is somehow different than back then?"

Andy fiddled with his pen some more, feeling the eyes of the class upon him. He had been perfectly willing to sit obediently in class, not saying a word, minding his own business. Sure, he occasionally added his two cents. But generally he cruised in silence, out at the edge of Andromeda, dreaming his dreams and planning his plans.

But Ms Pickering seemed hell-bent on pushing him.

Otherwise she would have left him in peace.

So he decided to hit her point blank with his phaser banks.

"Well...back then almost all of America's immigrants were Europeans. Today they're mostly from Mexico, Latin America, and Africa. So that's what I mean when I say we don't get served steak anymore."

Before it happened, Andy knew it would: the class erupted with laughter.

"I see," Ms Pickering said, her voice sharp as glass. "So Europeans are...steak? Is that it?'

Andy Hupp said nothing, his eyes a challenge.

"And the plate of grits? Africans, perhaps?"

More laughter, but this time with an uneasy edge.

"And the bowl of beans? Could that refer to Mexicans?"

This time there was no laughter. Now Ms Pickering's students were looking elsewhere–at their fingernails, a fly on the wall, empty space–anywhere but at the boy with the shaggy brown locks and the forthright glance. No one wanted to be accused of guilt by association, even by so much as a wayward glance.

"Well," Ms Pickering said, pushing her ass away from the desk and strolling to the front of the classroom again. "Andy has brought up a good lead in to point number three: that Race is only skin deep. Whether immigrants come from Europe, Africa, or Mexico, class, the only difference that separates us is superficial skin color."

"You mean like we're all steak, Ms Pickering? That nobody's a bowl of beans?" a dimwitted student by the name of Alan Birch remarked, hoping to win brownie points with his teacher and maybe firm up his shaky C- average. But she ignored him, even as his remark brought another unwanted bout of nervous laughter.

Pursing her lips, Ms Pickering darted a glance toward the handsome boy who had derailed today's multicultural Social Studies lesson. At the start of the school year she had mistakenly believed he might serve as a manageable example of America's new breed of smart, progressive student—one devoted to social justice and unquestioning service toward the underprivileged.

How wrong she was.

How–

"What is it now, Andy?" she snapped.

Timidly, every student in the room turned a collective eye toward the upraised arm of Andy Hupp.

"About what you said..."

"*About–?*" she echoed, confused and perturbed.

"You know, about skin color being the only thing that makes races different."

Ever so subtly, Ms Pickering's eyes dilated, like the aperture of a camera adjusting itself, though no one noticed it save for Andy. She did not like being challenged–*ever.*

"We are all the same under the skin, Andy. We all bleed red." She turned away, assured that a trivial matter had been easily dismissed and could not possibly be questioned further.

"That's right, Ms Pickering," chimed a snooty girl named Vivian Markham, haughtily ensconced at the head of the far row, nearest the teacher's desk. She was a member of the Youth For Social Justice Club, as well as an after-school volunteer at the town's new refugee facility. She had hoped Andy Hupp would join because she had a bad case of the hots for him. But when he hadn't, he became her number one class enemy. (even though she still had the hots for him)

"If race were only skin deep, " Andy pointed out, "then how come criminal forensic scientists can examine a skeleton and tell you if it belonged to a white person or a black person? They shouldn't be able to if skin color was the only difference between us." He looked around the class. "Right?"

He'd discovered that little fact while doing research for his crime film *Bust Out*–as explained to him by Jim Piker, a Titanisville police officer who had appeared in it.

"Is that true, Ms Pickering?" another student asked.

Other students were now wondering if Andy Hupp had just made their teacher out to be a fool.

Or worse: a deliberate liar.

"Class, class. This is not the proper time or place to discuss—" Ms Pickering started to say, when a green light came on next to the classroom speaker, signaling a school-wide announcement:

"ATTENTION ALL SENIOR STUDENTS. AS YOU KNOW, TODAY IS THE THIRD FRIDAY OF THE MONTH AND TIME FOR ANOTHER *FEEL THE HUG* GROUP SESSION OUT ON THE WEST QUAD. ALL STUDENTS IN THAT GRADE LEVEL ARE REQUIRED TO ATTEND. CLASSROOM TEACHERS ARE ASKED TO MAKE CERTAIN THAT THEIR STUDENTS MAKE IT TO THE DESIGNATED AREA WHERE DR. ROTHMAN ADLER OF THE CENTER FOR HUMAN UNDERSTANDING WILL CONDUCT THE MONTHLY EVENT. ANY STUDENT FAILING TO ATTEND WILL BE ISSUED A CLASS 1 INFRACTION. THREE INFRACTIONS WILL MERIT A THREE DAY SUSPENSION. SO PLEASE OBEY SCHOOL RULES AND ABOVE ALL...HAVE FUN!"

Ms Pickering glanced up at the classroom clock.

Three minutes left until end-of-period bell.

"We'll leave it here for today, class." She briefly shifted her glance toward Andy Hupp and held his eye for a telling moment, then pivoted back toward her desk, ass in sync, and sat. But even from his position, Andy could see a sliver of cleavage as she leaned forward and needlessly shuffled some papers, reminding him of the way she had pushed that same cleavage toward him that day she'd invited him to become a refugee shelter volunteer.

A woman scorned?

Odd that that particular phrase should come to mind.

He, a seventeen year old boy, and she a thirty-something school teacher who wore tight skirts. Oh, Jesus, he thought, the realization only now dawning. Please tell me that Ms Pickering is not into teenage boys!

The bell rang, jarring Andy's thoughts back to the present.

"Alright, class. Everyone head for the West Quad. No visits to lockers, no restroom breaks. And this time," Ms Pickering added, "no lies about having to call your stockbroker, Roger." The class chuckled and joked and snickered as they began to file out, earning Ms Pickering a small measure of redemption. Andy Hupp, many of them concluded, had been unduly mean to challenge their teacher.

As Andy rose from his desk Ms Pickering directed a glance his way. "And remember, everyone, I will be stopping by the West Quad later to make certain *all* of you are in attendance."

Hefting his backpack as he made for the door, Andy Hupp knew one thing: one session of last month's Feel The Hug had been one too many for him; it had been the school's first experience with the Federally-mandated *Stop The Bullying!* program, and more than a few students had suddenly disappeared along the way to the West Quad or within five minutes after arriving and ordered to hug each student standing left, right, forward and back of them, whether they wanted to or not.

Andy had been forced to hug a fat girl with questionable hygiene on his left, and then a boy of ambivalent sexuality on his right.

Christ in a lunch box!

Once out of sight of Ms Pickering, he'd implemented evasive maneuver 12 and split. It wasn't until a minute before the hour-long session of exercise, happy-talk, and social justice lecturing was nearing its end that she'd noticed his absence; too late, however, to tag him with an infraction.

But this time...

This time she would be searching the quad like a hawk.

And if he wasn't there—

"There's the cocksucker!"

"Get him!"

Startled, Andy Hupp jerked right just in time to see Tony Scarletti, Brodie Henshaw, Jamal Perkins, and T-Bone Ramirez bursting out of a side corridor. Didn't matter to any of them that it was Feel The Hug time.

Oh, no.

Now it was Feel The Fist time.

"Fuck!" Andy thought, this just ain't my day!

And before anyone could bat an eyelash, One Buck For A Suck Hupp was off and running.

Again.

CHAPTER 5

Rodney Crutchley began life as a large, eleven pound new-born with a somewhat oversized head, eventually evolving into a large, brooding youth, older-looking than his seventeen and a half years. But with his larger than average size came a correspondingly larger than average IQ, one that he kept well-concealed from almost everyone, save for his teachers at test grading time, when he always did better than they would have expected for such a silent, sullen youth.

As Rodney Crutchley often did, he spent whatever free time he had roaming quietly among the back aisles of Titanis High's modernistic school library, there among the tall book-shelves where he lurked, far from the prying eyes of the school librarian and her prowling student assistants. Usually he came to the library only during his one free period of the day, or sometimes in the middle of his one-hour lunch, when the prying eyes of his fellow cafeteria students became too much. Or now–during the school's monthly Feel The Hug event. For it was only during these errant moments that he felt he could let down his guard and finally be himself.

As he drifted among the back aisles, his dark, unkempt hair looked–to any curious eye–as if it had never been comb-ed, beneath which two thick eyebrows hovered above dark, watchful eyes. Even his face held a shadowy cast, since by necessity he had been shaving ever since entering his fif-teenth year. And because he appeared several years older than his chronological age, rumor had it that he was, in fact, actually in his mid-twenties–but was passing for seventeen for purposes unknown.

His appearance of accelerated maturity might have been envied by the others boys at Titanis High, had he not been "Rotten Crotch Crutchley". Once so tagged, it had kept other boys from befriending him, lest they too be shunned. And girls absolutely went out of their way to avoid passing him in the hallways, often leaving a trail of muffled giggles in their wake.

His rejection hurt less than it might have.

A loner from as far back as he could remember, his ponderous bulk had always set him apart, whether on the playgrounds of childhood, or later on in the classrooms and hallways of high school. Even so, Rodney was not muscular. Nor, on the other hand, was he obese; he was simply outsized, much like the 5XL stained white cotton briefs he wore.

At six foot three, he was one of the tallest boys in school. Yet he walked with a characteristic slouch, partly hunched, eyes downcast, moving like a silent shadow through his days.

It was better that way.

Better not to see the eyes that stole sly glances at him, not knowing what he was all about. Was he a threat? His mere size suggested it. Nevertheless, Rodney Crutchley had never threatened anyone. Instead, he possessed almost a bovine complacency, save for his eyes, which were ever watchful, and missed nothing. "*Ewwww!* He creeps me out," was a common refrain among the girls. As for the boys, he was simply "Rotten Crotch", or more often than not some disjointed combination of rapist, mental retard, undercover narco agent (a favorite) or "something".

Yes.

Or something...

That's what he was.

But if it kept other students from knowing much about him, it also kept teachers at bay as well. Saying little in class, Rodney Crutchley did whatever was required of him, and passed anonymously through his days. With his secretive manner, it was inevitable that some teachers would suspect him of cheating on tests, since he always performed better than expected, this brooding hulk sitting at the back end of the class in dark silence. But even on pop quizzes, where no chance to cheat had been possible, his performance equally surprised. Nevertheless, no teacher made any attempt to break through whatever barrier Rodney Crutchley had erected around himself. For in all truth, they too were vaguely frightened of him.

So he meandered through his final year at Titanis High doing as he pleased, invariably ending up in the school library among the tall shelves of books he so loved. Some thought it strange, seeing such a behemoth among the racks, since Rodney did not have the look of a bookworm, a nerd, or a geek. For most, his appearance was more in line with that of a serial killer, perhaps a latter day Edmund Kemper III.

And though Rodney read books on many subjects, he primarily focused on just three: robotics, military weaponry/firearms, and...grisly serial murder. Of the first subject, he never needed to worry about being seen perusing the shelves related to robot design, computers, or the burgeoning field of private-sector drone technology, of which several remote-controlled quad-copters he now owned. Nor the military and firearm section, since most Texans saw nothing amiss about having such interests. Still, his frequent visits to the firearm section might have raised a few concerned eyebrows, had it been known by his teachers or school counselor.

But the murder section...

Now that was another thing.

As it stood, Titanis High had a surprisingly extensive collection on the subject of homicide, chronicling the history of murder across the centuries, from Baron Gilles de Rais to Countess Erzsébet Báthory. From more recent times, there were books on many infamous killers: Jack the Ripper, Belle

Gunness, H.H. Holmes, Carl Panzram, Richard Speck, John Wayne Gacy, Ted Bundy and many more. Rodney Crutchley had read them all. As it stood, his extensive knowledge of such murderous individuals might have raised red flags, had it been known, especially in post Columbine High School America.

Only, no one knew...

No one but the librarian, who alone saw his choice of subject matter as she scanned his books through the checkout counter.

But Rodney had read somewhere along the way about how military aircraft, in times of danger, could release a certain material called "chaff", small aluminum-coated glass fibers that would temporarily confuse and reflect enemy radar signals in order to avoid detection by incoming missiles.

Using that idea as a metaphor, he devised his own "chaff" to confuse and disguise what might otherwise be construed as an inordinate interest in homicide: never checking out such books without also checking out other subjects, ranging from gardening in Central Texas to the works of Shakespeare to clay pot making, none of which held the slightest interest to him. But by so doing, he was able to camouflage his true interest, on the off chance the librarian or one of her smarmy student assistants should happen to take more than passing notice in the kinds of books he read.

Perhaps it was unnecessary, he thought.

But even here, in the only sanctuary he knew, he chose to be careful. He tread softly, here among the back aisles of the library, pulling one book after another and thumbing through, his dark eyes quietly alight as the fingers of his large hands moved with surprising gentleness across the pages.

He had come here after the end of his last class, even though, as a senior, he was required to attend the monthly Feel The Hug session out on the West Quad. For here he could prowl among the tall shelves of books, knowing there was no welcome for anybody called "Rotten Crotch" at any school function.

He reached up and pulled down a book.

Since its publication three and a half years ago during his freshman year, he had checked it out several times. Standing there, he momentarily allowed his dark eyes to linger over the lurid title: *Shot, Stabbed, Strangled, and Snuffed: Unsolved Murders & Unexplained Disappearances In America's Heartland.* Written by a well-known crime writer, of which several television documentaries had already been produced based on his homicidal research, Rodney had, time and again, returned to Chapter 17 of the thirty-two chapter book—each chapter chronicling various cases of unsolved serial killings and strange disappearances around the country.

Even now, tell-tale evidence left by a succession of chocolate-stained and cheese-smudged thumbprints marked the many times he had taken the book home and relived the strange disappearances of Titanis High's two teenage victims, there inside his locked attic bedroom as he devoured jumbo-sized Hershey bars and bags of Cheetos.

He flipped forward a couple of pages, studying again the tantalizing paragraphs in Chapter 17:

Where Did All The Pretty Girls Go?

"...the disappearance of three pretty girls from Austin, Texas, along with half a dozen more from surrounding towns, would eventually lead local law enforcement to suggest the possibility of a serial killer operating in their midst. These particular disappearances were especially troubling, since all the missing teens were from good families, with no known history of drug abuse or prostitution which might have placed them in a high-risk category. Nor did they seem likely candidates as runaways, since all were good students, from upstanding families. In fact, they belonged to not a single high-risk category, other than for being female and attractive.

Yet, they all vanished without trace, the last one only a few months before the publication of this book. And though there remain vestiges of hope from the grieving families, authorities in private now assume the girls are the likely victims of a particularly deadly and clever homicidal maniac every bit as elusive as the wind.

More puzzling still, two additional teenage disappearances have left authorities baffled, though it remains uncertain if they are related. Both involve disappearances in nearby Titanisville, an upscale community nestled among rolling, oak-forested hills some thirty-two miles northwest of Austin.

What is known is that both of the Titanisville teenagers vanished under similar circumstances as the Austin area cases: sudden abduction by person or persons unknown. One involved a sophomore by the name of Tina Sawyer, who fit the same demographic background as the other missing females. The other, however, involved a good-looking teenage boy by the name of Brett Hinkle, who vanished on the same foggy evening as Sawyer while in her company, leaving authorities baffled as to why he too was taken, unless he was also to be used as an unwilling sacrifice in some sinister sex cult ritual, one culminating, perhaps, in twisted, sadistic murder, of which tenuous rumors have long floated about the Texas Hill Country like foul vapors seeping from an open grave...

Rodney Crutchley had not known the two teenagers who vanished from Titanisville, other than they had both attended Titanis High, just before he began his freshman year. Tina Sawyer had been a cheerleader for the Titanis Terror Birds, the school's football team, and remembered as a good if not outstanding student.

As for the boy, he was known to have been a casual friend of Tina's, although it was not believed, according to the book, that they had been romantically involved. The night they vanished, along a lonely country road just outside of Titanisville, they had been traveling together to another student's house, to attend a Christmas party. When Tina's empty car was found, in the wee hours of a mist-shrouded morning, authorities discovered her purse, along with Brett

Hinkle's wallet, stripped of cash and tossed in a nearby ditch. No trace of them was ever found.

Since then, Rodney Crutchley had spent many idle hours wondering as to their fate, knowing they had once walked the very same school halls as he.

Walked them...*and then vanished...*

Perhaps he was obsessed, but he could not help but wonder who had taken them. Himself an outcast, only being dead made one even more so. And maybe that was why he couldn't let it go—why he endlessly pondered what had become of Tina Sawyer and Brett Hinkle. Had they pulled over to help someone who'd waved them down along a night-darkened road, only to be robbed, abducted, and murdered–then dumped in shallow graves in some godforsaken place? Maybe. Then again, had it all been a ruse, part of a plot by the two teens to fake their disappearance, afterward to set out and wander the highways and byways of America–perhaps to hitchhike out to the mountains of Montana or down to the sun-drenched beaches of Florida...?

But no, he thought.

It hadn't been either.

Perhaps it was his dark side, that shadow of deep suspicion in which he perpetually lived, that made him certain they had met a different, stranger fate. And that somehow, somewhere, someway, someone at Titanis High knew what had really happened...

Suddenly, Rodney Crutchley turned around.

Coming from somewhere beyond the rows of bookshelves, a loud commotion drew his attention. Then came a sound of someone rapidly approaching from around the corner, at the far end of the book aisle. It was that good-looking kid who always sat two tables over in the cafeteria, always with the same boy; and today, with a very pretty girl as well.

Without realizing it, Andy Hupp came skidding to a halt three feet away from Rodney Crutchley, his green eyes flashing wide with surprise. Nevertheless, there was something else in the shaggy-haired boy's glance that Rodney also sensed—something that said he too was an outsider, albeit for different reasons. However, neither had time to weigh this unexpected encounter, for just out of sight Rodney heard the muffled rush and hissed commands of others involved in this frantic teenage drama, moving through the library helter-skelter, as if searching for something—and that something had to be Andy Hupp.

Without a word, Rodney tucked his book under his armpit then wove his thick fingers into a stirrup, jerking his dark eyes upward.

Instantly, Andy understood.

Placing one foot into Rodney's cupped hands, he felt himself boosted swiftly upward, enough so that he was able to heave both himself and his backpack atop the massive, three foot wide bookshelf, immediately sliding toward the middle and flattening himself out of sight.

And not a second too soon—

For in the next instant came the sound of scuffling feet, gasping lungs, and then a tangled confluence of muscled arms, thick legs, and broad chests crowding and pushing and shoving into the aisle.

"Where'd he go?" someone grunted.

"Swear the mothahfuckah came—"

And then all the confused utterances came crashing to a halt as four pairs of eyes became suddenly aware of the ungainly youth standing stock-still at the opposite end of the aisle.

A second of indecision passed.

Then, with an air of blustering contempt Tony Scarletti broke free of the other three and sauntered toward the six foot three dark-haired teen holding a book. Coming to a stop three feet from Rodney Crutchley, a lopsided grin grudgingly worked itself onto Scarletti's face.

"Hey, hey, hey, ladies. If it ain't ol' Rotten Crotch, our very own shit-stained wonder boy."

Behind Scarletti, two of his three companions came ambling down the aisle, all beefy and cocksure, their shoulders rocking like seesaws, one wearing a pair of two hundred dollar Adidas, the other a similar priced pair of Pumas, and the third, Jamal Perkins, circling around to the adjacent aisle in his three hundred dollar shoplifted Nikes. A moment later the negro football player came up behind Rodney and stood within sniffing distance, effectively blocking his escape.

"Like, where'd he go Rotten?" Scarletti asked, taking another step forward, his football-toughened body sheathed in hundred dollar jeans set off by a pair of four hundred and seventy-five dollar black, tan, and green camo-patterned Reeboks.

Rodney glanced at Brodie Henshaw and T-Bone Ramirez standing behind Scarletti, both eyeing him with contemptuous but eager smiles, like dogs awaiting a treat.

"Sucka ain't back this way," a puzzled voice mumbled from behind Rodney. "I done looked up and down the mothafuckin aisles. He gone."

Jamal Perkins, Rodney knew.

The one responsible for his ignominious christening.

And all because a bad combination of events had come about the previous school year: a case of the flu which had beget a touch of diarrhea, and then those six fat, succulent bean burritos he had been unable to resist that day in the school cafeteria. Afterward, as the flu churned its way through his increasingly-upset intestinal tract, fueled by a gutful of spicy frijoles, he made an unsuccessful effort to squeeze out a desperately-needed emergency fart in geometry class, on full-silencer mode, only to hear instead a horrifyingly-long, loud, juicy, wet *brrrraaaaapppp!*

To say the least, Mr. Nithercott excused class rather abruptly, as unseen tentacles of stench worked its way around the room in a matter of seconds. His excuse for doing so was that the air-conditioning had failed, a feeble attempt to coverup the real reason, even as students staggered out, some gagging, others sniggering at Rodney, the latter already hinting at the scorn yet to come.

Not having a change of underwear, he had been forced to endure the resultant effluent as it radiated outward from his ass-crack all the way forward to his crotch, even as he lumbered his way awkwardly toward his next class, which thankfully was gym. But even as he had hurriedly reached his locker and began shucking his jeans, he failed to realize that other boys nearby might be slyly observing him.

And that's when they all saw his shit-stained underwear.

They—and Jamal Perkins, standing nearby.

In an instant, he'd caught sight of Rodney's massive anal blowout, letting out a war whoop louder than a Ubangi warrior at the sight of a cannibal feast, urging all the other boys to take a look: "Hey suckas! Check it out! That mothafuckah's got skidmarks like you ain't never seen! So big and wide they's loopin' all the ways 'round to his shit-stained crotch!"

A week later, after being absent from school with the flu, he returned only to find himself indelibly labeled as Rotten Crotch Crutchley. But considering he had no friends anyway, his subsequent humiliation and further ostracization had cost him little. Except, that is, for being an endless target of scorn and ridicule by Tony Scarletti and his gang...

"You don't hear so well, do ya Rotten? I asked you where he went."

The big youth stood silent, his eyes unmoving.

Scarletti' shot out a hand, snatching hold of Rodney's shirt.

"Don't fuck with me, you overgrown asshole. We saw him come down this aisle."

Rodney made no move to pull away, nor did he say anything further.

Scarletti chuckled.

"Nah, you're too much of a wuss to lie." He looked over his shoulder at T-Bone and Henshaw. "The motherfucker gave us the slip somehow. Fucker runs like a jackrabbit." He released his grip on Rodney. "Whatcha doing back here anyway, Rotten? Jackin' off or just waitin' to jump out from behind these books and rape some girl? Huh, Mr. Skid-marks?"

Jamal Perkins reached from behind and snatched the book from underneath Rodney's armpit. As the heavy-footed youth turned toward his antagonist, the negro kid tossed the book high over head where Scarletti nonchalantly caught it, star quarterback that he was.

"Whoa," he said, "get a load of this, dudes: *Shot, Stabbed, Strangled, and Snuffed: Unsolved Murders & Unexplained Disappearances In America's Heartland.*"

They all turned their eyes toward Rodney Crutchley.

"What the fuck you doing reading shit like this, Rotten?" Scarletti asked, a glint of interest in his eye.

"It's for a class report I'm doing," Rodney answered.

"Class report my ass. More like a training manual for after school rape & murder."

There was a chorus of chuckles.

Rodney said nothing.

"He look like a mothafuckin' rapist," Jamal said, leaning in close behind Rodney's ear as he voiced the accusation. So close Rodney could smell the negro's cheap, sickeningly-sweet cologne.

Scarletti, aware of his own school reputation of having committed a few borderline rapes—albeit none that could be proven—let go a crooked-smile. "Take it, chump," he said, tossing the book back at Rodney with a dismissive flick of his wrist. "But if I find out you helped that Andy Hupp ass-hole get away, you and me have got a date behind the school gym. Got it?"

Jamal leaned in close again. "Yeah, mothafuckah. Got it?"

Before Rodney Crutchley could react, the four school jocks faded away, all shoulders and biceps and husky legs jostling down the aisle as they beat it out of the library.

As soon as they were gone, Andy Hupp deftly slid his legs

over the side and dropped easily to the floor, nimble as a cat burglar.

For a moment the two youths stood silent, each viewing the other in a different light than before. For Rodney, this was the first in a long time that he'd faced anyone whose eyes were other than full of contempt. As for Andy, it was the first time he had ever had any close contact with this enigmatic youth. But he knew one thing: even when faced with four of Titanis High's toughest jock-yard thugs, Rodney Crutchley had not given away his hiding place.

"Thanks," Hupp said, a note of respect in his voice.

"No problem," Crutchley managed.

"It would've been had they found me," Andy countered. "You saved my ass."

"Somebody had to."

That brought a quick grin to Andy's face. "Yeah, well. Sometimes I get myself into jams." It was then he noticed the book clutched in Rodney Crutchley's huge hands. "I'm kinda interested in crime myself," Andy ventured, nodding at the book. "You see, I'm doing another film and I'm looking for ideas." He glanced at the big youth, speculatively. "You know much about the subject?"

Rodney dropped his dark eyes to the book. "Some," he tentatively replied. "Right now I've been analyzing the Sawyer-Hinkle disappearances."

"Analyzing", Andy thought. How many teens used that word nowadays, anytime at all during their brain-dead existence? But Rodney Crutchley had–a rare find indeed. "Who were they?" he prodded, always impatient to cut to the chase.

Rodney looked up. For a long moment, his dark eyes considered whether or not he should lower his guard, to allow someone else to enter his private little world. It had been a long time since he had.

Not since that girl...and that long ago ride into darkness.

But he tried not to think of her, or how it had ended.

After all, she had been dead for so long now...

Silently, Rodney parted the book to Chapter 17, then handed it to the handsome youth. Taking it, Andy skimmed through the chapter at breakneck speed, picking out all the salient points in a matter of seconds. Then he let go a soft whistle.

"Shit. I never knew about this. It says here that Tina Sawyer and Brett Hinkle disappeared from Titanis High several years before my family moved up from Austin. I mean, I had heard of other high school kids disappearing from the capitol area, but I hadn't known our own little town had lost a couple too."

"Nobody likes to talk about it," Rodney said.

"Why not?"

"Because the killers were never caught."

"Meaning...?"

"Meaning they may still be around. At least, that's what the author of the book believes."

Andy slowly nodded. "Yeah, I suppose you're right. Two high school kids like Sawyer and Hinkle don't just walk away and never come back. Not if they're still alive."

In silence, both boys regarded each other.

Both thinking.

Both seeing dark possibilities.

"Hey," Andy finally said, handing the book back to Rodney with a burning glint in his eye. "Could you write up a two page synopsis over the weekend regarding everything you know about the Sawyer-Hinkle case? You know, everything you know about the circumstances of their disappearance, their personal details, their life here at Titanis High, any people who knew them—students, staff, anybody? Finally, any ideas you may have developed as to what may have really happened to them?"

"You mean...you're interested in this case?"

"I am now, Rodney. Just bring that book along with a detailed report about what you've found out so far. And any ideas as to what—or whom—may have been responsible for Sawyer's and Hinkle's disappearance."

"Bring it...where?"

"To my lunch table next Monday. At noon. That's when I'll introduce you as the newest member of our film production team." Andy slapped the big youth on the shoulder. "See you then."

A second later Andy Hupp was gone.

For a long time the ponderous youth with the dark eyes merely stood there, thinking.

Thinking of one thing above all else:

The fact that Andy Hupp had called him 'Rodney'.

CHAPTER 6

"How was your day, Andy?"

It was the usual table talk banter from Andy's father, Peter Hupp, who made a ritual every evening at dinner to ask his son the same question. Andy figured it was akin to saying "nice day, isn't it?" or "how's the weather?" because no real interest lay behind it, or even a response beyond "okay" or "just fine".

And there hadn't been.

For years.

Once, long ago, things had been different. Back then, Andy's dad had taken a real interest in the affairs of his wife and two children, happy to see them every evening, all of them gathered around the dinner table and genuinely interested in how their respective days had gone—Andy and his younger sister Amanda at school, his mother's at the upscale Austin department store where she served as manager of the cosmetics section. That had been back in the days when they had still lived in Texas's capitol city, before moving out to Titanisville seeking "better schools" when Andy knew all along it was to escape the city's burgeoning "enrichment" by hordes of Mexicans and other Third Worlders.

Sometimes, Andy wondered why life was this way; why happier times and the way a family interrelated to each other gradually slipped away, like leaves on a slow-moving stream, each going their separate way. Why life itself often seemed that way. Human existence, even. Perhaps the universe itself, for all he knew. Big questions that his seventeen year old mind had not yet fully figured out.

"Same old same old," Andy mumbled, taking a bite of roast beef. "Except that me and TJ fought off a Muslim terrorist attack right after third period."

"Is that so? Sounds like you and your buddy had a very interesting day," his father murmured, absorbed in the latest news as he absentmindedly thumb-scrolled down his iPhone screen between halfhearted bites of mashed potato and gravy.

"As usual," Cynthia Hupp interjected, dishing herself some peas, "you're not much interested in what your children actually have to say." She reached for a dinner roll. "Nor I."

Peter Hupp raised his head and blinked twice, as if emerging from a dark cavern into bright sunlight. Or so it seemed to Andy, as the brilliance from the overhanging chandelier flashed once off his wire-rimmed spectacles, behind which two muddy-green eyes stared out. Not the same shade of green as his son's, which were a deeper, purer green, but more world-weary in appearance, as if the original color had been worn thin by the abrasive passage of time.

"Alright, Cynthia," Peter Hupp patiently responded, looking down the table at his wife, "how was your day?" The words came out in snipped little pieces, as if Andy's father were parsimoniously measuring out each individual syllable. Clearly, he was irritated at having to look up from his iPhone, as evidenced by his exaggerated politeness.

"How was my day?" Cynthia Hupp sarcastically echoed, her voice taking on an uncharacteristic edge. "Try asking me that after you've spent your whole work week trying to make black women look beautiful or some squatty Mexican woman believe she'll come out looking like Taylor Swift if she buys $300 worth of makeup and blonde hair-dye. Try doing that, Peter, then ask me how my day was."

Everyone at the table paused, dollops of mashed potato, precariously balanced peas, or chunks of roast beef poised on forks as they all looked quizzically at Cynthia Hupp. Still a very attractive woman, even at thirty-nine, Andy's mother possessed mid-length, golden-brown hair—almost blonde, but not quite. With eyes falling somewhere along the gray-blue continuum and dotted with random flecks of gold, she turned heads everywhere she went. And save for Andy's deep green eyes, he clearly bore the mark of his mother's good-looks stamped upon his own, albeit in a more masculine way.

Peter Hupp, having momentarily halted a bite of roast beef halfway to his mouth, regarded his wife as one might an unexpected knock at the door: "What brought that on?"

"Nothing I'm sure that would interest you," she said, her voice edged with...*what?* Contempt? Disgust? Andy wasn't sure, even as he tried to read meaning into her words, as if she were auditioning lines from a film script whose title and plot were unfamiliar to him.

"Are you ill, Cynthia?"

"No—!" She let go a sigh of exasperation. "Maybe I am—who knows? I just...just had a terrible day is all." She looked disconsolately at her food, all of which had been expertly prepared by her own hand. But then, I'm what they call a Super Mom, she thought. Career woman, housewife, mother. Hardworking, beautiful, dedicated; both her children admired her as much as their father, perhaps more.

"So what's this all about?" Peter asked, trying to decide if he should finish his bite of food or wait for her answer.

"I'm just wondering if I've reached the end of my rope," she said, looking off into the distance. "Career-wise, that is..."

"You're not thinking of quitting, are you?"

She turned her eyes back to her husband. "What if I am?"

"Cynthia, if we lose your income... I mean, that is...my landscape design business is not bringing in the kind of money it used to. Over the last few years I've lost clients that haven't been replaced with new ones. And with the mortgage and car payments and—"

"And what, Peter? Exactly what? In case you've forgotten

it was you who wanted to move out to the country and shackle us with a two million dollar mortgage, remember? Buy this eight bedroom house with built-in pool and five acres of land just so we could live like the landed gentry. All because you needed to impress clients who kept leaving you anyway for other design firms."

Peter Hupp's eyes darkened. "That's not my fault, Cynth. Austin and the surrounding area has been drawing in more landscape architects due to its high growth rate, many willing to undercut older firms like mine just to get a piece of the action. So if we lose your income we'll lose the good life we've worked so hard to achieve. Right now our kids go to nice, safe schools, we're respected in this small community, and we're hap—" Peter Hupp's last word caught in his throat, like a piece of gristle, Andy thought.

"Happy? Is that what you were about to say, Peter? That we're happy? You've said so yourself: your landscape design firm isn't getting the kind of business it used to five years ago. And now you're working harder and harder just to keep what few clients you have left while struggling to maintain that overpriced downtown Austin office of yours. That, while living in a two million dollar house with a beautiful swimming pool on five tree-covered acres that we're finding harder and harder to afford. And all for what? Just to show others how "successful" we are at the cost of our sanity? And today at work I really thought I was losing mine."

"But you can't just quit—!" he blurted, then recomposed himself. "I mean...you should think this through, Cynthia."

Cynthia Hupp dawdled with her peas. "Oh, don't panic, Peter. I'm not going to quit because I'm well aware we'll sink like a rock without both of our incomes paying the mortgage and car payments. What a mess we're in. But lately I've felt so blah about where my life is going and what I'm doing." She gazed off for an instant. "And yet, how can I go on doing makeup demonstrations on faces that look like lumps of brown clay?"

Andy stifled a grin; this was getting good. But then, grown-up talk at the dinner table usually was.

Peter Hupp sat contemplating his wife's words, as if he'd been asked to resolve a complex mathematical equation. Andy too wondered where all this was leading.

"Well, Cynth, I've never given such world shaking problems as makeup demonstrations much thought."

Cynthia's hand came unexpectedly crashing down, rattling the tableware. "I'm goddamn serious, Peter! How are my saleswomen expected to run their cosmetic counters and demonstrate their expertise when all the beautiful products we used to sell are becoming less and less needed! When the skin tones of my customers have become so dark that all the beautiful blushes and powders and eye shadows look like fucking clown make-up on their faces!"

Oh, boy.

Mom's got our attention now, Andy thought.

Especially after using the "f word".

Peter Hupp slowly set down his fork.

"You've obviously had a rough day, Cynthia."

"You're goddamn right I have, Peter! Do you even know how I feel? Every day, watching my saleswomen strain to speak expertly about proper cosmetics when their own faces often don't match those of their customers? Lipstick, eyeliner, blush? Dear God, Peter! I'm just finding it harder and harder to relate to some black woman wanting to use any cosmetics. I mean, makeup was designed for white skin, not something that looks like shoe leather. Lipstick was made to accentuate Caucasian lips, not smear across ones that look like a pair of over-inflated inner tubes. I mean, why are we being made to pretend that blonde or red or brunette hair dyes, or makeup developed for white skin, or eye shadow intended to highlight brown or blue or green or gray eyes—rather than the tar-colored ones of every black and brown customer that I'm seeing more and more each day!"

Peter Hupp, landscape design architect, brought his logical

mind up to full speed. His wife, normally so serene, was having a major meltdown.

"I guess...I guess that's just the way the cosmetic business is headed, Cynthia. After all, you more than anyone should know these things. Probably just a passing business trend, anyway. That kind of thing. None of this should come as a surprise to you."

Dear old dad, Andy thought. Always quick with an answer. Always ready to explain the mysteries of the universe, like all dads. Too bad he was full of shit, he thought.

"I think the issue that's troubling mom is changing demographics, Dad," Andy murmured, forking another mouthful of mashed potatoes into his mouth. "And it's not a passing business trend either. Not according to Ms Pickering, my Social Studies teacher."

Peter Hupp regarded his son from behind the twin lenses of his wire-rimmed eyeglasses, his jaw muscles working. Andy's sister also glanced his way, while Cynthia Hupp looked down the table as well; all four of them seated there in their spacious dining room overlooking their half acre backyard with its built-in swimming pool and lushly landscaped terrain—all that the combined income a business owner and a cosmetic department manager could buy.

"What do you mean by that?" Peter Hupp brusquely asked, a grave tone to his voice.

Andy shrugged. "Nothing much, dad. Just explaining why mom is having a problem selling cosmetics just to make shoe leather look attractive."

Amanda Hupp, aged twelve, giggled and spit out a pea.

Peter Hupp leaned forward. "That was uncalled for, Andy."

"Just saying."

"Saying what, exactly?"

"Just saying that's where the country is headed, according to Ms Pickering. For one thing, she taught us that Austin is a Sanctuary City."

"What's that?" Amanda Hupp piped in.

"A Sanctuary City," Peter Hupp explained, "is a safe haven for refugees, sweetie."

"You mean illegal aliens," Andy interjected, taking another bite of his dinner roll.

Peter Hupp locked eyes with his son, his thoughts awhirl. Of late Andy had been challenging him more and more on matters such as this: Politics, social issues, foreign affairs, and the like. Maybe it was natural, he thought. All part of growing up. After all, the boy was seventeen now, stood an inch taller, and had a lucrative, part-time job working as a fashion model, owned a Mercedes Benz van, and to top it all off, was an excellent, straight-A student. Were it not for all those facts he might've reached across the table and smacked him a good one.

Just like *his* father would've done...

Kids, he thought.

So fucking insolent today.

But Andy...

He had to admit the boy was a phenomenon.

Weird, quirky, hard to nail down.

Not a punk. Not a nerd. Not a fuckup.

Too good-looking for his own good, god help him.

And yet...not conceited either.

At least, not in the usual manner.

No, Andy had a confidence and a *certainty* about things.

Peter Hupp slowly pulled back and calmly ventured another bite, thoughtfully chewing his food for a moment as his mind mulled over how to respond. Finally, he said, "We live in changing times, Andy. And changing times bring changing ways of expressing things. Calling undocumented workers "illegal aliens" is just not socially acceptable anymore. Besides, they're not the ones buying cosmetics at your mother's department store anyway."

"Then who is, dad?" Amanda Hupp queried.

"I don't know. Maybe your mother can answer that."

Amanda turned toward her mother.

"Your father's right," Cynthia Hupp said, her calm demeanor somewhat restored. "My customers are not not illegals, dear. That is, they're not undocumented workers—they couldn't afford to shop at my store. But ever since our advertising department started aiming for the minority market, we've been getting more and more from that demographic. We've also brought in a whole new line of less expensive makeup products created by Ever Darkening World Cosmetics. It wasn't my idea, even though I'm the head of the department. I guess I'm still a bit upset that our corporate office went over my head without even consulting me."

"Okay, Cynth—so now you sell makeup for a growing market of darker-skinned customers. What's the big deal?" Peter said, dipping into his peas. "After all, money is money. Besides, there's only one human race."

God, Andy thought. My dad's more cucked than I thought. But even as the word popped into his mind, he wondered from where it had come. Somewhere, he guessed. Maybe the Internet. Or school...

"The problem is not that we sell them, Peter. Please understand. After all, we've been carrying some makeup brands aimed at minority customers for several years now. But until recently, they've been a very small part of our overall cosmetic inventory."

"And now?"

"Now Ever Darkening World Cosmetics has become our number one seller."

"Bravo, Cynth. Congratulations. Break out the champagne. There's probably a raise in it for you."

Good ol' dad, Andy thought. Always the bean counter. Always thinking only of the money angle, and nothing else.

"Is that all you think about, Peter? The money?"

Bullseye, mom.

"What else is there, Cynthia? After all, you and your store are in business to sell products and make money, right? Who cares if you're selling more makeup to black and Hispanic women now."

"But *I* care, Peter. I care very much. All my training is with light skin tones. With blondes and brunettes and red-heads."

"With white people, you mean."

"Oh, Peter. I know very well how it's making me sound. Dear God–I really do. But...I once took a lot of joy bringing out the best qualities in the faces of women... You know, faces that I could relate to. Faces...well, like mine. But with each passing day I'm finding it more and more difficult to gaze into some black face with oversized lips and a flat nose and convincing myself that there's no difference between our standard of beauty and theirs. That somehow I'm supposed to make faces like that look pretty by Caucasian standards when it's just impossible. Oh, god, Peter. It's–it's beginning to make me feel like a total–"

"Fraud?" Andy gently ventured, looking up slowly at his mom with sympathy in his eyes.

"Andy!" Peter Hupp shot back.

Cynthia Hupp turned toward her son, a look of tenderness in her eyes. Sometimes he was like her in so many ways that it hurt. Her first born, after all. And the bond was still strong.

"Please, don't jump on Andy, Peter. He's right. It's exactly how I feel. Like a fraud. That's because I and my saleswom-en are not black or brown. We're not African-American, Mexican, or whatever. We're white women and all these new faces are alien to my sales staff. And now I'm being pres-sured by upper management to retire some of my best sales-women and replace them with 'people of color'. My god, aren't white people a 'color' too?"

"Welcome to the real world," Peter dryly retorted, pushing his dinner plate aside. "It's called progress."

"Then why'd we move out to Titanisville, dad?" Andy asked, trying to keep his voice innocent-sounding. Because there was a gunsight behind his words, and he was about to squeeze the trigger. "You know, what with all the Mexicans and blacks moving into Austin these days, we should've stayed behind to enjoy some more progress, right?"

"We came here for the fresh country air and better schools, Andy," his father snapped. "That's why."

"Whatever, dad," Andy said, picking up his dinner plate, glass, and utensils and heading for the kitchen. Once there, he placed them in the Bosch 500, one of the best dishwashers money could buy.

A moment later a hand made contact with his shoulder.

Turning, Andy saw his mom.

"Thanks, Andy. Somehow I knew you'd understand."

"I just know what it's like to feel out of place, mom. I've always felt that way."

A sad mist passed over Cynthia Hupp's bluish-gold eyes. "Have you, dearest? Always? It hurts me to think that."

Andy shrugged. "Pretty much. At least, as far back as I can remember."

"You were always so different, Andy. For the longest time I never knew if I had a little boy running around the house or a pint-sized rocket scientist."

Andy smiled. "You're lucky it wasn't the latter, mom. Otherwise I might've blown up the house."

"Well, there was that time when you were eight or nine and tied a plastic bucket stuffed full of firecrackers and Roman candles to a helium balloon, remember? Then lit the fuses and sent it skyward. When it finally exploded and came tumbling down, firecrackers bursting in mid-air as Roman candles went flaming down on half a dozen rooftops two blocks away we were lucky half the neighborhood didn't burn down."

Andy grinned. "Must've been practicing special effects for a future movie, mom. Good thing nobody ever found out who did it."

"Yes, good thing young man. And good thing too no houses caught fire either," she added, a stern look in her eye. For a long moment she stood there, regarding him in silence. Then she gently reached out and touched his face. "Try not to argue with your father, Andy. Though he hasn't come out and said so exactly, Hupp Landscape Design is having some difficulties. Do you understand what I mean?"

"Sure, mom. I understand. Austin is one of the fastest growing cities in America right now and there's a lot of building going on. That's brought in a lot of new landscape design firms, some much bigger than dad's operation. So the competition is getting fierce. So, yeah, I get it."

Cynthia Hupp slowly nodded, once again impressed at her son's grasp of things. How quickly they grow up, she thought, with just the faintest tinge of sadness.

"That's right," she said. "And he's worried about meeting all of our commitments."

Andy's face grew serious. "All he thinks about is money."

"Not true. It's just that he's a hard-working man with big responsibilities. He wants the best for us. And for me."

Andy sighed. "Yeah, okay. It's just that—"

"Yes, dear?"

And for an instant the face of Ms Pickering entered his consciousness, knowing how she would've lectured his mother over her career concerns. Then he shrugged and forced a smile onto his face. "Never mind," he said. "And don't worry. I'm still part of the Hupp family team, mom. You know, hip hip hooray and all that."

"Thank you, Andy."

Then she kissed him and slipped away.

─────

The Hupp family residence sat on five acres of land at the end of a long paved road, effectively isolating it from both the town of Titanisville and any surrounding houses. At a cost of two million dollars, it came with the land, eight bedrooms, six baths, and five thousand square feet of richly appointed amenities. Beyond the house, six car garage, and built-in swimming pool lay two outbuildings, completely finished in the same style as the neo-modern main house. One, the smaller of the two, served as Peter Hupp's "man-cave" and workshop, which he seldom used, since he did most of his landscape design at his downtown Austin office. The other, larger outbuilding included a two thousand square foot workshop with a second story guest apartment, which Andy Hupp used as his own residence. The first floor work-shop once housed the original owner's forty-five foot Emer-ald Coach motorhome, a sixty-one foot Viking Sport Cruiser power boat, and various off-road vehicles. Now the large, high-ceilinged interior served as Andy Hupp's film studio.

With earnings gleaned from lucrative modeling jobs, the enterprising teen had equipped it with a sound-proofed recor-ding booth, various camera dollies and tripods, overhead stu-dio lights, and its own fully-equipped prop and wardrobe shop. But just to demonstrate his seriousness and commit-ment, he also insisted on paying his dad a five hundred dollar a month rental fee.

It was here that Andy now sat, amid all the film equip-ment, power cables, and high-intensity lights, reflecting on his earlier encounter with Rodney "Rotten Crotch" Crutchley inside the school library. Had the big youth with the mop of dark hair not literally lent him a hand today, Tony Scarletti and his football thugs would've made short work of him. Still, he wasn't out of the woods yet. Come Monday morn-ing, he'd be thrown right back into Titanis High's arena where Tony would be waiting for him.

Sighing, he looked around his studio. Other teen boys usually put their money and effort into cars, stereo systems, expensive smartphones, and the latest fashions, but Andy had little interest in them. They were tools to his way of thinking, and the more practical they were, the better. That's why he'd purchased the Mercedes Benz van, now parked at the far side of the studio space, sitting like a silver shuttlecraft on the landing deck of the starship Enterprise.

So much equipment, he thought. And yet here I sit unable to come up with a goddamn film project! Almost as if he'd sent a telepathic message, his silver and gray Cisco 8845 video phone atop his desk trilled. Startled from his reverie, he reached for the handset and hit the answer button. An instant later the freckled face of TJ Sully flared into view.

"What's up?" TJ queried, nibbling a candy bar.

Affecting a snobbish English accent, Andy said, "I say, old boy, perchance did you mean 'whuddup'?"

"Sorry, dude. I don't speak Ubangi."

Andy made a gun barrel and directed it at the video image of his friend. "Just for that crack, Mr. Sully, Ms Pickering will be paying you a visit tonight."

"Tell her not to bother, bro. I'm fresh out of condoms."

Andy broke out laughing. "You? Out? What happened−you use up your last box on Mr. Whippendell?"

TJ flipped him off: "Eat shit, motherfucker."

Again, Andy laughed. "Speaking of eating," he asked, eyeing the candy bar in his friend's hand, "is that an Almond Joy your mouth is busy raping?"

"Just snackin' on my favorite health food," Sully retorted, crunching into an almond.

"Coming from someone who'd classify a Big Mac as part of a balanced diet, that isn't saying much."

TJ feigned an expression of confusion. "You mean it isn't?" he said, his eyes going cross-eyed.

Andy chuckled again as he leaned back lazily, hands crossed behind his head, feet tossed atop his desk, his eyes wandering the twenty-foot high ceiling with its tangle of movie lights and electric cables.

"So how's Jinky, Mr. Stud?"

TJ grinned. "We've got a date to see a movie next Saturday."

"Way to go. Better treat her right or I just might have to move in on her myself."

And TJ Sully knew Andy Hupp could, if he wanted.

"In case you've forgotten, dude, I own a gun."

"You mean your dad does," Andy corrected.

"But which I have easy access to," the freckled teen countered, popping the last morsel of chocolate-covered coconut into his mouth. "Including three boxes of hollow-point ammunition."

Which was true, Andy thought.

The same gun they'd brought onto campus last year when shooting *Bust Out*, along with Andy's father's shotgun. Good thing Principal Meevers hadn't been a hard-ass about it. Otherwise they'd both have jail records now...

"So what're you doing?" TJ asked. "Plotting a bank robbery or something?"

"Got that planned for next week. Right now, not much. Gotta go into Austin early tomorrow. Doing a six am photo shoot for a series of fashion ads. The usual bullshit. From jeans to underwear. Probably gone all day."

"Lot of pretty models gonna be there?"

"Always."

"Lucky dog."

"Not really. Most of them don't dig male models."

"Why not?"

"Beats me, dude. Maybe it's because they don't want to be seen with someone better-looking who might draw attention away from them."

"Yeah, must be a terrible thing. You know, being so goddamn fucking good-looking that you scare chicks away."

Andy chuckled. "You said it, compadre—not I."

"Yeah, well. Jinky was checking you out too. Made me kinda jealous."

Andy waved a hand in dismissal. "Don't worry. She's safe from my predatory ways, buddy. Besides, I got my eyes on someone else."

"Let me guess: Lyla Van der Velden."

"You got it."

"Then why haven't you made a move on her?"

Andy sighed. Oh, the inevitable sigh. Maybe life was just one great big fucking sigh. The sound of lost dreams, he thought. The unreachable, the might have been, the never was, the too chicken to ever find out.

"Unfortunately, she's heard rumors that I occasionally run around campus waving firearms. And that I hang around with an equally nutty best friend. Kinda puts a damper on things, if you know what I mean."

"Shit, Jones. What are you talking about? You're a campus rock star."

"Yeah, right. What I am is a guy who's gonna get his ass beat come Monday morning."

"Look on the bright side, Andy. Lyla probably digs guys with purple and blue bruises. Black eyes too. Not to mention swollen lips. Maybe even a couple of missing teeth. You know, to give you that sexy macho look."

"If only that were true, smartass. Because if Tony Scarletti gets hold of me I'll be looking so sexy and macho my own mom won't recognize me."

"Nor your modeling agency..."

Though Andy smiled at this back and forth banter, TJ's crack had given him cause for sudden concern. And maybe he was right. Should he get his ass kicked come Monday morning, that might very well short-circuit his modeling career for weeks to come, if not months. If not forever. And he needed to maintain a steady flow of cash to insure his next film project got off the launchpad.

"Well, if an ass-kicking looks inevitable, TJ, I'll just tell Scarletti to spare my face. Then again, come Monday lunch period I'll be adding a new member to Hupp Film Productions. He stands about six foot three and two hundred pounds."

Puzzled, TJ exclaimed: "Who–?"

"Rodney Crutchley."

"Dafuq?" the freckled teen muttered, bringing the palm of

his hand up to his forehead with a slow-motion gesture. "I can't believe it. It's just not possible. But One Buck For A Suck Hupp strikes again..."

Andy yawned and grinned at the same time, quite a feat in itself. "Well, gotta go, amigo. Like I said, have to get up early and drive into Austin tomorrow morning."

"Okay, catch you on Monday," TJ said in parting. "You, me, Jink and–God help us–Rotten Crotch Crutchley."

The video phone went dark.

Sitting there, Andy Hupp stared out the blank screen for a long moment, thinking. Then, his thoughts turned again to Rodney, and the intriguing tale of two Titanis High students who had disappeared several years earlier. Biting his lip with sudden curiosity, he spun in his high-backed office chair and faced his twenty-five inch computer monitor.

Clacking rapidly on his keyboard, he quickly brought up images of Tina Sawyer and Brett Hinkle. Dozens of them, in fact–most captured several years ago by various regional and national news outlets as well as local, state, and federal law enforcement agencies. Intermixed among them Andy discovered photos of other teens, mostly girls; all now linked inextricably to Sawyer and Hinkle.

For a moment Andy just sat there, regarding the images in silence, his fingers poised motionless above the keyboard. All these vanished lives, he thought, cut short by person or persons unknown. And yet, two of them had once lived right here in Titanisville, walking the very same school hallways he now did.

Now they were gone.

Without a trace.

But to where...?

Clicking on a succession of photos and websites, he eventually alighted on one particularly obscure web page. It was much the same as the others, except that something new stuck out: a single photo, claiming to have been taken several months earlier by an unknown person while on vacation;

someone the vacationer claimed was a recent photo of missing high school student Brett Hinkle, who had disappeared years earlier. Hazy, barely discernible, the individual cited in the photo had been caught moving in the company of two swarthy-faced men as they made their way through an outdoor market. More bizarre still, was the alleged location of the photo: a crowded jungle town down in Guatemala called Mazatenango.

A slow breath of astonishment escaped Andy's lips.

Leaning closer to his computer monitor, he struggled to confirm with absolute certainty that he was indeed looking at the face of Brett Hinkle, some four years after vanishing and presumed dead from Titanisville, Texas.

Mazatenango, Guatemala...

He fought back an eerie shudder, even as all the implications came rushing in at once. For if that really was Brett Hinkle, then something very, very strange was going on.

Only...

The photo was just too hazy.

And the source was an unknown person whose only identity was listed as "Traveler".

Altogether, not much to go on.

Most likely a sick prank.

Still...

What if it was Hinkle?

On the other hand, it might just be someone who closely resembled him, Andy reasoned. We all have our doppelgangers, he knew. After all, even the author of Rodney's crime book believed Hinkle to be long dead.

If so...

Then how could that three month old photo possibly be him?

CHAPTER 7

Outside the rundown beer joint, a thin drizzle was falling over the seedier streets of Houston, but neither man bothered to look beyond the smear of blue and red neon outlining the establishment's grimy plate glass window. And though it was well past midnight, there was still a steady beat from the battered jukebox and shrill laughter oozing from the darkness, of glasses tinkling and flabby, middle-aged breasts and thighs being fondled and groped by unseen hands.

"Still on for Halloween night?" the burly man asked, leaning forward as several greasy strands of blondish hair fell limply over his sun-browned forehead, acquired from countless hours staring through the cockpit window of a cargo plane into endless vistas of sun-blazed sky.

"It's a go," the other man confirmed. "As planned, you'll drive the van on the night of the pickup. Together with our other man, you'll load the merchandise and deliver it to the airstrip, then place it aboard your plane. Once you're airborne, he'll take the van, sans all prints, and dump it in some ghetto neighborhood—keys in the ignition. Any questions?"

The cargo pilot nodded, then took a long swig from his bottle of Coors. "Same beaner helping me?"

"He's cartel, so yes. They like to have at least one of their own involved in these kinds of transactions."

"He's an asshole."

"True, but a dangerous one. So keep it businesslike."

"Ya got the fee?"

"Right here," the other man acknowledged, patting the left

93

side of his tweed jacket, the kind with leather-patched el-bows. "Half now and half when the merchandise reaches its final destination."

The burly pilot started to reach forward.

"There's one other thing..."

The pilot's eyes narrowed. "Yeah?"

"Another matter has recently come to my attention. One that will require an additional service from you."

"Like what?"

"It concerns a rather nosy high school kid. He's been snoo-ping around where he shouldn't and finding out things that we don't want him to know."

"Not my line of work, babysitting asshole punks."

"The cartel has authorized me to grant you additional funds for looking into this matter."

"Yeah? So what's the kid done? Shit his pants and needs a diaper change?"

"No, but you might shit yours if we allow him go on look-ing into the disappearance of Sawyer and Hinkle."

That gave the pilot reason for pause; he'd already done enough to get the needle ten times over and wanted to live a little longer to enjoy all the dough he'd made.

"What's he know?"

"It's what he might come to know that's the danger. Ap-parently, he's been going around school collecting data and storing it on his laptop computer. Data concerning the Saw-yer-Hinkle disappearance: talking to students who knew them, asking questions of teachers, even snooping around town. And now we suspect he's been putting two and two together, and we don't like it. But to be sure, we need to know what this kid is up to. And exactly what he's found out. We've al-ready looked into his school library record, and it's clear he's definitely been sticking his nose into their disappearance for some time now, judging by how far back the check-out dates on his library card go. But why, we haven't been able to figure out. Could be just youthful curiosity..."

The cargo pilot—whose name was Schmidt—slid his eyes off to the left, considering, one pale brown iris reflecting the blue and red neon like a baleful autumn moon. For a moment there was only the beat of the jukebox pounding out Alan Jackson's *Chattahoochee* and a drunken argument up at the bar, away from the booth where the two men sat.

"Could be—?"

"Or could be something else."

"So ya want me to snatch the laptop?"

"No, someone else will take care of that. Once he has it, it will be delivered to you. And once you have it, we want your computer hacker girlfriend to examine its contents and see what she can find. That will probably require her to crack a difficult password, since this kid's real paranoid I'm told."

"No prob. The bitch is a whiz."

"The additional fee is contingent that she is. Now, once you have access to this individual's data, look over everything he's collected—names, dates, places, and then decide if he and any others who may have seen this data is a threat to us. If so..."

As Schmidt listened, his booze-blurred mind thought back.

Hinkle...

Yeah, he remembered the punk kid.

Four years ago, wasn't it?

He had taken him south of the border, gagged, blindfolded, and hog-tied in the cargo hold of his twin-engine Aero Commander 500S Shrike. For some clientele, Hinkle was prime merchandise: Blond. Slender. Good-looking. With a 'bubble butt' favored by certain men of 'other proclivities'.

Rich foreign faggots, in other words.

Four years ago...

A lonely country road.

Hinkle and a girl; they had taken them both.

Leaving police without a clue.

"A photo's turned up online," the other man went on. "Apparently taken by a tourist. Someone, it turns out, who knew

Brett Hinkle rather well—in more ways than one. But for personal reasons he kept that connection secret during the initial police investigation into Hinkle's disappearance, which is just as well. Anyway, no matter what we do about this snoopy high school kid the cartel wants the photo, the website, and the tourist to vanish—permanently."

Schmidt caught the jiggly bar maid's eye and twirled a finger into the air. As she went off to fetch him another bottle of Coors he looked hard at the man seated across from him: "Wet-work will cost ya," he said. "Why not get some MS-13 gangbanger to do it on the cheap?"

"They want this to look 'accidental' so they're willing to pay more for a polished removal. That said, are you turning down the job?"

"Didn't say that." He'd wanted to add: "Asshole".

"Then?"

"Okay," he said, swiping a rough hand across his mouth after sucking down another sloppy gulp of beer, "I'll do it."

"Good. I've come prepared." He reached into the inside pocket of his tweed jacket and withdrew a cash-stuffed envelope. "Half up front, and the remainder once both assignments are completed."

"Is the guy in the area?" Schmidt asked, taking the envelope and sliding it through the open collar of his khaki shirt, resting it snug against a thick mat of chest hair.

"Just down the coast from Galveston. Should make a pleasant drive for you." As he spoke, the tweed-jacketed man reached into another pocket and withdrew a second envelope and tossed it at the pilot. "Here's his photograph, along with the name and address of the individual in question."

The bush pilot took the envelope and cracked it open, scanning the photo and enclosed information. Then he looked up: "Jeeze. With a name like 'Lance Butterfield' I'm surprised the faggot hasn't already been killed..." He pushed the information back into the envelope, and deposited it inside his shirt. "Ya want me to contact ya when it's done?"

"If you wish, but I'll be monitoring the news. When I see a media report that he's vanished and his house has burnt to the ground, I'll contact you for delivery of the remaining payment."

"So ya want a torch job too?"

"Don't worry, next time we meet there'll be a little extra bonus in your pay packet on top of everything else. You see, we want to insure that any incriminating photos or other evidence the target may have hidden away in his house is incinerated. That way, you'll be spared a tedious room to room search of the premises, thereby eliminating the possibility that you might overlook some critical evidence." The tweed-jacketed man took another sip of his highball, then added: "If you plan it right, the murder and house fire of a homosexual man will likely be written off by law enforcement and the media as just an act of spiteful revenge perpetrated by some unknown gay lover Lance Butterfield jilted. As such, it will never be solved. Which means they'll never suspect what really happened. Besides, nobody cares anyway—especially the public. Case closed."

The cargo pilot grunted as he took another swig of beer.

"Within a day or two the laptop will be delivered," the tweed-jacketed man continued. "Have your girlfriend look it over. Then let me know what you've found out. In the meantime, make certain Hinkle's photo, the website, and Lance Butterfield doesn't cause us any further concern. Clear?"

The bush pilot massaged his mustache.

Lotta money, he thought.

Then again, lotta risk.

Death penalty kind of risk.

But greed and a crooked grin cut across his ruddy, whiskered face. A moment later, he got up and left the bar.

Five minutes after that, so did the other man.

"Here he is, ladies and gentlemen," TJ announced, soon as Andy Hupp slid into his familiar cafeteria seat the following Monday. "Titanis High's most famous movie mogul has arrived."

Setting his tray down and quickly situating his ham, turkey, and Swiss cheese on rye, Styrofoam bowl of spicy brown mustard potato salad, and 17 ounce bottle of Sparkling Ice pomegranate-blueberry flavored water, Andy Hupp looked up and asked: "Where's Jinky?"

"I left her with Mr. Whippendell right after drama class. Said she wanted to talk to him about the play she tried out for last Friday. You know, *The Crucible*. Told me to go on and not leave you hanging."

"Not even married yet and already she's bossing you around."

"Guess I'm just pussy whipped."

"Guys like you were born to be."

"And I hope that sandwich you're about to eat has Ebola."

Chuckling over TJ's jibe, Andy emptied his tray and set it aside, then reached for his Hupp Film Productions notebook. As he did, he muttered to his friend across the table, "Hope the future Mrs. Sully won't be too long... We've got a lot to talk about."

"With girls you never know," TJ soberly reflected, reaching for his own food.

Andy nodded at the truth of it all as he took a hard bite of sandwich. Then, grinning at his best buddy from across the table, he said: "Fuck vegans."

"Hell yeah," Sully agreed, his own face now stuffed full of cheeseburger and bacon. "Being a carnivorous bastard is the way to go, bro."

As they waited for Jinky to show, both boys dug methodically into lunch, Andy silently thumbing through his production notebook and scribbling notes as he ate. As he did, he absentmindedly cracked open his bottle of Sparkling Ice, taking occasional sips between bites of food. Sully in turn took

long swigs of Coca-Cola, like an old-time TV cowboy tossing back shots of whiskey down at the Long Branch Saloon.

After an interval of self-absorbed silence between the two,
Andy's moss-green eyes suddenly jerked up, as if he'd forgotten something, and briefly scanned the bustling cafeteria
like a German U-Boat captain.

Still no sign of Scarletti.

Strange...

He hadn't seen him all morning.

"You seen TS around?" Andy asked, using code-speak for
Tony Scarletti.

"Saw him earlier. Just after third period."

"And?"

"And nothing. Just rushing 'round school with his thug-
sters."

"Where to?"

"Dunno. Out toward the South Quad last I saw."

"Any idea why?"

"Nope. Not a juvenile delinquent like he is. But they seemed in a hurry, like they were after something."

"Or someone..." Hupp murmured to himself, with an uneasy feeling. "Which reminds me..." he said, glancing around
the cafeteria again, "where's our newest production member?"

Sully paused mid-bite, remembering their Friday evening
phone conversation. "You mean Rotten Crotch?"

"Listen, TJ. Rotten saved my ass last week. Seriously. So
from now on he's strictly Rodney to me."

"If you say so."

"I do. Because let me tell you something, amigo: beneath
all the ridicule he's taken Rodney's still got a pair of cast iron
nuts. You should've been there. Scarletti had me cornered in
the library with no way out. Were it not for Rodney I'd be
sitting here right now with three front teeth missing and two
black eyes. So he's not rotten to me anymore." His friend
looked across the table at him, his gray eyes doubtful. "I mean

the guy's really sharp," Andy went on. "Trust me, I talked to him. He's just gotten a bad rap, is all."

"No, Hupp–he just got a load of shit in his pants."

"Okay, so he had a minor blow out. No different than a semi-truck blowing a tire on the freeway. I mean, you don't fire the driver for that, do you?"

"Except that Rodney's tire blew out in the back of his pants."

Andy started to laugh, almost spitting out a bite of potato salad. "Goddamn it, TJ. Quit trying to crack me up."

"Okay, bro. But consider this. What if we're shooting a really important love scene and right as our star goes in for the kiss Rotten blows another tire?"

Son of bitch, Andy thought, this time unable to stifle an outburst of laughter. Rising from his seat, he walked a few steps away until his mirthful convulsions were brought under control. *Damn it!* Sully could zero in on his funny bone like a fucking laser-guided cruise missile!

Finally, he turned around.

"Okay," he sighed, walking back and sitting down again. "I hope you've had your fun."

"One more thing..."TJ said, smacking down the last of his bacon cheeseburger.

"Yeah?"

"Maybe Rotten never showed because he blew another tire on the way here."

Damn my semi-truck-blown-tire metaphor! Andy thought, trying not to laugh again, even as he caught sight of Jeena Kirtland weaving through the lunchroom crowd. Noticing his glance, TJ turned as well. A moment later the cute girl with the dazzling blue eyes straight off a Hitlerjugend poster, came up and tossed her backpack on the table and plopped into a chair.

A sad frown on her face.

CHAPTER 8

"Well guys. Happy New Year. Just so you know my life is totally fucked."

Both boys looked at her, then at each other.

"I lost the part," Jinky said, tears in her eyes.

"No way!" TJ blurted.

"Yes, way," Jinky affirmed. "Whippendell told me."

"But...how could you?" TJ said. "You're the best actress in all of Whippendell's drama classes!"

"Doesn't matter, TJ," she replied, eyes downcast. "Not in today's world."

Wondering why Jink's words should suddenly make him think of his mother, Andy suspected the answer lay behind Whippendell's drama class rejection.

"Exactly what happened?" Andy pressed.

Slowly, she raised her eyes and looked across the table at Andy Hupp. "Something to do with the school's new Inclusivity Policy," she muttered.

"The inclusi-*what?*" Andy said, not liking the sound of that.

"Mr. Whippendell explained it to me. Somebody by the name of Dr. Rothman Adler had Titanis High adopt it a couple of months ago, at the beginning of the school year. Because of it Whippendell has to cast at least one minority in a lead role once a year in order to be in compliance. And since *The Crucible* is the only play scheduled for this year he had no choice but to–"

"What?" TJ Sully demanded, his freckled face showing a

101

side of anger that few ever saw in the otherwise laid-back teen.

"Cast a Mexican girl in the role," Jinky said.

For an instant the shock on TJ's face jarred against Andy's Friday night memory of his mother, a woman desperately trying to make sense of why she no longer felt her job had any meaning–or, for that matter, much of anything else...

"What Mexican girl?" Andy asked.

"Oh, I don't know. Just some pushy Mexican girl. "Cheesy Gordita" or "Nachos Bellgrande" or some other stupid Mexican Taco Bell name." She wiped another tear from her cheek. "Guys, I was really counting on getting that role. Really, really counting on it. Now I won't be able to add it to my theater credits when I transfer to Texas State next year. And I studied my ass off for the past two weeks, learning some of Abigail's best lines for the audition. Just listen–"

"Hey, Jinky," TJ comforted. "It's okay. We believe you."

"No, listen!" And in a flash she changed the expression on her face, becoming cold and evil: *"Now look you. All of you. We danced. And Tituba conjured Ruth Putnam's dead sisters. And that is all. And mark this. Let either of you breathe a word, or the edge of a word, about the other things, and I will come to you in the black of some terrible night and I will bring a pointy reckoning that will shudder you. And you know I can do it; I saw Indians smash my dear parents' heads on the pillow next to mine, and I have seen some reddish work done at night, and I can make you wish you had never seen the sun go down!"*

Andy had to admit: he was impressed.

No doubt about it. Jink could emote like a pro.

Just add a period costume and all the trappings of the stage, and she would've made an equally good impression on the audience.

"You're good," Andy admitted, without one speck of charity in his voice. "Really good."

"I told you so," TJ quipped excitedly, proud of Jinky and

proud he had a friend who could recognize her talent.

"Thanks a bunch, Andy," she said. "It means a lot. Really." And the look in her shattering blue eyes revealed a deeper, more heartfelt sincerity than Andy had expected; one that for the briefest of moments intimated, perhaps, of something more...

"This shit just ain't right," TJ mumbled, diddling with a stray french fry in a way that suggested he would've killed it, had it been alive.

"That's why I'm so disappointed, TJ," Jeena Kirtland shot back. "I mean, I practiced for two friggin' weeks in front of a full length mirror, polishing every little emotion and every tiny mannerism. And you know what? Last week I totally aced that audition. Really, guys. Even Whippendell said so. But today he told me he's got to give the role of Abigail to a minority student."

Andy chewed his lip. He'd read *The Crucible* in junior high and had seen both the 1957 and 1996 movie versions, suddenly recollecting some black character or another. He looked at Jinky: "Wait a sec, Jink. Isn't that 'Tituba' character you mentioned black? A slave or something?"

"Yep. In *The Crucible* she plays Reverend Parris's slave."

"There you go – Whippendell's minority part. So why didn't he give you the role of Abigail? After all, the part's written for a white woman."

"Fuck yeah," TJ chimed in. "Why didn't he—?" He'd almost added 'babe' at the end, but wasn't brave enough yet, still not sure if he and Jink were that far along in their budding relationship. Even so, that wouldn't have stopped the ol' Huppster, he thought, with a mixture of admiration and envy for his best friend.

"Because the part of Tituba is a minor role, guys. And Dr. Adler's Inclusivity Policy requires that either a male or female minority be given at least one starring role from now on, no matter if all the characters were written for whites. So..." Jinky shrugged, her voice trailing off, renewed disappointment in her voice.

"Who the hell," TJ wondered aloud, his voice edged with anger, "is Dr. Rothman Adler?"

Andy Hupp knew.

Thinking back, he remembered Ms Pickering's words to him at the beginning of the school year: *"You really should join our school's new Youth For Social Justice Club, Andy. It meets every Friday after school in the high school theater. Oh yes, none other than Dr. Rothman Adler of the Center For Human Understanding in Austin is involved. Yes, the very same Dr. Adler you may have seen on CNN news from time to time..."*

"Dr. Rothman Adler," Andy informed, looking from TJ to Jinky, "runs Titanis High's Youth For Social Justice Club. He's also the one who got that new refugee facility built right on the edge of town."

"Not to mention our wonderful Feel The Hug indoctrination program," Jinky sniffed, wiping another tear from her cheek. This was the one thing she sometimes hated about being a girl, that her emotions were too often on display.

"You mean he's the one behind that fucked-up shit?" TJ blared, looking indignantly from Andy to Jinky.

Despite their mutual disappointment, both Andy and the girl couldn't help but laugh.

"Like, hello there, TJ!" Jinky said, reaching over and pinching the cute, freckled faced teen on the cheek. "It's the current year!"

"Meaning the fuck what?"

Andy shook his head, with a mixture of amusement and disgust. "Just some asinine expression Social Justice Warriors like to use."

"Social what—?" TJ echoed, looking across at Andy.

"You know, what they call guys like Dr. Adler—a real honest to goodness Social Justice Warrior. People like him spend their lives forcing their social engineering bullshit down the throats of the rest of us. Only trouble is they've convinced a lot of morons to fall into lockstep behind them."

Jinky looked at TJ. "I think your friend's gone full college professor on us."

"How do you know so much about this Dr. Rothman, bro?" TJ asked, curious.

"I don't. I just know what Ms Pickering, my Social Studies teacher, told me."

"Why'd she even bother?"

"Who knows? Maybe to entice me into joining the school's Youth For Social Justice Club. Guess she thought someone like me might jump at the chance to hobnob with somebody famous like Dr. Adler."

"*Oooo*, watch out everybody! Andy's wants to be a big-time hobnobber!" Jinky teased.

"Hobnobbing is what big-shots do," Andy explained. "You know, like what the three of us are doing right now."

They all laughed.

"And what a happy bunch of hobnobbers we are!" Jinky squealed, her eyes dancing with mirth. "But tell me something, Andy. I heard only the smartest kids get asked to join." She elbowed TJ beside her. "You ever get asked?"

"What? A dumb schmuck like me?"

"But a very cute one," she said, her eyes twinkling.

She looked back at Andy. "Like TJ, I wasn't asked either. But someone I know was. She and I take Ms Pickering's third period Social Studies class."

"I take her fifth period one," Andy pointed out, taking another sip of Sparkling Ice. "She must be recruiting from all her classes."

"What's her name?" TJ asked, looking over at Jinky.

"The girl?"

"Yeah."

"Lyla."

TJ suddenly glanced across the table at Andy.

In turn, Andy looked across the table at him.

Then they both looked at Jinky.

"What?" she said, looking at each boy disconcertingly. "Did

I say something bad?"

"What's her last name?" TJ asked.

Jinky thought a moment. "Jeeze, I should know that. Uhh...Van Dyke, maybe. No! Van Velden. One of those odd German names."

"It's Van der Velden and it's Dutch," Andy corrected.

"But I thought 'Van' was German."

"You're thinking of 'Von'."

Jinky glanced at the boy beside her: "Is he always this precise and infuriating?"

"Always," TJ nodded, with a shrug.

"Always," Andy Hupp added, with a particularly pointed grin.

"Why do you ask?" she asked.

TJ cut in before his friend could respond: "Cuz Andy's got a thing for her."

Jinky darted a sly glance toward TJ's handsome friend. "Oh, really? Tell me more."

Andy never liked talking about girls–especially to other girls. Dangerous territory, he thought.

"TJ's jumping to conclusions," Andy said, pulling his notebook forward.

"Like hell," his friend shot back. "You've had the hots for her all semester."

"Big mouth," Andy countered.

"Chicken shit.

"Big mouth's worse."

"Not asking her out is."

Andy looked up, sighed. "Round one to the big mouth in the far corner."

Jinky giggled.

"Boys, boys. Settle down. I know Lyla pretty well. Like me, she's sassy, classy, and for the right boys we both offer something else with a double 's' in it."

A look of momentary puzzlement clouded the boys' eyes. Then, understanding dawning, they suddenly looked across the table at each other and mouthed a single word, one normally not said in the presence of girls.

But Jinky's quick eye caught it. "That's right, guys," she said, with a wink and a knowing look, "I read lips too."

"Okay, okay," Andy said, spreading his hands in surrender. "I give up. The big mouth across the table is right. I do sorta have the hots for Lyla Van der Velden."

"Andy, I do believe you're blushing."

"Just a sudden case of indoor sunburn. Comes with too much exposure to fluorescent lighting," he weakly defended, knowing this girl had him pegged. Distractedly, he reached again for his production notebook. "Anyway, doesn't matter. She probably already has a boyfriend." Then, reaching for his pen, he scribbled a quick note: *This chick sure knows how to embarrass a guy...but sure love that laugh of hers. Kooky girl, too, but has a sharp wit and perceptive eye. Can't wait to direct her in a movie..."*

"Well..." Jinky said, "Lyla once told me she sometimes goes out after their meetings with a few of them, including Ms Pickering. Doing who knows what. Sounded kinda mysterious, if you ask me."

"Well, Ms Pickering is kinda weird," Andy murmured, "so I'm not surprised."

"On the other hand," Jinky went on, "Lyla told me she finds you way cute. Especially the time you walked into class with your zipper down."

Andy looked up. "She mentioned *that?*"

"More than mentioned. She even described the color of your underwear."

"Which was?"

"Gray with black stripes. Convinced?"

Got me dead to rights, Andy thought, tossing the pen aside. And here I sit listening to TJ's girlfriend describe the color of my underwear—underwear that another girl privately described to her. And doing it right in front of my best friend. That can only lead to trouble.

"And you say she's a member of the Youth For Social Justice Club?" Andy pressed, trying not to sound too curious.

Only Jinky had his number, knowing exactly what he was thinking: "Well, she did tell me several times how disappointed she was after finding out you'd turned down Ms Pickering's invitation to join." Upon hearing that, she noted a questioning look in Andy Hupp's alpine green eyes. "Oh yes, Ms Pickering told her." She giggled conspiratorially: "That's right, Andy. We female students often share gossip with our female teachers and vice versa. So we've got you boys under observation all the time."

Maybe so, Andy thought.

Still, he wondered why.

There was no obvious reason to, so it made him pause and reflect on Jinky's words for just a fleeting wisp of a moment. But somewhere at his deepest level, he sensed there was more to it than just telling one student that another had chosen not to join the Youth For Social Justice Club. Something that was not readily apparent, but there just the same.

"Andy–?"

"Uhhh...sorry, Jink. You were saying?"

"I was saying that Lyla had hoped you would join Ms Pickering's after-school club. Had even thought of asking you herself. But she's way too chicken because she says you're so good-looking you'd probably act like a real asshole if a girl asked you something like that."

"Gee, thanks a lot, Jink. Now I can go home and cut my throat knowing Lyla thinks I'm an asshole."

"But a cute one," Jinky amended. "In fact, Ms Pickering herself mentioned something to Lyla about asking you again. You know, to join." And for a moment Jeena Kirtland examined him cryptically, her pretty head cocked to one side, as if her blue eyes were twin fluoroscopes: "So would you? Join them? Ever?"

Andy wondered why Jeena Kirtland was so curious to

know, Lyla Van der Velden aside. But what puzzled him most was Ms Pickering, especially since she had gone all ice cold on him since he'd declined to join the Youth For Social Justice Club the first time around. So why the change of heart? Why was she still determined to have him join? He just couldn't figure it.

Not yet, at least..

Funny, though, how life so often turned out to have so many subsurface connections that you never even knew existed until you stumbled upon them by accident—as he just had. In this case, the odd connection between Ms Pickering, Dr. Rothman Adler, Lyla Van der Velden, and himself. All interconnected. But just his luck; all this time he had been thinking about how to get in good with Lyla, positioning himself to ask her out, when all along there she was, thinking about asking him out—and yet neither had known of the other's secret desires. Somewhere in there was another movie script, he fleetingly mused, even as he suppressed his newfound disappointment at finding out that Lyla Van der Velden was just another Titanis High Social Justice Warrior.

Resignedly, he pulled his film production notebook forward again. Then, assuming a more serious expression, he tapped his pen against the Formica tabletop: "Okay, my fellow hobnobbers. I'd like to call this meeting of Hupp Film Productions to order. Any opposed?"

Jinky glanced at TJ. "Am I officially a member of the production team now?"

"That's what I was just about to ask, Jink," Andy said. "Seeing as how you're not going to be in *The Crucible* now, do you want to be?"

"Before I answer I want to say something..."

"What girl ever fails not to," Andy joked.

"Well, for one thing, I think you two are probably the weirdest boys in school..."

"We've been called worse," Andy admitted. "That is, TJ has."

"...and that you two seem to get into a lot of trouble."

"Again, mostly TJ's fault," Andy further explained, as if stating an undeniable fact.

"What Andy really means to say," the freckle-faced boy across the table shot back, "is that most career criminals like him always make that excuse."

"Which reminds me, TJ: have you told Jinky the good news yet?"

"What good news?" she queried.

"That TJ's five year probation period ends next week."

She shot a glance toward the boy beside her. "Five year pro–?"

Both boys burst out laughing.

"Oh!" she exclaimed. "I should've known!" When the laughter died down, she added: "You see, that's what I mean! You're both weird!"

"But cute," TJ said, poking her in the side. "You said so yourself."

"And real ladies men," Andy put in. "So much so the editors at Playboy send us a free copy every month."

"But not very modest," she bandied back. "Especially you, Andy."

"Movie people seldom are."

She rolled her eyes.

"Does that mean you've signed on to our production team?" Andy asked, grinning.

Just as she was about to answer a gangly youth skid to a halt next to their table. It was Lawrence Micklethwaite, the school's inveterate snoop.

"Huppy! You're still alive!"

Pushing back lazily in his chair, Andy adopted his best Mark Twain impression, speaking in the convincing drawl of an elderly man, "The report of my death has been greatly exaggerated, son."

"Pretty good, Andeee!" Jinky squealed, clasping her hands together. "I didn't know you could act!"

Andy canted one eyebrow, a debonair glint in his eye. "I'll have you know that I'm more than just a teen wonder movie director, Jink. Not to brag but I have many other talents as well." Too late, he thought, realizing his words might be interpreted in more ways than one.

"I'm sure you do," she softly replied. And for an instant Jinky held his glance, eyes wide with meaning, before abruptly looking away.

Andy too looked away, hoping Jinky had not seen anything in his return glance that she shouldn't have. Turning once more to Micklethwaite, he asked, "What happened?"

In response, the lanky teen jittered around like a spastic for a moment, as if he were an electrically-charged wire about to tear loose from its power pole. "All I know," he blurted, never liking to see the initiative lost when it came to spreading gossip, vicious rumors, assorted lies, character assassinations, and–on rare occasion–a nugget of truth, "is that Tony and his three thugs caught up with Rotten in the South Quad and tore him a new asshole. Scarletti called it payback for marking up his locker door again."

"What do you mean *again?*"

"Didn't you hear? Turns out Rotten's the same guy who marked up Scarletti's door first time around. Only this time he left his initials behind—RC. Better check it out before that dimwitted janitor removes it."

Andy rose from his seat. "I can't believe he did it."
Or did!

After all, he knew next to nothing about the hulking teen.

"Maybe you can't, but Scarletti sure can. And his fists just proved it. So watch out, Huppy. He'll be kicking your ass next."

It had to be a frame-up, Andy reasoned.

After all, nobody but a fool would leave his initials behind after doing something like that. Unless...unless they were looking for a fight. On the other hand, if Rodney Crutchley hadn't done it—who had?

And why were they trying to frame him?

As far as Andy knew, even Principal Meevers hadn't discovered yet who had marked up Tony Scarletti's locker door, or else the school grapevine would've heard about it by now.

No, Andy thought...

He was convinced the quiet kid he'd met in the library couldn't have done it. If so, then who among the student body hated him so much that they had? Any one of them, he was forced to admit—which meant Rodney Crutchley was vulnerable to every sadistic asshole at Titanis High.

But whether the big lunk of a kid had actually marked up Scarletti's locker door or not really didn't matter—because merely seeing the initials 'RC' was all the proof a jerk like Scarletti needed. For in the football quarterback's unthinking mind, it would never occur to him that it might be a setup; that Rodney Crutchley might be innocent and that he was being framed by some unknown enemy.

In the end, however, Tony Scarletti didn't like anyone defying him, and by now had figured out that Rodney had somehow helped Andy Hupp escape last Friday—and the marked-up locker door with Rodney Crutchley's initials was all the excuse Scarletti and his thugs needed to beat him up.

"Where's Rodney now?" Andy asked.

"Stevie Warren says he's in the school library licking his wounds."

"What's Principal Meevers done about it?"

"Done? Ha! What a laugh! Meevers' done nothing, dude."

"What*?!* After beating up Rodney Crutchley?"

"That's not the whole of it! Turns out Jamal got his arm bro–" At that instant, somebody called out from across the vast cafeteria: "Hey, Lawrence! Get your dumb faggoty ass over here and tell us what happened to Rotten Crotch! My girlfriend's having an orgasm just waiting to hear!"

Laughing insanely over being the bearer of more Titanis High drama, Lawrence Micklethwaite sped away toward a group of other boys and girls at the opposite side of the cafeteria, dancing a spritely little jig along the way.

Turning glumly toward TJ and Jinky as he gathered up his notebook and backpack, Andy said: "Meeting's canceled. And now we know why our fourth production member never showed up."

TJ looked at Andy: "What was that last thing Lawrence said?"

"Didn't quite catch it," Andy replied, "something about Jamal Perkins, I think. But it's Rodney whom I'm worried about."

"What do you mean 'our fourth production member'?" Jinky interrupted, looking from one boy to the other. "Did I hear right? Rodney Crutchley is now part of our movie production team? For real?"

Andy looked at her: "If he is does that mean you're not?"

A moment of hesitation passed over Jeena Kirtland's face. Still torn up after losing the part of Abigail Williams in *The Crucible* to a Mexican girl, she was looking for something else to dig her teeth into. But did she dare hook up with Andy Hupp and TJ Sully, two way cute but totally whacked-out boys that trouble followed everywhere?

"Well..."

Andy held her eyes, waiting.

"What's his job going to be?" she timidly asked.

"Your co-star and main love interest," TJ quipped, unable to resist.

"*Ewww—*gross!"

"Script development," Andy corrected, shooting a visual rebuke toward his friend.

"Sorry, Andy," TJ mumbled, gathering up his own books.

"Script development?" Jinky said, incredulous. "You mean like the idea for our movie is coming from Rodney Crutchley? From Rodney "Rotten Crotch" Crutchley? For real?"

"For real," Andy replied. "At least, the basic idea. But TJ and I will write the screenplay. And you'll be the star."

Now they were talking her language.

"Top billing?" she asked, in a teensy-weensy voice.

TJ burst out laughing. "Oh boy, Andy. I think she's hooked."

Andy hefted his backpack. "Are you, Jink?"

She gave a rapid nod, as if having just agreed to submerse herself in icy water, but still apprehensive about doing so.

"Good. And yeah, top billing. Now I've got to run off and check on our fourth team member. He's smart and I think he can help make our movie project a success. I just hope you two can treat him like a friend and partner instead of a piece of shit."

"Promise," Jinky meekly agreed.

"Okay, bro. No more "Rotten Crotch" outta me," TJ assured. "Just hope he doesn't blow another tire."

"Blow another—?" Jinky began, glancing from boy to boy.

"Never mind," Andy said, with a warning glance directed toward his friend. "In the meantime, I'm going to find Rodney and see what happened."

"Watch yourself, Andy," TJ cautioned. "If Scarletti went after Rodney you can bet you're next."

"TJ's right," Jinky added, her blue eyes reflecting female concern; that, and maybe something more—

But Andy mentally strangled the emerging possibility before it could fully develop. After all, he'd never do anything to hurt his best buddy. Not in that way. Not ever... That is, if Jink could just keep her distance and stop looking at him with those absolutely mesmerizing eyes.

"Gotta go," Andy said, pushing his chair in. "Rodney saved my ass and I never forget a favor."

"Then I'm going with you," TJ insisted. "That is, me and my one puny muscle."

Andy chuckled, but there was a grim note to it. "Thanks, amigo. But now's not the time to ditch that way cute girl sitting next to you just to be a hero."

And before his friend could object, Andy Hupp spun away and dashed out the exit door.

CHAPTER 9

On his way to track down Rodney Crutchley, Andy Hupp made a quick detour to his locker to dump his backpack. After he did, he turned around and noticed Tony Scarletti's lime-colored locker across the corridor, where the previous week Principal Meevers had discovered the "One Buck For A Suck Hupp" message, scrawled there by person or persons unknown. Now here it was again, this time defaced with an even more obscene message.

Walking over, he read:

> "After you suck Hupp for a buck, I've got a fat dick 4 U 2 lick. All you need to bring is some of your famous Scarletti lip lube. So look for me in the boy's bathroom, faggot–I might even let you fuck my shit-crusted crack. Signed, RC–your friendly neighborhood queer sex provider."

Making sure the coast was clear, Andy pulled out his smartphone and snapped a quick photo; he wasn't sure why, only that the printing style looked strangely familiar and that it might come in handy later. Besides, Gibb Galloway, the elderly school janitor would soon be along to erase all evidence of the vandalism, just like last time. Then again, he thought, glancing up at the surveillance camera at the far end of the corridor, there should be a video recording of the perpetrator committing the act. If so, Principal Meevers must already know the identity of the guilty party. With that in mind, Andy Hupp raced off in search of Rodney.

Five minutes later he discovered him seated in a remote section of the library, tucked away in a little alcove behind eight-foot-high shelves of books. As he approached the hulking figure seated at a small study cubicle, Andy noted the left side of his face: bruised, swollen, with a cut just above his right eye. Long ago, his vivid cinematic imagination had likened modern American high schools to prisons in all but name. They were crowded. They were violent. And they were under strict government control. All that was missing were prison uniforms and machine gun towers, and maybe those weren't far behind...

Pulling up a chair, Andy sat down.

"Hey, Rodney. You 'kay?"

Staring straight ahead, Crutchley remained silent.

Deciding not to push the sympathy bit any further, Andy cut right to the chase: "Hey, listen. We had our meeting in the lunchroom and I hit up TJ and Jink–that is, Thomas Sully and Jeena Kirtland–with the idea about bringing you on board as our script developer. They're way cool with it."

Crutchley slowly turned his eyes toward Hupp. He saw the kind of face that girls fall all over, framed by carefree, light-brown hair, friendly green eyes, and a quick and easy smile. Everything he himself lacked. So it just didn't make any sense why a popular kid like him would want to hook up with a loser named "Rotten Crotch". Was it pity? Curiosity? A set-up designed to get his hopes up that he had finally found a friend, only to end up as the butt of a cruel joke when he was later rejected and scorned? If anything, Andy Hupp asking him to join his movie making project made far less sense to him than Tony Scarletti's fists punching his face while T-Bone Ramirez and Brodie Henshaw held his arms behind his back as Jamal Perkins pranced about poking and jabbing while making homoerotic suggestions at him.

"What about...*the girl?*"

"Jinky?"

"Yes."

"Like I said, she's cool with it. So is TJ. They don't like Tony Scarletti any more than you or I do."

The big youth lowered his eyes; dark, forlorn, unreadable. Andy could tell talking was difficult for him, especially talking to someone who wasn't acting hostile.

"Is she...*your* girlfriend?" Rodney asked, looking down at his hands. Big, clumsy hands.

Now that question caught Andy off guard. "Uhh, no. TJ's. Why?"

Rodney shifted his dark eyes, so dark Andy hadn't realized they were actually a deep midnight blue. He didn't think eyes could be so dark and still be called by that color.

"Girls don't usually—" he started to say, before his voice trailed off.

Realizing he was dealing with someone who had taken so much shit from so many people for so long a time that he was almost paralyzed, Andy proceeded carefully: "Hey, don't worry Rodney. It's not going to be that way with Jink. Believe it or not, she's a lot less vicious than most girls."

That brought a curious look from the big kid. "Less?"

Andy chuckled. "What I mean is that all girls have a streak of viciousness in them, right? That's because they're physically weaker than guys so they've got to maintain a sort of balance of power, if you see what I mean." For a moment, Andy looked inward, thinking of a certain Social Studies teacher. "At least, that's my theory, for what it's worth."

"I've always felt that way too," Rodney ventured, surprised that someone else saw things the same way. "But I still want to like them."

Andy grinned. "Join the club, dude. We all do." He leaned slightly forward. "Look, I know girls have given you a rough time around school."

"How...how do you know?"

"I've got ears," Andy replied. "I've got eyes. I've heard

things. And I've seen the shit they've put you through."

Rodney said nothing.

"Anyway," Andy went on, as the big kid concentrated on his hands again, "why did Scarletti come after you?"

There was another long silence before Rodney Crutchley finally looked up again: "Because I helped you get away."

Andy thought about that. Then: "But how was he even certain you had? I mean, he never saw me hidden atop that book shelf, out of sight. And you kept your mouth shut, right? So he had no proof. No way to know."

"He didn't need any."

Slowly, Andy nodded. "You've got a point." Now for the big question: "Did you do it?" he asked. "You know, mark up Scarletti's locker? Personally, I don't care one way or the other. I just want to know."

Rodney looked at him, and this time his perceptive intelligence was evident, there in his fathomless dark eyes. "The forgery was good," he softly replied, almost as if he were alone and thinking aloud. "The printing resembled mine."

Andy's eyes sharpened. "*Resembled...?* Are you saying what I think you're saying?"

"I'm saying whoever wrote that message on Scarletti's locker door went out of their way to imitate my style of printing."

"Can you recall giving any students anything with your writing on it?"

"No one," Rodney said. "Ever."

Andy digested that, knowing it was probably true; Rodney had long been a secretive individual among the Titanis High student body, always keeping to himself. Most school pariahs were.

"Then maybe you lost a piece of paper with your writing on it somewhere along the way. Anyway, we need to go to Principal Meevers and explain to him how somebody else wrote on Scarletti's locker door and not you."

Rodney shook his head. "I don't want to do that—"

"Why not? Meevers is pretty cool. Last year he cut me some serious slack after he caught me and TJ with firearms on campus. He could have had us both arrested and sent to juvenile detention. So I'm sure he'll listen to us."

"I don't think that's a good idea. Whoever did this got a sample of my writing by another way..."

"I don't follow you."

"What I'm trying to say..." He broke off and looked up at Andy, his eyes plaintive. "What I mean is..." He halted again, knowing if he said it Andy Hupp would look at him oddly, if not walk away laughing.

"Go on."

"Never mind..."

"Go on," Andy repeated.

Rodney shrugged. "I don't think a student wrote those words on Scarletti's locker."

Andy blinked.

Didn't write the−?

For an instant his mind failed to grasp what the big youth was suggesting.

Then it dawned on him.

"Wait a minute. You're not saying it was...*a teacher?*"

Rodney slowly brought his head around. "For a long time something's been going on around this school. Before you or I ever got here. I've felt it for a long time. Like a sixth sense. Like that. And it's got something to do with the Sawyer-Hinkle disappearance. What, I'm not sure yet. But it's there just the same."

Oh god, Andy thought. He hoped Rodney wasn't the conspiracy theory type. Lawrence Micklethwaite was into that shit and could easily drive you crazy going over the Kennedy assassination or 9-11 or secret Nazi bases at the South Pole or even whether or not Traci Hochstedt wore crotchless panties under her skirts just to drive all the male teachers crazy by sitting in the front row and spreading her legs at strategic moments−all the while theorizing on these various subjects from fifty different angles.

"But you must have an idea," Andy prodded.

Rodney hesitated.

"Look, Rodney—let's get it all out in the open: what the hell's going on?"

"I'm still not sure yet."

Andy sighed and pulled back, examining Rodney Crutchley. Such a dead serious guy, he thought. He wondered if he ever laughed. Ever smiled. Ever once cracked a joke.

"Okay," Andy said, not sure it had been a good idea anyway. "For the time being we'll hold off going to Meevers. In the meantime, I came here to find out if you're still in?"

Two dark blue eyes regarded him, momentarily puzzled. He had taken four hard blows to the head while his arms had been pinned, and his brain was still a little foggy.

"You remember," Andy explained, "the movie project we talked about—that Tina Sawyer-Brett Hinkle thing? After mulling it over I think it has potential."

Understanding, Rodney reached into his binder without a word and pulled out a two page, typed synopsis and fact sheet on the Sawyer-Hinkle disappearance and handed it to Andy Hupp.

Andy took it and looked it over, his eyes vivid with interest. After a minute he glanced up, a glint of respect in his eye that the big youth couldn't fail to see. "This is really excellent, dude. With a whole lot of new details that neither the book nor my Internet search dug up. Really, this is college level research."

"So you looked up Sawyer and Hinkle? On the Internet?"

"Yeah, over the weekend," Andy murmured, absorbed in the paper, his mind slipping into analytical mode.

"Did you come across the photo of Hinkle taken by that tourist?"

"Yep," Andy confirmed. "Still, there's no proof it really was him. Even the crime author believes Hinkle's dead, along with Tina Sawyer. So what does a tourist know that he doesn't?"

"What do you think?"

Andy looked off, still unsure. "Let me answer that after TJ and Jinky have had a chance to go over this report of yours." He tapped the paper. "Okay if I make copies?"

Silently, the big youth reached into his binder again and withdrew two more copies, one each for TJ and Jinky, and handed them over to the good-looking teen.

"Hey, cool. Man, you're really on the ball, Rod. I like that. Too bad you and I don't share some classes together. I bet we could give certain teachers headaches playing tag team. I know one that hates students always maneuvering one step ahead of her."

"Which one?"

"Ms Pickering."

Upon hearing the name Crutchley looked askance, his mind seeming to work.

"Something wrong?"

Vaguely, Rodney shook his head, but Andy sensed that the mention of Ms Pickering had troubled him in some indefinable way. Then again, she often had that effect on certain students, especially male ones. Maybe she had given him the hungry eye too, since Rodney Crutchley wasn't bad looking really, albeit in a decidedly unkempt, menacing, and strangle-you-in-a-dark-alley sort of way. Then again, some brain-dead females were often drawn to such "bad boys" and Rodney definitely had an edgy side to him, in an *Outer Limits* kind of way. If he'd just lose that serial killer vibe he just might—

"About that photo..." Crutchley said, bringing Andy Hupp back into focus.

"Yeah?"

"Did you get a chance to visit the website?"

"Sure. Gotta admit that photo of Hinkle really creeped me out. That is," Andy went on, his voice colored with doubt, "if it really was Hinkle. I mean, *Mazatenango, Guatemala?* That totally blew my mind, dude. But when I tried to find out the name of the website owner I hit a dead end. No contact email, no name, no clue at all to his identity. Wait– There was one thing: I remember seeing the word "Traveler" at the end of all his web pages. You know, like it was his signature or something. But no actual name or contact email. Almost as if his website was intended only for people he personally knew. Probably because he doesn't want weirdos and conspiracy nuts contacting him."

He knew it was a mistake the moment he said it, because Rodney lowered his eyes and glanced away.

"Hey, I...uhhh....didn't mean you."

Rodney looked around again. "Maybe you should have. Because over the last few months I've been trying to hunt down the identity of "Traveler", stalking bits and pieces of him all over the Internet."

"And–?"

"Maybe it's better if I show you."

"Okay. Where to?"

"My locker. Over in C Corridor. That's where I keep my lap-top. Everything I've discovered is on it."

Andy rose from his chair. "Let's do it."

CHAPTER 10

They left the library just as the first bell marking the end of lunch period echoed up and down Titanis High's long, sleek, polished corridors. As Andy Hupp and Rodney Crutchley moved along, students rushed to and fro on their way to next class.

"Yabba dabba doo! There he goes! One Buck For A Suck Hupp!" a boy called out as he passed, sparking raucous laughter from passing students. "Hey, Andy!" another called out, "the price drop to fifty cents yet? That's all the spare change I got!"—inciting even more rowdy amusement.

"You like being made fun of?" the big youth asked, looking shyly at Andy—one of the most popular guys in school and here they were walking together, almost like—*like they were friends*. He had not known such a feeling for a long time.

"Mind? Hell yeah. And I gotta admit it's getting a bit old," Andy wearily confessed. "But it'll pass. In the meantime I just try to ignore it. Besides, most of them don't mean anything by it. It's just that being a teen seems to make a lot of us assholes, if you know what I mean. At least, that's what my dad likes to say. Something to do with brain chemistry, hormones, that kind of thing." He chuckled. "No wonder our parents can't wait to get rid of us once we turn eighteen."

"But you don't act that way."

Andy chuckled, thinking of the guns he and TJ had brought onto campus—not only against school policy, but state and federal law. "I don't? Try telling that to Principal Meevers."

"No, I didn't mean it that way. I meant that you seem to have," Rodney paused, searching for the right phrase: "a real purpose in life."

Andy glanced at him, his green eyes more alert.

"Sitting in the cafeteria," Rodney went on, encouraged by his companion's curiosity, "I sometimes hear you talk from where I sit two tables over. It's why I always sat nearby, you know, just to hear some of the intelligent things you say. I don't hear that kind of talk from too many others in our age group. I mean, you talk about movie projects and things like that, instead of the stupid things that everyone else does. Like future plans and stuff. Like what you're going to do with your life. Like...like you were already a thirty-something adult out on your own."

"Don't you have any plans?"

Rodney shrugged and looked off. "I don't think much about the future," he said, his voice trailing off.

They walked on—one a good-looking boy who turned female heads everywhere he went, the other a taller, heavier built youth with a brooding countenance and blackish-blue eyes, like water reflected from the bottom of a deep, dark, unfathomable well.

As they walked, girls looked at him too, but turned quickly away from the clumsily trodding giant. For many of them, just a brush of his watchful, brooding eyes seemed too intimate an intrusion.

A moment later, as the two boys approached a cross corridor, the second and final bell rang, indicating classes had begun.

"Guess we're late," Andy said, with a nonchalant grin.

Rodney looked toward him. "You don't really care, do you?"

Andy released a mischievous chuckle. "Nope. And I don't think you do either."

Rodney thought about it, even as the faintest hint of a

smile pushed outward onto his face, like a flower struggling up through a crust of snow seeking the first warming rays of the sun; and the sun, he realized, was Andy Hupp.

"No," Rodney slowly admitted, more to himself than to the boy beside him, as he looked straight ahead again. "I don't think I do."

"Besides," Andy went on, "when I'm busy putting together a movie project I don't let little technicalities like class attendance get in the way. Believe me, that counts for more than Ms Pickering and her fifth period Social Studies class."

Twenty feet further on Rodney glanced up at yet another poster stuck to the wall, one of many that seemed to be in perpetual rotation along the corridors of Titanis High. This particular one showed a white, All American family standing in front of the school entrance with their two white teenage children standing left and right of them, with both the parents' arms draped over the shoulders of a third child, a charcoal-black boy with dreadlocks. Emblazoned across the poster was the slogan:

ONE COLOR FAMILIES ARE BORING

And beneath it, in smaller font:

PUT AN END TO THE BOREDOM
ADOPT AN AFRICAN CHILD TODAY

Brought To You By
The Center For Human Understanding
and the Inclusivity Project
Dr. Rothman Adler, Director

"About what I was saying earlier..." Rodney softly began, lowering his eyes from the poster.

"Yeah?"

"About things not feeling right around this school. And not just here. It's all over the place. On those posters lining the hall, for instance. And every Feel The Hug meeting. Everywhere. Like something dark and unstoppable. Closing in on us."

"What kind of something?" Andy asked, intrigued by the way this weird kid's mind worked.

"Like–" and he paused, his eyes searching inward. "Like that old movie, what was it called? *Invasion of the Body Snatchers?*"

"Which version?" Andy asked, his formidable movie trivia knowledge kicking in. "The black and white version starring Kevin McCarthy or the color version with Donald Sutherland?"

"The first one," Rodney said, never having seen the color remake.

"Yeah, I've seen it. At least five times."

"Well, it's like the feeling you get when you watch that movie for the first time. You know, where everything seems normal. People going about their business. That kind of thing. But later on you begin to realize that things aren't normal. That something's not quite right in the town of Santa Mira." Rodney looked ahead. "Nor here in Titanisville. Or at this school. Or down in Austin. All over, in fact. Like...like people's minds and bodies have been taken over by something, just like in that movie."

He'd felt it too, Andy thought.

Some kind of creeping, cloying thing.

Recalling his mother's job concerns, he realized now that both hers and Rodney's words had spoken to a long-held feeling–that of a nagging, pervasive sense that something was not quite right. But no matter where he looked, not one single thing seemed to be the cause. And yet, here he was beside the only other person he'd ever met at Titanis High who shared that same sense of...*foreboding?*

But then, I'm weird too, Andy thought.

That had to be it. And this guy beside me is even weirder.

Then again, his weird best friend TJ had never brought it up, so how could that be? All he knew was that things didn't seem right anymore, just like in that Kevin McCarthy movie.

Like the whole school, even the whole town, and maybe even the whole country was fast approaching some sort of fracture point with no way to stop...

"Turn left," Rodney instructed. "My locker's down at the far end."

As they made the turn, bank after bank of purple, green, and yellow lockers came into view, their high-density polyethylene façades like so many sticks of multicolored chewing gum lining both sides of the twenty foot wide corridor. To Andy's eye, it looked as if they had stepped through a rip in the spacetime fabric straight into the psychedelic sixties, at least the sixties he had seen in old documentaries. He half expected some dope-smoking, long-haired hippie to pop out and flash him the peace sign as he and Rodney proceeded down the long sweep of corridor. Instead, he saw three students, one standing on the top rung of a step ladder while the other two, all electric with teenage exuberance, chattering excitedly among themselves. That is, until they turned and saw Andy Hupp, wisecracking school hotshot, and someone they had never expected to find walking at his side: Rotten Crotch Crutchley.

"Get a load of that combo," the boy whispered out of the corner of his mouth to the chubby female beside him. "Dr. Frankenstein and his monster."

It was then that the girl atop the ladder happened to turn and glance down; it was Lyla Van der Velden.

"Hi, Andy," she cheerfully called out, as he went passing by, causing him to stop dead in his tracks; for when it came to Lyla Van der Velden, Andy Hupp couldn't help himself. Rodney came to a stop too, standing silent and mute as he looked askance at the girl atop the ladder, as if fearing a verbal onslaught.

Flashing his wintergreen green eyes upward, Andy gave her the kind of look that put a bounce in any girl's heart.

"What are you up to?" he casually asked, "besides that ladder?"

In answer, she turned and proudly displayed the poster she was holding:

NO MORE BORDERS!

Beneath the bold statement, emblazoned in red font five inches high, was a secondary statement in smaller font:

BECAUSE NO HUMAN'S ILLEGAL!

The sight of the poster, with its message of—*just what, exactly?*—that pro-illegal, US-law-be-damned was a good idea to teach high school students? Andy wondered. If so, that was pretty fucked up, to say the least. Then again, he wasn't so sure how to take such posters, having always viewed them as just another silly way adults mucked up kids' minds. But now, seeing it suddenly through the eyes of a burgeoning seventeen year old mind on the threshold of adulthood, he wondered if something far more sinister was afoot, as Rodney had suggested. Trouble was, he had never been too political, letting such propaganda usually go ignored.

"Good thing you're wearing jeans standing up there," Andy quipped, channeling his uneasy thoughts into safer waters, even as he purposefully directed his eyes up the length of Lyla's svelte body.

"What? Oh goodness, you're right! Had I worn my usual skirt today you'd be getting quite an eyeful right now, wouldn't you!" She laughed, bringing her free hand up to her lips. "I can't believe I just said that! I'm soooo embarrassed!"

Andy laughed in return. "Say, wasn't that you putting up posters in the cafeteria last week?" Posters, Andy suddenly recalled, promoting an upcoming LGBTTQQIAAPO (lesbian, gay, bisexual, transgender, transsexual, queer, questioning, intersex, asexual, ally, pansexual, otherkin) seminar in the school's auditorium—a mandatory one that every ass bandit in the school was surely looking forward to, he thought, which is why he was going to play hooky that day.

"Yeppers. There–and the auditorium–and the main entrance–and everywhere else. Busy! Busy! Busy! Bee! That's me!" She gave him her most alluring smile. "It's all part of our "No Room For Racism" campaign that Dr. Adler and Ms Pickering put together. They're both great inspiration, Andy, especially Dr. Adler. Really, a smart guy like you should meet him. Say, why don't you join me at our next meeting? Ms Pickering told me she's already invited you to become a member, so you'd be welcome. And it's really fun. As a bonus Ms Pickering signs passes that gets us out of class all day whenever we're doing a project like this."

"I get out of class too," Andy grinned. "It's called ditching."

"Andy!"

"That's my name alright."

"Oh, Andy. It really is so fun to belong."

"You make it sound like the high school equivalent of Club Med," he replied, but the subtle jab of sarcasm floated right over her pretty little head.

"Oh, it is!" she said, then added: "What in the world's Club Med?"

The chubby girl assisting Lyla shot a hard glance up at her, "It's just a playground for the decadent bourgeoisie, Lyla! "

"Where'd you learn that word?" Andy mildly asked, "Marxism 101?"

"In our Youth For Social Justice Club, wiseguy–if you really must know," she shot back, a poisonous look directed at the boy too handsome for his own damn good. Now she despised him all the more, since she'd seen him checking out the lithe form of Lyla, perfectly encased in her tight designer jeans–a look he had not given her–nor ever would.

Where was the equality in that? she angrily thought.

Like Lyla, she too kept her eyes on Andy, but her glance remained venomous. And the boy beside her, a geeky kid with furtive eyes, looked on from behind thick-lensed glasses–his thick moist lips frozen in a permanent sneer. They both knew who Andy Hupp was: a devil-may-care student who lived by his own rules. But in today's PC world, that was the Mark of Cain...

Lyla, looking uncertainly at the hostile girl below, wondered why she was so disapproving of Andy Hupp.

"Well, better shove off," Andy finally said, sensing Rodney's growing unease. Then, tipping a hand at Lyla in farewell, he directed a parting glance at the rude-mouthed girl and her geeky sidekick: "After all, wouldn't want a couple of junior Bolsheviks like you running off to turn me and Rodney in for cutting class."

And with that, Andy and Rodney hustled on, even as Lyla van der Velden called out, "Remember, Andy! This Friday! October 31st! Five o'clock! I'll save a seat for you right next to me! Please! Come!"

Andy twirled around, waved one last time, then continued along his way.

"Was that your girlfriend?" the big youth beside him cautiously asked, as they moved on down the corridor.

"No. Why do you ask?"

"I don't know..." He looked ahead again. "She kind of acted like she was."

"Well," Andy confessed, "let's just say she's a girlfriend in training."

"She's very pretty."

Andy cocked an eyebrow in helpless agreement. "Lord Jesus but that's the gospel truth..."

A moment later he and Rodney Crutchley came to a stop in front of a purple locker door. As the big kid worked the combination, Andy stood by, keeping an eye out for any teachers prowling the corridors looking for truant students. Seconds later there was a 'click' followed by the sound of a locker door swinging open.

Then—dead silence.

Puzzled, Andy drew his attention away from the corridor and turned toward Rodney, who stood there with his hulking shoulders slightly bent forward, staring into the rectangular opening of his locker.

"It's gone," he muttered. "Somebody—"

"What's gone?"

"My laptop," Rodney said, slowly turning around and facing Andy. "Somebody got into my locker and...*took it.*"

But it wasn't that which unsettled Andy Hupp so much, unexpected though it was. No, it was something altogether different: the look of some inward sense of peril that only Rodney Crutchley could see...

CHAPTER 11

Crowding in front of Rodney, Andy began rummaging through the interior of the big youth's cluttered locker.

"Are you sure you didn't leave it in the library?" he called over his shoulder, even as he continued to sift through the locker's contents: a wadded up sweater, a jumble of books, a half-eaten bag of Fritos, a partially consumed bottle of Dr. Pepper, and a small plastic jar containing a few dollars in small change. Andy made note that the money, little as it was, hadn't been taken; certainly a student thief would have done so, along with the laptop–but not necessarily a Titanis High staff member.

"No," Rodney answered, "I'm certain I left it my locker right after third period. I don't forget things like that."

"Does anyone else know your combination?"

Rodney shook his head. "Nobody." But his eyes were looking into the distance. "Nobody except..."

They both looked at each other, thinking the same thing: the school office kept every student's locker combination number stored in a computer data base. That meant the entire school staff, from principal to teacher to office secretary, had potential access to the information.

Finally, Andy shut the locker door and spun the combination. "Not there," he concluded, sighing halfheartedly. "Boy, this is getting weird, Rodney. Really freaking weird."

"Maybe somebody else broke into my locker," Rodney softly suggested, with that same look of unspoken peril in his eye. "Somebody other than the school staff."

Andy let go a weak grin. "You mean, like a safe cracker?"

But Rodney Crutchley made no further comment, even as he glanced back at his locker, his mind working in directions Andy could not fathom.

Andy too remained silent, mentally following paths of his own as he scanned the banks of student lockers, all yellow and purple and green, their doors running off down the long polished corridor. Colorful and garish, he half-expected Willy Wonka and his chocolate factory Oompa Loompas to come traipsing down the slickly-burnished floorway, tossing bright jellybeans and gumdrops along the way.

Yet his mind kept coming back to one overriding question.

Who had broken into Rodney's locker?

Sure, it was possible some petty thief had wandered in from off the street and used some devious criminal trick to get inside a few random lockers–Rodney's being one of them. If so, the theft of his laptop might be no more than mere coincidence, with the thief lacking any knowledge of its contents. Still, would such a petty thief have passed up the small jar of nickels, dimes, and quarters? Not likely, Andy reasoned, leaving only one other possible explanation: that Rodney's laptop had been deliberately targeted.

The realization sent a sudden chill down the teen's spine: if that were true, then somebody out there must have known what was on the lumbering youth's laptop–information pertaining to the Sawyer-Hinkle disappearance and the alleged sighting of Brett Hinkle himself down in Central America. If so, then something really fucked-up was going on.

But what?

And more importantly–*who was behind it?*

"What exactly did you have on that laptop?" Andy asked, packing all his thoughts, suspicions, and fears into one tight ball.

Rodney Crutchley's dark, blackish-blue eyes slowly scanned the hallway, then came back to Andy, restive and brooding."Nothing much. Just class reports, things like that."

"That's not what I meant," Andy clarified. "What exactly did you find out about the Sawyer-Hinkle case that wasn't in the crime book?" As he saw it, someone willing to steal Rodney Crutchley's laptop must have had good reason. If so, he was determined to find out.

"Nothing new on Tina Sawyer," Rodney quietly intoned. "But–"

"But–?"

"I found a lot more on Hinkle..."

"Well?"

"For one thing, I tracked down an email for "Traveler". That led me to his real name. From there I paid $39.95 to an online search company called "Find That Fucker" and–"

"You're joking, right?"

Rodney Crutchley regarded Andy Hupp with serious consideration. "That's what it's called."

"Find. That. *Fucker?*"

"Yes. Just go to www.findthatfucker.com and you'll see."

Andy shook his head, sighing.

The modern age...

"Okay, go on."

"Like I was saying, I found out "Traveler's" real name on a website connected to an Alaskan cruise line he once traveled on a few years back. He's traveled all over, in fact. Europe. Africa. Asia. Australia." He moved his eyes into the distance. "Even down to Guatemala..."

Andy's eyes widened. "Then the photo...?"

"Might be authentic," Rodney confirmed.

"Authentic, maybe," Andy carefully reasoned. "But we still have no proof it was Brett Hinkle."

Rodney remained silent for a moment. Then he said: "It's Hinkle. I'm sure of it."

Andy felt a cold chill.

So was he.

If so, the missing Titanis High School youth who'd vanished four years ago from a foggy country road was still *alive*.

My God, he thought–what exactly did they have here?

"Later," Rodney continued, "I located "Traveler's" home-town..."

Andy's eyes sharpened. "What about his home address?"

Rodney Crutchley solemnly nodded. "That too."

"Where?"

"A place down on the coast called Jamaica Beach. Not far from Galveston. About two hundred and fifty miles from here."

Andy ventured a step away, then turned. "If we go with this idea we'll need to pay him a visit. What's his name?"

"Lance Butterfield."

"Okay, let's add up what we have so far: an Internet website with a photo of Brett Hinkle that reveals he's possibly still alive. Second, the name of the guy who took the photo while on vacation down in Central America. And third, the address where he lives. With all that, we can get a good start on developing the script, once we finish talking to Butterfield."

"That is, if he's willing to talk to us..." Rodney cautiously ventured.

Andy considered that, knowing Butterfield likely would-n't. Even so, they might still learn something simply by paying him a visit. Only then did he notice Rodney's strained silence.

"What is it?" the junior movie mogul asked.

The hulking youth seemed to struggle over some inner in-decisiveness, then slowly regarded the boy facing him: "Shouldn't we...that is...shouldn't we go to the police with this? Tell them what we found."

Andy just looked at him. "You're not serious, are you? Just because you and I believe that photo is of Brett Hinkle doesn't mean anyone else will. Get real, Rodney. The cops won't listen to a couple of dumb high school kids. Besides, they may already know about it."

"But–"

"But what?"

"There are...other photos. On my laptop, that is. Ones I thought you should see before we go ahead with this movie idea. Photos that you...well...*need to see*."

"Like what?"

"Like photos of Brett Hinkle. Taken before he disappeared. Ones I also uploaded to my photo storage account."

"Okay...cool. But why would you want to take these photos to the police?"

Rodney looked uneasy.

"Well...?"

"Because...because of..."

"Yeah, go on."

"Because of what I saw..."

"C'mon, spit it out, Rodney."

"Because Brett Hinkle was–naked."

Andy paused, uncertain he had heard right. "Hold on a sec: Did you just say that Hinkle was...*naked?*"

The big youth nodded.

Andy swallowed.

Just by the look in Crutchley's eyes he could tell something new and terrible was about to be revealed–eyes that stared at him like darkened tunnels out of which a midnight train was fast approaching."You mean, like at some pool party with some girls or something? Like that?"

Rodney dropped his brooding eyes. "No...these photos were found on a website that I had to pay $99.95 to access. A website that I discovered Lance Butterfield is a member of."

Andy's eyes widened. His dream of using the story of Brett Hinkle as the brave teenage hero destroyed by unknown forces was fast sinking, and he knew it. With ever sickening dread, he slowly asked: "What kind of website, Rodney?"

"Something called–" Rodney started to say, then pulled

out a small notepad from his pocket and methodically scribbled down some words, then handed it to Hupp.

Andy read:

"Cock Sucking Teen Boys Go In Deeper And Cum Out Harder"

Oh. My. Fucking. God. Andy thought.

For the longest moment he just stood there, totally fucking freaked. This couldn't be happening, he thought. Finally, he looked up from the scrap of paper.

"So Hinkle was an ass bandit..."

"More like his ass was burglarized by one," Rodney quietly reflected, without any trace of irony.

"But the crime book never mentioned anything about *this*."

"Maybe because somebody sold the photos to the porn site after the book was published."

"Like who?"

"Like...Lance Butterfield."

"What makes you say that?"

Rodney glanced left and right, his eyes shadowed with growing paranoia, almost as if were half-expecting someone's approach. "Because...because in several photos Lance Butterfield is the one being sucked off by Brett Hinkle."

"No way, dude!"

But he saw the truth reflected in the tall youth's eyes.

Standing there, taking it all in, Andy Hupp wanted to gag, to find the nearest bottle of bleach and rinse out his brain, to run and grab the nearest toilet plunger and do a quick Jim Carrey impression by suctioning out the bottom of his stomach. Something. Anything. Whatever it took to remove the thought of Brett Hinkle fagging off with some guy probably old enough to be his father.

And now Andy understood why Rodney had suggested going to the police: because if this information wasn't in the crime book, then it was equally possible the police were unaware of the gay photos in Lance Butterfield's possession—the same gay photos he must have had during their initial missing persons investigation–which probably hadn't been much of one to begin with. After all, many homosexuals were terrified of any scandal that might draw attention to them and their sordid activities, especially when it involved teenaged boys from respectable families.

If so...

Then maybe there was an underlying motive to target Rodney's laptop after all, beyond mere random theft. Which might now explain the look of unease in the bulky youth's eyes, since he'd already put the missing pieces together. Because if they could get to his laptop, Rodney must've reasoned, then they could also get to him. And if they could get to Rodney Crutchley, then they could also get to TJ Sully, Jeena Kirtland, and–ultimately–a budding teenaged filmmaker named Andy Hupp...

"Earlier you said you uploaded Hinkle's nude photos to your photo storage account, right?"

Rodney nodded.

"And you've told no one else about them but me?"

"No one."

"Then we better get back to the library right now and sign on to a student computer," Andy said. "I want to have a look at them myself."

Rodney nodded, and they took off back the way they had come.

"By the way," Andy asked, as they hustled down the hallway, "do the photos clearly show the face of Lance Butterfield?"

"Some of them do. But most are close-ups of his dick," Rodney shyly confessed. "But there's two or three where you can clearly see his face while he's humping Hinkle from behind. And about a dozen more of Hinkle himself, either sucking Butterfield off or getting fucked by some other guy."

Jesus Christ, Andy Hupp thought, as they rushed on. What a clusterfuck this was turning out to be, in more ways than one. Ahead, with classes now in full swing, the school corridors were all but empty. Even Lyla Van der Velden and her poster crew had moved on, leaving no one in sight. Then, from out of nowhere, Andy heard the clicking of high heels on the polished floor behind. That, and the duller thud of heavy, flat-soled leather shoes, at least two pair.

"Stop right there, boys!" came a sharp command.

Oh shit, Andy thought.

Caught.

Red-handed.

Crime: ditching class.

Both boys froze in their tracks, hesitated, then slowly turned around. Behind them, at the far end of the corridor, stood Ms Pickering. And flanking her, one on either side, were two sheriff's deputies.

An instant later three sets of shoes came rapidly down the corridor, tip-tapping and thud-thudding with determined authority, the kind intended to scare the living shit out of recalcitrant teenage delinquents.

This is serious, Andy thought, already calculating his next tactical move. But coming up with an escape plan wouldn't be easy, he knew, since he and Rodney were outnumbered three to two, and two of the three were armed with Glock 9 mm's.

A moment later Ms Pickering came up, as usual exquisitely sheathed in an ass-tight gray flannel skirt and sleek nylons, which made scritchy-scratchy sounds as she walked.

"You're in serious trouble, Andy," a mouthful of gleaming teeth said. "I'm taking you to Principal Meevers office right this minute. We'll decide there what happens next."

Andy started to say something when one of the two sheriff's deputies stepped forward and directed a hard-eyed glance at Rodney: "Is your name Rodney Crutchley?"

Rodney slowly nodded.

"You're under arrest for assault."

Before Andy could say a word in the big kid's defense the other deputy moved in to pat him down, going first for his armpits then quickly to his front and back pockets before sliding down the length of his grimy khaki pants, as if he were some big-time thug just captured on an episode of *Cops*. Only, Rodney just stood there, looking straight ahead, no emotion on his face.

"But he didn't start the fight—" Andy started to say, when the first deputy cut him off: "I'd advise you to keep quiet, son. We could just as easily take you in for attempting to help this individual escape."

Andy looked from the deputy to Rodney to Ms Pickering, who stood there watching him with cool interest in her honey-colored eyes, two hard black pupils like flies caught in prehistoric amber.

"That's right, Andy," Ms Pickering echoed, as if she too were a deputy. And in a way she was, Andy realized. As government employees, all public school teachers were, and they were always on the lookout to make a bust.

Like now.

"Okay, Andy," Ms Pickering ordered, even as one of the deputies snapped cold steel cuffs on Rodney Crutchley before both officers turned and marched him away, "let's go."

As the deputies faded away with their prisoner in custody, Andy and Ms Pickering set off in the opposite direction, straight for Principal Meevers office.

As they walked along, one a seventeen year old boy who stood five feet ten and a half and the other a thirty-something, five foot seven unmarried high school teacher, Andy could sense some indefinable electric tension from the woman beside him, as if she had always wanted to get him alone—as she had now. But no sooner had the thought entered his mind than she maneuvered him toward an alcove where stood a trio of recessed water fountains. Stopping abruptly, she leaned forward to take a drink. As she did, she stretched the fabric of her skirt to new levels of tautness, until the cleavage of her ass was clearly delineated. She must know what she's doing, Andy thought. She had to—even as he watched the cold arc of water splash against her lip-glossed mouth. When she finished she slowly raised again, turning toward him as she did. They were now both ensconced in the alcove, alone, set off from the main corridor. And with classes in session, they would not likely be disturbed by any passersby.

"I had no fifth period class today," Ms Pickering said, answering the unspoken question in Andy's eyes. "An unexpected teacher's meeting. But then, had you shown up to class like you were supposed to, you would've read the note on the door instructing you to go to the library multimedia room with the rest of your classmates."

Andy said nothing. He was standing on dangerous territory, he knew, in more ways than one.

"No comment, Andy? In my class you never have trouble speaking your mind, do you? Or making the other kids laugh with your intelligent and witty remarks, even when they're at my expense." Her teeth glistened, and Andy wondered if it was the residual coating of water from the drinking fountain or some animal lust within her over the sight of cornered prey. When he said nothing, she studied him, her fly-in-amber pupils pinpoints of sharpness.

Emboldened by his silence, she took a step closer; she had never before been this close to him. He was an incredibly good-looking boy, and yet she sensed an innate shyness that belied that fact; a shyness that made subtle tingles race through her body. She had noticed him from the first minute on the first day of his first ever attendance of her fifth period Social Studies class. And from that point on she could not get him out of her mind. Not once during the school day. Not once when she drove home to her Austin apartment. Not once during her off hours or her weekends, even when she was in the throes of lukewarm passion with her thirty-five year old social worker boyfriend. A boyfriend, she reminded herself, whose face became the face of Andy Hupp whenever she gazed upward into his pleasure-wracked eyes just as he climaxed.

And now here she was, almost as close, looking into her star pupil's mist-green eyes; she saw curiosity in them, and the hint of forbidden possibilities—exactly the thoughts she wanted him to have.

"I took you aside, Andy, to offer you some advice before we report to Principal Meevers' office. To say the least, he won't be happy that you have been hanging around a violent trouble-maker like Rodney Crutchley. Oh yes, I know about him. He takes my Social Studies class too, during second period. He's silent and never speaks, and yet somehow he always seems to make grades almost as good as you. As such, I have reason to suspect he cheats, although I have not yet found out his method." Her mouth widened, teeth cold and crystalline. "But in time...I will."

"Rodney's very intelligent, Ms Pickering," Andy defended. "He doesn't need to cheat."

A short laugh escaped her. "Oh, so it's 'Rodney' now, is it? I thought you and your little sidekick TJ Sully amused yourselves by calling him 'Rotten Crotch'."

"Who told you that?"

"Certain students," she said, eyeing him with radioactive intensity.

That gave Andy reason for pause. What students? Who among his friends and acquaintances had overheard him using that nickname for Rodney? And why would they have reason to tell Ms Pickering anyway, or her to have reason to want to know? But any answer he could come up with disturbed him.

"We used to call him that," Andy confessed. "We don't anymore."

"Very commendable, Andy. Unfortunately your new friend is not someone who reflects well on your own academic record. After all, I wouldn't want to entertain any suspicions that you yourself have been less than honest during my tests, now would I? After all, such disclosure could hurt your own chances of getting into a good college."

Her eyes held his, and there was no doubt he saw a threat in them. A threat he could not report, since she could deny she had ever said anything—and they both knew it. She must have read his thoughts, for she added: "Just friendly advice from a teacher to a student, Andy. That's all. After all, you're an exceptionally bright boy, and rather mature for your age. I've no doubt you intend to go on to college. And every one within a hundred mile radius of Titanisville I have contacts, or know important people who do. And that applies even beyond Texas, as I work closely with Dr. Rothman Adler writing university recommendations for my brightest students."

Her eyes drifted aside for a moment, as if looking at something of interest. Then, sweeping her amber eyes back again, she said: "In a past talk I had with you I pointed that out, but you seemed disinterested. That won't work anymore, Andy. Not for those who go on to higher education. Not in this country. Not anywhere in the Western world. We're all interconnected now. We're all...*obligated*. That is, those who, like you, want to become somebody someday. You won't get there without the rest of us...*letting you*."

"Who's 'us'?" Andy asked.

She smiled cryptically. "In time you'll learn. You're learning now. How do you think I found you and Rodney?"

She saw the answer in his eyes even before he spoke.

"Lyla Van der Velden..."

"Exactly, Andy. She's one of the 'us' I've been speaking about. Beautiful, intelligent—*and one of us*. And totally enamored of Dr. Adler. As you too can be..." She took a step closer. "As I...want you to be."

All at once he smelled her perfume, the fragrance of shampoo in her hair, the freshly laundered scent of her clothes, a fleeting trace of baby powder between the cleavage of her ample breasts, and then the taste of her lip-glossed mouth as it closed tight against his. For a long moment the kiss lingered, intensified, became a hot suction against his own mouth, even as a billion thoughts rushed through his mind. A long time ago, as a kid, he had seen a movie called *Summer of '42*, and now he was living it—in a twisted sort of way.

When Ms Pickering pulled away her eyes were closed, and if Andy didn't know better he'd swear she was having some serious clitoral satisfaction at that moment.

Oh god, he thought.

I've just fallen victim to a cougar.

For a moment both looked at each other in silence.

"We'd better go now, Andy. Principal Meevers will be waiting."

Andy dropped his eyes, then slowly raised them again. "Ms Pickering—?"

"I'll expect you this Friday at our Youth For Social Justice Club meeting. Lyla wants you there." She held his glance in a telling way. "As do I..."

"Ms Pickering—?" Andy repeated, still reeling from the effects of the sensuous kiss.

"Yes?"

"Why...why was Rodney arrested?"

"Surely you must know."

He shook his head.

"Because," she answered, "he broke Jamal Perkins' arm..."

CHAPTER 12

Titanis High, like many modern high schools, had a large, central reception area located near the front entrance—more akin to an industrial command center or urban, high-rise law firm than the typical high school office of old.

Here there was no doughty, middle-aged secretary with thick glasses seated behind a wooden desk flanked by banged-up metal file cabinets, but instead a long, sweeping curve of raspberry-colored Formica countertop spanning a good thirty-feet, behind which five attractive, fashionably-dressed women worked, meeting and greeting and assisting and directing an endless flow of visitors, students, delivery people, and parents—all amid a background of ringing telephones, paper-churning photo copiers, and yammering voices.

And located on the back wall were twelve 32 inch flat-screen TV's, in two rows of six, each displaying a different part of the school, from the cafeteria to the hallways to the main entrance, insuring little escaped the purview of the five females tasked in keeping Titanis High functioning at top proficiency. For if ever a high school could be said to have a *Star Trek* "bridge", then this was it, Andy thought, as he and Ms Pickering, of the huge and hungry mouth, entered the bustling office.

Still stunned by the unexpected and savagely lustful kiss, he found himself surprisingly obedient for once. Something terrible had happened, he thought, some invasive power had been asserted over him, and he wasn't quite sure what to do about it. His two choices came sluggishly to the forefront: remain silent about the incident in the hallway, or tell the principal he was about to meet. And yet, one thing mitigated against the latter—that it would be his word against a school teacher's. But then, he realized that wasn't the only reason: because he had enjoyed it.

Yes, he thought.

I enjoyed Ms Pickering's kiss...

I enjoyed it all: from her scent, to her firm and lustful mouth, to the press of her ripe breasts against my chest, to the insistent need he had sensed, behind which a deeper need hungered to be fulfilled.

> *"I'll expect you at this Friday's meeting of the Youth For Social Justice Club, Andy. Lyla wants you there...as do I."*

Ms Pickering came up to the counter, Andy beside her. He knew the office well, having been escorted here on several occasions.

"Good afternoon, Ms Pickering," one of the office staff greeted, after finishing with a postal clerk making a delivery. "How can I help you?"

"I'm here to speak with Principal Meevers. He's expecting me."

"I'll let him know," she said. A moment later she returned. "Go right in."

Ms Pickering led Andy around the sweep of counter and toward a raspberry-colored door with a gold name plaque and the words PRINCIPAL BUDD MEEVERS etched in black enamel. From Andy Hupp's point of view, it might as well have been the lethal injection chamber at some Texas penitentiary, considering how he had promised Principal Meevers he would stay out of trouble since being granted a reprieve for bringing firearms onto campus. Now here he was again, and he knew what the charges would be: repeatedly ditching Feel The Hug assemblies out on the West Quad, roaming the school hall-ways without a permission slip, and, finally, attempting to help Rodney Crutchley escape law enforcement, even though he hadn't realized sheriff's deputies were looking for him.

Didn't matter, he concluded.

Meevers would probably no more believe he hadn't known than if he told him about his strange hallway encounter with Ms Pickering. For it was just a fact of life that teenagers were generally considered guilty until proven innocent—usually the former.

As Ms Pickering grabbed the doorknob and swung wide the door, her other hand firmly pressed against his back and guided him into Principal Meevers' inner sanctum—a large, modern room spanned by floor-to-ceiling windows on two sides, lush maroon carpeting, burled walnut paneling on the remaining two walls, an expansive teak desk, an eight foot leather sofa, and several thickly-padded, wing-backed chairs with deep-cherry upholstery. All in all, it could have passed for a suite at an upscale Austin hotel, Andy thought, even as he followed Ms Pickering over to Meevers' desk, where he sat, pushed back lazily in his high-backed office chair, chatting with some unknown person on the other end.

"...Yes, yes, we're doing everything we can to increase racial diversity at our school, Commissioner. But you must remember that most of the students at Titanis High come from high-income families and there's just not enough low-level employment opportunities in town to sustain a more diverse population. Yes, yes, that's exactly right. Titanisville has only three fast-food joints, one Pizza Hut, and two mom-and-pop cafes, but no factories whatsoever to employee new immigrants, and certainly no agricultural in the immediate area. Yes, yes, I know, there's some agriculture around twenty miles away, which accounts for the few minorities we do have at my school. Of course, of course. We're still working closely with Dr. Adler trying to get that Chicken Lickin' poultry processing plant approved and built, but quite frankly there's some serious town council opposition to it. Yes, I'm well aware that Titanisville as a whole does not reflect the changing face of America. At least, not yet. Yes, yes, it's a terrible thing. But let me get back to you on this matter in a day or two, since I have a meeting right now with one of my teachers. Yes, yes, that sounds fine. Give my regards to your wife and family. Will do. So long."

As he hung up the phone Principal Budd Meevers swiveled around and pulled himself into a more restrained, businesslike position. "My apologies, Ms Pickering. You know how these calls can run overtime. Please, both of you have a seat."

As Ms Pickering folded smoothly into one of the cherry-leather chairs, followed by Andy in the one next to her, Budd Meevers leaned forward, hands clasped in front of him. "Well...what is it you wanted to discuss with me, Ms Pickering?" But even as he said it his eyes focused on the teenaged boy seated in front of him.

Ms Pickering gracefully slid her amber eyes toward the handsome youth she had only a short time ago indulged with a passionate, lingering kiss, the merest wisp of a smile tracing her lips. "Well, Andy?" the smile seemed to say. "Here's your chance to tell Principal Meevers about our little hallway tryst—so speak up. No...? You don't dare? Good boy, Andy. You're learning. And those who learn are those who are rewarded...in very exciting ways."

And it was then that Andy knew she was safe, because the whole idea of telling Principal Meevers anything was out of the question, even though it had happened. Another lesson learned on the long climb upward to adulthood, he realized: truth wasn't always the ultimate defense. Sometimes, only position, power, and authority mattered.

"First of all, Mr. Meevers, I just wanted to introduce Andy Hupp as the finest student in my fifth period Social Studies class, and perhaps in all my classes."

Andy Hupp shot a glance toward Ms Pickering as Budd

Meevers nodded approvingly. "Way to go, Andy. I see you do more around school than just—" run around wildly across campus waving shotguns and semi-automatic pistols, he almost let slip, then let go a sly grin instead: "—chase after pretty girls."

What was going on here? Andy wondered. He had come in expecting to be crucified by Ms Pickering and yet—

"But there is one minor issue, Mr. Meevers..."

Uh-oh, Andy thought—here it comes.

Deflector shields up, Mr. Sulu.

Principal Meevers turned his tennis-player-tanned face toward Andy's teacher. "Oh?"

"It seems that Andy doesn't like to attend our school's wonderful and enriching Feel The Hug assemblies."

"Is that true, Andy?"

"Guess I've missed a few," Andy quietly admitted, in his most respectful tone of voice. "...here and there."

"Attendance is mandatory, you know."

Andy was about to ask "why" then thought better of it; the last thing he needed was to go into full smartass mode.

"However, I have a solution, Mr. Meevers," Ms Pickering went on, looking again at Andy. And this time there was an absolute look of triumph in her eyes. "As I see it, Andy should be excused from all Feel The Hug assemblies from now on—"

Hey, Andy thought, I could get behind that!

"—and instead join my after-school Youth For Social Justice Club. We don't have nearly enough bright boys like him and he would be a welcome addition."

Wait a minute—! Andy started to blurt.

"And why do you feel this is necessary, Ms Pickering?"

"For one thing," she primly explained, "I'm concerned that Andy has started hanging out with certain boys and girls who aren't, well, part of the program, you might say."

"And what program is that, Ms Pickering?" Principal Meevers inquired, even as he studied Andy Hupp.

"The program of love thy fellow man, Mr. Meevers. Where we all get along."

"We?" Andy echoed, not liking the sound of that.

"Why yes, Andy—*we*. You. Me. African-Americans. And our newest students from Mexico, Guatemala, Somalia, Syria, Pakistan, Cambodia—all those places. Like a great big banquet table where all sorts of dishes are being served, instead of just—" and her eyes sharpened to pinpoints— "steak." In that instant it became clear to Andy that this inquisition inside Meevers office was Ms Pickering's revenge for his classroom behavior.

But she wasn't done yet, oh, no.

"Or, if you prefer, imagine it's a new computer program called America 3.0. You know, like a fantastic new video game we all get to play."

Andy Hupp looked askance, seeking some mental rock to cling to, some way to escape this stormy sea of Ms Pickering's coolly delivered social justice warrior assault.

"But what if some of us don't want to play, Ms Pickering...?" Andy innocently asked. Yet, a subtle thread of steel had now woven itself into his voice, even as he wondered what Principal Meevers thought of this.

Ms Pickering leant forward, her eyes narrowing, as if studying Andy for the first time, like a new form of life. "We're all going to play, mister. On that you can bet your life. Because to get along—is to go along. That's the unofficial motto of Titanis High." Then, turning toward Principal Meevers, she added: "I also recommend that Andy stay away from certain bad influences—like Rodney Crutchley, for instance. As you know, he was arrested only minutes ago for committing a violent assault against another student. In fact, I've long suspected that particular student of cheating in class, as well as noting clear signs of antisocial behavior. And today has proven me right."

"Well, Ms Pickering," Meevers said evenly, "I feel confident Andy has gotten the message." He flicked an eye toward the teenager. "And if he hasn't, by the time he leaves this off-ice–he will."

"Very well," Ms Pickering said, rising smoothly to her feet. "And that concludes everything I needed to see you about, Mr. Meevers. After I've departed, I'm sure you can round off this discussion by convincing Andy of the absolute necessity of being a little more–shall we say–involved with the human race."

Turning, she made for the door and pulled it open, pausing one last time to look back, a glint in her eye intended only for the teenage boy: "Remember, Andy: I'll expect you this Friday, five o'clock. Halloween evening. In the school auditorium." Then, ass-tight woolen skirt and all, she was gone.

"Your teacher must think very highly of you, Andy, if she made a special trip to my office on your behalf. I'm rather impressed."

Andy shrugged. "Yeah, well. You know how it is."

Except you don't, Andy thought.

Especially the part about us making out in the hallway.

"Good to hear," Meevers remarked affably, pushing back in his chair as he regarded Andy Hupp. A winning combo, he thought: good looks, smart, with a real talent for filmmak-ing. On the other hand, he was a certified troublemaker; he'd already proven that. He–along with that freckled-faced imp–TJ Sully. But their school grades were excellent, especially Andy's. Certainly so, if he had impressed that ball-biting bitch Ms Pickering.

He had to keep that in mind at all times.

And what the hell, he thought: he had done some pretty crazy things back in his high school days, remembering the time he and some buddies had torn down their high school flag and raised a Playboy banner up the flagpole in its stead. Or that other time, during his early college years, when he and two others had taken that can of gasoline one chill night and...

But he suddenly blocked the thought.

That was the old, long ago Budd Meevers.

The one that didn't count anymore.

The one he had safely buried long, long ago.

Besides, the authorities never found out who burned down old Mr. Fitchins' house and now, after so many years, they never would...

Sealing off the memory as he leaned forward with his friendliest high school principal grin, Budd Meevers remarked nonchalantly: "So...you really don't like our little Feel The Hug assemblies, do you, Andy?"

Andy gauged Principal Meevers warily.

Could be a Klingon trick, he thought—trying to get me to go on a tirade against Ms Pickering, Titanis High's stealth cougar, or maybe Dr. Adler's Inclusivity Project, of which Feel The Hug was only a part. The other—the Youth For Social Justice Club—he'd thus far managed to elude. But Ms Pickering had set a clever trap, first stunning him like an electric eel in the hallway with the fiercest kiss he had ever experienced, then leading him here, dazed and disoriented, to be trapped into joining her Marxist 101 after-school shitlib brainwashing project.

Conflicted by indecision, he wryly asked himself: what would Jesus do? Then he remembered, with a feeling of astonishment: he'd actually enjoyed Janelle Pickering's kiss—a lot. For whatever else that evil mouth was capable of, it could kiss like there was no tomorrow.

"Guess I'm just not into group hugs, sir," Andy managed to say.

Meevers chuckled. "Neither am I, Andy."

Andy managed a smile; Principal Meevers wasn't a bad warden at all. Truth be told, he actually liked him. And when he was transferred at the end of the school year and sent to a maximum security state university, where the prison guards (in the guise of teachers) would really go to work on his mind, he'd almost feel sorry. For when that day finally arrived, he'd look back on his time at Titanis High like it had been a Sunday school picnic.

"I just hope you'll keep your end of the bargain" Budd Meevers went on. "You know, by attending Ms Pickering's Youth For Social Justice Club this Friday." He leveled two unwavering gray eyes on Andy, suddenly hard as granite. "You see, I've cut you some pretty serious slack before and here I go doing it again. Kinda makes me a nice guy, don't you think?"

Andy slowly nodded.

"You betcha, Andy. I can be as nice as all hell."

Meevers pushed back in his high-backed chair, wrapping his hands behind his suntanned neck. For a penetrating moment he studied the teen. Then he said, in that vaguely indefinable drawl that lay somewhere between his native Mid-Western accent and the southwestern twang he'd picked up living down Texas way for the past twenty odd years: "Seeing as how I saved you and that smartassed partner of yours from expulsion and possible jail time, I think you owe it to me to be there at Ms Pickering's Youth For Social Justice Club this Friday, promptly at five. Otherwise she's liable to think I talked you out of it, and boy I don't need someone like her on my case. So make it a point not to ditch."

Again, Andy Hupp nodded.

Besides, after what had happened in the hallway between he and Ms Pickering, he was now just a little bit curious about her Youth For Social Indoctrination and Leftist Brainwashing Torture Club, and what they were actually up to, especially if a gorgeous chick like Lyla Van der Velden was going.

"Okay. Good deal, Andy. Now that that's squared away, I guess you know what happened between some of our students earlier out on the East Quad."

"I heard something about it," Andy cautiously acknowledged, not wishing to reveal too much.

"Well, earlier Ms Pickering notified me that you and this Rodney Crutchley fellow were seen roaming the hallways together. After classes had started. Without a pass. And just minutes earlier this Rodney character had gotten into a tussle with four students and injured one of them pretty seriously. Flipped him up and over his back before he slammed down on the concrete, breaking his arm. To say the least, he succeeded in frightening Scarletti and his bunch so thoroughly they've now asked my office to protect them from any further confrontations. I mean it, Andy—Scarletti is one scared kid. So are the others. Now, the fact that you were seen with this student so soon after that incident just doesn't look too good. Maybe you should tell me what you two were up to."

"Nothing, Mr. Meevers. Just hanging out."

Meevers slowly nodded, then cocked an inquisitive eye toward him. "Ms Pickering claims he's the one behind marking up one of our brand new school lockers—twice. Know anything about that? It's important you tell the truth, because I've been asked to give my findings to the sheriff's department. So, what's the scoop, Andy?"

Andy leaned forward. "I don't think Rodney Crutchley did it, sir. I think he was framed."

"What evidence do you have?"

Andy considered that.

Not much, really.

In fact, not any.

Then he remembered: the surveillance camera. Certainly it had caught the person who had marked up Tony Scarletti's locker.

"There must be video, Mr. Meevers."

"Video?"

"You know, from the surveillance camera in the row of lockers where Tony Scarletti's is."

Meevers eyes froze for an instant, as if looking beyond the walls of his office, as if something had escaped his mind that shouldn't have. Then, gradually, he brought his eyes around to Andy Hupp again: "Why...of course. The surveillance camera. As soon as I'm able to get our video technician here we can...pursue that possibility."

"Shouldn't that clear Rodney Crutchley?"

"Not necessarily, Andy. Our surveillance cameras have many hallways and corridors to cover, not to mention the four quads, the front entrance, the cafeteria, auditorium, and so on. What you may not know is that they rotate their surveillance perspectives, in order to provide coverage to all areas of the school. But as they do, some areas are temporarily left without video surveillance, though no one can tell when they're being watched and when they're not. Since that's the case, whoever marked up Tony Scarletti's locker may have done so during one of those periods when it wasn't under active camera surveillance."

"But even if that turns out to be true, Mr. Meevers, I know Rodney couldn't have done it."

"Again, what proof do you have?"

"Maybe I don't have any solid evidence that he didn't do it," Andy went on in his best junior attorney's voice, "other than his claim that he didn't."

"Don't most guilty people deny their guilt, Andy?"

"Some. Maybe even most. But Rodney's different, sir."

"How so?"

"He's pretty smart, for one thing. Smarter than people realize. So why would he write a nasty message on Tony Scarletti's locker door then leave his initials behind?"

"Hard to say, Andy. But as a former teacher and a principal of many years, I know that kids will often do a lot of things like that, if their intent is to taunt and antagonize someone. And letting the victim know who's taunting them is part of the fun, isn't it?"

"Take a look at this, Mr. Meevers," Andy said, tugging his smartphone from his jeans. He thumbed through his photo gallery and brought up the picture he had taken of Scarletti's locker door, then handed the device to the principal.

Meevers took it and examined the photo for a long time, until his eyes seemed to glaze over, as if he were seeing something other than the image.

"Why'd you take this?"

"Evidence, I guess," Andy answered, shrugging. "Besides, I knew the school janitor would remove it just like the last time."

"And did you photograph Scarletti's door the first time?"

The question seemed important to Principal Meevers, although Andy couldn't figure out why.

"No, not the first time. I didn't think to."

Meevers nodded, lowering his eyes to the photo again. "Good job," he said. "As it stands, I may need to hold on to this. Just for a few hours. Until I can take it to the sheriff's department. They'll need to see it."

"Couldn't I just forward a copy to your email?"

"I'd rather not do that, Andy. You see, it might give the impression that I took the photo myself instead of a student. I don't want it to seem like I'm biased or 'out to get' Rodney Crutchley. Understand?"

Andy nodded.

Sounded reasonable.

Sort of.

"Better to show that a student took the photo," Meevers went on. "Besides, it might help Rodney. That is, if he's innocent."

"What exactly is he charged with, Mr. Meevers?"

"Well, he hasn't likely been charged yet, judging by similar incidents I've dealt with. For the moment, the sheriff's department is probably just holding him, since he's a minor. Even so, I fear that Rodney could eventually be charged with aggravated assault, which in this state constitutes a second degree felony."

Andy swallowed.

If so, that would mean serious prison time.

As well as one less production member...

Shit.

"Where is he now?"

"Most likely at the county juvenile detention facility."

"For how long?"

"I'm not privy to that information. He'll either be held indefinitely or released to a parent or guardian."

It just occurred to Andy that he knew nothing about Rodney Crutchley's family life. Maybe no one did, secretive as he was.

"Mr. Meevers–"

"Yes?"

"Tony Scarletti started this whole thing. He and his three football buddies: Brodie Henshaw, Jamal Perkins, and T-Bone Ramirez."

"'T-Bone'–?"

"Carlos Ramirez, sir. But everybody calls him T-Bone."

"Everybody," Meevers managed a weak grin, "except principals not in the know..."

"Anyway," Andy continued, "Scarletti goes around campus shaking down any student he thinks he can use for his personal ATM machine. I was his latest victim."

"Any reason why?"

Andy shrugged.

"Well," Meevers said, reaching idly for a glass paperweight, "there remains the fact that Tony Scarletti's locker door was defaced on two occasions, and the most likely suspect we have is Rodney Crutchley."

"He didn't do it, Mr. Meevers. When you turn over that photo to the sheriff's department have them compare the letters printed on Scarletti's locker door to a sample of Rodney's style of printing. I'm certain they won't match."

Meevers cradled the paperweight in one suntanned hand, rolling it back and forth contemplatively. "You realize they may not be able to prove or disprove it's Rodney's writing. If he's as smart as you say, he may have been clever enough to disguise the letters to make them appear someone else had written them. If so, he'll likely remain the most likely suspect." He put the paperweight down. "And still be on the hook."

"But even if the cops can't prove it's not Rodney's writing, Tony Scarletti is still the one who started the fight."

"How do you know that, Andy? Did you witness what happened today?"

Andy shook his head. "No, but Scarletti threatened both of us, Mr. Meevers. Last week he and his goon squad chased me into the library and Rodney saved my ass."

"How so?"

"By boosting me atop one of the library bookshelves just in the nick of time, where I hid out of sight. Otherwise Scarletti and his football thugs would've pounded me into the floor."

"I see."

"That's why they took revenge on Rodney."

Meevers nodded, assessing everything the teenaged boy had told him. Then he said: "Two minutes before the town commissioner telephoned my office, I received a cellphone call from Ms Pickering apprising me of the East Quad incident, while she and the deputies were still roaming the hallways searching for you and Rodney. According to her, Tony Scarletti and his friends tell a different story. They claim Rodney instigated the attack—not them."

Andy pushed back in his chair and let go a sigh. "I'll bet."

"Not so fast, Andy. Hear me out. Scarletti told the sheriff's deputies that he only warned Rodney not to write on his locker door again. That's all, before starting to walk away. That's when Rodney threw the first punch, hitting Scarletti in the jaw. True, the other three jumped on him after he struck the first blow, and that's when they said he went totally berserk, flipping Jamal Perkins up and over his shoulder when Perkins grabbed him around the neck. The fall broke Perkins' arm, which effectively puts him out of action for the rest of the football season."

Meevers leaned forward, hands clasped in front of him. "That's a bad deal for Titanis High, Andy. Let me tell you.

What's more, a lot of students aren't going to be happy about this, once the story gets out. As it will by tomorrow, if it hasn't already. Nor will the team's business sponsors be thrilled, since they were counting on the Titanis Terror Birds to finish out their unbroken winning streak this season. But without Jamal Perkins, their star line-backer, that's not likely to happen now. So that's what you need to understand. This isn't just about Rodney Crutchley, innocent or not. Nor is it just about you, Andy. It's about our school, our students, and our team spirit. And none of what's happened reflects well on us or our town. That's the big picture, Andy."

Budd Meevers had gone full warden on him, Andy Hupp realized. And the message was clear: Rodney was a nobody, just another worthless con in the high school prison yard, even if he was innocent. What mattered was 'team spirit', that amorphous, nebulous miasma that he and jillions of other students had been forced to worship since their first year in high school, going all the way back for untold eons. Even now, he still had no idea what it was. But if Tony Scarletti, Jamal Perkins, Brodie Henshaw, and T-Bone Ramirez were the embodiment, then it was nothing but a vacuous, evil thing.

"I don't care what Scarletti said," Andy Hupp quietly stated. "He's a liar."

Meevers said nothing for a long moment. Maybe good-looks and brains weren't really the source of Andy's magnetism, but this–this insolent courage he possessed. Where did he get it? He was far from a "bad ass" and yet there was something he had: *a certainty*. And that translated into a special kind of toughness, Meevers concluded, that went beyond mere muscles. He himself had not been so self-assured at that age; nor any of his old high school buddies.

But this kid–

"One other thing you should know, Andy. Dr. Rothman Adler of the Center For Human Understanding monitors this school for this very kind of incident. And Ms Pickering will no doubt report it to him. And when she does, if it should turn out that Rodney Crutchley started the fight, then Adler will insist on hate crime charges being filed against him, which could up the ante to first degree felony."

"But why would such charges even be filed?"

"Because of who–and *what*–Jamal Perkins is."

Andy slowly rose from his chair, a cold determination in his eye. "The only hate crime that's been committed here, Mr. Meevers, is the one committed by Tony Scarletti and his gang of thugs." That said, he turned abruptly and headed for the door.

"I haven't excused you yet, Andy."

Andy stopped and turned. "You didn't have to, Mr. Meevers–I excused myself."

A stunned look clouded Meevers face. "You–*what?*"

Andy grabbed the doorknob.

He was done here.

As he opened the door Budd Meevers called out, "Be careful, Andy. You don't want to get on the wrong side of history."

Andy wasn't sure what that meant, except for one thing.

It had sounded like a threat.

CHAPTER 13

Andy Hupp left Principal Meevers office without looking back. He still liked Meevers, even though the principal had gone all hard-ass on him. Maybe that was just part of his job. Still, the idea that hate-crime charges might be leveled against Rodney Crutchley made him angry.

As for the rest of the day, he still had two more classes to attend, but he knew he would ditch them too, criminal recidivist that he was. Still, he was troubled by his delinquent behavior; troubled by his flaunting of the rules, when his mind was so orderly, precise, and generally respectful of them. Civilization had been built on rules, he knew, and would not long function without them. And yet, there were countless times throughout history when rules had been defied, and men had gone off to make their own, sometimes for the better, sometimes not.

Yes, he respected rules, and yet had always felt constrained by them, ever since he had been a child and his mother had placed the cookie jar far above his reach on the top shelf of a kitchen cabinet. When, at age four, she had caught him with his dad's step ladder heisting the cookies red-handed, she had said, "Andy, you must be ashamed of yourself!"

And he had solemnly replied: "No, mommy. You always taught me to go after what I wanted, remember?"

And she had laughed, helplessly, for it was true.

"Yes, Andy, that I did. Just don't start giving the neighborhood bank any thought, okay?"

Along the rocky road to seventeen, going after what he wanted hadn't always been as easy as heisting cookies. At four, life had seemed immortal, with no thought of that distant twilight to come. But now, at seventeen, and on the brink of adulthood, he knew life wasn't immortal. He knew that life was finite, and that one only had a handful of decades, if that, to accomplish one's dreams.

Unlike so many other boys, Andy Hupp had never gone through the attendant stages of wanting to be a fireman or a soldier or an astronaut or a gynecologist, but had wanted to make movies since as far back as he could remember. Funny, that. No one in his family worked in the film industry; nor were his parents enamored of it. Quite the opposite. His dad thought it a foolish long-shot, and urged him to "grow up" and pursue something "practical". His mother was more understanding, having worked as a fashion model, a profession occasionally drawn into the orbit of Hollywood. But she had not been the source of his cinematic ambitions, for long before he had even learned of his mother's former career he had decided he would one day make movies.

"Why am I always pretending to make movies?"—he'd relied to his mother's curious question, one day in his tenth year after she'd come upon him methodically directing several playmates in an imaginary film production in the backyard. "Because," he'd solemnly intoned, "it's like...like saving my thoughts so..." Whereupon he hesitated, cocking his boyish face upward, eyes squinting against the summer sun, two burning pools of green fire, even as he groped for just the right words: "...so that whenever I look back, when I'm very old, I can still hold all the things I ever loved..."

And though Andy never knew it, his mother had never cherished him more than in that one moment. That had been when they had still lived in Austin, before it became overly "enriched" and his dad proposed they "seek good country air", although even then Andy knew the quality of the air had nothing to do with it.

After moving to Titanisville, and determined to begin making real movies, even if only at an amateur level, Andy Hupp took his first real job at a local fast-food joint. Too young to work the counter at age fifteen, he labored for a year cleaning up around the place, dumping trash, wiping down tables, sweeping floors, and keeping the parking lot picked up, until he had saved enough money to buy his first video camera.

Taking note of the growing strength of his ambition, and knowing he was seeking a dream far higher and far more difficult to attain than even the heights she had scaled in the cutthroat world of fashion modeling, his mother knew he needed far more capital to explore his youthful dreams, something she knew his father would never finance. That was when she'd suggested he try fashion modeling, telling him she still had the requisite contacts to open doors for him.

At first, Andy had been resistant to the idea, having neither an interest in the profession or wanting the stigma of being involved in what was generally considered a female pursuit. But after weighing all other reasonable options to earn large amounts of money, and realizing it would take years of menial labor to save the necessary funds to buy all the equipment he needed, including a professional-grade movie camera and a van for transporting actors, crew, and equipment—as well as the cost of converting a large motor home storage garage on his family's new five acre property into a viable studio—he acquiesced.

Nevertheless, he'd set out for his first interview at his mother's former modeling agency disguised with dark sunglasses and a rakish scarf looped thrice around his neck—only to find out a mere five minutes into the interview, to his utter astonishment, that he'd been hired.

A week later, called to begin work on a photo spread for a major clothing retailer, he was offered more money for a few days work than he could have earned in six months of afterschool clean up duty down at the local Spee-Dee-Burger.

Thus began Andy Hupp's double life: high school whiz kid during the week, fashion model in his off hours high atop the 25th floor studios of the BrightStar Modeling Agency in downtown Austin. It was a profitable, albeit uncomfortable new identity for the photogenic teen, one known only to his family and his best friend.

Or...*was it?*

Andy had to wonder, pausing in the empty hallway and glancing back over his shoulder, remembering the way Meevers had looked him over, almost as if...

Yes, he thought.

The possibility that Titanis High's principal may have chanced upon one of his magazine ads suddenly occurred to him, perhaps even a recent one for Mann Hunt underwear, which Andy half-ashamedly felt had always bordered on soft porn. Even so, his mother had assured him it was just part of the business, although admittedly some of her old lingerie ads that he'd come across in one of her modeling scrapbooks had certainly given him cause for red-faced embarrassment, along with the uncomfortable knowledge that his mother had once been one hell of a sexy woman. But the thought that Meevers may have come across one of his less modest ads made Andy feel a bit uneasy, although he couldn't say why.

Discarding the thought, he proceeded on down the empty hallway, his mind turning again to Rodney Crutchley and the information he'd discovered about Brett Hinkle–especially the vanished youth's strange involvement with a mysterious, middle-aged homosexual by the name of Lance Butterfield. As he mulled over what he had learned, images of John Wayne Gacy and Randy Kraft flashed through his mind at the mere thought of what Hinkle might have been involved in, during all those "after-school" hours of his own: activities that sucked him off before ultimately sucking him down into some seedy, dark memory hole from which he never returned. It was disturbing information for a seventeen year old teen to possess, something that the dark corners of his mind whispered might ultimately be dangerous.

But if nothing else Andy Hupp was persistent, whether it came to heisting cookies or following a promising new lead for a movie. And if that meant ditching classes with Rodney Crutchley or walking out of Principal Meevers office without permission, then so be it. Because he had something here; something he was just beginning to feel the vague contours of, dark and shapeless though it was.

But what next?

And where?

He wasn't sure, other than to find out what happened to Rodney. With that in mind he–

Voices.

Somebody coming.

One sort of familiar, one definitely not.

Quickly, One Buck For A Suck Hupp dodged sideways through the door of the nearest Boys Bathroom just before whoever it was came around the corner.

"I told you never to contact me at this school," the familiar voice echoed, low and deliberate.

"But I had to see you, uncle," said the unfamiliar, heavily-accented voice.

"And I warned you never to call me that! Never, ever call me that! Do you understand? You could cost me my job if they ever discovered my connection to an illegal alien...*like you!*"

They were standing outside the bathroom door now, going back and forth in low voices. By sound alone, Andy confirmed one of them had to be "No Way" José , aka José Ortega, one of Titanis High's eight athletic coaches. Ortega, along with one other coach, taught senior gym classes, which meant he was Andy's gym teacher, and if he caught him in here without a pass he'd be right back in Meevers' office in no time flat.

Come on! Andy's mind shouted.

Quit babbling and move on!

But the heated conversation continued, momentarily slipping into Spanish:

"¡Por favor, tío José!" pleaded the unknown voice. "Pepito vino al norte para encontrarse con una chica blanca y casarse con ella. ¡Él no quiere secuestrarlos! ¡Tampoco quiero−!"

Coach Ortega shot back: "¡Callate idiota! ¡Tú y Pepito son analfabetos campesinos! ¡Estás aquí para recibir órdenes y hacer lo que te dicen!"

WTF? Andy had only rarely heard Coach Ortega speak Spanish, and never with such vehemence. Was it a student he was talking to? He sure sounded about high school age, but Ortega's tone was not that of teacher to pupil−

Then he remembered: the unknown youth had addressed Coach Ortega as "uncle". So whatever was going on, Andy thought, none of this shit sounded any good,. Because whoever this kid was−nephew, illegal alien, whatever−Ortega was definitely upset about him being here. And if he was that upset, Andy doubted he would be happy should he discover a truant student had been standing right behind the bathroom door all along−eavesdropping.

Jerking his head around, he looked for someplace to hide. Scanning the four toilet stalls, he thought of darting inside one, latching the door, then hopping atop the toilet. But a closed door with no feet visible below would alert Ortega immediately, should he come in. And if Andy just closed the door and sat on the toilet, the lower part of his legs and feet exposed, Ortega would challenge him to come out and show a pass−so that idea was screwed.

Any moment now...

Ortega and the kid would come in.

Andy's eyes darted around the tiled bathroom: all sinks and mirrors and panicked reflections of himself−

A door.

At the far end.

Janitor's supply room.

Just maybe−

Dashing light-footed toward it, he made a double-handed grab for the handle.

Locked.

Damn!

Behind him, the door pushed a quarter of the way open, then paused, four brown fingers wrapped around the edge, hesitating, as another spurt of dialog shot back and forth between the gym teacher and the kid.

"Listen to me, Raul," Ortega kept saying, "you and Pepito are going to do exactly what I tell you. It's easy money for a couple of dumbass shitheads from Chiquimula. *¡Comprende!*"

"But José! Pepito told me he is afraid to come along. He says he has never done such a thing. You know, what the gringos call *keednapping*. He is afraid of what might happen. Besides, he is only fifteen—"

"And what are you, my little cockroach? A wise old man at seventeen? You and your brother Pepito begged me to come north and now that I have arranged it, all I ask is a small favor in return. Don't let me down, you little chickenshit!"

"I am forever grateful but—"

"But nothing, you little donkey turd. We cannot talk out here anymore, even with the hallways empty."

The door pushed halfway open then paused again, exposing part of Ortega's hickory-colored arm.

Andy whipped his head around.

Where?

Where...?

Then he saw the square-sided trash can.

Large enough?

"Come on, you little wetback. I have to take a piss."

—and the door pushed all the way open.

Peeking through the crack afforded by the tent-shaped metal cover above his head, Andy watched from his vantage point inside the trash can just as "No Way" and the youth entered.

Just in the nick of time, too, he breathed, crunched down as far as possible inside the receptacle, with just his neck and head sticking above all the wads of discarded paper towels, candy wrappers, soda cans, test papers with "D's" and "F's" slashed across them by sadistic teachers, and, finally, some putrid item that appeared to be a freshly discarded, still-oozing condom—clinging ickily to the left arm of his two hundred dollar gray leather jacket that he dare not reach over and remove lest he give himself away. Instead, he concentrated two green eyes on Coach Ortega and the kid, peering at them through the narrow, horizontal slit along the bottom of the disposal container's tent-shaped lid with cat-like intensity.

Ortega moved toward the row of urinals, but not without slowing down to admire his dark, meticulously groomed reflection in the long span of mirrors.

"Soy muy guapo, ¿no?"

"Yes, Unc—I mean, José. Mamá always says you are the best looking uncle in the family."

"So true, so true. Which is why your papá and all the rest of my brothers always keep their eyes on me whenever I fly down for a visit, pipsqueak. Because they all know how the senioritas must have me, even if they are married," Ortega said with a sly grin, as he grappled with his pants. Unzipped, he reached in and pulled. "Ah, the prize," he chortled, withdrawing a brown appendage. The sound of yellowy piss began to splash against white ceramic.

"You do not have to go?"

The youth nodded, looking around anxiously.

Shit, Andy thought.

If he didn't know better, the kid seemed to sense he and Ortega were being watched; perhaps some animal cunning he possessed. But then, if he was an illegal alien, as he and Ortega's conversation seemed to suggest, then he had good reason to be on the alert.

"Are there cameras in here, José? Like in the hallways?"

Ortega laughed, shot his last spurt of piss against the ceramic, then let go a long "ahhhhhhhh."

Zipping up, he shook his head.

"*Caramba*, Raul. But you sure are a dumb country motherfucker, you know that? Why would there be cameras in here? So the principal can check out all the gringo boys' pink peckers?"

Raul seemed not to hear, as his oily black eyes darted about the bathroom. Here, there, under the doors of the toilet stalls.

Nothing.

Still...

He had that feeling.

The same one he and his brother Pepito had had as their 'coyote'–their smuggler–had moved them across the US/ Mexican border in the dead of night. Yes, the coyote... The one who had cost Uncle José *muy mucho dinero*. A debt that now made he and his scared little brother beholden–not only to their uncle–but perhaps to other, darker things he dare not name...

Ortega ignored his jittery nephew, disdainful as any gringo of such a fresh-over-the-border wetback, as he sauntered over to one of the mirrors. Pulling out a comb, he leisurely stroked his thick, black hair, thinking back to the time when he had come to El Norte at age seven, alone with his mother, after she had abandoned his four older brothers to the care of their abusive, drunken bastard of a father, and set out to make a new life in America.

Since then, none of them had fared well back in the mother country. Five years ago his father had been abducted by one of the drug cartels, tortured, eyes gouged out, then beheaded. At the end of his ordeal, the machete must have been a blessing, Ortega thought.

The oldest brother was in prison, serving a thirty year sentence for killing a local politician. And though the other three had escaped similar fates, they did little more than eke out a living in the employ of a secluded banana plantation, one owned by nameless business interests, which were in turn owned by the Sinaloa Cartel.

Only he, José Manuel Ortega, had seized the American Dream and squeezed its fat, juicy *cojones* for all it was worth. Growing up in the new land of Texas, stolen by the gringos in 1848, he went on to college coasting on a free government grant, got enlisted into a new government diversity program seeking Hispanic teachers, and somehow ended up with a teaching degree—although just barely—considering his sketchy grades. In the end, he opted for "athletic coach" as his teaching specialty, since he knew little else.

For ten years he taught in dangerous, low-income barrios in San Antonio, coaching an endless succession of students through an endless routine of pushups, chinups, long-distance running, basketball, whatever The Man demanded, just to build his cred.

On one occasion, he broke up a knife fight between a nigger and a Mexican in the gym locker room, after the nigger claimed the Mexican had "rubbed his dick" against the crack of his ass while they were both in the shower. Pulling a knife from his locker, the nigger, still naked, backed the Mexican against the wall. Ortega, seeing the altercation, waded in with lightning speed, punching the nigger to his knees.

Earning a police commendation as well as school board recognition, he managed to disguise how much he had enjoyed humiliating *el negro*. But outwardly, his quick intervention demonstrated to the gringo that he was "one of the good spics", and "a minority who could be trusted".

Yet, José Manuel Ortega never forgot his roots, or his early years as a member of *Los Buitres de la Sangre—The Blood Vultures*—a violent San Antonio street gang, where he was known among his fellow drug dealers and pimps as "Ricky Ricardo" for his Latin good looks and deceptively easy manner. What was less known about Titanis High's gym coach was that he had never forsaken his street connections.

Instead, he had expanded and strengthened them.

And was now bringing in family members...

"Since you are here, I have something else for you to do," Ortega said, his eyes flicking over his handsome image, first turning his head one way, then the other, as he made minor stylistic touches with his Ace comb.

"Sí, José. I will do anything you say."

Ortega, satisfied he was one hot chili pepper, turned to his skinny wetback nephew. "How did you get here?"

"By car."

"Since when does a penniless border jumper like you have a car?"

"Since last week. But no need to worry. I have already changed out the license plates and repainted it. It was red but now it is black. Black is my favorite color."

Ever so slightly, Ortega smiled.

Black was his favorite color as well.

And the little wetback fuck knew it.

"Then you know not to keep your new car more than a week or two, *comprende*? Use it for a short time, maybe to hit a few convenience stores for some quick cash, then get another one as the need arises. That is the way to go about it." He looked over the kid. "But I know the real reason you took the car, Raul."

"You do?"

"Because you knew I used to be so good at it. So good, never once was I caught. Your mamá must have told you that."

"Sí, José. She told me."

"And you took the car for one other reason..."

Raul looked at him, his eyes expectant.

"Because you wanted to prove you had the *cojones*, you little *puta*."

Raul barely nodded; his uncle could read him like a book.

"So maybe there's hope for you yet, shithead. Now listen

up: I want you to follow me back to my office in the gym. I have something I want you to deliver to a Mr. Schmidt. It's a laptop and he has been told to expect it. Do you know what a laptop is?"

"Sí, it is a little machine."

Ortega chuckled darkly. "Yes, you simple-headed country fuck—it is a little machine. Back where you come from you don't see many of them. But all the gringos have them. And they use them to hide information they don't want anyone else to know about. So never trust a gringo."

"Is not this Señor Schmidt a gringo?"

"A useful one, for the moment. A smuggler and a pilot. But one day the cartel will exchange him for someone new; someone who does not know so many names and so many secrets. And then he will be rattlesnake food."

"And the laptop?"

"I will give you instructions where to deliver it. And a note explaining who you are. Once you leave here, you are to take the laptop directly to Señor Schmidt. Without delay. He is expecting it."

The youth nodded, but his eyes told the boy in the trashcan that he still sensed he and Ortega were being watched. If he should act on his suspicions and search the only possible hiding place left in the bathroom...

Then Andy would be found.

And if he was, Ortega would instantly realize that one of his own gym students had heard everything about his criminal past, his car thefts, and–

Something about a kidnapping...

Sitting there hunched in the trash, Andy broke out in a cold sweat. Something very bad was going down here, something he couldn't quite grasp, some criminal conspiracy that he had inadvertently stumbled upon. Because he knew right then the "little machine" referred to Rodney Crutchley's laptop, and that Coach Ortega had gotten into his locker and stolen it.

Only—*why?*

Then his mind began to put the pieces together.

Stolen cars...

Purloined laptops...

But of course.

A theft ring!

That had to be it!

And somehow a kidnapping was part of it all. Clearly, Ortega must be engaged in some complex criminal operation, one involving a teacher/student theft ring like others he had read about.

"Time to go," Ortega ordered. "Fifth period will be ending soon and it's better if no one sees us together."

The youth nodded, still looking apprehensively around.

"For a macho car thief you sure look jittery."

It was then the youth's eyes halted on the trash can.

"Let's go," Ortega repeated, heading for the door and pulling it open.

"I have to pee," the youth suddenly said, still eyeing the trashcan.

"Now you tell me. Well, go ahead. I will wait for you down the hallway at the water fountain. But hurry."

As Coach Ortega departed and his footsteps echoed down the corridor, the youth moved toward a urinal, still keeping his eye on the trashcan.

Andy watched him every step of the way.

He could tell the youth's mind was working.

Studying the trashcan.

Considering the possibilities.

Wondering if the receptacle held two peering eyes.

After a short pee, Raul zipped up his pants.

Moving to the sink, he placed his hands under the faucet, letting an automated sensor gush water over them. Then, bypassing the bank of automatic hand-dryers mounted along the wall, he instead moved toward a bank of paper towel dispensers provided for those who preferred them, since they were quicker. Taking the automatically ejected length of paper towel, the youth dried his hands methodically, all the while keeping his dark eyes on the trashcan. Finally, wadded towel in hand, he approached it.

Andy froze.

Coming to a stop, Raul looked down at the trashcan's swivel-mounted lid, which required only the lightest push to expose the waste receptacle's interior...

And whatever lurked within.

Stooping forward, he cautiously lowered the crumpled paper toward the swivel-mounted lid—

Andy exploded upward.

In a flash, the lid went flying toward the ceiling and One Buck For A Suck Hupp was up and out, discarded paper towels, soda cans, test papers, and used condoms flying in twenty different directions at once. Grabbing the shocked youth by his baggy *cholo* shirt, Andy swung him sideways into a stall, crashing him headlong into a toilet bowl. As the mestizo punk cried out in pain, Andy burst out the door and skidded sideways into the corridor. Down at the water fountain, Coach Ortega whirled around at the sudden commotion.

Got to keep my back to him, Andy thought.

Mustn't let him see my face!

In another instant he rounded the corner and rocketed down the side corridor, bolting for the exit door that led to the East Quad.

Somewhere behind, he heard Ortega's running feet and the bathroom door shoved open. Then, an instant after that, the sound of two pairs of feet in hot pursuit.

But if nothing else, Andy Hupp was one fast motherfucker. For by the time Coach Ortega and his nephew made it to the exit door and searched the quad from left to right, he was long gone...

CHAPTER 14

A hundred yards away, bent over and gasping for breath, Andy Hupp took a moment to reflect on his near escape. Goddamn he was fast, but boy did it burn out his dilithium crystals. Still, he had gotten himself to the opposite side of campus at superluminal speed, finally coming to a halt somewhere near the auditorium. Classes would soon end, and then once more the school would crawl with students. Safety in numbers, he thought, his lungs still heaving as he finally straightened up and moved away on impulse power, plotting his next move.

Drifting cautiously out of a side corridor, he checked to see if the coast was clear, then began to weave his way through the labyrinth of hallways toward the student parking lot, where his Mercedes Benz sat. As he did, he was pretty sure Coach Ortega hadn't caught a glimpse of his face as he tore out of the Boys Bathroom and shot lickety-split across campus.

On the other hand, the kid named Raul had.

But Andy probably looked like just another faceless gringo to him, so it likely didn't matter.

He hoped...

A minute later the end-of-class bell rang, signaling a flood of teenage boys and girls off to their next period.

But professional juvenile delinquent Andy Hupp had other plans, as the good-looking teen with the arresting green eyes and mop of tawny brown hair moved with shark-like swiftness through the student crowds.

"Hey, *Andeee!*" a voice called out.

Oh god, Andy thought, here it comes: another One Buck For A Suck Hupp joke—at his expense.

But no—

"Wait up, Mr. Junior Movie Mogul!"

Andy half turned, buffeted by onrushing streams of students headed to and fro. And bobbing toward him in that sea of tumult was Jeena "Jinky" Kirtland, books in hand, long strands of hair rippling like molten gold. In another instant she was at his side, Nazi-blue eyes all aglitter and shining like the Lord Jesus Christ himself had just come down to earth to ask for her hand in marriage.

Or something like that, Andy thought, now walking beside her as they were carried along by the river of students.

"Where you headed, Mr. Big Shot?"

"Got to run an errand," he answered.

"I see—ditching class again."

"What do you mean 'again'?"

She giggled, looking up at him through thick golden eyelashes. "TJ's given me a complete dossier on you, buster. That's what I mean. What you do, where you go, what you like, even the girls you've—"

"Hold it, Jink. Just hold it. You're about to say something guaranteed to embarrass me. So just pretend you're my kid sister and I'm your older brother, 'kay? And talking about what boys and girls do together just isn't proper etiquette."

"How old are you?" she demanded.

"Seventeen."

"Same here, smartypants. So you're not my older brother and I'm not your kid sister."

"Jesus Christ on a Big Mac—" he said, exasperated.

The walked on, even as Jinky realized that—underneath all his know-it-all bravado—Andy Hupp was actually kind of shy. And yet, according to TJ, he never went a day without some girl in hot pursuit...

"So what happened to Rodney?" Jinky finally said, her voice turning serious.

"He got beat up."

"I already know that, Mr. Brains. I was there when Lawrence Micklethwaite went blabbing all over the cafeteria about it, remember?"

"Yeah, I remember. Anyway, Rodney got into some bad trouble. Real bad trouble."

"What kind of trouble?"

"He broke Jamal Perkins' arm."

"Oh my god! That must've been what Lawrence Micklethwaite was about to tell us! You know, before he took off for that other table!"

"I'm on my way to see Rodney now."

"Where—to his house?"

"No—to the Juvenile Detention Center."

"The Juvenile De–? You mean they *arrested* him?"

"Yeah. And they might charge him with felony assault."

As they approached a cross corridor, one stream of students funneled left, another funneled right, and the rest continued onward, like lemmings headed toward oblivion.

"Well, gotta go," Andy said, nodding leftward in the direction that would take him out to the school parking lot. But even as he broke away from Jeena Kirtland he heard her rush up from behind: "Oh, no you don't!"

"What?" Andy said, moving with purpose toward the far exit that would lead him outside to his van.

"If you think I'm going to stand by while one of our production team's sitting in jail you're dead wrong, bubbo! I'm coming with you!"

And together they rushed out the door.

Two minutes later Andy Hupp shot out the parking lot with Jeena Kirtland at his side, glad his best buddy TJ hadn't been around to see their departure. If he had, he knew how it would've looked: good-looking boy, way cute girl, speeding away. Jesus Christ—enough circumstantial evidence to get any guy the electric chair.

What was it with him and trouble?

Because this was mighty thin ice he was skating on.

Mighty thin...

Even now he could hear it cracking beneath his feet.

But he willed himself to set his guilt aside and concentrate on the task ahead.

"You know how to get there?" Jinky asked, kicking her stylish athletic shoes off and propping her ankle-socked feet up on the dash.

In answer, Andy leaned toward the GPS system in the middle of the dash and spoke in the name of the detention facility—watched the screen pop up the travel route—then glanced casually over at Jeena Kirtland: "Why don't you make yourself at home?"

She wrinkled her nose, flitting a sideways glance at him. "Just did, rich boy."

Andy shook his head, half amused, but half not. "Get this straight, Jink. I'm not rich."

"Says you, Mr. Brainiac. My eyeballs say otherwise. Daddy buy you this cool set of wheels?"

"I—" he started to say, almost blurting out that he had earned every penny that had gone into buying the expensive German van. But knowing Jink's inquisitive mind, she would have demanded to know with what kind of job—sweeping floors down at the local burger joint, maybe?

And what could he tell her?

The truth?

That part of his earnings had come from posing in expensive designer underwear while some middle-aged bearded guy shot countless photos of him—including close-up crotch shots?

God help him if *that* ever got out.

"Go on," she prodded. "You were saying?"

Andy pretended to study the map on the GPS screen, even while he struggled to come up with an answer.

"I–I inherited some money."

"Uncle? Aunt? Or is that too personal?"

"Uhhh...my grandmother."

"Mother or father's side?"

Jesus Christ on the RMS Titanic, Andy thought, who is this girl—the US Attorney General?

"Uhhh...father's."

"How old was she when...you know."

"Hundred and five," Andy said, with an inward grin, deciding it was time to yank Jinky's chain a bit in retaliation for putting him through the third degree.

"Hundred and five! What happened?"

"It's a sad story," Andy said, his voice turning convincingly mournful.

"If you'd rather not talk about it..."

"It's just the way she...went."

"You mean, an accident?"

Andy nodded, then dramatically looked off at the passing Texas countryside, as if he were too choked up to go on. In reality, he was having one hell of a time keeping her from seeing the big grin on his face.

"Yeah," he finally whispered. "An accident."

"Slipped and fell? Something like that?"

"No...hit a semi-truck while riding down the highway on the back of a Harley with her boyfriend."

"With her *boy*–!"

"Toward the end she liked 'em young. He wasn't a day over seventy-five."

"Wow."

"It's the Hupp genes, my dad says. We're driven to squeeze the last juices out of life, no matter how old we get."

Jinky leaned back, reflecting. "That was a beautiful story, Andy. Really. No wonder you want to make movies. You have a certain poetry about you."

Oh god, now I've done it.

She bought it—hook, line, and sinker.

If only I had the Brooklyn Bridge to sell...

They drove on.

Ten minutes earlier, as Andy Hupp hunched over catching his breath in a secluded corridor at Titanis High, Coach José Manuel Ortega and his nephew Raul hurried across the school headed toward the gym.

"Did you get a good look at him, Raul?" Ortega demanded, his obsidian-hard eyes sizzling with anger as they headed back to his office.

"Sí, José. But he was just another gringo to me."

"I'm asking you what he looked like, you little fuck! Don't you know he heard everything we said?"

Yes, Raul knew. He had sensed something or someone had been spying on them, certain at first it must be one of those black metal "eyeballs" stuck to the ceiling that he saw everywhere he went in this strange new country. Why, just the other day, as he was shoplifting all that good shit from Walmart, he'd been overly-aware of the "bubble" cameras lurking over his head as he prowled the aisles looking for anything stealable. So fucking nosy, these Americans. Why do they need so many spies on their ceilings, on their walls, everywhere they go? It was not that way back home...

As they rounded a corner, Raul said: "Just a gringo with light hair and pale eyes, José. About my age, I think. So he must be a student here."

"Lot a help that is, *pequeño bobo*," Ortega snapped under his breath, as they hurried the last stretch toward his office, hoping to beat the bell that would signal the end of the class period. Raul winced. His uncle had just called him a "little fool" in their native tongue.

He did not like being called a little fool.

Normally, he would've cut someone up for that.

And had.

But one did not challenge Uncle José. He was the hero of the Ortega family, the one who had made it big in America. The one they all looked up to. And finally, the one with connections to Mara Salvatrucha—otherwise known as MS-13.

And no one ever challenged *them*.

That is, and died an easy death.

"Wait. I remember now..."

"Then out with it!"

"His eyes—they were *verde*."

"Verde? Green? Are you sure?"

"Sí, José—green."

Ortega chewed on that for a moment.

Green eyes...

How many students did he know with such eyes?

Quite a few, actually.

As they continued on, Ortega ran a few dozen faces through his brain, searching his memory. He needn't recall any female students, since the person he'd glimpsed running away had clearly been male. But with a student body of close to a thousand, roughly half of them boys, he failed to bring up any immediate suspects.

But one way or the other...

"Yes, I know of a few green-eyed boys around school," he said, his dark eyes calculating. "If I come across the right one, I will know."

"But how?"

Ortega let go a slow grin.

"Because I found a trace of blood on the trashcan lid, you little shit. Whoever cut his hand when he jumped out is the one we're after."

Raul nodded.

His uncle was *muy* smart.

That's why he was where he was, working as a teacher in

Norteamérica while his brothers toiled back home on the banana plantation. So he would respectfully accept being called a little shit and a little fool—for now. That is, until he could prove to his uncle that he was a real *hombre*.

And somehow, some way, he would.

Perhaps, very soon..

Arriving at his office, the gym teacher shut the door and went immediately to his file cabinet. Sliding open a drawer, he retrieved the laptop he had taken from Rodney Crutchley's locker, after accessing the combination via the school's computer data bank. Turning off the hallway camera before removing it had been a little trickier, but that too had been taken care of. After all, a favor given is a debt waiting to collect—and he had given many favors to certain office staff in need of certain street drugs.

And today he had come to collect on one of them.

Taking the laptop, he set it on his desk then went over to the closet, digging through it until he found just the right sized box. Returning, he slid the computer inside, then taped it shut.

There.

As for the now-packaged device, he had only an inkling as to what was contained on its hard-drive, having merely been ordered to remove the computer from a certain student's locker. Chain of command, Ortega thought: one hand always scratching someone else's back, all down the line, while the other was always at the ready, knife or gun poised to strike.

But it had to be that way, he knew.

Simply because there was too much money at stake, too much lucrative sex-trafficking, too much meth and cocaine dealing—in the end, too much dangerous good living that the fools of everyday life never suspected went on behind their backs, in hidden places and hidden rooms, where darker souls ruled...

Even so, his nephews wanted a part of it.

Then again, perhaps only Raul did, for already he had stolen a car. A good sign, Coach Ortega thought. On the other hand there was his younger brother Pepito. A scrawny weakling by all accounts. If so, his stay in America would be short.

And cruel.

"Here," Ortega said, handing the boxed laptop to his nephew, along with written instructions to Schmidt's remote airstrip. "Remember, do not delay in delivering it."

Raul took the box. "Thank you, José. I will do as you say."

The gym coach leveled a cold black eye: "You'd better. I was to deliver it myself but I have a *muy caliente* date tonight. So I do not have the time. But this way I can see how well you follow orders. Just remember: do not stain the Ortega name with cowardice like your brother."

Raul solemnly nodded.

As he started away José called out one last time: "You should get yourself a gun, little gangbanger. You might need one sooner than you think."

Raul locked eyes with his handsome uncle, who had once belonged to San Antonio's deadliest street gang. "I already have," he quietly stated, with the thinnest touch of pride in his voice. Then he took the box and left, leaving José Ortega looking after him for a long, silent time—a shrewd, diamond-hard glint in his eye...

A minute later, Raul was almost out of the school when the bell rang, flooding the hallways with mostly gringo kids. How he hated them with their multicolored eyes, of brown, blue, gray, and green instead of obsidian like his own—and hair rarely black like his, but instead mostly brown, blonde, and red, with every shade in between. So many colors, he thought—so much diversity—true diversity! How different these gringo kids looked from the rest of the world—the mestizos, the orientals, and the *mayates*—the niggers. But though he hated gringos, how much he wanted what they had, and how he was determined to get it.

One way or the other...

As he headed for the exit leading to the parking lot, he was briefly engulfed by the Anglo students, pushed and shoved and buffeted as he clung tenaciously to the box containing the laptop, as if it were a lifesaver in a stormy sea. And in a way it was, for he was determined to prove to his uncle that he was not a timid little goat like his brother, but a real *hombre*.

Hopping into his stolen car a minute later, he revved up the engine. What did these rich gringo kids have that he didn't, now that he too had a car? And soon, he would also have *mucho dinero*.

More, perhaps, than they'd ever dreamt.

Sí, he thought.

Muy mucho más...

Putting the stolen car in gear, he tore out of the parking lot behind a fast-accelerating silver van, feeling the blood of manhood pumping through his veins. If only his mamá, **papá**, and other uncles down on the banana plantation could see him now! He—Raul Domingo Ortega, aged seventeen. Here in America. With a hot car *and* a cold gun.

¡Olé!

"Wonder who's behind us?" Jinky drowsily asked, lolling back in her seat, but with one blue eye casually trained on her side-view mirror.

"Beats me," Andy said, tilting a green eye at his rear-view mirror. "Just a black car."

"Probably another kid ditching school," she murmured, now moving her attention to the passing countryside.

"Probably."

"Ever think you might be a bad influence on the morals of Titanis High?"

"You never know."

"You sound like you don't give a shit."

"I don't."

She laughed, liking this back and forth picking and teasing with TJ's best friend.

After a moment of silence, she turned her face toward him, studying his profile. She loved his long eyelashes, something many girls would kill for. And his nose, with its subtle upturn ending in a blunt little tip. Strong, yet somehow irresistibly cute. And that hair, thick, carefree, with three shades of medium brown interwoven through it: mostly chestnut and auburn, but with occasional strands of deep copper, as if hinting at richer hues beneath.

"You ever think of being a model?" she asked, out of the blue.

"Who? Me?"

"Who else is sitting here beside me, bozo?"

"I'm just the chauffeur."

"No, really. As a blossoming young actress I like to study faces. And I've seen faces like yours in the women's mags my mom sometimes reads. You know, like *You Go, Girl!*, *21st Century Woman*, *It's Our Time*, etc, etc, etc."

Andy swallowed.

He'd just completed a lucrative photo spread for *21st Century Woman* four months earlier, featuring him shirtless in Buccaneer Jeans, an ad for a hip new smartphone, and his back-by-popular-demand Mann Hunt Underwear series of ads, in one issue wearing black briefs, in another purple ones, in still another posing with a girl in semi-sheer lace panties reaching around his waist toward his—

Geeze, Andy thought.

Just thinking about the things he'd done to earn this high-priced van and movie equipment almost made him blush. That, and having to lie to Jinky.

"I mean, ever wonder why so many women's magazines feature men's underwear ads...?" she murmured, gazing off at the passing Texas countryside.

"Not really," Andy said, briefly darting his eye at the GPS screen. "Studies have shown that two thirds of men have their underwear bought by women—wives, girlfriends, even mothers. So it makes sense to advertise men's underwear in women's magazines."

"You don't say, Professor Hupp?" she remarked, in a credible English accent.

"Oh, but I do," he replied, in an equally credible, but overly-stuffy aristocratic one.

Again they laughed, and for an instant their eyes sparkled with reflections of each other.

"Anyway," Andy went on, turning his eye back to the road as he assumed a more serious tone, "I wouldn't be caught dead working as a model."

"But why not, Andy-Pandy? It's kinda like show business in a way, isn't it? I mean, they create make believe, don't they?"

"'Andy-Pandy'?" he echoed, pronouncing each syllable with slow emphasis as he turned a gimlet eye toward her.

"That's my special name for you. I just made it up. See? I can write too."

Again, they laughed, in the aftermath drifting once more into silence. A pleasant silence, Andy thought. Strange, with most girls he'd always felt an underlying strain to keep talking, to keep the conversation going, to be a non-stop showman. Maybe because girls got bored so easily, something he knew from experience.

Must be a genetic thing...

But sitting here next to Jeena Kirtland, it was somehow different. She was more than mere words. She was clever gestures and eye movements, sensuous twists in her seat, enticing shiftings of thighs, occasional soft sighs momentarily lifting her breasts, all unconsciously designed, it seemed, to draw subtle glances her way, disguised as they were whenever he looked over to check the GPS screen.

"Same boring black car still behind us," Jinky remarked several miles later, as the road whispered beneath their wheels.

Andy glanced again at his rear-view mirror. "Guess he's going the same way since the main highway's just ahead. Probably going to veer off toward Austin."

A little farther on Jinky let out a wistful sigh. "Do guys ever stop to wonder just how difficult a girl's life can be?"

"How so?"

"Well, for one thing Mr. Know-It-All, we have to go pee more often than boys."

"Let me guess," Andy said, "you need to use the lady's room."

"Gee, Andy-Pandy, anyone ever mention you might be psychic?"

"As a matter of fact," he said, "I've been told by several notable experts that I have exceptional psionic abilities. I just don't brag about it. Anyway, there's a crummy gas station about a mile down the road."

"Crummy? For high society like me?"

"Well, I don't know what else to call it. But it does have a bathroom—batteries and toilet paper not necessarily included."

She held up her small purse, dipped in a hand, and pulled out some perfume-scented Kleenex. "Ta-Da!"

Girls, Andy thought.

God, but they were another species.

CHAPTER 15

As the crummy gas station/convenience store hove into view—aka Spot-N-The-Road—Andy activated his right turn signal and decelerated.

Behind him, the black muscle car closed rapidly on his rear bumper, showing no sign of slowing. Andy hated tailgaters, and turned toward his driver's side window for an instant, hoping to catch a fleeting glimpse of the asshole as he zipped by. Then, at the last second, the black car snaked around his van, almost clipping it, as it whizzed on past. For a split second Andy caught sight of a shadowy figure seated behind the steering wheel, obscured by tinted windows. Even so, he had the distinct and eerie impression the driver was suddenly looking straight at him, as if he somehow knew Andy.

"Anybody you know?" Jinky asked, as Andy wheeled into the graveled service area of the run-down gas station.

"I don't know anyone who owns a black Mustang," Andy hesitantly replied, a note of puzzlement in his voice.

She looked at him. "What?" she said, addressing the unspoken concern in his voice.

"Nothing, I guess..."

"But–?"

"But I got the strangest feeling that whoever was driving that car recognized me."

"Okay, buster, you're creeping me out. I'm not ready to end up on an episode of *Forensic Files.*"

Despite his concern, Andy chuckled. "Don't worry, it's no

longer on the air." He pulled the van to a stop. "Want a soda?"

"Long as you're paying, rich boy."

"Sure, but don't consider this a date. Our mutual friend TJ wouldn't like it." Especially, Andy thought, if he knew I was with his girl right this instant...

Yet they couldn't help but look at each other, bringing home all the unspoken implications that had ridden with them after leaving Titanis High—implications only now rising to the surface. But just as quickly Jinky looked away and hopped out of the van, as if she had wanted to say something but suddenly thought better. Andy hopped out too, wondering what had been started here...

Between Jinky, his encounter with Ms Pickering, Principal Meevers, and the asshole driving the black Mustang, it all gave his teenage mind plenty to chew on, even as he crunched across the graveled drive toward the rundown excuse of a convenience store, pushing open its banged-up door. As he and Jeena Kirtland wove their way through tightly-packed shelves of potato chips, snack items, and canned goods toward the soda cooler, a hundred yards down the road a black car pulled sharply into a thicket of mesquite trees. Inside, an illegal alien who had no right to be in the country leaned back over the seat of his stolen car and stared at the gas station, where a lone van glinted silver in the sun.

By sheer blind luck, or perhaps the will of *Ah Puch,* fate had led him here, down this road, past a certain silver van, to glimpse for but a fleeting instant a certain gringo face. For there was no doubt now who he'd seen: the trashcan boy from the school—and with him some slutty blonde *puta,* as his sharp eye had observed.

Twisting back around, Raul reached for the glove compartment, snapping it open.

A brown hand reached in.

Fingers clutched cold steel.

Bringing out the Belgian-made, FN-57 semi-automatic pistol, prized by the Sinaloa Cartel as a "cop killer" because of its penetrating power, he and some other wannabe gang-bangers had ripped it off, along with a crateful of other weapons last month, from a Houston gun store. The crime remained unsolved, the perpetrators unknown, but not the desire of one Raul Domingo Ortega.

And that desire was to make his Uncle José so proud of him that he would never again call him a dumb shit or little fuck. For before the day was done, the seventeen year old border jumper knew, looking once again at the dilapidated gas station as the trashcan boy emerged, he would make his bones.

And finally become a man...

⁂

A few minutes later, Andy Hupp and Jeena Kirtland cruised out of the gas station sipping transparent green bottles of cinnamon-flavored *SNARK!*, even as they settled in for the remainder of the twelve mile drive to the Burnet County Juvenile Detention Center.

As they drove past the spot where Raul Ortega lay concealed behind a roadside grove of mesquite trees, he cautiously waited until they traveled some distance down the road before pulling out after them, keeping himself out of visual range. For if the occupants of the silver van saw him at all, it was only as an indistinct grayish blot in their rear-view mirrors.

Now he would follow them, looking for just the right spot.

And there, lying on the seat beside him, sat the FN-57, black as a deadly scorpion.

Hungry to sting...

⁂

Fifteen minutes later Andy and Jinky spotted the County

Juvenile Detention Center and veered toward it.

"So you're convinced Rodney didn't do it?" Jinky said, her voice tinged with doubt as she gazed toward the approaching concrete facility.

"Pretty much. For one thing, I got a good look at the writing on Scarletti's locker door. I even took a picture of it. Then I compared it to a sample of Rodney's printing when we met up in the library. Gotta say they didn't match. Close, but not quite. But whoever did it made certain to write 'RC' at the end so that Rodney got blamed for it—which he did. Hopefully, the photo of Scarletti's locker door I gave to Principal Meevers to pass on to the sheriff will help clear him."

"You gave Meevers a copy?"

"Well, not actually. Instead, he asked for my entire cellphone. Told me something about not wanting to appear like he was 'out to get' Rodney by making it seem like he'd taken the photo instead of a student."

"Let me get this straight," Jinky said, turning her blue eyes toward him. "You just handed your smartphone over to Principal Meevers? Just like that? No search warrant—nothing?" There was an edge of something in her voice, like she couldn't believe how easily he had done so.

"Didn't have much choice, Jink," Andy explained, as he wheeled into the Detention Center parking lot. "I mean, he's the principal, after all. Besides, he could've had me arrested for bringing real guns onto campus last year but didn't. So I kinda owed him a favor by not being a dick about it when he asked for my phone. Anyway, he said he needed it to show Scarletti's locker door to the sheriff. That it might somehow help Rodney."

She puffed out a skeptical breath. "You really believe that?"

Andy had to wonder, still troubled about turning over his cellphone without much of a protest—mainly because it had lots of personal information on it. And now it was in the hands of Principal Budd Meevers and...who knew else?

"Right now I don't know what to believe, Jink. But when

you're a seventeen year old con summoned to the warden's office you haven't much choice."

"Seventeen year old con? Summoned to the warden's office...?"

He grinned. "Just some prison lingo me and TJ like to use."

She rolled her eyes. "You and TJ have some serious weirdness problems, you know."

"Yeah, I know," Andy agreed, as he pulled the van into a parking spot, unaware that a black Mustang with tinted-windows had come to rest beneath an oak tree farther down the street, blending in with several other parked cars, including two others that were also black—the perfect camouflage for a predator lying in wait.

As Andy and Jinky exited the van and headed for the glass-fronted entrance, the girl beside him suddenly patted his shoulder. "Andy, wait a sec. Isn't that Rodney Crutchley? Over there?"

Andy turned in the direction of her glance and saw a large, clumsy-looking youth walking alongside an old, white-haired guy toward a battered green Ford pickup, splotched here and there with gray primer. Reaching it, they paused a moment and exchanged a few words before the elderly man handed over a set of keys. As Rodney took them and climbed into the pickup, the old man wandered off toward a nearby gold Toyota Camry where an old woman waited, seated behind the steering wheel. A moment later the two of them drove away. Seconds later, the Ford pickup chugged out of the parking lot and turned in the opposite direction, Rodney Crutchley at the wheel.

"Come on," Andy said, grabbing Jinky by the wrist and darting for the van, just as the pickup accelerated down the road. "Let's try to catch him."

"Was that old guy who I think it was?" Jinky asked, as Andy Hupp spun out of the parking lot a moment later.

"Yeah, I think it was."

"Kinda weird, don't you think? I mean, the school janitor

busting Rodney out of the Graybar Hotel."

"What's even weirder is a girl named Jinky talking like a con."

She stuck her tongue out at him.

"Watch it. TJ might spank you for that."

"I like to be spanked."

Oh, boy, Andy thought–better not go there.

He looked ahead again, his face as chaste as a monk.

Somewhere behind, a black Mustang fired up and pulled out after them, staying at the outer edge of visual range. Andy briefly noticed it, but since it was no more than an indistinct, darkish-gray apparition in the fading October afternoon, he paid it no mind.

"Not much daylight left," Jinky observed.

Andy noted the time on the dashboard, then glanced at the blonde profile next to him. "You need to call home or something?"

"Nope. Mom's still at work and so's dad."

"Your parents both work?"

"Well, they're not exactly drug addicts you know. But then, rich boys like you probably lounge around the pool all day so you wouldn't know." She glanced over at him. "You do have a pool, don't you?"

He did.

And it'd cost his dad a bundle.

"I'm afraid to answer on the grounds it might incriminate me," he replied, looking ahead again. "You know, as a rich boy."

She smirked at him. "TJ's already told me," she fired back, one eyebrow raised knowingly. "So no use lying."

Rotten traitor, he thought.

"Maybe you and TJ can come over some weekend for a swim."

"Why–just so you can gawk at me in my bikini?"

"No–so TJ can."

She laughed. "He gawks at me fully dressed."

"Why not? You're worth gawking at."

Her blue eyes fixed on his. "Really?"

Danger, Will Robinson!

At that moment the pickup carrying Rodney Crutchley flipped on its left turn signal, sparing Andy from answering.

"Any idea where he's going, Sherlock?"

"To his house, I guess. But who knows?"

"Why do you suppose his dad and mom didn't come bust him out of lock-up instead of the school janitor?"

"Beats me. Maybe they're both drug addicts."

She reached over and punched him. "Smartass." Then, leaning back comfortably, she added: "What's taking you so long to catch up with him, gramps?"

"Just curious, maybe."

She slid an eye in his direction. "Curious?"

"About where he lives."

"And I thought girls were nosy."

Behind them, the black Mustang maintained its distance, trailing the silver van as it curved left. Was it just a coincidence, or was it following the truck?

It had to be, Raul suddenly realized.

If so, why?

Then something occurred to the highly suspicious mestizo: maybe the occupants of both vehicles were together, headed to a secret hiding place to discuss what the trashcan boy had overheard he and Uncle José talking about; to decide whether or not to go to the police, which could end up getting his uncle arrested. If so, he would lose his job, his home, maybe go to prison...even have a contract put out on him by MS-13.

Raul's eyes darted feverishly to the gun.

Only you can save the Ortega family from dishonor, he realized, snatching the weapon and tucking it forcefully between his thighs. Then he drove on, his black eyes growing sharp as cactus needles; the moment had come.

"Funny..." Jinky casually remarked, glancing over her shoulder, "that same car's still behind us. And it's turned left too..."

"Now you're starting to creep me out," Andy said, keeping his eye on the pickup ahead.

"Ever think it might be the same black car?"

"Is it?" There was a growing edge to his voice.

She squinted. "Can't tell..."

"Never mind–look. Rodney's pulling off the road. I think we've been made."

"Made? You mean, like were cops or something? And he's a wanted criminal? God, you should make movies!"

"And I thought I acted weird."

"Oh, but you do, Andy-Pandy. In the weirdest, cutest way I've ever–" she blurted, before realizing she had said far too much.

"He's getting out," Andy said. "Waving us down."

As Andy slowed and pulled up behind Rodney Crutchley, Jinky grabbed another look at the vehicle behind as they exited the van.

It was closer now.

Much closer.

Engine roaring.

Streaking toward them like a bat out of hell.

"Andy, the black car–!"

Gunshots cracked and whizzed.

Three, four, five bullets zinged past their heads, even as Andy grabbed Jinky and twirled her down into the dirt. Nearby, Rodney ducked behind his truck, as three more slugs pierced its battered metal side as easily as an ice pick punching through a beer can.

From where he lay, lying there in the dirt beside Jinky, her arm clutching his waist, Andy estimated the black Mustang must be doing at least 80 mph as it streaked past.

In the next instant it looked as if the car's driver tried to execute a movie-style, sliding U-turn, in order to set-up for a second drive-by.

But *tried* was the operative word, Andy thought.

Because one second later the powerful machine screeched and rolled, flipping sideways across the asphalt before bouncing off the road into an outcropping of granite boulders. A hellish shriek of tortured metal and shattered glass followed, then what looked like a mini-nuke going off as the gas tank exploded in a huge, high-octane fireball.

"Oh my god, Andy–*why!?*"

But Andy had no time to answer, even as he yanked Jeena Kirtland to her feet and ran, hand in hand, over to Rodney. Both boys looked at each other, their eyes wide with possibilities.

"Me and Jink were worried about you so we drove out to the detention center," Andy gasped. "But when we got there you had already taken off–"

For a moment Rodney Crutchley said nothing, looking silently from Andy to Jeena, the dark pools of his deep blue eyes filled with a momentary trace of emotion, one that seemed to acknowledge something he had not experienced in a very long time–a sense of gratitude toward someone who had shown concern for him. But to this he could add no words, so unaccustomed he was to any kindness. Instead, he simply turned and gazed down the road at the furiously burning car. "He tried to kill us."

Andy glanced at Jink, then back at the big kid. "Whoever he was, I'm pretty sure he's been following us ever since we drove out of the high school parking lot."

"Why?" Rodney asked.

"We don't know," Jinky offered, still trembling from her brush with death. "But I think that's his body lying by the side of the road..."

The two boys looked again, squinting against the fading light.

"Yeah," Andy confirmed, "I think I can just make it out." He glanced at the blonde girl. "Jesus, you must have eyesight like a hawk."

"An eye doctor once told me I have 20/15 vision," she

said. "As a little girl I've always been able to see better than others."

Andy nodded, thinking her eyes were more than just bewitching. Then he turned back to the hulking, dark-haired teen with the night-blue eyes: "Grab your truck and follow us. But we've got to hurry before another car comes along and finds us here."

With that, Andy turned and snatched Jinky by the wrist, dashing toward his fifty-thousand dollar cargo van. A moment later they were racing down the road toward the burning Mustang, now a charred, twisted hulk roiling with black smoke.

"There it is," Jinky said, indicating the dead body.

Andy saw it too, and whipped his van off the road just opposite the burning wreckage.

Behind, Rodney Crutchley pulled up.

Hopping out, Andy and Jinky darted across the road, followed more warily by Rodney.

"Wasn't wearing his seatbelt," Andy murmured, crouching next to the body, one knee dug into the rocky dirt. "Not that it would've made any difference..." he grimly added, looking over at the still burning, charred interior of the Mustang.

"He was thrown through the windshield," Rodney dispassionately observed, as he walked up from behind.

"How do you know?" Jinky asked.

"Look at the bits of glass embedded in his scalp. And the lacerations down his arms. Like he was shot through a cheese grater."

"Thanks for the visual, Rod," Andy dryly commented. "You'll definitely make a fine addition to Hupp Film Productions special effects department."

"Just sayin'," Rodney quietly remarked, shrugging. His dark eyes continued looking about for other clues.

As he did, Andy slowly reached for the bloody corpse.

"*Ewwww*, Andy! You're not going to roll him over, are you?"

In all truth, he didn't want to.

He had never touched a dead body.

At seventeen, death just didn't seem real.

And yet...here it was, lying there before him.

Mortality.

Swallowing, he took hold of the dead driver's shoulder and rolled him over–and stared straight into the bulging, death-shocked eyes of Raul, his face spiked with splinters of windshield glass; the same eyes that had sensed his presence in the high school bathroom. Eyes that were now staring off into the emptiness of nonexistence; or, perhaps, into the meaningless void of his own short, filthy, criminal life.

For a long moment Andy remained silent, as if there were some unspoken lesson here, before finally rising again.

"We've got to get out of here–now."

Jinky looked anxiously at Andy: "Do you recognize him?"

He recognized him, alright.

He wished he hadn't.

And if ever Coach Ortega connected him to this...

But he couldn't think of that now.

"Let's go!" Andy snapped, startling the girl.

"Wait," Rodney interrupted. "There's something over there."

A few yards down the shoulder of the road lay a box, partly scorched, with a dark object half sticking out.

Then the green-eyed teen recognized what it was.

Moving rapidly toward it, he got down on one knee again and examined the flame-blackened box and the partly ejected object. Behind him, the big youth and Jinky came up.

Slowly, Andy lifted the box and handed it, along with the object it contained, up to Rodney. "I think this belongs to you."

Recognizing his laptop, Rodney looked from Andy to the burning car to the dead youth, his indigo eyes overflowing with dark implication.

"This has got to be our secret," Andy grimly said, looking from the tall youth to the blonde girl to the dead mestizo lying in the dirt.

In acknowledgment, Rodney made a slow nod.

Jinky, her blue eyes wide with fear, swallowed.

But she too nodded.

"In the meantime," Andy instructed, "you better head straight home Rodney. Say nothing of this to anyone. As for me, I'm taking the long way back into town. Once there, I'll drop Jinky off then head straight home. Later on, I'll call a special meeting of Hupp Film Productions at my place." He took Jinky's hand without even thinking, "Now let's get the hell out of here."

And with that, Andy Hupp darted back across the road with Jinky in hand.

Five seconds later two vehicles tore off in a cloud of Texas dust, leaving the burning Mustang and one dead car thief lying half-charred by the side of the road.

"Just in time," Jinky gasped, checking her side-view mirror. "There's a car way behind us, but it's coming up fast on the wreckage."

"Hopefully they didn't see us," Andy said, gritting his teeth as he raced up to 75 mph.

"I don't think so. I think we got away in time." For a moment she fell silent, then looked toward the boy beside her, her eyes forlorn. "You recognized him, didn't you?"

Andy wanted to lie, to spare the girl beside him.

But this time he couldn't.

"He's coach Ortega's nephew."

"No way!"

Solemnly, Andy nodded.

"But–!"

"Listen up, Jink: I secretly overheard Ortega and his nephew talking about some crimes they'd committed only minutes before you and I met in the school hallway." He jerked his head back over his shoulder. "That burning Mustang? Raul stole it. He's an illegal alien and he and his uncle are part of some kind of crime ring. My guess is he recognized me as I slowed down to turn into that gas station. Afterward he followed us, looking for some lonely spot along the road to kill me."

"Because he feared you might talk—?"

"Probably. And you and Rodney just happened to be unfortunate witnesses. That meant both of you had to die too. Besides, I pissed the punk off when I threw him against a toilet bowl inside the boy's bathroom. Cracked his skull like a cheap piñata."

"Andy, you didn't!"

"Had to. He left me no choice."

Way behind, so far behind the smoke from the wreckage had become a barely visible wisp against the fading yellow-gold of the Texas sky, Jinky's sharp vision spied two tiny pinpoints of blue and red light twinkling rapidly toward the wreck.

"The cops," she said. "Somebody must've called in the accident."

Andy turned a sharp, no-nonsense eye toward her.

"Remember, Jink: no matter what happens, we've got to stick together on this. Because my life, yours, and Rodney's may depend on it. For real." He clasped her shoulder, searching her eyes with his. "Maybe...maybe even our families."

"I...I won't tell a soul. I promise."

"Sorry you ever got mixed up with a wild-ass kid like me."

Involuntarily, she took hold of his hand and pressed it tenderly against the skin of her face, her eyes gazing deeply into his. "Right now I'm glad I did. Because I'd follow you anywhere, Andy..."

"Jink, you can't mean—"

"But I can," she countered, holding his gaze.

After a long moment, Andy slowly pulled away, his mind awhirl.

Driving on, the boy and girl said no more.

But both their thoughts were on TJ...

"I'm very sorry, Mr. Hupp. Really, it's most regrettable. Admittedly, your landscape architect firm has been a valuable asset in our downtown Austin office building for several years but now that we're under new ownership we are compelled to collect all past due rents or initiate the eviction process. As the record shows, and in light of your recent business difficulties, we have extended you a generous grace period these past three months regarding your overdue rental fees. But our corporate office has now made it clear that all unpaid office rent must be collected in full by no later than the first week of November or we must begin the eviction process..."

Listening in silence, Peter Hupp sat alone in his darkened study, blinds partly drawn against the fading October glow. Thin vertical stripes of yellowish-orange light slashed his emotionless face, like virtual prison bars, as his leasing agent finished his grim litany: his office rent was now three months behind and his creditors were demanding immediate payment—or else his landscape architect firm would be thrown out on the street. To avoid that fate meant thousands of dollars in back rent that he just didn't have, unless he defaulted on his mortgage, auto, and credit card payments. Yes, Cynthia had been right; they had been living way beyond their means for far too long.

And now...

He slid open a desk drawer.

There, lying amid a clutter of odds and ends, lay the only way out that he could see. Slowly, he reached toward the object, only to pause—fingertips mere centimeters from the 9mm pistol; for suddenly he remembered: his old friend had made it clear that he might be willing to buy a certain asset of Peter's for a very generous price—were he only willing to sell. If so, then there just might be an alternate solution after all.

That is, if he agreed...

Abruptly, Peter Hupp said: "I'll have the money to you no later than November fifth." With the call ended, he reflected a moment, his face ribboned by the dying October sun, before dialing his old friend.

"Okay, I'll do it," he quietly said. "When do you want to take delivery of the merchandise...?"

CHAPTER 16

Right in the middle of pumping his girlfriend's waxed vagina, José Ortega's cellphone rang.

Damn!

But since it was never wise to miss a call, he blew his load sooner than planned and quickly rolled off, snatching his Android off the nightstand as he did; it might be the cartel regarding Halloween night's merchandise pickup.

Instead, it was his *gringa* wife, Alison.

Bringing his heaving breath under control, he said, "What is it, *mi alma*?" straining to keep any trace of irritation out of his voice.

"You must come home, José. Right away. Something terrible has happened."

"Tell me." There was a sudden hardness to his voice.

"Pepito just called. He told me Raul was in a bad car accident..."

The little shit, José thought, glancing around the darkened room for his underwear. Behind him, a feminine hand appeared out of the gloom, holding forth a pair of Mann Hunt briefs. Taking them, the gym coach wiggled them on even as he continued speaking to his wife, "What hospital did they take him too?"

As his eyes searched for his trousers on the floor, his wife answered: "Don't you understand? He's dead, José. Killed. And now Pepito tells me the police are looking for him."

Dead, José thought, an icy glaze descending over his coal-black eyes. Driving dangerously, no doubt. Like the

203

little fool he was. Lost control. Just another dumb beaner the gringos like to make fun of...

Then he remembered the laptop.

Had the police found it?

If they had, questions might be asked.

People investigated.

Which might lead to him.

But one thing he knew for certain: the cartel did not like mistakes like this.

"Why are the police looking for him?"

"I'm still not sure, José... When Pepito called, he acted crazy with fear. Said Raul and some others forced him into robbing a gun store...that he didn't want to go along. That they were trying to make a man out of him and–"

"But the cops–*tell me!* What led them to Pepito!"

"He–he told me something about the police finding a stolen pistol in the wreckage of Raul's car. Taken from a gun store burglary in Houston a couple of weeks ago. Somehow they connected it to several other stolen guns which eventually led to Pepito and a bunch of their friends..."

Yanking his trousers on one leg at a time, José continued dressing as his girlfriend got out of bed and padded naked into the bathroom.

Dios mío!

She had an ass that wouldn't quit!

But now this!

"Where did the accident happen?"

After giving him the location, José Ortega reached for his boots, slipping them on.

"I'm going out there to look," he told her.

There was a pause, then she quietly said, "When I called you seemed out of breath..."

José had his game down. "You would too *muchacha* after running a mile around the high school track with three of your best runners! That's because I'm still at school getting them in shape for next month's track meet!" He glanced at his girlfriend as she emerged from the bathroom, an amused smile on her Latina face. "Let me tell you," he went on, his eyes dropping to her hairless vulva as he kneaded his sore crotch, "it's been a really hard day for me. Really, really...*hard*." A twisted smile came over his girlfriend's face as he winked at her; doubly funny since it mattered not to him that his nephew was dead, only that he had obviously failed to deliver the laptop as directed.

Then again, perhaps it was still out there, thrown from the wreckage and lying in the scrub. If so, he had to find it or else he would be blamed for losing it—not his idiot nephew. And one did not want MS-13 pointing the finger at you.

"What's more," he added, with a note of pride, false though it was, "I beat them all. That's why I was so out of breath."

Silence.

He hated his wife whenever she pulled that shit. Because it always implied that he was a liar (which he was) but that was beside the point; what irked him was that she dared imply it in the first place. But one day, when he grew really tired of her...

"I'll be home late," he abruptly snapped, cutting her silence off and hanging up.

On the way out of his girlfriend's apartment five minutes later, his head jerked around at the sight of a mirror, something his obsessive vanity could seldom ignore. Whipping out a comb, he neatly shaped his sex-mussed hair, stroking it until it glistened black and shiny like a gun barrel. *¡Qué demonio guapo!* he thought. No wonder you worshipped your handsome uncle so much, my dearly departed nephew. But ahhhh...how you will miss me so, burning down there in the fires of Hell!

Hair in place, he raced off into the night, hard at the wheel of his Chevrolet Camaro ZL1, headed for the location where his nephew had crashed and died.

Poor little fool.

But maybe the laptop was still lying out there.

And maybe other things too, José Manuel Ortega thought; things his suspicious eyes might find...

———————

"You're late, Andy. Where were you?" Peter Hupp asked, as his teenaged son slipped quietly into his dining room chair.

Playing it cool, Andy reached calmly for the meatloaf. "No where in particular, dad," he murmured, forking two thick slices onto his plate. "Just had to drop off a classmate." Reaching next for the bowl of peas, he added a large heaping, followed by one of his mother's dinner rolls. Okay, so they were store-bought. Even so, his mom was a whiz in the kitchen, but with her busy career she had to cheat here and there. Still, her meals were never something to complain about.

"Who? Your buddy TJ?"

"Nope," Andy replied, digging into his meal. "Just someone else."

His mother looked up from her plate. "Oh?"

Being the rebellious one in the family, Andy was often the focus of dinner table conversation.

"Just a girl."

"Was it Lyla?" his mother delicately inquired. "You know, the one I overheard TJ mention the last time he was over? The one he said you were too shy to ask out?"

"Nope," Andy replied, taking another hefty bite of meatloaf. He didn't like talking about girls to his family, especially with his nosy sister looking on. Not since that evening last year when she'd blurted out over her dinner-time bowl of strawberry ice cream: "I bet Andy got naked with that girl he took out on a date last night!" to the shocked expressions of his father and mother, as well as to his own everlasting certainty that his evil little sister must surely be psychic—since that was exactly what he had done.

Peter Hupp glanced over at his wife. "Wonder what the big

secret is?"

"No secret, dad," Andy said, sighing. "Just a girl, okay? She needed a ride home and I gave her one."

Yeah, he thought, after she and I almost got our brains blown out by an illegal alien who also happens to be involved in a crime ring with my gym coach. Not to mention I left him dead by the side of the road like a sack of shit then split before the cops showed up.

"Did you get naked with her?" his sister Amanda coyly asked, dawdling innocently with her peas. But she knew full-well she had fired a nuclear-tipped ballistic missile straight for her brother's side of the table.

"Amanda!" her mother admonished, reaching across the table and slapping her arm. "That will be enough!"

But all it did was make Amanda smile and lower her devious eyes, triumphant. On the other hand, Andy noticed his mother now regarding him speculatively, as only mothers can. Conversely, she knew how females regarded him, which worried her at times. As a full-grown man it might bring considerable trouble from too many unscrupulous girls vying for his favors—trouble from jealous boyfriends and even irate husbands. As it stood, she reasoned, too much in the way of good looks, just like too much in the way of money, gave problems all their own.

From across the table, Andy directed an eye toward his sister: "Don't you have a terrorist bomb to make or a voodoo doll to stick pins in? Besides, it just so happens it was TJ's girlfriend."

Uh-oh.

Maybe he shouldn't have said that.

But upon hearing it, his mother's scrutiny intensified, even as she examined him with concerned eyes. For she loved TJ Sully like a second son, and was so very glad he was Andy's best friend. Yet when it came to girls, her son coursed through the sexual waters of Titanis High like a shark, even when his motives were outwardly innocent. Knowing that, she certainly didn't want anything to spoil her son's friendship; for despite his good looks and winning smile, his quirky personality garnered few friends. And when it came to Andy and TJ, she knew, the only thing that could wreck their friendship would be a girl...

"Was TJ with you?" she calmly asked, averting her eye as she took a sip of water.

"Mom, it was innocent."

Lie #2,934,378, he thought.

Oh, boy. They're adding up.

Because it wasn't innocent, and he knew it.

Something had happened—some look in Jinky's eyes had told him so. That, and maybe the way she'd clung so tightly to him as they lay there beside the road, bullets tearing over their heads.

"I haven't said otherwise, dear."

For a while the Hupp family went on eating in silence, until Amanda murmured to no one in particular, "I don't want to grow up."

That brought three pairs of eyes in her direction, as well as a sober comment from her father: "We all grow up, Amanda. None of us have a choice. And with it comes responsibility."

"Responsibility?" she echoed.

Peter Hupp waved a hand around. "This."

"You mean, like having to eat icky meatloaf?"

"No, I mean work. Hard work. Work and more work. Rushing to and fro every day. Getting up out of bed every morning whether you like it or not. Rain or shine. With one driving motive—to make money and more money so you can pay your bills. Which never stop, by the way. Followed by more work. And more. With only one goal: so you can live away from all that's bad in this world. Crime, poverty, crowded cities...even...even bad memories." For a moment his eyes turned distant, as if, Andy thought, he were gazing back into time.

Then Andy noticed his mother staring at his father.

"What bad memories, Peter?"

Peter Hupp paused and came back into focus. "What was that?"

"You mentioned something about bad memories."

"Did I? Must've been thinking aloud again. You know me. Mind always wandering." He resumed eating, his bespectacled eyes vague and adrift, the thinnest trace of concern furrowing his brow. "Nothing meant by it...nothing at all." He let go a sigh. "Just a financial problem I've been struggling with." He glanced obliquely at his son, just for an instant, his mud-green eyes wide with scrutiny, before quickly flicking them away again, "But I may have found a solution..."

"I hope so," Cynthia Hupp answered, albeit doubtfully, for Andy could see she was unconvinced, though he couldn't say what any of this was all about. Then again, he recalled a night several weeks ago when he'd overheard an ugly bedroom argument between them, something to do with dad's "cash-strapped business", "competition from cheap Mexican labor", and "loss of clients". All kind of vague, he thought, like so much else adults rambled on about. But by the look in his mother's eyes a moment ago, she too had been remembering that same conversation.

Finally, Cynthia Hupp turned toward her son. "On the way home today several emergency vehicles went racing past out near Kilbane Road. Every time I see something like that I worry sick about you, Andy."

"Don't worry, mom. I intend to stick around for awhile."

Yeah, he thought, if I'm not killed in a drive-by shooting first...

Cynthia Hupp smiled at her son, and went on eating.

Andy's my rock, she thought.

Without him...

"Must've been that wreck I caught on the news driving home from the office," Peter Hupp said. "Apparently, some car thief tore up a Mustang out that way. Probably hot-rodding with another teenage hoodlum. Anyway, cops found a stolen handgun lying near the burnt-out wreckage they claim was stolen from a Houston gun shop a while back."

Staring down at his plate, Andy casually asked: "Any witnesses, dad?"

"Witnesses?"

"Just wondering if anyone saw it happen."

"The news report didn't say. Why?"

"No reason."

Lie #2,934,379.

Because he had every reason for wanting to know. Especially if a beat-up Ford pickup and a spanking new Mercedes-Benz van had been seen racing away from the scene.

"Oh, by the way, Andy..."

Andy glanced up.

"Got a call from Principal Meevers just after I left the office."

Andy's fork paused midway to his mouth.

"Andy's in trouble, Andy's in trouble," his evil little sister chimed, her eyes twinkling with expectation.

"Hush," her mother said.

"Nothing like that. On the contrary, he told me that your teacher Ms Pickering made it a personal point today to tell him you were a star student in her Social Studies class. Meevers said he makes it a policy to inform parents whenever he gets a good report like that. "

"Why, that's wonderful, Andy," his mother complimented, beaming.

"Oh, yes. He also mentioned that you were selected by Ms Pickering to join her prestigious Youth For Social Justice Club. Meevers says it's a great honor." His father regarded him from behind two spectacle-covered, swamp-green eyes— a shade far less attractive than Andy's own emerald ones. "Well, I for one am glad to see you're finally growing up and taking an interest in the real world instead of just running around playing big-shot movie director. You see, it's very important to develop a social conscience, Andy. You'll find that out once you finish college and start a real job." He gazed off for a moment. "Like I was forced to..."

"But why, dad?"

"What do you mean *why?*"

There's that annoying habit of my son again, Peter Hupp thought. Always questioning what others take for granted. Why couldn't he just shut the hell up and do what he's fucking told like the rest of us peons?

"Didn't mean to sound like an asshole, dad, but why is it necessary for me to care about people who are nothing but a burden on society? You know, just asking as a hypothetical question."

Peter Hupp slowly set down his fork, adjusted one side of his eyeglasses with his left hand, and looked gravely at his son. "Because you won't make it far in this shitty world without caring, that's why." His dad rarely cussed, but when he did it was worth noting, Andy thought.

After a moment, Andy slowly nodded, knowing it was wiser to just leave it at that. He went on eating, staring at nothing, his mind cruising out at the edge of the universe. Yet he couldn't help but wonder why his dad's remarks had reminded him so much of Ms Pickering, and in the eeriest sort of way. Then he suddenly recalled Rodney Crutchley's words: *"About things not feeling right around this school. And not just here. It's all over the place. On those posters lining the hall, for instance. And every Feel The Hug meeting. Everywhere. Like something dark and unstoppable. Closing in on us."*

Dark and unstoppable.

Closing in...

Yes, he too had felt it, and for a long time now. Even here, at the dinner table. And maybe as far back as the ninth grade. Like in that movie, *Invasion of the Body Snatchers;* a perfect metaphor for what he sensed all around him. There, and yet to most, still shadowy and unnamed. But whatever it was, this feeling in the air, this palpable miasma, it was growing like the alien pods down in the basement, ripening and almost ready to burst...

"Oh, one other thing", his dad went on, "Meevers said to drop by his office tomorrow afternoon on your way to lunch..."

Andy froze—just as his mother slowly moved her eyes toward him and his sister's face gradually evolved into a maliciously delightful grin, gleefully anticipating disaster.

Had Meevers called his dad to report Andy's insubordination? Walking out of his office without being dismissed?

Andy steeled himself for a Romulan broadside.

"Something about picking up your smartphone, he said. Told me you'd understand."

Slowly, Andy started breathing again, even as his mother's eyes dropped back to her dinner plate and his sister's smile faded into gray disappointment.

Hooray.

One Buck For A Suck Hupp slips the hangman's noose...

Again.

Five minutes after Andy Hupp sat down to dinner with his family, José Manuel Ortega's Chevrolet Camaro ZL1 came to a gravel-grinding halt beside a charred spot on the lonely, night-darkened road. Killing the 650hp engine, he sat there in silence for a long time, staring out at the charred rocks, scorched earth, and scattered bits of metal, glass, and melted plastic. The car itself had been hauled away, no doubt to some police impound, along with the grisly, charred remains of his nephew—to the county morgue.

But Ortega shed no tears.

He had seen violent death too often, on the mean streets of San Antonio—sometimes caused by others, sometimes inflicted by himself. Long ago, he'd seen his *cholos* cut down in drive-by shootings, their faces punched out like cancelled subway tickets by bullets, then scattered like chunks of dog vomit. No, there was nothing here to shock a *vato* like him...

And then there was Raul.

The punk had wanted to be a gangbanger and now had paid the price. Well, my little fuck. Life is hard, then you die. And that was the only eulogy the thirty-seven year old high school gym teacher felt like giving, even for his own kin.

Finally, he opened the door and got out of the car.

Beneath him, the heels of his eight hundred dollar vaquero boots, hand-stitched with a Central American sun god design, crunched in the hard gravel. He never wore them on the job, never let his mostly gringo students see his personal, off-the-job side, the side that refuted everything they were—in so many ways they could not even guess...

Shoving his hands into the back of his jeans, Ortega walked over and examined the charred spot more closely. The little shit must've really torn the fuck out of the Mustang, he thought, a tight grimace twitching across his savage lips as he imagined the owner's face—most likely a gringo—the instant he showed up at the impound yard to reclaim the car the police had "recovered".

As he paced the glass-strewn stretch of scorched earth, Ortega pulled a small flashlight from his shirt pocket and flicked it on, playing the beam over the ground. As he did, he tried to recreate the cause of the wreck in his mind, running through the possibilities. But none of it made sense. Why a wreck? Why here? Why on this lonely stretch of road going in the opposite direction than he should've been?

Turning on his boot heel, he sent the flashlight beam out across the asphalt road. There. Skidmarks. Curious, he walked out onto the road and examined them with poisonous black eyes. It looked like Raul had been driving at high speed only to suddenly hit the brakes, skidding along the pavement as his rubber tires scorched an inverted 'J' across the asphalt.

As if—

As if he had been trying to make a high-speed U-turn to go

back the other way.

But why?

Ortega looked up, thinking.

Then it became clear.

Raul had not been alone at the time of his crash.

Another car had been out here too.

And something...had happened.

Perhaps Raul had come across a rival gang. Maybe one that had recognized him from a previous encounter. Certainly possible, considering how many gangs were moving into the area as America swelled with millions of illegal aliens–selling drugs, burglarizing homes, committing a rape here, a murder there, the usual shit. Even so, they were no threat to MS-13's overall grip on the Southwest, especially here in Texas. When such upstart gangs got in the way they either joined Mara Salvatrucha–or died. Sometimes by gun, but very often by machete, after being kidnapped and taken to a remote spot.

But no...

It couldn't have been a rival gang.

It just didn't feel like it.

Then...*what?*

Playing the flashlight beam around, his hope of finding the laptop rapidly faded. Either it had been destroyed in the crash, or the police had found it.

Or someone else...

It was then that José Manuel Ortega noticed a green plastic bottle lying on the opposite side of the road. Curious, he crossed over, the heels of his vaquero boots clicking on the hard pavement, and played the flashlight over it. Then, crouching, he slowly rolled it back and forth. Still half-full, he observed. How long had it lain here–months? Weeks? Days? His eyes narrowed; there was one way to tell. Clasping the bottle, he shook it vigorously, and had his answer.

Fizz.

The soda had not gone flat, but was still strongly carbonated, telling him it had been only recently discarded. Very, very recently. Perhaps even today.

Whoever the soda had belonged too, he reasoned, it had either been deliberately or accidentally dropped on the shoulder of the road, perhaps as someone exited a vehicle. Someone who might have had something to do with his nephew's death.

And taken the laptop...

Taking the half-full bottle of soda with him, he walked back to his car. Seated inside again, he examined the bottle's label in the pale light of a rising harvest moon: SNARK!

A thin sneer worked itself onto his brown face; a face made superficially handsome by a strong infusion of Spanish conquistador blood, and yet made all the more cruel by its more dominant Tz'utujil Indian heritage.

Examining the brand of soda, Ortega thought: what a stupid, guttural, Anglo-Saxon word it bore. But then, what had that English teacher once said–? That it was a "portmanteau" created from "snide" and "remark". A made-up word, one that all the gringo kids used everywhere he went. But now the word had found renewed fame as a hipster soft drink, especially popular among white kids. Maybe it was the name, maybe it was the spicy cinnamon sting of its formula or the weird colors that changed and coalesced, turning from pink to lime green to turquoise-blue through some trick of gringo chemistry.

Whatever.

All José knew was that gringos were always complicating life, coming up with new ways to do things just for the hell of it. For instance, who would invent a machine to fly through the air over a hundred years ago while the rest of the world was content to stay earthbound? Who would blast themselves off to the moon just so they could stick their fucking racist flag into the dust?

Only loco gringos, that's who.

Fucking up the world.

Thinking their magic gave them the right to rule.

He held up the bottle of *SNARK!*, thinking.

Where was the nearest store that sold this gringo shit?

Find it, he told himself, and make the clerk reveal who had come in to buy it. Then he would discover who had been here the instant Raul was killed—and taken the laptop.

With that in mind, José Manuel Ortega fired up the Camaro's powerful engine, knowing just the people to do it. Old friends, he thought, one side of his mouth slowly curling into a cruel mestizo grin, even as he reached for his smartphone and tapped out a number.

Far away, a phone began to ring in San Antonio...

CHAPTER 17

Friday morning, October 31st—and still subdued from his near-death experience earlier in the week, Andy Hupp exited Mr. Furtmeyer's second period calculus class and headed for the Computer Science department, located next to the library. Walking along, his eyes downcast in thought, he relived last Monday's incident out on Kilbane Road: the attempted murder of he, Jinky, and Rodney by a gun-crazed gangbanger. Were it not for their quick reaction in diving for cover, combined with the sloppy shooting of Coach Ortega's nephew, all three of them would be dead.

But what now?

Andy didn't know, but he knew one thing for sure: Jim Kirk had never faced a problem like this, even when he'd fought the Gorn in hand-to-hand combat out on Cestus III. Nor had most seventeen year old boys. So who could he turn to? Not his family; their lives were already in danger, although he dare not tell them. *The police?* An option, maybe, but Andy doubted it was a good one. As every negro rapper in America made all too clear, snitches got stitches—often fatal ones.

One question still nagged at him, however: what if Rodney Crutchley's laptop hadn't been stolen for its objective street value—*but for what was on it?* Because there was no doubt in his mind that what Rodney had dug up about Brett Hinkle was explosive: Naked pictures. Gay suck offs. Butt-slamming fag-fuckings. And finally, a tantalizing photo taken down in Mazatenango, Guatemala, in what appeared to be an older

Brett Hinkle, seen in the company of two swarthy Guatemalan men, his demeanor strangely docile. How was that even possible? Andy wondered. Drugged? Very likely. But what kind of circumstances had led someone to kidnap him to begin with and then take him so far from home?

Dangerous questions to even ask, he knew.

And now he was faced with a hard decision.

Because with TJ, Jinky, and Rodney now on board, the four of them had to decide whether Hupp Film Productions should proceed with the Sawyer-Hinkle story.

And do it...

No matter where it led.

When the bell rang and the great cattle herds of Titanis High emptied once more into the hallways, hundreds steered toward the parking lot and off-campus fast-food joints while hundreds more made for the cafeteria–Andy Hupp among them.

As he was pushed and shoved along, jostled and bumped amid that great youthful tide, he occasionally felt the smooth caress of a feminine shoulder brushing past, trailed by a fleeting scent of perfume, before it too vanished into the crowd.

Kinda like life, Andy suddenly realized.

Fleeting.

Ephemeral.

Because in some fundamental way, he thought, we really only get a transitory glimpse of each other over the years, maybe a brief touch here, a passing smile there, and before we know it we're married–our children born, grown, and gone–almost in the blink of an eye. Then onward we go, churning toward oblivion. All these kids, Andy Hupp thought, most he'd never get to know. Girls he'd never get to kiss. And once this final year of high school was over, they'd all be scattered to the four winds, most never to be seen again.

Much like Tina Sawyer and Brett Hinkle...

Once, they too had walked these very halls.

With dreams, aspirations, and thoughts of the future.

Now, they were gone.

Gone–

And all but forgotten.

Some thought him strange, Andy realized, in a moment of self-reflection. Yet, ever since childhood, he'd dwelt on the impermanence of life. For joyous as his early years had been, he'd known that one day it would all end–childhood friendships that had once seemed immortal would irretrievably fade away. Cherished pets he'd held so dear were left to cry over as tenderly he lay them in their graves. And fond farewells to cherished homes and autumn-leaved neighborhoods told him all was ephemeral, and would ultimately pass away.

For Andy Hupp, even at such a young age, forever took note of life's passings, even while other children never seemed aware of them. And through it all he began to create a small little wood deep in his heart, one filled with a melancholy mist, very private and sweet and lovely, into which he would retreat at times, beyond the reach of others, lost in a world of his own.

For while other kids seemed to bask in what they perceived as the eternal sunshine of youth, unaware of the future, or even caring, some dark cloud had always hovered on the horizon for him, even then, at so young an age. And thus he found himself drawn to anything that seemed to hold at least a semblance of permanence, taking an early–and to his parents–surprisingly precocious interest in art and sculpture, eager to visit the museums of Austin so that his little six year old eyes could behold the sculpted objects and painted visions of men who had lived centuries before. And though they were gone to dust, their statues and paintings lived on, he realized, leaving his young and inquisitive mind in awe.

For Andy, it was a startling revelation.

Yes, the ancient statues and paintings told him: life did not have to be lived without rhyme or reason, only for the moment, like the beasts in the field, or the wayward winds, here today and gone tomorrow, with no trace left to grasp. For here were things that could live on, at least in one sense, if one but had the will.

Later, at the age of ten, his fascination with museums sated, he discovered old movies–and a whole new world opened before his young eyes as he watched films made decades before he was born, vibrant with faces and voices still crisp and alive, although he was assured everyone who laughed and sang and danced before his eyes were long since dead.

Yet, here they were: 'Rhett Butler' from *Gone With The Wind*, 'Charles Foster Kane' from *Citizen Kane*, 'Joe Gillis' from *Sunset Boulevard*, all living on, as were so many, many others, both real and imagined. For here, he realized, was life–life captured and bottled; all the sunny, long ago days, all the once-upon-a-time rains, all the faraway mountains, trackless deserts, and mysterious jungles, as well as all the imagined worlds of unexplored space. In the end, all the panoramic sweep of Man's entire existence on Earth–wherever it had led him down through the centuries. For when the true magnitude of this technological miracle sank in, little Andy knew he had found his quest in life...

"Whoa, cowboy," a familiar voice called out from the rushing crowd, bringing Andy to an abrupt halt as he turned and looked into the tanned and handsome face of Principal Budd Meevers.

"Oh, hey Mr. Meevers. Guess my mind was elsewhere."

"Daydreaming again, Andy?"

"Uhh, yeah. Guess so."

"Well, I've a quick errand to run," he said, an attractive smile flashing forth. "In the meantime, go have a seat in my office and I'll be right back. I've instructed Mrs. Rath to let you in."

"Uhh, sir?"

"Your smartphone, Andy. Remember?"

Now he did.

"Sure, Mr. Meevers. I'll head right over."

"Good deal."

And the tall figure whirled away into the crowd.

At least the warden didn't seem upset with him any longer, which was a good sign. And with that, Andy put lunch on hold and veered right down Corridor A, heading straight for the principal's office.

When he walked through into the reception area a minute later, Mrs. Rath, a pleasantly attractive woman in her fifties, greeted him with a cheerful smile. She knew him by sight, good-looking teen that he was. Especially in today's school culture, where many boys went out of their way to look "stylishly" unkempt and grubby, or, in the case of the girls, like street hookers. Andy Hupp, on the other hand, was an iconoclast. With his expensive designer jeans, two hundred dollar gray leather jacket, and clean good-looks, he turned female heads everywhere he went, regardless of age.

"You always look so nice," Mrs. Rath complimented, secretly wishing she was thirty years younger. "I swear you could be a model."

"Psst!" Andy whispered, raising a finger to his lips as he slid his eyes left and right. "Don't tell anyone, but that's exactly what I do for an after-school job."

Mrs. Rath tittered. "You're such a cut-up, Andy," she said, even as she led him toward Principal Meevers' office door. "Just have a seat inside until he returns. It shouldn't be long."

As Andy stepped past the threshold, Mrs. Rath quietly pulled the door closed.

Alone.

In the principal's office.

Every teen's worst nightmare.

Oh, well.

Chill-out time, he thought.

And with that, he flopped down onto a leather sofa. Sitting there, listless, his green eyes began to wander. Nice wood paneling, he observed. Real teak, by the looks of it. Your taxpayer dollars at work.

His survey moved slowly around the wall, clockwise, past a painting depicting a yacht crashing upward into the crest of a wave, ocean spray dashed against the wind as the prow of the vessel jutted boldly against storm-gray skies.

Dramatic, Andy thought.

I like it.

Moving onward, his eyes drifted next to a cluster of plaques, the kind with brass plates attached to squares and rectangles of dark walnut. Various awards, Andy assumed; Kiwanis Club, Titanisville City Hall, one or two others. Boring. Moving further around, onto the adjacent wall, was a collection of framed certificates; it was clear that Budd Meevers wanted to make visitors aware of his accomplishments. One frame displayed his college diploma, with all its fancy scroll work, signatures, and gold metallic sticker–just to make it look official–all in accordance with a well-planned, orderly, and successful life.

University of Michigan, Andy read.

Interesting.

His dad had been born in Lansing, hadn't he?

Even graduated from the same university as Meevers.

Small world...

His eyes next arrived at some more wall art, then a modernistic clock, the kind without numbers, so that it forced your mind to engage in complex fourth dimensional physics just to figure out what the fuck time it was.

Potted plants occupied the corners, he noted.

Rubber plant here.

Palm tree there.

They too looked good juxtaposed against the teak wood.

Where the hell was Meevers?

If he doesn't come soon they'll find me staring up at the ceiling babbling home décor tips straight out of *Better Homes & Gardens*.

Andy shrugged.

Sighed.

Twiddled his thumbs.

Looked around some more.

Hell of a big desk, he thought.

Pretending he was circling above in a miniature helicopter, he imagined himself hovering over the vast rectangular expanse, as if on a recon mission in some war-torn country. A double-decker paper tray became an enemy bunker, a crystal pen holder an anti-aircraft gun, that jar of candy mints an ammo dump.

Oh shit, he thought.

He'd already lost five minutes of lunch time.

He got to his feet, restless.

Nice carpet, though. You could feel the richness beneath, nice and cushiony.

Oh shut the hell up about the fucking carpet.

And quit cussing so much.

Fuck!

He glanced at the Twilight Zone clock again.

Another minute gone.

Jink and TJ and Rodney waiting for him.

He began to pace.

They do that in movies a lot, he remembered.

Shows tension.

Uncertainty.

Classic cinematic display of character angst.

Get hold of yourself, he thought.

Life isn't a movie.

And this isn't a movie studio where you have a camera on you as you pace back and forth.

No, but I've been shot at, he thought.

With real bullets.

So maybe life is more like a movie than any of us want to believe.

After all, life imitates art, he remembered.

He shoved his hands into the back of his pockets.

Paced.

Stopped.

Paced some more.

Stopped again.

This time looking curiously at Meevers' desk.

In so doing, he noticed the bottom side drawer stood partly ajar, just by an inch or so. Something lavenderish was sticking out, as if it had been hastily wadded up and shoved inside, preventing the drawer from closing all the way.

But against the dark teak, walnut, and mahogany background of Meevers' otherwise masculine décor, the lavender blotch contrasted jarringly. Standing there, Andy wondered what he was looking at. And as so often happened, curiosity got the better of him. Sidling closer, his eyes examined the lavender oddity, even as his eyes darted toward Meevers' office door once or twice, simultaneously listening for any approaching footstep.

So far so good.

Still wondering what he was looking at, Andy circled slowly around and stopped. That can't be what I think it is, he thought. Glancing one last time at the door, he lowered his hand and slowly pulled open the drawer.

Then, reaching down, he tugged out a pair of—

Lavender panties.

Whoa.

Major shock value here.

Spreading open the wadded material, the scent of a popular teenage perfume wafted upward. That, and a contrasting lime green trim, with the words: 'No Unauthorized Entry' imprinted over the crotch.

Oh, boy.

The first thought that came into Andy Hupp's mind was: what the hell are *these* doing in Principal Meevers drawer? Was it possible his wife had left them? Perhaps dropped them out of a shopping bag on a brief visit to her husband's office?

Not likely, Andy thought, since this was not the kind of underwear the average middle-aged wife of a school principal would likely wear. No, this was something altogether different...

Hastily, he wadded up and stuffed the panties back into the drawer, exactly as he had found them. Then, returning to the leather sofa, he quickly grabbed a sporting magazine and flipped it open, as if he had been sitting there all along, reading.

But his mind was ablaze over his discovery.

What were some teenage girl's panties doing in Meevers' drawer? Had he found them by accident, just lying around? "Oh, look. Some poor girl dropped her panties in my office. Better keep them here in my official Lost & Found Panties Drawer I created just for that purpose!"

Then Andy took notice of another door, one that on previous visits to the principal's office he had always been curious about. It stood in the far corner, flanked by two potted plants, which partly obscured its presence. Judging by its location, Andy figured it must lead out into a side corridor, which in turn led to Corridor B. Anyone entering or exiting that door could do so without ever being seen passing through the main reception area.

Such as a high school girl.

One missing her lavender panties...

Andy swallowed.

What did he have here?

But no sooner had an alarming implication entered his mind than the main door to Meevers' office burst open, as if a wind had blown it wide, and in stepped tall, handsome, smile-a-minute Budd Meevers.

Andy, demonstrating admirable aplomb, calmly looked up from his magazine. Meevers, in turn, swept his eyes quickly around the office, as if to assure himself that everything was as he'd left it, then brought his glance back to the teenaged boy.

"Didn't mean to keep you waiting, Andy. Unfortunately, I had to deal with an issue that took a bit longer than I had expected."

"No problem, Mr. Meevers. I've just been sitting here reading this cool article about Tyrone Lucretius Washington's football career. Did you know his original dream was to be the inventor of the world's first starship drive?"

Meevers' eyebrow went up, in an act of feigned interest. "Really? A starship drive? Why no, I hadn't known that. I guess what science lost the world of football gained."

"Well, football ended up losing too."

"How so?"

"Because he was just sentenced to twenty-five years in state prison for seven counts of child rape."

Meevers slowly nodded. He often wondered if Andy Hupp was yanking his chain, saying things just to get a rise out of people. The kid was far from politically correct, which one day might cause him a world of hurt.

"Shame," Meevers murmured, "a great loss to the black community."

Andy folded the magazine shut and set it aside as Meevers took his seat.

"Here. Let me get your phone so you can run off to lunch," the principal said, unlocking his top center drawer with a key. As he did, Andy noticed his eyes suddenly flick down and to the left, toward the side drawer where the wad of lavender panties had been carelessly stuffed. A momentary flash of concern appeared in Meevers' eyes, but so subtle no one unaware of what the drawer contained would have noticed.

Meevers' eyes then flicked upward to Andy, searching the teen's face for any hint that he too might have seen them. But the boy's face was respectfully attentive, and no more. Deciding he had not, Meevers deftly fingered the panties down into the drawer then quietly slid it shut, all the while as his other hand rooted into his top drawer and brought out Andy's smartphone.

"By the way," Meevers asked, as he brought out Andy's smartphone and laid it atop his desk, "have you and TJ come up with a new movie project yet?"

"We're working on one," Andy replied, rising from the sofa and approaching Meevers' desk.

"Oh? What about?"

"Another crime movie. This time based on a true story."

"Interesting. When it's completed, I hope you'll give the school a free showing."

"We will, if you give us permission to shoot some scenes on campus."

"You drive a hard bargain, Andy."

"No guns this time. Promise."

Meevers chuckled. "Then you've got a deal."

"In writing."

Meevers' smile faded. "I see... You're taking no chances, are you?"

"No different than Hollywood, sir."

Meevers studied Andy with a shrewd eye. "Yes, yes indeed. Nothing's done there without a written contract." He regarded Andy with a touch of respect. "Okay, you'll have it in writing. I'll have my secretary draw up the permission form and then add my signature to it. Deal?"

"Deal."

Meevers pushed back in his chair, regarding the teen standing in front of him, casually, yet almost with the bearing of a soldier.

"You aren't like most kids, you know, because sometimes I think I'm running a prison camp here rather than a school. But whenever I come across a student like you..." He shrugged, offering forth Andy's cell phone. "Anyway, here you go."

Stepping forward, Andy took it.

"And please accept my apologies the last time we met in this office, Andy. Sometimes an ugly authoritarian side arises in me and I become a bit," he puffed out a sigh, "overbearing."

"No hard feelings, Mr. Meevers."

"Good, good. Glad to hear that. Because like you, I'm not into all this new-fangled lovey-dovey stuff going on in our schools today. Still, I think it's good that you give Ms Pickering's Youth For Social Justice Club a fair chance. They really do try to do good by this school and this community, and they need the kind of youth we have too little of: intelligent, idealistic, filled with ideas. Like you, Andy." He flicked a glance toward the side drawer again, as if to confirm he had fully hidden the panties. So quickly, Andy had almost missed the eye movement.

Almost.

"As always, youth is our future. But only a handful come into this world like you, Andy, ready to meet the challenge head on. So make the most of your time, abilities and talents. Use them for the betterment of mankind."

"Always on my mind, Mr. Meevers. And don't worry. I'll be at Ms Pickering's meeting right after school—like I promised."

"Good, good. If nothing else, take it as a learning experience. Because things that refuse to learn and...evolve...often die, Andy." He nodded toward one particular painting on the wall that the teen had been curious about, that of a prehistoric landscape populated with several enormous, frightening birds with huge, parrot-like beaks. "Like Titanis there, our school's namesake and mascot," he said. "Also the name behind our school's football team—The Titanis Terror Birds—a frightening creature that once prowled parts of our state during the Pleistocene era, some five million years ago, killing everything in its path. Were it alive today, it could easily kill any land animal alive, lion, tiger, elephant...," his gray eyes hardened on the youth, "even you." Then, walking up to the painting and studying it for a moment, he softly added: "And yet, it was only a bird. Now it's gone. Like you, it was strong, fast, and clever, and yet it attempted to defy the world that it lived in, and came to an abrupt and tragic end. That's because it refused to evolve, Andy–until it was too late."

Turning, Budd Meevers gazed back at the handsome youth, his eyes cool and reflective, and for an instant the teen wondered if his words had been a warning of things to come, or, perhaps, a strange confession of some fate that had already come to pass...

Andy didn't know.

All he knew was that, for the first time, he wondered if he had reason to fear Principal Meevers. Then, certain the feeling must be due to nothing more than an overactive imagination, he bade farewell to the man standing next to the prehistoric killer bird and headed for the door.

But just as he pulled it open, Principal Meevers called out: "Oh, by the way, Andy..."

Andy turned.

"There's something I almost forgot. That photo you took of Tony Scarletti's locker door? Somehow, it got accidentally erased. Down at the sheriff's office, they tell me. Beats me how it happened. Sheriff wasn't too clear. Some sort of cellphone glitch or something while one of their technicians was examining it. Anyway, please accept my apologies."

For a long moment, Andy studied Budd Meevers, recalling Jinky's earlier words about the inadvisability of turning over his cellphone.

Oh well, he thought.

What's done is done—hopefully Rodney will be exonerated at his upcoming court hearing.

Time would tell.

In the meantime...

"Not a prob, Mr. Meevers," Andy cheerfully replied, but for a telling moment his eye lingered on the man before him, his glance alert and considering. "Besides, you know what they say, sir."

"And what's that, Andy?"

"Shit happens."

"That's right, Andy," Budd Meevers softly affirmed, as he slowly settled down behind his massive desk. "Shit does indeed happen."

Then Andy Hupp turned and left.

CHAPTER 18

Five minutes after leaving Budd Meevers' office, Andy Hupp settled in at his usual cafeteria table, bearing a tray of food and a solemn look.

"Bout time," TJ quipped, finishing off the last of his lunch.

"Where were you?" Jinky inquired, a trace of anxiety in her voice that only Andy and their newest production member, Rodney Crutchley, could detect.

"In the principal's office," Andy replied, reaching for his sweet onion chicken Teriyaki sandwich and distractedly taking a bite, "again".

Across the table, Rodney sat with his big clumsy hands folded in front of him, unmoving, his dark eyes staring down at an indeterminate spot on the table. But Andy could tell the big youth's mind was still filled with their roadside brush with death and, perhaps, other things as well.

"Hey," Andy said, nodding toward the next table over, "who're our new neighbors?"

"Haven't you heard?" TJ replied, "Titanis High just got a new shipment of refugees courtesy of Dr. Rothman Adler and the Inclusivity Project. And that's some of them."

Andy briefly studied the newcomers. "Syrians?"

"Nope, those came last week. These are Afghans."

At the mention of their nationality, two of the swarthy-faced refugee 'students' slowly turned and looked their way, dark malice in their obsidian eyes. In that one glance, Andy saw the scorched hills of the Hindu Kush, back-dropped by the snow-capped Himalayan mountains rising twenty-five thousand feet; a forbidding land burnt brown in summer and bitterly frozen in winter. A land that had made of its people a suspicious, superstitious, and violent breed, long hateful of outsiders, murderous in their hearts toward any wayward stranger and foreign invader. But whatever circumstances had made them leave their war-torn land, Andy knew one thing for certain: America was no place for them.

And never would be.

So why were they here?

Looking away, he went back to his sandwich, thinking again about Rodney's words, about something taking over, something moving insidiously through the land, everywhere one looked.

Glancing once more at the Afghans, he saw the manifestation of that feeling, there in their dark, merciless faces. They had come from a ruthless land, with ruthless ways, and no amount of "Americanization" would ever change that fact.

Dr. Rothman Adler...

Syrians—and now Afghans.

And before them, Somalians and Haitians.

And *before* them, a never ending flow of Mexicans, as if a turd-choked sewer line had broken that nobody cared to fix— all overflowing into the cesspool of nearby Unity Gardens, there at the edge of town. But the sewage hadn't stayed there, Andy knew. For it was already seeping into surrounding neighborhoods, until now it was here, in this school, sitting at these very cafeteria tables...

For day by day more and more non-white refugees began to be seen, he realized, even though Titanisville was supposed to be a haven for high-paid white professionals and affluent entrepreneurs. Somewhere, perhaps on the Internet, he had once come across a cryptic phrase, the context long since lost:

Diversity Means Chasing Down The Last White

What did that mean, anyway? he wondered, even as he flicked a final glance at the table of Afghans. And what kind of people were behind it? One day, some inner voice told him, he must find out.

"Andy...?"

Andy looked up, sandwich poised in hand. "Uhh...yeah, Jink?"

"Looked like you spaced out for a moment."

"Just...thinking."

"Brainiacs usually are." She crunched down on a carrot stick, her eyes keen. "You get your smartphone back?"

Vaguely, he nodded, not looking over at her.

"Mind if I see the photo you took of Scarletti's locker?"

His green eyes moved, making contact with hers. Only for an instant. But in that instant she knew: the photo had been erased.

"I knew it. *I knew it!* It's connected, isn't it Andy? The photo and–*what happened...*"

"We don't know that it is, Jink. So let's not jump to conclusions."

"What's connected?" TJ piped up, suddenly looking from Jeena to Andy. Nearby, Rodney shifted uncomfortably in his seat, but remained silent, thoughtful.

"Hey," TJ repeated, looking around the table. "What gives? C'mon, everybody! What's the big secret?"

"You didn't tell him, Jink?" Andy said.

"No! You made me promise not to open my pretty pink mouth, remember?"

"He made you *what–!*"

Now TJ Sully was really getting hyper. "One of you better spill the beans!"

"Or what?" Andy teased. "You gonna beat it out of us?"

"I might!"

Jinky laughed, which had been precisely Andy's intent. It seemed to have worked, since her edginess eased, and TJ settled down, gazing questioningly toward his best friend.

"Well?"

Andy glanced at Jink and then Rodney, finally turning back to his friend. In a lowered voice, he said: "Here's the lowdown, TJ. A couple of days ago something bad happened out on Kilbane Road."

TJ slowly moved his eyes around the table, filling in the blanks as he did. And he wasn't liking what he was seeing. "You were out on Kilbane Road? All three of you?"

Andy could see his friend running the equations through his head, computing all the possible permutations: Jinky alone. Andy alone. Rodney alone. Jinky, Rodney & Andy together. Andy & Rodney together. Jinky and Rodney together. And, finally: *Andy & Jinky together...*

Finally, TJ's eye fell on Jeena Kirtland once more—lingered for a moment—then swung full around to Andy again. "You mean you and Jinky were out there? Together? Just the two of you?"

Jinky took hold of TJ's arm, trying to head off the direction his voice was taking. "Listen, TJ! Andy was just going out to the detention center to check up on Rodney. I saw him leaving and hitched a ride at the last second. Okay!"

But TJ's eyes remained on Andy.

"That's what happened, TJ. Jink wanted to go along and see what she could do for Rodney. When we found out he was released we caught up with him out on Kilbane Road and that's when—"

"Wait a sec!" TJ interrupted. "Now I remember! Kilbane Road was mentioned on the news a couple of nights ago! Something about a fatal car crash and—!"

Andy slowly nodded.

"Then—?"

"That's right," Jinky interjected. "We were out there when it happened."

"Do the cops know?" TJ asked, looking from her to Andy.

"That's all we can tell you right now," Andy said, his voice speaking in cautious tones. "You'll learn all the rest at tonight's meeting."

"But–"

"Give it a rest, TJ. You'll understand the reason for the secrecy tonight. Cross my heart."

"Since when have you had a heart?" TJ shot back.

Jinky snickered. "Good one, poncho!"

Andy, TJ, and Rodney all stopped and looked at her.

"What? You three got a problem? Just because I like to make up nicknames!"

That brought a much needed chuckle from Andy and TJ, both of whom had been on the verge of mentally squaring off over Jinky Kirtland being out on a lonely road with another boy. But for the moment, Andy inwardly sighed; that little time bomb had been defused.

"So what's this about a photo of Scarletti's locker vanishing?" TJ asked, trying to keep his voice low. "I mean, what's the big hullabaloo?"

"Big hullaba-*what?*"

"Name of an old TV show Andy once tricked me into watching on YouTube, along with two others called *Shindig* and *Hootenanny*. Still haven't paid him back for that."

But Andy hardly heard, however, his mind momentarily drifting away to the surrounding cafeteria, with all its churning hustle and bustle, as he listened to hundreds of voices speaking, laughing, and joking all at once. If nothing else, it served as good background cover, save for the suspicious Afghan newcomers seated at the next table over. From now on, his table would have to be cautious when speaking around them.

"Meevers found out I'd taken a photo of Scarletti's locker," Andy finally explained, coming back into focus. "The one Rodney supposedly marked up."

TJ flicked a glance toward the big kid. "Did you?"

"Tell him, Rod."

Rodney Crutchley shifted in his seat, uncomfortable with three pairs of eyes focused on him. It was a strange feeling to see that none were hostile, only curious and attentive. It had been a long time, however, since such beautiful female eyes had gazed upon him with anything other than wary disquietude.

"No," Rodney answered, "I didn't mark up Tony Scarletti's locker. Neither this time nor the first. But the printed letters closely matched my style. So someone had to have studied a sample of my writing." He lowered his eyes for a moment, then looked up. "I think a teacher did it."

"No shit?" TJ gasped.

"It's possible," Andy confirmed.

"Okay, then," TJ bounced back, "so where's the proof?"

"We'll have it once we get hold of the hallway video," Andy countered.

"But if some teacher wanted to frame Rodney," Jinky cautiously put forth, looking from boy to boy, "wouldn't he or she have made certain beforehand that no video would ever turn up?"

"Yeah," Andy slowly had to admit, remembering how something had clicked in his brain just as he was leaving Meevers' office. "Just like somebody made certain no smartphone photo of Scarletti's locker door would ever turn up...at least, not for long."

All four of them suddenly glanced at each other, as a moment of disquietude settled over the table.

"Okay, guys," TJ murmured, looking from face to face, "this shit's gettin' real." Now a glint of unease was evident in his eye too.

And then Andy remembered.

The lavender panties.

How did they fit?

And just as importantly...*on whom?*

At the risk of sounding like a pervert, he decided to mention what he had found.

"Okay, something else, guys," Andy cautiously began, "while sitting in Meevers office I came across an unusual and embarrassing discovery..."

The other three looked at him, waiting.

"Any females present be forewarned."

"Nothing to do with little ol' me!" Jinky chirped. "Cause I'm just sitting here with my three fellow dudes!"

TJ poked her with an elbow. "You just registered a nine point five on my cute-o-meter."

She twinkled an eye at him, then gestured at Andy: "Lead on, maestro."

Andy nodded, glancing down at his folded hands as he searched for the right words. Finding them, he took a deep breath and said: "Okay, here goes. Not twenty minutes ago I found a pair of girl's panties in Meevers' desk drawer and−"

Jinky's jaw dropped like the trap door of a gallows. Beside her, TJ broke out in a shit-why-couldn't-I-have-been-there grin. But it was Rodney's sudden flash of eyes that froze Andy's words in their track.

"What color were they?" he asked. Spoken in his slow, deep voice, the question came out sounding kind of kinky, causing Jinky and TJ to giggle.

"What color would you like them to be?" she teased in a low, sultry voice, batting her eyes at him.

Rodney looked over at her, his dark blue eyes guarded. But when he saw that there was no female malice behind the question, just girlish playfulness, a rare but uncertain smile worked itself onto his face. Then he looked away, shyly, because girls like Jeena Kirtland were just too pretty for his eyes to endure.

"Why?" Andy asked, addressing Rodney.

Rodney remained silent for a long moment, one big hand clasping the other, as if deciding whether or not he would answer the question. Then he inhaled a long, slow breath, like someone about to jump off a cliff.

"Because," he uneasily began, "two years ago, during my sophomore year, I was sent to Meevers' office. And when I sat down on the sofa..."

"You mean the big brown leather one?"

"That one."

"Why were you sent?" TJ interrupted, always interested in the gritty details.

Rodney hesitated, then opened his notebook and scribbled rapidly on a piece of paper and shoved it over to Andy.

The teen read:

For Staring At Girls

Oh, brother, Andy thought.

In some high schools, that would get you the electric chair.

Folding the paper, he slid it back to Rodney.

"Well?" TJ pressed, "Tell us your big bad crime."

Rodney glanced at Andy.

Andy shrugged. "Hey, we all do it, Rodney. So you might as well confess."

He needs to, Andy thought.

What's the word—cathartic?

"I got caught...staring at girls."

TJ grinned. "Way to go, dude! Andy and I are experts at it!"

Jinky, trying to alleviate Rodney's discomfort, chimed in, her voice soft and sweet, "Was I one of them?"

That brought a round of laughter, and even Rodney barely stifled a chuckle.

Success, Andy thought.

We'll thaw this kid out yet.

"Who sent you to Principal Meevers?" Andy asked.

Again, Rodney Crutchley hesitated, as if considering whether or not he should answer. Then, gradually, he raised his eyes to the handsome youth across the table: "Ms Pickering."

Almost imperceptibly Andy nodded, and for an instant he felt something cold and disturbing, creeping stealthily closer, as if toward some darker understanding.

But...*what?*

"Were you?" Jinky asked. "Actually staring?"

"I guess. But not to be rude or anything."

"Okay," Andy said. "Go on. You were in—"

"Mr. Meevers' office, sitting there while he lectured me about inappropriate staring. I was kind of nervous and slid my hand down between the cushions, you know, kinda fumbling about. That's when I touched a pair of..." He swallowed and looked askance. "You know..."

"Panties?" Jinky gently assisted, with a sparkle in her eye.

Oh god, Andy thought. *If you don't stop with the sexy routine you're gonna cause Rodney to blow a load.*

Rodney nodded, studying his hands. "Yes...those."

"So what color were they?" TJ prodded.

That brought a poke from Jinky. "Like you need to know."

"They were black—" Rodney began, then hesitated.

"Go on," Jinky cooed, as if she were a mother encouraging a six year old to unwrap a gift.

"Black," he continued, "and...lacy."

"Ooo la la," she purred, faking a French accent.

"Was Meevers aware you had found them?" Andy asked.

"Get a load of Perry Mason over there," TJ snorted, a big grin on his freckled face. "Giving poor Rodney the third degree like he's on the witness stand."

"No," Rodney answered, "I don't think so. You see, my left thigh concealed the space between the cushions and I only barely pulled them up. Just enough to see what they were. Made me think they had been taken off in a hurry and then stuffed between the cushions."

Taken off...

In a hurry?

Now the lavender panties, hastily stuffed in Meevers' desk drawer, suddenly began to make more sense. And before anyone else, Andy Hupp put the pieces together and grasped why Rodney had wanted to know the color of the panties he had found: to see if they were the same pair—only discovered in a different place.

Clearly, they weren't.

And that begged the question: just how long had these way-ward panties (and the girls to which they belonged) been turning up in Budd Meevers' office, stuffed between cushions and inside desk drawers? What's more, which Titanis High female students had 'misplaced' them there?

Breaking the silence, Jinky asked in a sensual voice: "And what color were the panties *you* found, Mr. Andy?"

The question caused Andy to reach for his pen, and for a moment he tapped distractedly at the table, sure sign he didn't care to talk about girly things around a girl, especially with other boys present.

"I don't know. Just some color," he murmured, sorry now he had mentioned them.

"Pink? Red? Polka dot?" Jinky probed. "See-through, maybe? Am I getting a teensy bit warm?"

Andy sighed. "Lavender or something, okay? With a lime-green waist band. Satisfied?"

"Now we're getting somewhere. Anything else?"

"They also had some kind of slogan. Stitched in lime green letters."

"Oh? Do tell."

"It was nothing, really. Just...some words."

"Which I'm sure you read, being the analytical person that we all know you are."

Andy sighed. "Okay, okay. So I read them."

"Naughty boy." Jinky's blue eyes glittered. "And?"

Andy mumbled something no one could make out.

"Say again?" she pressed, taking an eager sip of soda, thoroughly delighting in Andy's discomfort.

Exasperated, he repeated himself, more distinctly this time: "No Unauthorized Entry."

Jinky spit soda from her mouth. "*What?!*"

TJ's jaw dropped.

Rodney examined an indeterminate spot on the table, his mind absorbed in some private thought of his own.

"Oh. My. God." Jinky suddenly blurted, causing all the

boys to look at her. "I just remembered a girl who wore a pair exactly like that only last week. Two lockers down from me while we undressed for gym and—" She suddenly broke off and pretended to concentrate on sipping her soda.

"And what?" TJ prodded. "Who was she?"

Jinky lifted her eyes toward Andy, then quickly averted them again. "Never mind, TJ. Just some girl." She again stared down at her drink. "Besides, I wouldn't want to embarrass her by mentioning her name. You know how gossip travels around school."

Andy and TJ looked at each other, then shrugged.

The female mind, their glances seemed to say. The good Lord made 'em that way, and only He knows why.

"So they weren't the same..." Rodney mumbled, as if he were alone, analyzing an intriguing mathematical equation. "What's more, they were found two years apart..."

They all looked toward the brooding, mysterious teen with the hulking shoulders, then around the table at each other, the implication in the big youth's softly muttered words not lost on them.

Finally, Jinky spoke up, "What's going on here, Andy? I mean, I can't even—"

"Neither can I," TJ chimed in.

"Two different pairs of panties..." Jeena Kirtland went on, "found by two different boys in two different places—two years apart." She raised her Bavarian-blue eyes. "What's it all mean—?"

Andy couldn't answer, because he wasn't quite sure.

Then again, how many other pairs of girls' underwear were lying around Meevers' office, stuffed away in nooks and crannies? The very thought boggled the mind. Could it be that he and Rodney had inadvertently discovered the long-lost "Bermuda Triangle of Panties" deep in the bowels of Titanis High? Or was Principal Budd Meevers performing "unauthorized entries" of the student body (in more ways than one) in exchange for extracurricular credit?

Either that, Andy reasoned...
Or something far more sinister.

CHAPTER 19

"Look, guys," Andy said, folding his hands diplomatically atop the cafeteria table. "who knows what it all means? After all, girls sometimes lose their panties, right? You know, here and there. One or two might've accidentally dropped a pair of them from their gym bags or purses or something while visiting Principal Meevers office."

"More likely dropped 'em off their asses, bro," TJ shot back. "After which Meevers used 'em to wipe his cum stains off after banging 'em. And that's how they got stuffed in his desk drawer and beneath the couch cushions."

"TJ!" Jinky exclaimed, even as she too looked over at Andy, her face doubtful. "You really believe that, Andy? That it's all just innocent?"

"For the moment it's our only choice."

"But why?" TJ interjected.

"Because I like Principal Meevers, that's why. And so do you, TJ. Besides, he cut us some serious slack last year. Don't forget he could've sent both of us to juvenile detention, remember? But Meevers gave us a break." He looked around the table. "So we owe him a break too by not jumping to conclusions." Reluctantly, they all nodded, but their eyes still expressed doubt. "Anyway," Andy went on, "we've got less than fifteen minutes left before the bell rings, so let's put that aside and get down to business."

As he took out his film production notebook and cracked it open, he flicked an eye toward Rodney, who had remained on the fringe of the discussion while scrolling through local news headlines on his smartphone. "Rodney, have you finished the chronological fact sheet regarding the Sawyer-Hinkle disappearance so TJ and I can get started on the script?"

The lumbering youth glanced up. "It's done."

"Good. And what about you, TJ? Did you compile a list of possible shooting locations, cast and crew needed, as well as possible leads to play the main characters?"

TJ cracked his knuckles. "Mostly, except for the guy to play Hinkle. Since he turned out to be a faggot we may have trouble getting someone to play him."

"Not a prob," Andy calmly replied, with just the thinnest trace of a smile on his face, "since I had you in mind."

"Eat shit and die, asshole."

"Hold on a sec. With a little bit of help from Jink and a bottle of Clairol we could get your hair just the right shade of blond and then–"

"Double eat shit and die, asshole."

Andy chuckled.

TJ: Best friend. Filmmaking partner. Able to both take it and dish it out. They made an inseparable team.

Andy turned his attention to Jeena Kirtland.

"What about you, Jink? You finish your research on Tina Sawyer?"

"Almost. But there's just not much on the Internet about her. Nice girl, according to the news reports. That kind of thing. Member of the Titanis High cheerleading squad. Good student. Active in the school's Youth For Social Justice Club. Last seen on her way to a friend's Christmas party with Brett Hinkle four years ago. When they failed to arrive the police were called. Later, her car was found halfway in a ditch about a mile outside of Titanisville. But after a month-long search no trace of her or Hinkle was ever found." She shrugged. "And that's where the trail ended."

"I know...not much," Andy agreed, sighing. "Anyway, finish up the outline you're writing on Tina along with some key character points we'll need to incorporate into the script.

You know, things that will define her for the audience. Now, based on what Rodney's already found out, which is plenty, Tina Sawyer and Brett Hinkle were clearly ambitious and smart, but also clearly flawed. Tina was a bit of a slut, so I hear, and Brett...well, we know what he was into. So it's our job as filmmakers to show why and how they became what they were–and maybe shed some sympathetic light on the circumstances that made them end up as victims."

Jinky nodded as she scribbled something down in her notebook.

"Okay, that's gotta be it for now," Andy said, glancing up at the cafeteria's wall clock, showing they had only five minutes left until the bell. "Anyway, let's meet over at my studio this evening–around eight. And since tonight's Halloween, I'll have plenty of party snacks and soft drinks to go around." He looked over at his best friend: "TJ, if you can, bring some beer. Your dad will never miss a few six packs, since he stores the stuff by the crate out in his garage." He directed glances toward Rodney and Jinky. "And just in case you're both wondering, my parents are okay with it."

"But why wait until eight, bro?" TJ said, finishing up a few notes of his own then closing his notebook. "Let's meet around five, get our film business out of the way, then party 'til midnight."

"Have you forgotten?" Andy fired back, as he stuffed his production notebook into his backpack as students began to rise from their lunch tables and spiral away toward the row of cafeteria waste containers and out the various exits, trying to beat the last minute rush. "I promised Meevers I'd attend a Youth For Social Justice Club meeting after school. You know, as payment for all the times I've ditched. Anyway, it starts at five, so I've got to hang around school until then."

"Since when hasn't one good ditch deserved another?" TJ quipped. "Think about it, Andy–or else next time we see ya you're gonna have posters of Karl Marx, Che Guevara, and Hillary Clinton hanging from your studio walls."

Andy chuckled, shaking his head with amusement. "Hope not, amigo. But I've no doubt Ms Pickering already has them on hers. In fact, I think–"

"Shit..." Rodney Crutchley whispered, his softly uttered word causing all three to turn in unison, since no one at the table had ever heard him use a cuss word before.

In response to three sets of questioning eyes, the big youth silently extended his arm as he turned the smartphone's screen toward them. Across its glassy surface they saw a headline:

SPOT-N-THE-ROAD CLERK FOUND MURDERED

"What the–" TJ started to say.

"Oh. My. God," Jinky said, bringing her hands up to her mouth. In an instant her eyes shot toward Andy, seeming to say: "*They know.*"

But who were *they?* Andy wondered, although deep in his gut he already knew.

"Let me see that," Andy snapped, grabbing the smartphone from Rodney. He read, aloud:

AUSTIN AMERICAN-STATESMAN
TITANISVILLE, TX
WEDNESDAY, OCTOBER 29

COUNTY LAW ENFORCEMENT OFFICIALS STILL HAVE NO LEADS IN THE SLAYING OF A CONVENIENCE STORE CLERK NEAR THE TOWN OF TITANISVILLE, SOME THIRTY-FIVE MILES NORTHWEST OF AUSTIN. THE VICTIM, IDENTIFIED AS FIFTY-NINE YEAR OLD BURRIS NUNFORD OF NEARBY FOGERTY-VILLE, WAS FOUND EARLY WEDNESDAY MORNING BY THE RELIEF SHIFT. HE WAS DISCOVERED IN THE REAR STOCK-ROOM, BOUND TO A CHAIR. AN AUTOPSY INDICATED THE VICTIM HAD BEEN SEVERELY BEATEN THEN STABBED TO DEATH. HIS THROAT HAD ALSO BEEN SLIT.

SHERIFF'S INVESTIGATORS REVEALED THAT THE STORE'S CASH REGISTER HAD BEEN ROBBED OF APPROXIMATELY TWO HUNDRED DOLLARS, CITING THIS AS LIKELY MOTIVE FOR THE MURDER. IN ADDITION TO THE STOLEN MONEY, SEVERAL ITEMS OF MERCHANDISE WERE TAKEN, INCLUDING THE STORE'S VIDEO SURVEILLANCE SYSTEM, SEVERAL POWER

TOOLS, AND A TWO THOUSAND DOLLAR PORTABLE GENERA-
TOR. LOCAL LAW ENFORCEMENT IS ASKING ANYONE WITH
INFORMATION REGARDING THIS CRIME TO CALL...

Andy Hupp's voice trailed off as he slowly lowered the smartphone and looked silently at the other three.

Jinky was first to speak: "Someone knows what happened out on Kilbane Road, Andy. Somehow they know we stopped at the Spot-N-The-Road just before Coach Ortega's nephew was killed. And that we were there when he died."

"It's just a coincidence, Jink."

"Andy! *It isn't!* And we both know it!"

"She's right," Rodney softly interjected. "Because the motive for the murder wasn't money."

All eyes looked at him.

"Nor was it the power tools," the big youth went on, "or the generator. They were just camouflage to disguise what they were really after: the surveillance system DVR."

"The DV what?" Jinky blurted.

"The digital video recorder," Andy explained, drawing upon his extensive knowledge of various kinds of video equipment. "It's the system that records video images and sound from video surveillance cameras."

"You mean like a DVD player?"

"Pretty much. Except it records images directly to a hard drive without using a CD disk. So that's why they took the entire DVR system, to make sure they got the video they were after..."

"Video," Jinky ominously echoed, "*of what?*"

"Of you. Me. That day we went into the Spot-N-The-Road. Somehow, someway, whoever killed that clerk put two and two together and figured out that the last people to see Raul Ortega alive must've stopped in at that store—and been recorded by their security camera."

"If that's true," Jinky slowly reasoned, "then whoever it was must now—"

*Be looking for us...*Andy thought, silently finishing Jinky's unspoken words.

"But...*how?*" TJ asked. "I mean, it all sounds too far-fetched. What could've possibly led them back to that store?"

"I don't know..." Andy wondered aloud. Then he shot a glance toward Jink. "Wait a sec—when I got home that day there was only one bottle of *Snark!* left in my van's cup holder—mine. What happened to yours?"

"I don't know..."

"Did you have it when I dropped you off at your house?"

The urgency in Andy's voice frightened her.

She grimaced, thinking hard. Then she looked up, helplessly. "No...I thought I left it in the van with yours."

"When I got home it wasn't there—just mine," Andy said, with dark certainty. "So that means–"

"–that I must have lost my bottle of *Snark!* when I got out on the side of the road," she exclaimed. "Either absentmindedly dropped it or accidentally kicked it out, since it might have been lying on the floor next to my feet. But Andy—I don't remember!"

"Doesn't matter now. Somebody must have found it and noticed it was a new bottle. Then they put two and two together and backtracked it to the Spot-N-The-Road, where they–"

"Stole the DVR and played back the video," Rodney Crutchley somberly reasoned, following Andy's lead. "And then matched the video time stamp to the approximate time Raul Ortega was killed—and discovered two teenagers buying *Snark!*" He looked across at Andy. "Won't take much imagination to figure out what high school they attend, since we're the nearest one to that store...nor identify the students when they do."

When they do, Andy thought.

When.

They.

Do...

"Oh, when I think about that poor man!" Jinky cried. "Murdered because of a little green bottle I accidentally dropped!"

The bell rang.

Like H.G. Wells classic 1895 novel, *The Time Machine*,

students arose from surrounding tables like the siren-summoned Eloi and proceeded to exit the cafeteria.

But Andy, Jinky, TJ, and Rodney remained frozen.

"We've got to go to the police, Andy!" Jinky suddenly insisted, breaking their trance just as students began to jostle past. "You said so yourself you overheard Coach Ortega and Raul talk about stealing cars and God knows what else!"

Kidnapping was the 'what else', Andy wanted to say. But instead, he said: "Listen, Jink. We haven't a speck of proof Ortega had anything to do with the murder of the store clerk. Nor any proof he's a car thief–or ever was. Because that's what we need, Jink. Proof. Not what I claimed to have overheard from inside a trash can. Solid proof. Besides, who's gonna believe us? The cops? In their minds it would be the word of four trouble-making teens against the star coach of Titanis High. And who'd be accusing him? A guy like me. A guy with a record of bringing guns on campus, ditching classes, trips to the principal's office, and being an all-around high school smartass." Andy shook his head. "No, Jink. They'd laugh us out of the police station."

TJ leaned forward, hands clasped on the table.

"Andy's right. Without proof we ain't got jack."

"But this Raul guy tried to gun us down, TJ!" Jinky blurted. "What more proof do we need!"

"Sure," Andy acknowledged. "He tried to gun us down. And we even have the bullet holes in Rodney's pickup, right? On the other hand, the cops might see it differently. They might accuse us of making the bullet holes ourselves as part of some complicated high school prank."

Exasperated, Jinky glared helplessly around at the three boys.

"Besides," Andy went on, "guess what would happen if we said anything against Coach Ortega?"

Puzzled, all eyes turned toward the good-looking teen.

"Don't you see?" Andy explained, looking at each one in turn. "The cops could end up charging us with a hate crime. After all, we saw how quickly they turned on Rodney. Knowing that, it doesn't take a rocket scientist to see what they would think of our story." Three faces regarded him blankly. "C'mon, guys. Add it up. Four white kids. A gym coach who's a racial minority. One plus one equals two and Bingo–we might as well walk into the police station wearing white hoods for all the good it would do."

Sitting there, the other three considered Andy Hupp's words.

And knew he was right.

"Jeeze, I hadn't thought of it like that," TJ slowly acknowledged, looking askance. "If so...we're fucked."

"I hate to say it," Andy continued, "but in these times, any white guy who says anything negative about a black or Mexican is just asking for trouble. And trouble is exactly what we don't need right now. Otherwise, Principal Meevers will kill any chance we have of filming on campus."

They rose as one from around the table, hefting backpacks.

"Don't forget, guys," Andy said, tipping a hand nonchalantly at the other three as he turned toward the far exit. "Eight o'clock my place. Halloween party snacks provided by yours truly."

"See you tonight, Andy!" Jinky waved, almost wistfully, as she and the other two boys made for a different exit. Yet she got no more than ten feet before suddenly turning around, looking back at the boy who so tugged at her heart– only to see him standing stock-still, gazing past her toward the opposite end of the cafeteria. Puzzled, she turned and followed his gaze–only to see a solitary man standing by the far wall, unmoving, his arms folded across his muscular chest. Two cold, dead-black eyes cut the distance between him and the teen like a switchblade. In that moment, she had never felt such icy malevolence, or the unspoken threat of...

Murder.

"Oh, Andy–wait!" she called out, breaking free of TJ and rushing to his side. "*Wait!*"

Andy caught her in his arms, even as José Manuel Ortega abruptly spun away and disappeared.

"Andy–! I–I saw him! Coach Ortega. The way he was staring at you! *At me!*"

Andy had noticed it too, having turned around at the last instant, as if compelled by some sixth sense, just as he'd started to push through the exit door and head for class.

And now he knew why.

And yet, something else had happened, something far greater than the sudden realization that José Manuel Ortega was very likely involved in a cold-blooded murder–and that was the girl he now held in his arms. Despite his fear, he felt his heart thump as she gazed up at him with those incredible Nazi-blue eyes.

And then her lips were suddenly eager against his.

As they kissed, a last minute gaggle of boys strolled past, laughing and joking among themselves. Seeing the boy and girl in passionate embrace, one shouted out, "Look out everyone! It's One Buck For A Suck Hupp!" as another boy chimed, "And he scores!" before the group shoved their way out the exit doors in a raucous chorus of laughter.

"Oh, Andy..." Jinky whispered, looking up helplessly at him. "What have I done?"

Andy understood. For even as Jeena Kirtland's fragrant kiss lingered on his lips, his best friend TJ, standing next to Rodney Crutchley, gazed across the cafeteria at him.

Angry? Hurt? Betrayed?

For an instant, Andy Hupp couldn't tell.

And then the freckled-faced youth did the unexpected, and slowly raised a hand in salute, as if it had taken all his strength to do so, his gesture seeming to say, "It's okay, bro. No worries. I knew from the beginning she wasn't mine. So no hard feelings, 'kay? Cuz you're still the best friend any dude like me could ever hope to have. And no girl's ever gonna change that. Besides, you two look like you belong together..."

And with that, Thomas Jefferson Sully abruptly turned away, as if to conceal a momentary flash of pain he didn't want Andy to witness, before fading through the doorway with the big kid at his side.

And you're the best friend a guy like me could ever hope to have, Andy Hupp somberly returned, there in the silence of his own thoughts.

Maybe too good...

"I never wanted to hurt TJ," Jinky softly assured, a mist of tears in her eyes as she looked up at the handsome, green-eyed boy holding her. "But the first time I laid eyes on you I knew it would come to this."

But had *he* known? Andy wondered.

That it would come to this?

Standing there, with Jinky held tight in his arms, her breath sweet against his face, he knew the inescapable answer...

CHAPTER 20

At 3:45 the bell rang, signaling the end of Andy Hupp's final class of the day. Rising, he followed a rush of students out into the hallway, whipped a left, and made for Corridor B where his locker was located.

As he moved briskly along, the news about the murdered store clerk continued to trouble him. On the one hand, stores like Spot-N-The-Road had a long history of being unsafe places to work, especially at night. Clerks were robbed and murdered all the time, all over the country. Security cameras frequently captured such murders, then grimly posted them on YouTube for all to see.

Perhaps that was all it was, Andy reasoned: just a random murder by a random killer.

Nothing more...

With absolutely no connection to the disappearance of Tina Sawyer and Brett Hinkle.

But there his mind stopped.

Because he knew it was connected.

And knew that Coach Ortega's sudden appearance in the cafeteria was ominous proof of the grave danger he and Jinky were in.

Only, what would Ortega do next?

He didn't know, except that it would happen soon, by one means or another.

"We've got to go to the police, Andy! You said so yourself you overheard Coach Ortega and Raul talk about stealing cars and God knows what else!"

Yes, God knows what else...

Turning down Corridor B, Andy jostled his way past banks of lockers—all yellow, and green, and purple—past fellow students laughing and joking and shoving and pushing, glad the school day had finally ended. As for himself, he still had an hour and fifteen minutes to kill before reporting to the school auditorium and his first meeting of Ms Pickering's Youth For Social Justice Club. But since it was located next to the library, he might as well drop in there first, maybe hang around the book racks until the meeting started.

Finally crowding up to his locker, he spun through the combinations, flung wide the door, tossed in his backpack, and banged it shut again. Turning, he half started away when a hand caught hold of his arm.

Whirling about, he came face to face with Jink.

For the longest moment they stood there, looking at each other, saying nothing. But if their voices remained silent, their eyes did not. Everything that had happened was there in a single glance; and something more, something he knew from which there was no turning back.

"You're getting to be a real pest," Andy finally said, breaking the silence.

She came up close to him, almost nose to nose, a playful twinkle in her eye. "Trust me. You don't know what pest is, buster." She sunk into his arms. "But you will."

"Then I guess I might need to invest in a flyswatter."

"Just you try."

Tenderly, they kissed.

After a moment they slowly drew back, regarding each other between outstretched arms, as if to reconfirm what had happened between them in the cafeteria—and out on Kilbane Road—and what it all ultimately meant.

"Andy..."

"Yeah, Jink?"

"I decided to hang around after my last class, waiting for you. I—I just wanted to catch you before you left for Ms Pickering's Youth For Social Justice Club."

"You didn't have to, Jink. I think I'll survive one meeting with her."

"Let's walk, okay?"

"Sure..."

As they proceeded down the wide hallway, past students slapping lockers shut as they rushed off excitedly for home and a night of Halloween parties, Jinky seemed at a loss for words.

"What is it, Jink?"

Hesitating, she came to a stop beside a glassed-walled section of hallway overlooking the front lawn of Titanis High, its scattering of evergreen live-oaks burnished by the dying light of a fading October sky. Raising her eyes, blue cornflowers against the golden wheat of her hair, her voice was suddenly soft and earnest: "Andy, don't go."

Andy looked down at her, puzzled, his mouth moving as if to respond, but only silence came forth—and bewilderment. She seemed so beautiful in that moment, he thought; so vulnerable. This was a side of Jeena Kirtland he'd never seen before.

"Not to that meeting," she said.

"But I—"

"Please, listen to me. There's something...*unclean*...about Ms Pickering. About the way she looks at life. About...about all of them. You can't know, but I do."

"But how could you?"

"Because...because I used to be one of them."

Andy looked at her, his eyes like two pools of forest-dappled water. "*You?*"

"I know, I know. That day in the cafeteria I pretended I hadn't been asked to join Ms Pickering's Youth For Social Justice Club."

Andy looked up. "Pretended?"

"Okay—lied."

"But why, Jink?"

"Because I was ashamed. Ashamed of ever having been a part of Ms Pickering's communist brainwashing program, that's why. Because I could tell you weren't the kind of guy who would associate with their kind. Or *me*, if you knew I had." She looked out the floor-to-ceiling window at the waning day, her eyes momentarily lost. Then she looked back at him. "Because there was nothing else I wanted more than to be liked by you."

Andy slowly drew her toward him. "You really are a pest, aren't you?" he said, a teasing grin forming on his handsome face. "And for my sake, I hope you'll always be..."

A tentative smile brightened her face. "You mad?"

Andy shrugged. "How could I be? It'd be like getting mad at a butterfly."

"A butterfly with a stinger," she corrected, hugging him tight. "And don't you ever forget it."

"But answer me one thing, Jink: does this have anything to do with Lyla Van der Velden attending tonight's meeting?"

At the mere suggestion her expression grew pugnacious. "Are you accusing me of being jealous, Andy Hupp?"

"Well...yeah...kind of."

"Well, you're freakin' right, buster—I am. Today in gym Lyla bragged about you and she being together at tonight's Youth For Social Justice meeting. Sitting together all snug-gily-wuggily."

They started walking again.

"Andy, please. I know boys. And I know how easily they can be... manipulated...by pretty girls."

"Like right now?" he said, gazing pointedly at her.

She poked him.

"Listen to me. I've heard her talk. Boys like you think she's some sweet little innocent red-haired thing. She's not. She's cold and...vicious. In ways you don't even suspect. And Ms Pickering made her that way. All of them. They hate guys like you. Guys who don't sing the praises of gays and blacks and illegal immigrants."

As they moved on down the hallway, Andy glanced up at the glossy, professionally-printed posters lining both sides of the hallway—many of which Lyla Van der Velden had put up, along with her fellow Social Justice Warriors. At the time Andy had found their antics vaguely amusing, like some goofy high school prank that could be laughed at then shrugged off by next morning. Only now, looking at them–really looking at them–they began to take on a whole new, darkly ominous light.

As Jinky filled him in about Lyla, his eyes wandered down the long line of posters, interspersed between orange and black Halloween bunting, reading their proclamations:

- *'We Are One Race!'*
- *'Diversity Is Our Strength!'*
- *'Black Lives Matter'*
- *'Equality Is Our Sacred Heritage'*
- *'Grrrl Power! Come Get Some!'*
- *'We All Come From Africa'*
- *'You Gay? Then Jump For Joy Cuz That's Okay!'*
- *'Support Sanctuary Cities For Undocumented Immigrants'*
- *'We All Bleed Red'*
- *'Mix It Up! – Cuz A School That's All White Ain't Alright!'*
- *'We Are A Nation of Immigrants – Welcome, Mexicans!'*
- *'Slavery Yesterday? Then Reparations Today!'*
- *'Multiculturalism Enriches You – So Feel the Vibrancy!'*

Only, thinking about it, he honestly felt no such 'vibrancy', even as he studied the images and artwork, of blonde girls standing shoulder to shoulder with black boys as they huddled over a set of test tubes in chemistry class, or sat together at cafeteria lunch tables laughing and joking, or walked home, side by side, hand in hand, cheery and carefree, while every white student smiled ecstatically, as if they were part of some heretofore unknown Nirvana, even while the black and brown youths depicted in the posters strained to look studious, thoughtful, intelligent, and caring, as some teacher or group of white adult authority figures looked on from the sidelines, always with the same saccharin expressions of sickening, self-righteous approval.

Yes, Andy Hupp thought.

Invasion of the Body Snatchers indeed...

Only, it was really an invasion of the mind snatchers, the soul snatchers, and the racial identity snatchers, he realized, judging by the endless posters marching down both sides of the hallway like invading enemy troops–offering no escape.

How long had he ignored them? he wondered. How long had he failed to realize that those posters were not there by accident or idle whim, but had been strategically arrayed so that every student, coming to and fro down the hallways, day in and day out, could not fail to see them—could not fail to absorb their strident message of alleged 'brotherhood', and then to internalize it, until one day the poster and the student could not be told apart.

Like...

Like Lyla Van der Velden.

"And that's their goal, Andy," Jinky was saying, her voice more earnest than Andy had ever heard it. "To convert you. And everyone like you. To convert this school, this town... this country, until there's no place left to run. All I know is that they're an evil and a poison that wants to take over everything and everyone. That's what they teach in those meetings. Because it's the good and the strong that they hate the most. Don't tell me how I know. I just do. Oh, Andy, here I am making a speech when all I want is for you to hold me in your arms. So please, don't go to that meeting. I...I have this crazy feeling that if you do–"

"That if I do–?"

"That I'll never see you again. At least, not the same Andy that I'm seeing now..."

Gently, Andy took Jeena Kirtland into his arms. As he did, she leaned in toward his ear, her breath warm and soft and fragrant. "I love you so, Andy. I know that now. So please, don't be afraid of hearing it. Because...I do. For now... And forever. If...if you'll have me, I'll follow you anywhere, to college, to another state, up any mountain, across any sea, to the ends of the earth if necessary. And I'll stand at your side and help you with your work, to make your dreams–and mine–come true. And I'll never, ever leave you."

In a rare moment, Andy found himself at a loss for words. What was Jeena trying to tell him? he wondered. About never seeing him again? What made her say that? Words of love and now words of grave danger, all entangled there in her beautiful, wistful blue eyes. He didn't know how to respond, yet her strange concern troubled him.

"Don't worry, Jink. I'll see you and the others tonight, right after the meeting. Promise."

And with that, he kissed her fiercely one last time, even as his fingers softly slipped away. Then, turning, he walked away down the long corridor that led to the school theater...

And his meeting with the Youth For Social Justice Club.

Inside the school theater, Andy encountered a small gathering of around thirty students, roughly two thirds of them girls; more or less what he had expected, so no surprises there. Several students he recognized, from various classes they shared in common, among them Lyla Van der Velden, who was even now waving him over.

Andy headed her way, glad Jink wasn't there. Like she had told him back in the hallway, she was a 'butterfly with a stinger'–and he believed it.

Coming down the aisle between rows of thickly-padded, movie-style theater seats, yet another touch of high-end class the builders of Titanis High School had spared no expense on, he slid in beside the gorgeous redhead, even as he caught Janelle Pickering out of the corner of his eye making her way up to the broad stage and positioning herself behind a podium.

As he settled in, Lyla tilted cozily toward him, drawing him into a cocoon of girlish fragrance. "Oh, I'm so glad you could make it, Andy. You're in for a real treat. Ms Pickering is such an inspiring speaker."

Andy slowly nodded, offering no more than a vague smile. Glancing around without being obvious, he noted all the faces, quiet and expectant, almost religious in their countenance, with a distinctive touch of...*what?*

Smugness, perhaps.

Over the fact that here they were, 'specially chosen', honored to sit in the presence of Ms Janelle Pickering. And considering where he was, and with whom he was with, it seemed to fit. After all, hadn't that always been the aura Ms Pickering exuded, every time he sat in her class, looking down the length of the room at her. *Smugness*–over how America and the world was changing, and only the 'smart ones' (like her) were ahead of the curve, ready to meet whatever came their way. As for everybody else, well, they could just fall by the wayside and die, her attitude seemed to suggest.

Then again, maybe he was being unfair. True, Principal Meevers had ordered him to attend this meeting, when Andy really had better things to do. On the other hand, Meevers was a pretty cool guy, wasn't he? So what if he had some unexplained panties floating around his office? Maybe there was a logical explanation for that. Whatever the case, the least Andy could do was go along with Meevers' demand that he attend this meeting of the Youth For Social Justice Club without making a fuss. You know, give it a fair hearing.

So, yeah.

He could do that.

Sure...*why not?*

"Welcome to tonight's meeting of the Youth For Social Justice Club," Ms Pickering began, her eyes burning like small campfires glimpsed through a dark forest clearing. "As you all know, we have many projects now underway, besides this semester's ongoing poster campaign. It continues what we began five school years ago, spreading the ideas of social justice among the corridors and hallways of our school, so that our students and staff have no choice but to see them each and every day, wherever they walk, wherever they look, wherever they sit, think, and talk. And this year, with a whole new group of dedicated students now gathered before me, we continue our quest. As such, I am proud to guide this important project, knowing it will bear fruit in the eyes and minds of many Titanis students, even in years to come, as well as in the general public that they will encounter, as they enter the adult world, go on to college, to work, to the very seats of our government..."

As Andy sat there listening, his eyes on Ms Pickering, he felt an almost palpable energy emanating from her down to the gathered students, as if she were a self-contained power station and they just so many batteries waiting to be charged, their collective eyes glowing ever brighter as they were energized by her words:

"...and yes, let us live up to what Republicans and right wingers and immigrant-haters and racists call us, for we are exactly what they claim we are at their Tiki torch, Neo-Nazi hate rallies, boys and girls: Social Justice Warriors! Yes! We are exactly that–*Social! Justice! Warriors!*"

A fervent round of applause broke out around Andy as the gathered boys and girls cheered, with Lyla Van der Velden clapping so rapidly that all he could see beside him was a blurred motion of hands approaching Warp 9 velocity. It was then that he became aware that of all the students present, only his hands remained motionless. Knowing how that might look, he forced himself to halfheartedly slap his hands together a few times, just for appearances. He hated the dishonesty of it, but when behind enemy lines...

Lyla herself was totally enthralled, her eyes lit with an almost messianic fire, even as she reached over and squeezed his left hand: "Isn't she wonderful, Andy!" But then he heard another voice: *"And that's their goal, Andy! To convert you... to convert all of us."*

As Janelle Pickering rode the wave of enthusiasm, Andy Hupp unobtrusively looked around, realizing these fellow students–bright, engaged, and dedicated–were the future leaders of America. But what kind of leaders would they be? he wondered. Then he thought back, knowing now what Rodney Crutchley had meant when he spoke of 'a dark thing moving among us'.

And when he looked up again at Ms Pickering, he knew she was speaking directly to him, about there being no future for anyone like him, unless he became one of them, heart and soul: "...and there will come a time when anyone who opposes us and what we stand for–open borders, illegal immigrants, or *us*, will no longer be tolerated–anywhere or at anytime. Such a day awaits us! For today such people are only 'condemned'. Yet tomorrow, all of you–America's future leaders–will make new laws that will forever silence those who oppose us, as has always been our movement's goal right from the beginning. Because the time for debate is fast drawing to an end. The world that's coming is rushing up at us from south of the border, and we will and must embrace that world as America's dark-skinned future...!"

And then Ms Pickering's voice seemed to recede into the distance, leaving only her glistening teeth, like tombstones in a vast graveyard, Andy thought, behind which her enormous mouth gaped like a great carnivorous maw devouring all the student minds in the room except–not just yet–his own. And yet, he could feel the sway of their united purpose, their common goal, their sense of belonging...of the euphoria of their all-encompassing *belief* that the world would soon be theirs.

But as quickly as it had receded Ms Pickering's voice returned full force, blasting into his consciousness once more as she introduced the next speaker: Dr. Rothman Adler–from the nearby liberal stronghold of Austin–and that city's own august statesman of everything the liberal left stood for embodied in a single man.

"It's him, Andy," Lyla Van der Velden cooed. "The one man we in the club all live for. He's everything that's good and kind and decent. And most of all, he gives us hope for a better world..."

In the next instant, Dr. Rothman Adler took the stage, pausing for a moment to swing his sixty-year-old visage round the gathered youths below, his gray-streaked Van Dyke beard jutting outward like the prow of a 19th century ship. Then, in a slow, mellow voice, almost grandfatherly in tone, he began to speak—about all the nascent hope he saw in the young faces of his audience, especially the new ones who had joined since last he'd addressed the group.

As he continued with his opening remarks, his eyes kept coming back to Andy—eyes of no definable color, neither brown nor gray nor green nor blue, but something of no color he could define, like discolored water puddling after a rain. And for the next twenty minutes Andy listened, as Adler spoke of the great progress that had been made at Titanis High, as well as many other schools, both in Texas and afar. Then, toward the end, his voice became animated as he closed his speech by announcing the upcoming *'Hooray! We're All Gay Today!'* festival that his organization, The Center For Human Understanding, had created and gotten accepted by school districts statewide.

To Andy's barely-concealed horror, Dr. Adler described the upcoming event—a festive, school-wide carnival featuring a variety of 'social justice' amusements, including one he was particularly enthusiastic about called 'Bobbin' For Wieners' (as opposed to apples) whereby, as Adler energetically explained, boys could bob their heads in a tub of milk-white water and bite at floating wieners, in the hope of seizing one in their mouths and winning a prize. Great fun for all, he assured, to a round of student applause.

At the conclusion of Dr. Adler's talk, Ms Pickering took the stage beside him to announce a surprise—that everyone was invited to a special Halloween party at none other than an Austin television producer's private residence along the craggy banks of the Colorado River. "There will be many important people there," Ms Pickering explained, resting her eyes for a moment on Andy, "and it will be a once in a lifetime opportunity for everyone to meet some very interesting and idealistic progressives shaping today's social climate."

As Ms Pickering closed the meeting to another round of applause, she departed the stage and came winding her way through the milling students just as Andy was saying goodbye to Lyla, telling her he had to go because he was expecting friends over.

"But Andy!" Lyla pleaded, seizing hold of his wrist. "The evening's just begun and you heard Ms Pickering! We're all invited to a special Halloween party down on the river! Please don't go!"

"I've got to, Lyla," Andy said, as diplomatically as he could. But just as he was about to turn away he felt a hand alight firmly on his shoulder, only to turn around and find Janelle Pickering facing him.

"Now you'll do no such thing, Andy," she admonished. "Lyla is counting on you being there. As am I. So of course you'll go." And then she stepped in closer, the swish of her tight skirt hinting–it almost seemed–of things yet unseen, but soon to be discovered... "After all, Andy, I've already told Dr. Adler all about you and your interest in filmmaking and he–"

"Thinks you sound like a very bright and ambitious young man," Dr. Rothman Adler said, walking up with a jovial gust of enthusiasm. "Oh yes, indeed. And my organization, The Center For Human Understanding, knows a great many people with a growing need for talented young filmmakers like you. So it's really a golden opportunity, Andy, as there will be many well-known Austin filmmakers there, along with several Hollywood studio executives and film directors that a young man like you would do well to meet. And with my introduction, you will have the opportunity to establish some important contacts in the film industry, ones you might not otherwise so easily acquire, if at all."

Between the three of them, as well as the prospect of meeting professional filmmakers, Andy Hupp reluctantly gave in: "Okay, guess I'm sold. Let's do it."

"You and Lyla can ride with me," Ms Pickering said, as she primly led the two teens out of the auditorium.

A moment later, as they crossed the school parking lot toward Janelle Pickering's car, Lyla Van der Velden snuggled in close to Andy, whispering sultrily into his ear: "And tonight I've also a special surprise for you..."

But even as the redheaded girl said it, he caught a sideways glance from Ms Pickering, almost as if she had known what Lyla had whispered, even though she could not possibly have heard...

CHAPTER 21

Leaving the secluded Hill Country town of Titanisville behind, Andy Hupp and Lyla Van der Velden sat close together in the back seat of Janelle Pickering's sleek Jaguar XKE, a surprisingly expensive car for a small town high school teacher to be driving, Andy thought, even as they zipped through the night toward a waterfront mansion situated along a wealthy stretch of Austin's Colorado River.

For the first twenty minutes of the drive, Andy could hardly believe where he was–or with whom: seated behind none other than Ms Pickering, Titanis High's fanatical Social Studies teacher and clandestine sex predator of young teenage boys. But how the heck he had gotten himself into this jam in the first place he just couldn't figure. And to make matters even worse–so soon after Jinky had expressed her undying love for him–here he was with one of the hottest girls in school–Lyla Van der Velden–with her arm glued around his waist. He could even hear T.J.'s mocking voice right now: "One Buck For A Suck Hupp does it *again!*"

Oh, boy–had he ever...

As they rode along, the Jaguar grinding smoothly through the twists and turns of the famed Texas Hill Country, Andy kept noticing Ms Pickering stealing glances at him in her rear-view mirror, like a tawny-eyed predator biding its time. For with every glance, she exuded an animal sexuality he had never encountered before, an almost preternatural lust. And yet, she never uttered a word, even as she drove the winding curves between vast, rolling hills of live oak and cedar. Seated where he was, he managed to catch a glimpse of her well-toned thigh between a narrow gap in the bucket seats, as she maneuvered the accelerator and brake pedals back and forth, the hem of her skirt alternately hiking up, then down, with only the faintest whisper of nylon against wool.

But she knew he was watching, and that frightened him in a way he could not define. What's more, he realized, she's waiting to make her move. "Our hallway encounter was only a taste," he imagined her saying, in those brief stolen glances in the rear-view mirror. "Because now that I've cornered my prey I'm just waiting for the right moment...to pounce."

And when she did?

But Lyla drew him back into the present, to the rich smell of leather upholstery and the whisper of wind past the window and the night-darkened landscape beyond as she snuggled into him, sighing with pleasure. As she did, he could not help but think that not only had he been snared by the cougar in the front seat, but also by her well-trained cub in the back...

<hr />

After a long drive through rolling, oak-dotted countryside of what many considered the Lone Star state's most scenic region, the Jag and its three occupants arrived at Lake Austin, a section along the Colorado River fronted by countless Beverly Hills-style mansions costing, Andy had heard, as high as sixty million dollars. Here, poor people lived in million dollar homes beside their much wealthier neighbors, but all were far removed from Austin proper and the increasing influx of Third World people so beloved of the liberal rich— provided they didn't have to live near them. Of course, Andy could never make such an observation to anyone like Ms Pickering without triggering them, so he kept his heretical thoughts to himself.

A short time later, the Jag passed up a curved street lined with huge, sprawling mansions jutting two, three, and four stories high, all rising from thick masses of live oak, magnolia, palm, and other lush, waxy vegetation, lending this length of prime riverfront, as well as the house-studded granite cliffs beyond, an eclectic mix of Beverly Hills élan and Palm Beach flash, with just the right pinch of Texas nouveau riche.

As Ms Pickering cruised down the street, Andy observed architecture ranging from Mediterranean to French Chateau to Greek Revival to Palm Springs modern, along with a dozen other styles. And though his family wasn't exactly EBT users, this egregious display of wealth certainly made him feel like it.

"Andy, lighten up!" Lyla said, shaking him from his reverie. "We're here and it's party time!"

And with that, Janelle Pickering whipped her maroon Jag down a long, curving drive flanked by olive trees, cycads, and lush flowers, above which ancient live oaks stood juxtaposed against the looming hulk of a European-style mansion, craggy, dark and brooding, with gray stone turrets at the corners, long mullioned-windows, and stone gargoyles running along its four story high Gothic roof-line. At a quick guess, Andy estimated the house and riverfront property to be worth somewhere in the neighborhood of fifteen million dollars, so the residents had probably never heard of an EBT card, much less used one.

"Just look at all the cool Halloween decorations, Andy!" Lyla exclaimed, gesturing out the window as Ms Pickering pulled the car to a halt next to a waiting valet dressed in Halloween costume–that of a sinister, orange-haired clown.

As the three of them exited the car, the valet motioned for another costumed attendant to drive it away to a parking area, where some fifty cars were already parked, ranging from expensive German and British makes, including one Rolls Royce, to a collection of sports cars and high-end pickups–the last a sure sign this was a residence in Texas, and not somewhere else.

As they walked past a gurgling fountain brimming with

koi toward the main entrance, Andy and Lyla took in the elaborate Halloween decorations, including glowing jack-o-lanterns strung along the eaves, interspersed with gape-jawed skulls whose illuminated eye-sockets throbbed with eerie green light. Scarecrows, mummies, vampires, and other full-sized animated replicas were strategically placed among the gardens and entrance area, emanating howls and moans and hideous cackles, all expertly done. But then, this was a television producer's house, Andy reasoned, so that was no surprise.

"Oh, Andy–Ms Pickering–*look!*" Lyla cried, pointing.

They looked.

Overhead–streaking between two Gothic turrets–they saw a broomstick-riding witch in black hat and cape, her shrieking paroxysms of laughter and glowing green eyes causing Lyla to squeal with delight and amazement.

"She's flying!" the redheaded girl exclaimed.

But clever though it was, it was only a life-sized dummy riding an invisible wire strung taut between two turrets, pulled by a motor-powered tension line. A cool effect, Andy had to agree, but decided to keep silent about the mundane mechanics involved. Ms Pickering, for her part, remained non-committal, only once flicking an eye toward him as she led them up the mansion's wide sweep of granite steps where another costumed house attendant awaited, this one garbed as a medieval executioner, black hood and all.

"Before you enter," a middle-aged man's voice said from behind the hood, gesturing at a rack bedecked with hanging costumes, "you'll need to put on something more festive." Glancing at the teenage girl, he reached over and handed her a witch's pointed black hat and cape. "Should go nice with your pumpkin-colored hair," he added. Next, he handed Andy a pirate's tricorn hat affixed with a metallic skull and crossbones, along with a realistic metal cutlass. "Make sure you don't poke anyone with that, son." Finally, he glanced at Janelle Pickering, noting her imperious expression and then her tight woolen skirt sheathing, in his salacious mind, an equally tight, well-cleaved ass. "I think I have just the thing for you," he said, "something that should put you in a devilish Halloween mood," as he handed her a red cape and horned eye-mask.

After donning their impromptu costumes, Janelle Pickering, Andy Hupp, and Lyla Van der Velden were shown into the mansion proper by another costumed attendant. Once inside, Andy saw that most of the guests were also outfitted in basic costume accents, probably taken from the same rack theirs had come. Even so, a few of the guests wore elaborate latex masks, full-body costumes, and complex facial makeup, all strictly Hollywood grade. Over in one corner stood a *Star Wars* Wookie, drinking from a bottle of Heineken. And next to him reposed a full-blown, fanged Dracula, face made-up in pallid skintones, holding a mixed drink.

Everywhere Andy looked he saw monsters, demons, ghosts and zombies. One man wore a grinning, oversized pumpkin head with a bloody butcher knife protruding from the side of it, while another looked like some sort of horrifying, overgrown insect. There was even someone wearing a Trump mask, replete with reddish-blond wig, all mingling about in a ceaseless whirlpool of voices, drinks, and laughter.

Scattered amid the party goers were black-draped tables arrayed with generous platters of catered food, ranging from hors d'oeuvres to fried chicken to pizza to vegetarian dishes, all courteously served by costumed staff. There was even a live blues-rock band playing atop a raised platform, the main guitarist quite good as he filled the room with just the right level of background music.

"Glad you came, Andy?" Lyla asked, squeezing his arm possessively, as her beautiful face lit up with high-voltage excitement.

"Of course he is, Lyla," Ms Pickering said, her voice as prim and correct as if she still stood at the head of her class. "He heard opportunity knocking, and he answered." She glanced off through the milling crowd. "Speaking of which... I think that's Dr. Adler standing right over there."

They crossed the vast living room beneath a vaulted Gothic ceiling rising three floors high, at whose uppermost reaches a medieval-style wrought-iron chandelier hung suspended from multiple lengths of chain, its outer ring of electric lights designed to look like half-melted candles. Looking up, Andy wondered why the residents even needed to throw a Halloween party, when they already lived in a haunted house.

As they came up to Dr. Adler, they found him standing amid a semi-circle of important looking, older men and women, all wearing a variety of Halloween eye-masks; minimal in appearance, but nonetheless in keeping with the spirit of the party. Their collective demeanor, however, indicated they knew they were important and that outsiders should know their place while in their presence. But Adler's warm greeting made all that unnecessary as he grinned from behind his black eye-mask, atop which two nubby gremlin horns protruded.

"Ah, Ms Pickering, glad to see you made it—as well as these two bright young acolytes."

"We just arrived," Ms Pickering said, by way of greeting.

"Yes, of course. I only arrived myself just a few moments ago when these old Hollywood friends of mine waved me over. Until you three walked up we were just chatting about some new social projects we're putting together." After a round of introductions, among them a handsome, but rather effete actor starring in an upcoming HBO movie about "a sympathetic pedophile", Adler gestured toward a bespectacled gentleman wearing a green 'goblin' eye-mask he identified as one "Sid Glickstein", producer of educational films aimed at high school kids across the country:

"...as Sid was telling me before you three arrived," Dr. Adler smoothly informed, "he's at work on a new series of short films to be shown in high schools all across the country. I'd just mentioned to him, Ms Pickering, that you had a student who was a talented filmmaker and he immediately expressed an interest in meeting him. So–"

At this point Mr. Glickstein stepped forward, eyes bulging from behind a green mask as they roved hungrily over Andy's face, taking in his thick, golden-brown hair, green eyes, and photogenic looks. "Nice to make your acquaintance, kid. So Rothman here tells me you wanna break into movies, that right?"

Andy glanced at Ms Pickering, then at Lyla, then back at the squat man with the lewd eyes. "Uh, yeah. That was the idea."

"Tough business to get into, kid. Lotta young stuff have that dream nowadays but few ever make it. Sad, so sad. You see, talent's usually not enough anymore. Not like the old days. Takes connections now–the right kind." He let go a slow, crooked smile. "And the right people..."

"I figured as much," Andy said. Actually, he knew a great deal already about how difficult it was, and had been planning his career trajectory accordingly.

"Well, you figured right, kid. Now, let me tell you a little about what I'm doing, and see if any of it grabs you." After running on for five minutes about his company, MultiCational Films, which, he explained, made educational school films from a multicultural perspective, "a big thing nowadays, by the way, what with all the immigration pouring into this country. And I'm always looking for young, clean cut talent like you..."

Andy simply looked at Sid Glickstein, not sure where he was going with this. But he noticed Ms Pickering was observing him, carefully, gauging the effect of Glickstein's words on him.

"Right now I need young ambitious filmmakers who can learn my business from the ground up, take a script and put together the kind of quick, snappy films schools and students are looking for. But not just young talent directing these films will do. I also need directors who can get in front of the camera too."

"You mean...act in them?"

"Sure, kid. It's how we keep costs down and how young talent like you learns all the angles of the biz. Directing, acting, lighting, editing, running out for pizzas–whatever's needed. Sound good?"

But before Andy could answer Sid Glickstein went on: "Right now we're doing a short video about interracial dating, shooting next month right here in Austin. After hearing Rothman's recommendation, I decided to talk with you first but now that I have I think you'd be perfect."

"Perfect...?"

"That's right, kiddo. I've been looking for a good-looking white teen like you to play the boyfriend of a black girl. As the film unfolds, you at first reject her sexual overtures. Then she teases you a bit more. You know, maybe shows you a flash of panties as she bends over next to her school locker. That kind of thing. Next thing you know you find yourself out behind the school cafeteria making out like gunblazers, then later on, after class, in the back seat of her car. Afterward, you're sold. Later, at her house, you two go all the way, hot and heavy. Soon you have your jealous buddies chasing black girls all over your high school and...well, you get the picture."

Andy swallowed.

He got it alright.

And now all eyes were upon him.

Watching.

Waiting.

What would his reaction be?

"I–"

"It's going to be shown all over the country kid. In thousands of high schools. Maybe in Europe too. Even Australia. It's a ground floor opportunity for you."

"But–"

"Screen credit? That what you're worried about? Don't

sweat it, kid. When I'm done with you your face and name will be synonymous around the world with interracial love—guaran-fucking-teed."

"Andy!" Lyla chimed in, "Just think of it! You'll be a professional filmmaker even before graduating high school! And you'll be helping fight all the racists in our schools that claim black girls aren't as pretty as white ones! You've got a chance to change all that!"

Such a beautiful face, Andy thought, looking at her. It had taken untold thousands of years to bless her with those emerald green eyes, silken orange hair, and creamy white complexion. Knowing that, could he lend his abilities toward making a film that said her beauty was no greater than that of a random black girl? Is that what Sid Glickstein and Dr. Adler and Janelle Pickering all were asking of him—as well as all the white teens in America?

To accept this?

Was this, then, a glimpse of the thing that Rodney Crutchley had sensed was moving across America?

He looked at them.

They waited.

And he knew he was trapped.

For either he had to reject the offer or...

But wait—

What about Star Fleet evasive maneuver 9? If he immediately engaged it there was still a chance he could escape this Klingon trap. Decision made, he silently ordered the helmsman of his imaginary starship: "Prepare to fire photon deception-torpedoes one and two!" even as he opened his mouth and said, in a tone of pure teenage astonishment: "Wow. Just. Wow. I mean, I can't even," and let it go at that, hoping the art of youthful incoherency would work its magic. Otherwise, he'd never make it out of this sector of space alive.

"You see, Andy?" Dr. Adler said, beaming. "You've been here for only a few minutes and already you're being offered a professional job in the film business."

"That's because," Janelle Pickering said, with an almost sadistic gleam in her eye, "Andy has come to see the advantages of joining my Youth For Social Justice Club. Before now, he was one of my slow learners when it came to having a social conscience. But tonight has convinced him that social justice works for everyone, and not just minorities. Isn't that right, Dr. Adler?"

"Of course, Ms Pickering. That is, for those who play the game according to the rules. Otherwise, how would we all ever get along in this world?"

"Well," Lyla Van der Velden sweetly interjected, thrilled at Andy's good fortune, "if nobody minds, I think Andy and I would like to get something to eat." Besides, it would give her an opportunity to be alone with him.

The older adults nodded good-naturedly as they shooed them along, thoughts of "ah, these impetuous youth" in their minds, even as Andy thankfully allowed himself to be tugged away from this deep space enemy encounter that had almost destroyed the USS Huppsterprise...

After acquiring plates of food, Andy and Lyla circulated among their fellow party goers and Youth For Social Justice Club members, idly checking out the interesting variety of Halloween costumes as they admired the vast size and medieval décor of this television producer's house–whoever he was–all to the background beat of blues-rock music. If Andy had said he wasn't having a good time, he'd have been a liar. In all truth, strolling through this concentrated collection of nice-looking, intelligent, and talented people was a new experience for him. And doing it with a pretty redhead at his side was an added bonus.

As they strolled, mingled, and then moved on, heads turned whenever they passed, several convinced they had seen the attractive couple in recent episodes of *The Hunger Games*, based merely on their youth and good looks. Pausing at one circle of people, including, to Andy's delight, a man costumed as Captain Kirk and wearing the lesser-known green wrap-around Star Fleet shirt, they listened in as another man, bearing a marked resemblance to Rod Serling and dressed in his iconic 1960's dark suit and tie, exchanged TV trivia as they sipped cocktails. Yet no more had they stopped than Andy suddenly felt a hand tap him on the shoulder. Turning, he recognized the face of the TV actor Dr. Rothman Adler had introduced to them half an hour earlier, the one starring in an upcoming HBO movie about a "sympathetic pedophile"–whatever the hell that meant.

"Don't I know you?" the actor queried, glass of bourbon poised in hand.

Andy glanced at Lyla, then replied: "Yeah. Sort of. We just met a few minutes ago."

"No, I mean from somewhere else."

"Not to my knowledge."

"But I'm sure I've seen your face before...somewhere."

"People tell me that all the time," Andy said, dismissively, his tone of voice implying it was a case of mistaken identity, even though it clearly wasn't. It wasn't that he was 'famous' in the conventional sense, but there was no doubt that his teen model work had placed his anonymous, nameless face in countless magazines all over America, as well as Europe and abroad–for better or worse. Truth be told, and long before he'd gotten into the business, he'd always wondered who all those nameless people in clothing and appliance ads were, from Sears catalogs to copies of Better Homes & Gardens. Yet nameless though they were, they were also famous–in a weird, anonymous sort of way. And now, his face was one of them...

The actor took a thoughtful swig of bourbon, studying Andy. "No, no, I'm sure I've seen your face before. You ever do any film acting?"

"No," Andy said, which was true, at least in regard to Hollywood films.

"Even as an extra?"

"Nope."

Swirling his drink about, the actor again contemplated Andy. "Strange, but I don't forget a face once I've seen it. Ever. And I know I've seen yours before...somewhere. And not that long ago."

Andy shrugged. "Guess you're mistaking me for someone else, that's all. Happens all the time," he added, by way of explanation. Or, in his case—by way of lying.

"Wait a sec–! I think I got it! You ever do any modeling? That kind of thing?" He glanced at the floor, wracking his brain. Then he snapped his fingers and looked up. "Now I re-member! On the flight out from LA I saw your face in some kind of magazine. Let me see... Yeah, yeah that's it! You were in a Mann Hunt underwear ad. And you were straddling a Harley with some chick in a pair of panties. Yeah, that's what it was! You!"

Red Alert, Andy thought.

Beam me aboard, Scotty!

"Nope, sorry," Andy said, as he made an effort to move away with Lyla. But just as he did the actor reached out and snatched his arm. "Hey....now I get it." He chuckled darkly. "Sure, sure–I get it. Of course. You just don't want anyone to know who you are, do you?"

Without further comment, Andy–with Lyla in tow–left 'Captain Kirk', 'Rod Serling', and the "sympathetic pedo-phile" behind and moved away, even as the intoxicated actor called out, "Just so you know, I'm wearing a pair of Mann Hunt's right now. So tell your client his ads work! In the meantime, maybe he'll let me do a magazine shoot too!"

Placing as much distance between himself and the inebri-ated actor as he could, Andy brought Lyla to a halt next to one of a half dozen portable bars scattered about the first floor of the sprawling house.

"What was that all about?" Lyla Van der Velden asked,

breathless, looking back in the direction of the actor, now badgering 'Captain Kirk' and 'Rod Serling' about who knew what.

"Just a guy who's had too many drinks," Andy said.

She regarded him curiously. "Is there something you're not telling me, Andy?"

"Like what?"

"You know, like what he said."

"Not a thing."

"Seriously?"

"Seriously."

Add another lie to his tally, he thought.

She looked at him slyly. "Then tell me. What brand of underwear are you wearing?"

"What's underwear?" he coolly replied, feigning puzzlement.

Lyla giggled. Now this was the kind of talk she'd been hoping to get into all evening. "Well, guess we'll just have to find out a little later, won't we?"

Double Red Alert! Andy thought.

Thank God Jink wasn't here!

"You look like you could use a drink, Andy," Lyla teased, knowing she had made him uncomfortable–and loving it.

"Thanks. But I just had a cup of punch."

"Not that kind of drink, silly," she said, motioning her pretty head toward the portable bar, where bottles of beer, offered in a variety of foreign and domestic brands, sat in tubs of ice. "How about we have the bartender make us a couple of *piña coladas*?"

"Uh, I think you're forgetting something, Lyla."

"Like what?"

"Like the fact that we're not twenty-one."

"Has that ever stopped you before?"

"Only when there's a cop present."

She smiled. "Do you see any?"

Andy nodded at a man across the room.

Lyla turned, saw who he was looking at. "Him? Smarty-pants! He's dressed as a Keystone Kop!"

Andy laughed. "Okay, maybe he doesn't count. Still, the bartender will card us."

"That's what you think," Lyla smirked, turning toward the portable bar.

Shrugging, Andy followed.

CHAPTER 22

"Since my junior year," Lyla Van der Velden cheerily explained as they walked up to the portable bar, "I've gone to half a dozen of these Social Justice Club parties, and twice before they served alcohol. And when they did we club members were allowed to drink."

"Now that's what I call social justice," Andy murmured, as they waited for the Mexican bartender, who was busy serving another customer.

"Exactly!" Lyla agreed, totally missing Andy's sardonic import. "You'll find that everyone here is absolutely progressive in their thinking! And that's why I love being a volunteer in Ms Pickering's group. And you will too! That's because we're working to break down barriers all over our school and all over the country. It's so...so..."

"Marxist?" Andy suggested, glancing off at the Halloween partiers.

"Huh?"

"Nothing," he said, turning back to her. "You were saying?"

"I was saying that our club's mission is to break down barriers. Like getting to drink at this party, for instance. That's because Ms Pickering and Dr. Adler and the man who owns this house aren't a bunch of stuffy windbags like most people. That's because they're progressive, Andy. Really, really progressive. And that's the way the world is going."

"Meh ay helpchu?"

Andy and Lyla turned as the Mexican bartender, a man in his thirties, addressed them in mangled English.

"Yes," Lyla started to say, then exclaimed in delight: "Why, it's you, Armando! Remember—you served drinks at that Christmas party our club attended last year! In downtown Austin! You know—at the offices of The Center For Human Understanding!"

"I do not theenk so, Meese—"

"Of course it was you! Don't you remember? I was the one who spilt my drink all over my elf costume!" She moaned in feigned mortification. "And everyone laughed at me!"

Andy saw the Mexican's wary eyes shift left, then right. He clearly did not like attention being drawn to him. So Andy engaged Star Fleet tactical maneuver 367-A and stepped forward: "We'd like two *piña coladas*," he manfully asserted, "with extra shots of rum."

"Andy!"

He looked at her. "No—?"

"Yes!" she squealed, giddy and excited; she'd find out yet what brand of underwear he was wearing!

The bartender sullenly made the two gringos their drinks, adding extra shots of rum. What an easy life this focking *güero* and his *puta güera* had, he thought, as he handed them their *piña coladas*. Not like the hard life he knew back in México. But he didn't care, just so long as they weren't ICE agents. Not likely, though—too young. Besides, the proprietor of the catering service he worked for was a good friend of the house's owner, and would never set such a trap. Still, he had been jarred by her remembering his face and name...

"Isn't it wonderful?" Lyla cooed, taking a heady sip of her double-rum *piña colada* as they leisurely strolled away with their drinks toward more Halloween partiers.

Andy took a sip as well, felt an immediate jolt of rum hit his bloodstream. Wow, that's some good shit, he thought. Maybe this was Ms Pickering's little secret for luring students into her club. If only he had known!

"Sure," Andy said, venturing another sip, thinking a guy in a pinch could live on these things.

"Are you even listening to me?" she said.

"Sure. These are great."

"Not that, Andy. I was talking about Armando the barten-der. I mean, isn't it wonderful that Dr. Adler made it possible for him to get a job in this country? With that catering ser-vice? After all, he's not even here legally. But then, that's what what our Youth For Social Justice Club is really all about—justice. Justice and..."

As Lyla Van der Velden deliriously rambled on, Andy en-joyed his drink, especially since it deadened his mind to all her social justice spew. Still, not so much that his observant eye didn't take in the totality of where he was and with whom he partied: Austin's movers and shakers, its liberal glitterati, its arbiters of power and privilege—the ones like Sid Glick-stein who molded school kids' minds by manipulating them into believing that white teens could be psychologically lured into lusting after black girls. But why? he wondered. Why teach them *that?* And why the posters lining the hallways back at Titanis High? Were they and Sid Glickstein somehow connected in some metaphysical way, as Rodney Crutchley seemed to think?

Too many questions, he thought.

Ones for which his seventeen year old mind had no answers.

But the one question he needed answered most was the one that throbbed in his brain at that very moment, between the dreamy swirls and foggy intoxication of rum: *All to what end?*

Then he looked across the vast room at Dr. Rothman Ad-ler, smoothly talking among the older, more important guests. Guests that, for the most part, worked in television or movies or newspapers or magazines, all *writing things* and then care-fully pumping them into the unsuspecting consciousnesses of America's white youth.

Hazily, he examined Rothman Adler, standing there in his horned gremlin eye-mask, with his expertly manicured Van Dyke beard. And beside him stood Ms Pickering, in her red devil's cape and eye-mask, equally horned. Somehow, there was a special irony in that. All of it, in fact. And for the first time Andy Hupp questioned his long-held ambition to join these kinds of people, in these kinds of houses, talking about these kinds of ideas. But even as these doubts crossed his mind, his smartphone began to vibrate. Reaching into his pocket, he withdrew it and tabbed an icon, bringing a new text message into view:

> JUST CAME ACROSS THIS ON THE NEWS: LANCE BUTTERFIELD'S HOUSE BURNT TO THE GROUND TWO DAYS AGO. NEXT DOOR NEIGHBOR REPORTED HE OFTEN SMOKED WEED IN BED AND MUST'VE FALLEN ASLEEP. GUESS WE WON'T BE DRIVING DOWN TO SEE HIM AFTER ALL...
>
> RODNEY

Andy spoke into his phone's automatic typist: "Keep me posted," and hit 'send'. As he started to put his phone away it vibrated a second time. He tabbed the text icon once more:

> ANDY – THE THREE OF US JUST GOT TO YOUR HOUSE. ON THE WAY OVER WE'VE BEEN READING THE NEWS ABOUT LANCE BUTTERFIELD, WHAT LITTLE THERE IS. POLICE FOUND HIS CHARRED BODY IN THE BURNT-OUT RUINS THE DAY BEFORE YESTERDAY AND HAVE RULED HIS DEATH AN ACCIDENT. BUT TJ THINKS HE WAS MURDERED BY THE SAME PEOPLE WHO KILLED THE CONVENIENCE STORE CLERK. IF SO THEN WE'VE GOT TO GO TO THE POLICE, ANDY! RIGHT THIS MINUTE! SO PLEASE GET HERE ASAP!
>
> LOVE, JINK!

Andy sent a second message: "Delayed at meeting, Jink. (he winced at the lie) Relax and enjoy yourselves until I get back. In the mean time, everybody chill. We'll figure out what to do when I return. PS: Miss you too, Miss Kirtland!"

Just as Andy put his phone away Ms Pickering came walking up, red devil costume and all, the thinnest trace of a smile on her smug face. "I see you've discovered another of the benefits of our Youth For Social Justice Club, Andy. Will wonders never cease?"

"But it looks like I'm all out of social justice," he said, glancing mournfully into his empty *piña colada* glass, already feeling lightheaded. But then, double shots of rum will do that to you...

"So am I," Lyla drawled, with a big happy grin on her face, rubbing up sloppily against Andy and liking the feel of it. As she did, she thrust out her empty glass: "My dear Ms Plickering, would you be so kind as to get us both another shot of social justice?"

Andy chuckled, "Ms 'Plickering'? Ha. Ha. Pretty good, Lyla...only problem is she'll probably flunk you now."

Standing there, Janelle Pickering examined Andy Hupp and Lyla van der Velden with a critical eye: two vibrant teens too gorgeous for their own good. They had it all, she thought. Everything that too many of the world's less fortunate darker youths did not have: looks, brains, talent, and a goodness of the heart that disgusted her. But unless these kinds of teens were conquered, body and soul, heart and mind, then the plans of men like Dr. Rothman Adler would never be achieved.

Or, for that matter, her own...

"But of course," she murmured sweetly, taking their empty glasses and walking away through the milling partiers toward the nearest bar, until all but the tips of her red satanic horns vanished among the crowd of celebrants...

Fueled by a second round of *piña coladas*, and soon a third, Andy Hupp and Lyla Van der Velden wandered, albeit tipsily, throughout the vast, four story house, up and down stairways and hallways, in and out of strange rooms, even out into the spacious back garden and around the swimming pool—Lyla giggling sillily along the way as they encountered ghosts, goblins and ghouls, as well as other scary things—like left-wing journalists, social workers, and Cultural Marxists disguised as innocent Halloween guests.

Eventually, Andy lost track of time, as the passage of min-utes–and then hours–melted into a euphoric blur of rum and laughter and outright gaiety, as Lyla led him by the hand down a flight of basement stairs into another maze of hall-ways and rooms, leaving behind the Halloween party on the floor above.

Here there was softer laughter, and other sounds—sounds of hot, sweaty flesh pounding hot sweaty flesh, interspersed with long, tortured moans of pleasure and gasps of ecstasy. In one room, seen through an open door, Andy glimpsed eight to ten people slopped across sofas and overstuffed chairs, some drinking and laughing while others smoked marijuana or snorted white powder up their noses through tightly rolled dollar bills.

"Down here is where the real party's at," Lyla breathed, tingling with excitement over everything she saw and heard. "Ms Pickering told me to bring you down here after she brought our last round of drinks. Said we could find a room for ourselves."

A room–*for ourselves?*

Half lost in an alcoholic fugue, Andy tried to understand what that meant. And why was Lyla tugging him down an-other hallway, opening doors—until she finally pulled him through into an unoccupied room?

There, in the soft light of a low-wattage, medieval styled lamp, he saw a room furnished in the same period as the rest of the house, with a big, rough-hewn oaken bed set against the wall.

"I don't get it..." Andy mumbled, even as his half empty glass slipped free of his hand.

"Oh, but you will," Lyla chirped, pushing him back onto the bed, giggling, as she slid a hand under his shirt, her mouth clamping down on his. After that the rest came so fast he couldn't remember if Lyla or he had stripped off his pants and shirt and tossed them aside, or even how she ended up in her panties and bra so quickly, her reddish-orange hair cascading down her bare porcelain shoulders.

"Aha! So you *do* wear Mann Hunt underwear," she teased, snapping the elastic waistband against his skin before hitching them down and tossing them aside. "But you won't need them now," she assured, arching her back as she raised her arms in triumph. "because I told all the girls in gym this was going to happen–tonight!"

Thinking of Jeena, Andy tried to rise from the bed, but his head was spinning wildly, crazily, as if that last *piña colada* had stripped him of any will to resist, even as he watched Lyla unhook her lavender bra and let it slip away. In an instant, large, creamy white breasts of exquisite perfection sprung free of their lacy confinement. But as she began seductively peeling down her panties he suddenly took note of their distinctive lime-green waistband; that, and the pithy slogan printed provocatively across the V of her crotch: 'It Ain't Gonna Lick Itself!'

Suddenly he remembered: the panties he had found in Meevers office. Except for the different slogan–'No Unauthorized Entry'–they were identical in both color and style–apparently from a matched set. If so, it had been Lyla Van der Velden all along who had left them there...

And Jinky–*Jinky had known!*

But before he could comprehend how it all connected, her panties were stripped away and she was tilting forward, giggling deliriously as she mashed her exquisite breasts against his bare chest, letting go a low-throated moan. And then, without any remembrance of how it happened, he suddenly found himself pushing hard and deep into her eager mound, this dream girl he had so longed for. Now all those long, pent-up weeks of unrequited lust for the redheaded girl seated the next row over in his English class was forged into a molten shaft of pounding steel, his thrusts accelerating far beyond warp 9 as if the very end of the universe was nigh and they only had seconds left to achieve–

Faster-than-light orgasm.

At that instant, a white-hot plasma jet of semen shot upward into Lyla's hot moist hole, at the same moment she threw back her head in a long, shuddering moan of unbearable pleasure, even as he fell back—gasping, tumbling, so strangely dizzy now...his hands falling limply away from her naked body, his head spinning, spinning...

Out of control.

Almost as if he had been drugged.

Until he passed out.

An unknown time later Andy Hupp awoke.

Alone.

Except for the faint bluish glow of a nightlight, the bedroom lay in darkness. Then, after the longest time, he twisted his head to one side.

Where was Lyla?

She was gone; leaving behind only a wisp of fragrance. And now, beyond the darkened room, he heard distant voices, low and disembodied, like ghostly echoes of former inhabitants, now long vanished.

Again, he made an effort to move, then listlessly abandoned the effort once more, overcome by a strange sense of euphoria.

Languidly shifting his field of vision, he noticed the door to the room stood ajar, revealing a sliver of the hallway beyond. Distantly, he heard a woman's laughter, faint and hollow in the otherwise deadening silence, like a voice at the bottom of a well. It was then he saw the shadow appear in the doorway and pause for a moment.

Lyla?

Then the door soundlessly swung open, and Janell Pickering walked in.

"Hello, Andy."

"Ms Pickering..."

"Perhaps you were expecting Lyla?"

Was that a hint of mockery in her voice?

"I–"

"Well, she's gone. And now it's only you...and I."

Andy said nothing as his high school social studies teacher ventured another step into the room, then slowly closed the door behind. Now there was only the blue glow from the nightlight, but it was enough to cast the edge of her red cape and horned eye-mask in a rim of eerie spectral light. That, and tint her otherwise yellowish-brown eyes with an ethereal greenish hue, as blue wavelengths mixed with xanthic eye pigment.

"Well, Andy?"

Again, he remained silent, waiting.

"Did you enjoy your time with her?"

Her words seemed to momentarily shake him free of his strange lethargy, enough so that he became suddenly aware that he was sprawled there on the bed before her observant stare–stark naked.

"Oh yes, I knew she had you down here. Of course I did, since I was the one who told her about this special base-ment." As she spoke, Ms Pickering casually walked around the room, unfastening her devil's cape as she went until it fell loosely to the floor. "Actually, it was planned that way," she went on, her fingers slowly unbuttoning her blouse until it too fell loosely to the floor. "In exchange for her helping me drug you with GBH, she got to have you first. But that's alright," she added, unzipping her trademarked woolen skirt and letting it slip away, "because now *I* get to have you..."

And there Ms Pickering stood, with her huge mouth and glistening piranha teeth, wearing nothing now save for black lace panties and matching bra, topped off by a red-horned devil's mask.

The cougar had found its prey.

"GB...*H?*" Andy vaguely murmured, trying to comprehend what that meant even as he stared dumbfounded at his teach-er, who stood regarding him as casually as if she stood in broad daylight at the front of a classroom of thirty pupils.

"Gamma Hydroxy Butyrate," she answered. "Often called 'lolllipop' but sometimes it's known as Liquid X or Georgia Home Boy, among other names." She approached the front edge of the large bed, one hand skimming down her panties as she planted first one knee and then the other onto the thick mattress. "I provided the GBH and Lyla slipped it into your drink somewhere along the way, when you had your head turned. The mellow intoxication you experienced was only partly due to the alcohol in your drink. The rest was lolli-pop..."

Andy tried to move, to struggle upward, but the same sense of pleasant lethargy overcame him once more.

Ms Pickering smiled.

"GBH relaxes you, Andy. Takes away your inhibitions too. But at the same time..." She moved toward him, rocking her knees back and forth as she progressed up the bed toward him, "it amplifies sexual intensity to a point you've never ex-perienced before...as you found out with Lyla."

Straddling Andy's knees, Janelle Pickering now paused and looked down at him, as if at something reached after a long and arduous journey. Then, slowly, her eyes never leav-ing his, she reached up and unhooked her bra, letting it fall by the wayside. Now, save for the devil's mask, Ms Janelle Pickering, Titanis High Social Studies teacher, was completely naked.

She moved forward again, until she paused once more, this time over her objective. From his prone position, she appear-ed to tower over him, like an Easter Island statue or a silent Egyptian sphinx, her enigmatic eyes locked to his. All along, she had been working toward this, he suddenly realized. From the first moment of the first day he first stepped foot into her classroom and she looked up and saw him–*this* had been her goal–to be here, naked, her shaved pussy poised mere inches from his dick, now at rest after its long, hard pounding of Lyla's red-haired muff. Slowly, she lowered her hips, by small increments, until her pubic hairs, shaved to a mere quarter-inch, made the faintest contact.

"Yes..." she breathed, almost like a paean to herself, her head cantilevered back as she gradually began to rock back and forth, back and forth, rhythmically stroking Andy's flacid member with almost religious fervor.

For the next minute and a half, she continued to tease his cock, like it had never been teased before by any high school girl, stroking it with the merest touch of her pubic hairs, careful not to make contact with her already moistened vulva.

Just yet...

To Andy's shock, certain Lyla had taken everything he'd had to give, he incredibly began to stiffen. As he did, Ms Pickering looked down at him again, her cougar eyes looking as if they were lit from behind; luminescent, superior.

"*Why?*" Andy whispered, even as he fought against his growing erection, against what was being done to him, of hoping Ms Pickering would stop.

And yet...

Hoping not.

"Because I chose you," she answered. "Months ago, in less time than it took for you to walk to your seat on the first day that you entered my class, I knew it would come to this." Gradually, she allowed her vulva to make its first, brief contact with his stiffening organ. "As it always does."

"What do you mean?" he asked, some part of him afraid to hear the answer, even while another part fought against the rising pleasure. Because seventeen year old boys weren't meant to fuck their teachers, and yet time and circumstance had somehow brought him here; he had to know why.

"I know what you're thinking, Andy. About what we're doing. About the propriety of it. About your contempt for me. The way you tuned me out in class. How you manipulated other students to doubt what I said. But I bided my time, you see. Because I knew that one day I would be sitting astride you, as I am right now, giving you an exquisite pleasure you will not be able to repeat."

And she was right.

Moment by moment, as the intensity grew, his inability to reject what Ms Pickering's firm, taut body was doing to him, as her hips swayed hypnotically back and forth, back and forth, brushing the length of his cock like a pendulum, each pass forging an ever-harder alloy of blood-engorged lust just barely contained behind a rising wall of unbearable pressure.

"Now I know why Lyla wanted you so badly. That's because you represent every high school girl's dream boy. What they all want. What most will never get; that is, unless they look like a Lyla...or a Jeena."

She saw the sudden look in his eye.

"Oh, yes. I know about Jeena. Every bit as beautiful as luscious little Lyla. But it was not Jeena you fucked tonight, was it, Andy?" She saw a glint of regret, mixed with guilt, flicker across his face, coming through the fog of alcohol and GHB. "Come tomorrow, how will you ever explain Lyla...or me?"

Andy didn't know.

All he knew was that it was a not-too-subtle hint of blackmail. Because whatever he had done with Lyla would not change how he felt about Jeena Kirtland.

"I could just get up and leave," Andy murmured, the first edge of defiance in his voice.

"You could," she agreed, dipping her vulva toward his cock once more, skillfully sliding herself onto its throbbing head, yet only allowing it to penetrate no deeper than an inch. "But you won't."

"This isn't...right," Andy gasped, fighting against the growing intensity of pleasure, as she began rhythmically stroking him again. "Teachers caught doing this get charged with...rape."

"Do they? Funny. For someone being raped you're as hard as a block of concrete inside my cunt, Andy. My, my, I wonder why. Could it be that you've just achieved in reality what every boy in America fantasizes every day of the week but will never have: the chance to fuck the brains out of his teacher?"

What boy hadn't dreamt that? Andy realized—including himself. For as much as he despised Ms Pickering, the thought of fucking her blind had long been on his mind, from the first moment he saw the cleavage of her ass beneath her tight woolen skirt to the insistent push of her breasts against her equally tight blouse. Was that why he was here, willingly letting her have her way with him–*because he wanted it?*

Her teasing was becoming unbearable.

In that instant, he fought the urge to plunge the full length of his dick into her wet hole, teacher or not, but Ms Pickering was controlling everything, only allowing herself to be penetrated no deeper than a tantalizing inch, knowing the suffering it was causing him, even as she rocked his cock back and forth between her labial lips with a mocking smirk on her face.

"Feels good, doesn't it, Andy? Feels like you're learning cooperation, doesn't it? Because you have to go along to get along. You know, teacher, pupil, fucking like this. Just the right after-school activity, don't you think? After all, what healthy boy could resist?"

It does feel...good, Andy found himself thinking.

Faster, goddammit...*faster.*

"Ah-Ah-Ah, Andy. Don't you dare cream my cunt just yet. Because I've other duties for you."

"But...why me?" he gasped, his member pulsing at the edge of orgasm. "Why not some other guy?"

"Why you? Well, why not you? After all, you can't be thinking that you're the very first and only boy in one of my classes that I've fucked, can you? Oh, no. I've taken pleasure from three other Titanis High boys already. Did you really think otherwise? That you were that special?"

His dick nearing supernova, he didn't know what he'd thought.

"Still, one boy did turn down my charms, during a previous school year. And that was something I just couldn't abide," Ms Pickering said, her voice trailing wistfully. "Since then, he's become the school outcast and designated troublemaker. And now he may even end up going to jail. But then, I warned him there would be consequences..."

In a sudden flash of insight, Andy blurted: "The locker. Tony Scarletti's locker. Those messages. Rodney suspected they had been written by...*a teacher*." He looked up into Ms Pickering's enigmatic eyes. "That teacher was *you*."

Ms Pickering laughed and tilted forward, Andy's cock popping free of her pussy like a cork from a champagne bottle. "You've had enough of *that*, little boy," she said, her mouth coming to within inches of his face. "I'll let you come when I *say* you can."

She laughed again, delightedly, feeling in complete control."Of course it was me, Andy. And yes, as a teacher I have access to the school's security cameras, so I made sure no record was left of my two little visits to Tony Scarletti's locker. You see, two years ago Rodney was assigned to my home room, where he sat for the first fifteen minutes of every new school day while I took attendance. He was always quiet, always well behaved, although he tended to stare at girls. But once, just once, I caught him looking at me. And when I did I noticed a rather hard lump between his legs where none should rightfully have been. Suffice to say I've always been attracted to good-looking but socially awkward boys, or, in your case, rebellious misfits. But Rodney Crutchley, big, crude, roughly attractive boy that he is, rejected the greatest sexual experience of a lifetime when he rebuffed my overtures—and that's something I simply couldn't forgive.

"Nor was I pleased with your behavior in class, so that's when I decided to mark up Tony Scarletti's locker in order to have Titanis High's star quarterback teach you a lesson. And when I found out you had befriended Rodney, I decided to split you two apart for good by marking up Scarletti's locker a second time. Why I ever resorted to such juvenile tactics I'll never know. Perhaps it was a holdover from my own high school days, when I made it a point to always settle scores. In Rodney's case, he was my designated charity case that year, a big, hulking virgin I wanted to conquer. But he missed out. Now look where you're at, in the place he could've been, living the dream every high school boy dreams: fucking the shit out of his school teacher."

Andy said nothing.

But now he was listening more carefully.

"I have a knack for reading minds, Andy. Especially boys like you. And right now you're wondering if there's something wrong with me, aren't you? That as good as it feels, you're still thinking a teenage boy like you and an older woman like me shouldn't be here, doing this. Well, I suppose it's reasonable to consider that, looking back...For it is true that I've always had a 'thing' for young, good-looking teens like you. Even, on occasion, unpolished ones like Rodney. Insatiable, perhaps? Yes, that word sounds about right. And if I had to say where those desires came from, I'd have to confess it started with my brother..."

Andy swallowed.

Oh, Jesus.

"He was sixteen back then," Janelle Pickering went on, "and I was twelve. Very handsome, my brother. We lived in the Pennsylvania hill country, far from the nearest town. That can be torture to a sixteen year old boy, with no girls for three miles around. That is...except his cute little sister. And that's how it all started, I suppose. Looking back, I drove him to it. Coming out of the bathroom wearing nothing but my panties. Things like that. And yes, I did it deliberately, sort of as a game. And then, one thing led to another... That was the beginning, I suppose. Of my need. A burning, never satisfied need..."

CHAPTER 23

"My only regret was my brother," Janelle Pickering wistfully carried on. "You see, my father got home early from the coal mines one Saturday afternoon, and caught my brother grunting on top of me like a pig in heat, pounding me raw, and me gasping. He thought I was gasping in fright and desperation. To this day he never found out I was actually gasping with unbearable, forbidden pleasure. Sadly, my brother was sent away to reform school, after my father savagely beat him half to death, then on to prison for another ten years, once he turned eighteen..."

As Janelle Pickering spoke, she began teasing him anew, almost unconsciously, edging a bit forward as she stroked her shaved vagina gently along his abdomen. But Andy remained mute, unmoving, as she relentlessly went on: "I testified in court that he raped me, of course. As if I had any other choice. He said I wanted it–which I did–but in court I pretended otherwise. When the judge heard that–that my brother was accusing an innocent twelve year old girl of such evil lusts, well...that sealed his fate."

Still hard as rock, Andy realized he was having the strangest sexual encounter he had ever known, even as he continued listening to Ms Pickering's bizarre tale of childhood molestation: "During his second year in prison, my brother was gang-raped by four black convicts in the prison laundry then thrown over the third floor railing to his death. Not long after that, I left home, to live with an aunt and uncle in Philadelphia where I finished high school, before going on to college in Michigan. I wanted to be a teacher, you see. Looking back, I realize now why–because I could not help being attracted to boys. Not men, mind you, but boys like you. It was a need I could not deny myself. As I cannot deny myself now, Andy..."

She edged up his body a little more, her vagina now poised over the center of his chest, stroking, stroking, ever so delicately, as she went on with her recollection: "Since then, I've had many boys, as the years went by. From school to school, across many states. Which at times created problems for me. I taught for awhile in Omaha, until a boy I had wonderful sex with bragged to his friends, and they in turn told others. I left, after school authorities promised not to press criminal charges. From there, I moved on to other states, over the years, having my fill of boys along the way...boys just like you.

"But I was always fastidious in my choices, and seldom did I make an error in a boy I had set my eyes upon. Once in Nevada, true, while teaching in Las Vegas. And again with Rodney Crutchley, a boy I sensed a certain sexual longing that had long been repressed."

Andy struggled to find his voice, fighting against the lingering effects of too much alcohol spiked with 'lollipop' and his own confused, seventeen year old emotions: "Were you ever...married?"

Janelle Pickering edged up his chest a bit more as she answered: "Married? Let's just say that marriage was never in the cards for me, Andy. At least, not for what I wanted. And then, a few years ago, an old college friend told me about a teaching position at Titanis High, and so Texas became my latest home."

With that, she moved up to his face, touching her vaginal lips teasingly against his nose.

"What makes you think I won't report you?" Andy said, seeing something most teen boys would never see in their wildest dreams–their teacher's cunt in extreme closeup.

Ms Pickering laughed deliciously. "Report what? That you fucked Lyla Van der Velden and later invited your Social Studies teacher in for an encore performance? Just imagine what a local news sensation that would make." She laughed again, her eyes blazing down on him. "Because when I'm done with you, Andy Hupp, you'll be hanging around after class every day. Like a little puppy dog. Begging. Begging for another night like this. It will be the worst torture you've ever known, remembering a pleasure beyond what an amateur like Lyla Van der Velden could ever give. And then a day will come when I move on to another boy, as I always do, and then you'll want to take your own life–as one unfortunate young man did in Florida, when I taught school down in Miami."

Andy's eyes widened. "You mean...you drove him to suicide? Used him up and then–"

"Discarded him? But why not, Andy? What do you think the Youth For Social Justice Club is all about, anyway? I'll tell you. It's about the world that's coming. About free sex. Endless sex. With anyone. With everyone. At anytime. Anywhere. No more boundaries, Andy. Because that's what progressives like me and Dr. Adler are after. No more boundaries with our bodies or with our countries. Here, Europe, Australia, wherever. Free sex for everyone, free movement for everyone. Besides, why shouldn't teachers fuck their students? For that matter, why shouldn't brothers fuck their sisters? God is dead, you know. So why shouldn't Mexicans move here? Why shouldn't we all believe in equality too, whether it actually exists or not? It's our feelings that count, not facts. And you're starting to learn that, aren't you? And you're learning something else: that we can't be stopped. That's why fence-sitters like you better join us while you can, Andy. Because it's my philosophy and it's Dr. Adler's and it will be the philosophy of the world before we're done."

That said, she inched slightly backward as she repositioned her vagina directly over his mouth, until Andy had a magnified view of her pussy, sweet with the scent of perfume, like a honey-nectared Venus flytrap—waiting to ensnare its victim. Yet he also saw in her vagina a vertical reflection of her horizontal mouth, gaping and hungry, as it lowered toward his lips. Even as it did, he struggled to twist away.

"Don't fight it, Andy. Don't fight my pussy. It's your entire world now—my pussy. All that you will see for the next two hours." She exhaled luxuriantly. "Now eat it."

And with that, she ground her vagina hard into his mouth.

Andy twisted away, his will to resist strengthening.

"Eat it, Andy."

"No."

"Eat it."

Angered, she crushed her vagina down again, grinding her labial lips deep into his mouth.

"*I SAID EAT IT!*"

With all his strength, his lungs burst forth: "Fuck you, whore!" as he shoved her off. She thumped to the floor in the same instant he rolled off the bed, snatching up his clothes as he staggered to the door, drugged, disoriented and confused, but now determined to get away.

Hopping on one leg and then another as he yanked on his jeans, he stumbled down the hallway toward a door at the far end. Reaching it, he dug into a pocket and pulled out his cell phone. Time: 2:08 am. Stunned at how late it was, he tried to understand where the night had gone—until he realized that for the last eight hours he had been lost in a twilight zone of alcohol, 'lollipop', and cock-teasing sex—

Then he noticed he had a new text message and tabbed it open:

HEY, ANDY – WHEN YOU NEVER SHOWED UP TJ CALLED AND TRIED TO REACH YOU BUT THERE WAS NO ANSWER. SO HE CALLED LYLA VAN DER VELDEN'S CELL INSTEAD AND SHE SAID YOUR PHONE WASN'T WORKING BUT THAT YOU'D DECIDED TO STAY LONGER AT THE PARTY AND FOR US TO JUST GO ON HOME. SOUNDED FISHY BUT THEN MAYBE LYLA'S COMPANY WAS MORE INTERESTING THAN OURS. ANYWAY, WE DECIDED TO DRIVE UP TO KLIMMEN'S POINT JUST TO TALK. TJ HAD A COUPLE OF SIX PACKS

WITH HIM AND I BROUGHT A BOTTLE OF BRANDY I SWIPED FROM HOME. YOU KNOW, TO CELEBRATE OUR MOVIE PROJECT. NOW WE'RE OUT HERE AT KLIMMEN'S POINT, JUST THE THREE OF US, JOKING AND DRINKING AND TALKING ABOUT OUR FUTURE. WE'RE STILL SHAKEN UP ABOUT THE LANCE BUTTERFIELD NEWS. BETWEEN THE STORE CLERK AND HIM WE HOPE YOU'LL AGREE IT'S TIME WE WENT TO THE POLICE. DESPITE WHAT'S HAPPENED I'M STILL FEELING PRETTY GOOD. MAYBE IT'S BECAUSE THIS IS THE FIRST TIME IN MY LIFE I'VE HAD SOMETHING WONDERFUL TO LOOK FORWARD TO—YOU.

LOVE, ALWAYS, ALWAYS, ALWAYS!
JINK
💙 💙 💙

A follow-up text had arrived thirty-seven minutes later:

JEENA AND TJ JUST TOLD ME SOME HEADLIGHTS ARE COMING UP THE ROAD TO WHERE WE'RE PARKED. DON'T KNOW WHO IT IS. NOW THEY'VE STOPPED AND SOME GUY IS GETTING OUT. NOW TWO MORE. ALL MEXICANS. NOT SURE, BUT SOMETHING'S NOT RIGHT. WILL CALL YOU LATER.

RODNEY

But there was no 'later'.

No further messages had arrived.

Feeling queasy, with Rodney's and Jeena's words still echoing in his mind, Andy glanced forlornly back down the hallway, reliving all that he'd done during his long night of *piña colada*/Rohypnol debauchery, and for a moment lowered his head in shame, especially over his betrayal of Jink.

Better call them, he dimly thought, still unsteady on his feet.

But first, he had to get away from this house.

Far away.

But even as he pulled open the door, leading to who-knew-where, he heard a faint voice somewhere behind, as if someone were speaking urgently into a cell phone; someone who sounded a lot like Ms Pickering.

Hesitating no further, he lurched up a flight of concrete stairs until he reached the top, where he came up against a second door. Yanking it wide, he found himself outside, somewhere along one side of the four story Gothic house, standing beneath a massive orange moon hung low in the starlit sky. Darting his eyes left, then right, he sprinted off in what he reasoned must be the front of the house, the long curving drive–and freedom.

Then he noticed the van.

An old Chevy model, by the looks of it, boxy and window-less along both sides. A type of cargo van once commonly seen on America's roads, some thirty years ago. But what was a beat-up vehicle like that doing here, parked alongside this multi-million dollar house–at 2 am in the morning?

He had no idea, even as he slowed going past it. Suddenly, the twin doors swung outward and two men emerged. But what froze Andy in this tracks was the sight of a third person, lying in the back, naked and hog-tied.

Lyla Van der Velden.

Andy's shock froze him dead in his tracks.

Instantly, the two men rushed forward and seized him.

"Well, well, well. Looky here. One teenaged asshole signed, sealed, and delivered. Saves us the trouble of having to go back inside and pry him loose from that whore," the scruffy man with the deep tan and shaggy, dirty-blond hair said, as the other, a swarthy Hispanic, pulled out a pair of hand-cuffs from his back pocket. Only then, as he stepped out of the shadows, did Andy realize who it was: Coach Manuel Ortega. Stunned, speechless, he stood numbly as his arms were quickly pinned behind his back.

"Get the cuffs on him," the scruffy man said, in a tone of voice that indicated he was the one in charge.

"With pleasure," Ortega replied with a savage grin, snap-ping cold steel across Andy's wrists.

"Forget the duct tape around his ankles. We haven't got time. Just get his cell phone and wallet."

Handcuffed and stripped of his possessions, Andy was hustled into the back of the van alongside Lyla Van der Vel-den and the doors slammed shut. A moment later they were in motion, headed for the main gate. As they left the mansion grounds and swung a left, the scruffy man, at the wheel, turned to Ortega: "Damn. We forgot to tape his mouth."

"Like you said, wasn't time," Ortega reminded, glancing back at Andy Hupp. "But don't worry—that trash can punk makes a peep I'll shut him up." He flashed moonlit teeth again. "But good."

From where he lay, feet toward the back, head toward the front, arms handcuffed behind, Andy could just twist his neck around and make out stray blobs of bluish street light smearing past the front windshield, like distant stars drifting beyond the port of a starship moving through a lonely stellar void.

As the van drove on, keeping within the 25 mph speed limit as it moved slowly past multi-million dollar homes lining the upscale residential street, Manuel Ortega twisted in his seat once more, staring back at him, two bottomless black eyes glinting like a tarantula's from down a dark hole—cold, pitiless, evil; the eyes of a murderer. And he and Lyla, he realized with a sudden stab of fear, were now in his grasp.

Trying not to panic, Andy shifted his head in the direction of Lyla, lying beside him, naked save for her lavender panties. Handcuffed too, she was also duct taped across the mouth and ankles. Unnecessary, he could see, since she was out cold—either drunk or drugged or both. Checking his immediate surroundings, he saw a pile of clothes lying next to her, carelessly tossed aside.

Andy tried to process everything he saw and everything that was happening. As he did, a sickening feeling tumbled far down into his gut, like cold chunks of jagged ice, as the horrible truth sunk in: he and Lyla had been abducted.

Just like–

Like...

Brett Hinkle and Tina Sawyer.

And by a criminal gang so depraved, so evil, that it went beyond mere car theft and drug dealing into the nether world of kidnapping and, he now suspected—sex trafficking. If so, he and Lyla were entangled in a terrible nightmare, of the kind he had heard about but never believed could happen—*to him.*

Get a grip, he angrily told himself.

Or guaranteed you and Lyla are dead.

With great effort, Andy Hupp slowed his heaving lungs and let himself go still; he would need all his wits about him if he were to have even the thinnest chance of getting out of this mess alive. After a moment, he twisted his head around again, focusing on what the two men up front were talking about—

"The cartel wants these two flown out right away, Schmidt," Manuel Ortega said to the driver, as they progressed down the affluent street. "Tonight. No bar hopping, no getting high, no pussy, no nothing. Tonight."

"I don't need you telling me my job, Ortega. I'm the pilot, remember. You're just the muscle."

Ortega let go a sinister chuckle. "There's a rumor inside the cartel that you've been smoking a bit too much Grape Krush lately. They're worried you might start getting sloppy in your duties and miss a scheduled flight. So they thought you needed a friendly reminder." He pulled out a switch-blade and nonchalantly snicked it open, digging dirt from beneath a fingernail. "I'm the friendly reminder."

The man called Schmidt glanced obliquely at the blade in Ortega's dark hands, sharp and cold like a shard of ice. Almost, he knew, as sharp and cold as the man who held it. Of Ortega he knew little, except that he had killed a number of men the cartel did not like, especially those it suspected of dereliction of duty. Whereas Schmidt carried out contract killings made to look like accidents, for a tidy fee—such as that of Lance Butterfield—Ortega was rumored to be a cartel enforcer, who 'unhired' no longer needed personnel.

"Shit, I smoke Grape Krush even while I'm flying. So I'm usually pretty fucked up anyway by the time I land."

Ortega shook his head. "One day, Schmidt, you will go too far and smoke too much. And then you will have to answer to the cartel..."

Both men laughed, but not in a mutually friendly way.

But now Andy knew the name of the driver: Schmidt.

Schmidt and Ortega.

Both working for 'the cartel'.

And that meant—

"Hey, Hupp!" Ortega suddenly yelled back. "You shit your pants yet?"

Steeling his nerves, because he dare not let them see any fear, he shot back: "When I do I'll make sure you smell it."

Titanis High's star coach wasn't expecting bravado.

"Before we get through with you, *puta*, you will," he assured. "Because you're going for a long trip, Hupp. A very long trip. Down to where the bananas grow. And when you get there you're going to be strapped to a table, face down. Naked, Hupp. Do you hear me? Naked. And what happens next you don't want to know. But I think you can guess: they're going to make a punk out of you. A woman. A *puta*. And by the time they're finished—"

"Shut up, Ortega," Schmidt warned. "No need to let him know what's in store. Remember, I got to fly these two down and don't want them pukin' and shittin' all over themselves thinking about it."

Ortega chuckled, dark and ominous, his head lolling back with evil mirth. "Maybe you ain't shit your pants just yet, punk. But you will. *Sí*, my little trashcan snoop. That's because I know you killed my nephew. Out on Kilbane Road. Don't ask me how I know. I just do. And when my brothers and uncles get their hands on you you'll be sorry you were ever born...'

Ortega knew?

But how?

And then, through his drug-hazed mind, Andy remembered: Jinky's bottle of *SNARK!*—accidentally dropped at the scene where Raul crashed and burned. Somehow, Ortega had figured out what had happened, pieced it all together in his criminal mind. Then, traced it back to the Spot-N-The-Road convenience store and forced the hapless clerk to identify them, afterward, along with a fellow thug or two, slitting his throat and stealing the store surveillance video. All in a day's work for the ruthless Sinaloa Cartel, Andy grimly realized. And yet, if he hadn't insisted on sticking his nose in places where it didn't belong by making a movie about Tina Sawyer and Brett Hinkle, none of this ever would've happened...

Finally, feeling far from brave, Andy nevertheless decided to fake Manuel Ortega out: "I don't know what you're talking about."

"Hear that, Schmidt? The punk says he doesn't know what I'm talking about. Sounds like we got a fucking comedian in the back, eh? But he won't be laughing for long once he gets down to Guatemala."

Schmidt, the driver, blew out a breath of exasperation. "Brilliant, you dumb beaner. Now you've told him where he's going."

Ortega tapped the blade of his knife on Schmidt's brawny shoulder. "Don't call me a beaner again, gringo. I've killed *güeros* like you for much less."

Schmidt stared straight ahead. "Okay, then. How 'bout I just call you a goddamn spic?"

Ortega laughed, loudly, but Andy could tell it was not one of mirth, but a deadly warning. "Very funny, you dope fiend. But one day when all this land is filled with my brown *compadres*, as soon it will be, it is I who will be laughing. Besides," he added, "what does it matter if the punk knows where he's going?" He glanced back at Andy. "He won't be coming back."

"Why are you doing this?" Andy asked, from out of the darkness. He knew why, but he needed to keep Ortega distracted if his plan were to succeed. And he had to hurry, because once they left the neighborhood and reached the county highway, Schmidt would accelerate to the posted speed limit of 65 mph and then it would be too late.

Ortega chuckled. "Because you and the girl are prime merchandise, that's why. Personally selected by someone whose name can't be mentioned. You see, punk, certain people will pay big money to fuck prime merchandise. Or didn't a smartass trashcan peeper like you know that?"

Andy knew, alright.

Sex trafficking was a growing menace in certain parts of the world, and now America was a target zone too. And in this part of the world most of the abductions were being committed by the Mexican cartels, and those who worked for them.

Like one particular high school coach.

"What kind of people?" Andy asked, trying to sound both dumb and curious at the same time, even as he slowly scooched backward toward the rear doors. He'd once been inside an old cargo van like this, and knew that it had interior lever-style handles that could be pulled inward, unlocking the door latches. Easy, if only he could somehow get into a crouch and push his handcuffed arms against them, then use his fingers to pull. But he had to hurry, before his two kidnappers got onto the highway and went high-speed. At that point, it would be far too dangerous and far too late.

Without turning around, Manuel Ortega snickered with contempt. "Rich motherfuckers, punk. So rich you wouldn't believe it. And they have special tastes. Some like redheads like your *gringa* girlfriend. Others....they like pretty boys." He laughed again. "Like you."

If that was to be his fate, Andy thought, he'd rather be dead. And he'd kill Lyla too before he'd let her be subjected to that.

Lyla...

Poor little lost Social Justice Warrior.

Is this the world you wanted? he wondered, looking over at her. Because this is the world Rothman Adler and Janelle

Pickering want you to help them build. A world where illegal aliens, criminals, and moral corruption run rampant in our land, all in the name of "cultural diversity".

But now was not the time to lament all the confused and misled Lylas of the world—if he were to get away. To do so, he'd have to make his escape without her. As hard as that was, he knew it was Lyla's best chance as well—his getting free and going for help.

With that in mind, Andy Hupp slowly, silently, brought himself up into a crouch, even as he slid his feet steadily backward toward the van's double doors, his eyes locked to the back of Manuel Ortega's oily black head, praying it would not suddenly turn around.

"Now I know what happened to Brett Hinkle," Andy went on, by way of keeping the conversation going, "and Tina Sawyer."

Ortega let his head rock back against the seat's head rest, gurgling with obscene laughter. "Now there was some fine pussy, right Schmidt? Raped that high school whore but good before we shipped her ass south." He laughed richly. "Fringe benefits of the job, you might say..." He picked up his knife and began picking under his fingernails again, sighing, as if over fond memories. "Just like your *gringa* girlfriend back there, punk. Schmidt and I ripped her clothes off as soon as we got her in the van and banged her good. Then she got all hysterical while she was putting her panties back on so Schmidt knocked her cold with one punch. Must be all that dope he smokes. Fucking bastard doesn't know his own strength."

Andy glanced down at Lyla, she of the beautiful face but corrupted mind. As he did a stray beam of street light swept through the windshield down the length of the van, briefly touching her face. Now he saw the bruise, and finally understood the cause of her unconsciousness.

I've got to get out of this van, he thought. Up ahead, about two blocks, lay the county highway. Got to, his mind raged, because I won't have a second chance.

Without being able to see, his cuffed hands explored the metal surface of the van doors. There. The door handles. All he had to do was pull them inward, and the door latches would release. But when....*when?*

"After the stop sign, one more block to the main road," Ortega muttered. "Then a two hour drive to the airstrip and you and your cargo are off to the dope-smokin' paradise of Central America."

Schmidt just grunted as he slowed the van. The last thing the bush pilot wanted was to get pulled over for running a stop sign with two kidnapped teens in the back, both handcuffed and one freshly beaten and raped.

Gradually, Schmidt applied the brakes.

As he did, Andy tensed.

Out the windshield the teen saw the stop sign come floating up, its glossy red surface bathed in the ethereal light of a street lamp.

Slower, slower...

Now!

Instantly, Andy yanked the toggled door handles and bumped hard with his ass, knocking the doors outward. Falling backward like a scuba diver over the edge of a boat, he plopped onto the asphalt, rolled, and came to his feet.

"Motherfucker!" Ortega screeched, ripping his head around. "The punk got out!"

"Motherfucker is right!" the bush pilot shouted. "You dumbass beaner! You we're supposed to keep an eye on him!"

Andy wasted no time.

In a nanosecond he engaged warp 12, tearing zigzaggedly down the silent residential street of multi-million dollar homes, running for his life. Snatching a quick look behind, the man called Schmidt had popped out of the driver's side door and was already punching numbers into a cell phone as Ortega came sprinting after him.

Andy ran.

He ran in the street, up sidewalks, across lawns, around parked cars, hopped fire hydrants, hedges, and landscape boulders, darting here, darting there, looking for anyway to ditch the athletically-toned gym coach. Andy's only advantage was his longer legs, but he was certain that Ortega probably had more lasting power, as he made his living being physically-fit every day of the week. That is, when he wasn't dealing drugs, kidnapping people, or murdering convenience store clerks.

At the street corner Andy swung left, heading back up the street where the Halloween party had taken place. Though it was past 2 am there might still be a few partiers there. Knowing they all couldn't be involved in this criminal ring, he could get help. Reach a phone. Call the police.

Almost...almost out of power, he thought.

Behind, Manuel Ortega was gaining fast.

Then Andy saw headlights flaring in the distance, coming down the street toward him. Huffing and puffing, his dilithium crystals rapidly failing, he ran toward it, stumbling, gasping, yelling–

"Help!"

CHAPTER 24

At the sight of Andy Hupp's flailing arms, the car came to a screeching halt, simultaneous with the teen slamming sidelong against it, frightened and gasping.

A car window powered down.

"Andy...? *Andy?* Is that you? What the−?"

"Mr. Meevers!" Andy burst out. "I−you−behind−!"

"What happened, Andy? I saw you earlier at the party with a girl and then you wandered off somewhere...I thought you had gone home hours ago."

"I−I'm in trouble, Mr. Meevers. Please−can you give me a ride?"

"Of course. Get in."

Andy spun around, revealing his handcuffed arms.

"My God...what...how in the world−?"

"No time to explain, sir. Just open the door."

Budd Meevers leaned across the wide seat of his Lincoln Navigator and pushed open the door. Andy jumped in, squirmed sideways, and pulled the door shut again.

"Now go!" he pleaded.

Principal Meevers sped off down the street.

"Andy, what happened? The handcuffs...you...*out here!*"

Still gasping, Andy Hupp turned toward the school principal: "I need to call the police, sir. Right away. They took my cell phone and they have Lyla Van der Velden−!"

"Slow down, Andy. Take it easy. What's this about Lyla Van der Velden?"

"They took her!"

"Who took her?"

"Coach Ortega and somebody named Schmidt."

"Our coach? Coach Ortega?"

"The same. He's part of a crime ring that—"

"Whoa there, pardner. Those are some serious charges. Are you certain it was our Coach Ortega?"

"Yes! He and this guy Schmidt kidnapped us from the party. In a van I just escaped from a minute before I ran into you. And they've still got Lyla. I know how crazy it sounds but it's true!"

Principal Meevers nodded his head reflectively, then looked soberly at Andy: "I just left the party myself a few minutes ago, one of the last to leave. For the past few hours I've been sitting in our host's library with some friends enjoying some good conversation and even finer brandy while you younger people partied downstairs. And now here you are telling me this wild story about being kidnapped."

"It's not a wild story, sir! We were kidnapped by Coach Ortega and this other guy! Not only that, but I think Ms Pickering was in on it!"

Budd Meevers whistled. "Those are some pretty serious charges, Andy. Ortega is a respected athletic coach and Ms Pickering an established teacher. What proof do you have?"

Andy twisted in his seat, exposing his handcuffed arms. "These!"

Meevers smiled indulgently. "Look, Andy. It's okay. So you and this girl went off into some private corner and got a little kinky. You know, handcuffs. Bondage. That kind of thing. Nothing to be ashamed of."

"But I'm telling the truth!" Andy insisted. "You've got to believe me!"

Again Meevers nodded. "Maybe... But I need to learn more of the details before we call the police. Remember, I've not only the reputation of two fine teachers to protect, but also that of Titanis High. So let's get back to my house before we decide on calling the police. Okay? It's only about fifteen minutes away and that will give you time to calm down and get your thoughts in order. In the meantime, start from the beginning and tell me everything you did and everyone you talked to at the party. The police will want to know that too, so now's the time to get your facts straight..."

Andy told him everything, from his introduction to Dr. Rothman Adler to the illegal alien bartender to the drunken actor to his time with Lyla Van der Velden, censoring only the specific details of their encounter. Likewise with his encounter with Janelle Pickering, telling Meevers that she admitted drugging him with some sort of date-rape drug and forcing herself upon him.

"Forcing herself upon...*you?*" Budd Meevers echoed, his voice disbelieving. "But she's a teacher, Andy."

"That didn't stop her from climbing naked on top of me, Mr. Meevers," Andy exclaimed.

Meevers slowly nodded, let go a slow whistle, and said nothing for a long time. Then: "Okay, I've heard enough. When we get to my house we'll call the police. But first we need to get those handcuffs off. Deal?"

Wordlessly, Andy nodded.

They drove the rest of the way in silence.

When they reached Principal Meevers' house a short while later, the first thing Andy Hupp noticed was its isolation from the main highway, situated down a long, winding, graveled road accessed through a dense grove of live oaks. He'd never given a thought to where his principal lived, and somehow had imagined him residing in some sort of Leave It To Beaver type neighborhood of two story houses fronted by neatly manicured lawns. Indeed, such neighborhoods existed throughout the Texas Hill Country, but this house was not one of them, hidden as it was at the back end of thirty acres, as Meevers had pointed out on the way in.

When they reached the end of the road Meevers pulled to a stop in front of a sprawling one story house faced with irregular stones of craggy pink granite, with deep, recessed windows behind which murky splotches of yellow light glowed.

As they got out, Andy paused and looked around at the surrounding night, pricked with the cold light of distant stars. Nearby, gnarled oaks hovered against the raven sky like a black & white negative slowly emerging from a photographer's development tray, dark gray against an even darker background. It was as if all the color of the world had been drained away, leaving only shades of ash and pewter and charcoal. Then, with a sudden sense of disquiet, he realized that nobody knew exactly where he was at that moment, nor had any way of reaching him on his cellphone—now that it was in the possession of Ortega and Schmidt.

"Coming?"

Andy's mind suddenly jerked back to the present, realizing he had been lost in thought. "Yeah," he vaguely answered, following after Budd Meevers.

As they left the driveway and stepped onto the flagstone-paved walkway, Andy expected Meevers to veer left toward the front entrance, fronted by clusters of Mediterranean fan palms lit by ornamental green lighting. Instead, they proceeded straight ahead, along the right side of the house, toward a back gate.

"At this late hour Mrs. Meevers is asleep so I don't want to disturb her," Budd Meevers explained, as they reached the gate and proceeded toward the back of the property.

Andy made no reply as he diligently followed after his school principal, moving across a large expanse of dew-shimmered grass glistening beneath a huge harvest moon. Here and there massive oak trees arose, like giant black mushrooms against the starlit sky. And ahead, he caught sight of a small cottage, nestled in among the trees.

"What's that?" Andy asked.

"Just an old mother-in-law house," Meevers answered, as they started up a curved walkway leading toward it. "Until last year, that is, when she passed on. Now I use it for my personal study, rec room, and man cave."

Pulling forth a set of keys as he came up to the door, Budd Meevers unlocked it and motioned for Andy to follow. Inside, Meevers gestured toward a long black leather sofa and invited Andy to sit.

"Make yourself comfortable, Andy. In the meantime, I'll be out back in my workshop rooting up some tools. When I return, we'll have those handcuffs off in a jiffy."

Andy nodded and sat down, even as Meevers disappeared through a side door and closed it softly behind. But ten minutes later, with Meevers still absent, he started getting restless. Curious, his eyes began to wander about the room, meandering across the walnut-paneled walls, over the green-felt surface of a nearby pool table, past a 70 inch wall-mounted TV screen and, finally, coming to rest again on the fireplace mantle in front of him.

Where the heck was Meevers? he wondered. Swinging his head around, he looked at the door through which his principal had vanished. No sound. Nothing. Still restless, Andy got to his feet and started drifting around the small living room, running his eyes over end tables and wall shelves covered in vases and knickknacks and other odds and ends; the detritus of a lifetime. Wall plaques and framed photographs mostly reflected Principal Meevers life and achievements, just like in his high school office.

There were trophies from his junior high and high school days, from the Debate Club to his participation as a player on the school's basketball team to various awards from his years as a Boy Scout, eventually rising all the way up to Eagle Scout. Along a credenza were more awards, medals, and the like, including a Boy Scout knife engraved with his name and the year it had been awarded. Certainly more awards, medals, and whatnot than Andy had ever earned. But then...he'd never joined the Boy Scouts or a debate club or a basketball team in his life, so that was no surprise.

But where the hell was Meevers? he wondered again.

Or a telephone?

Only, strangely, neither was in sight.

And now it was past 3 am.

And here he was, miles from home.

Robbed of his cell phone.

Shackled like Kunta Kinte.

Totally alone...

Andy moved down the length of the credenza and came to a sudden stop, where a scrapbook lay. Idly, he twisted sideways and, stretching his handcuffed hands around, managed to flip it open. Just old photos, news clippings, and some long-faded ribbons, awarded during Meevers' school and Boy Scout days. Twisting and flipping more pages, he examined Meevers' high school years: Freshman. Sophomore. Junior. And then Senior. Mostly pictures of him goofing off with the high school kids of his day, with an occasional teacher standing in the background, looking on, not much different than now.

Funny, Andy thought.

Not much different at all...

Another flipped page and there was Budd Meevers again, attending his first year of college at Michigan State University.

He paused, thinking.

Michigan State...

Vaguely, he remembered hearing that name more than once over the past few months, here and there. Only, he couldn't remember exactly where. Maybe it was the lingering aftereffects of the Rohypnol and three rum-soaked *piña coladas*. But something about that name—or was it the place?—seemed important; something that he should strive to remember, as if there were some important connection he needed to make...

But what?

Unable to remember, he twisted sideways again and flipped over another page of the scrapbook, then stopped. What was this doing here? he wondered. A news article? About some long ago crime? Leaning forward, he examined the faded, yellowish-brown news clipping:

UNKNOWN YOUTHS TORCH HOUSE – MAN SEVERELY BURNED

Sometime during the night, a pedestrian out for a walk said he noticed several youths enter through a backyard gate via an alleyway along Red Oak Avenue. Thinking one of them must live there and the others were merely friends of his, the witness said he thought nothing of it and walked on. But an hour later the house was in flames and the actual resident of the house, a Mr. Henry Fitchins, aged sixty-nine, was found by firemen in his bedroom, unconscious and suffering severe burns...

After reading the article, Andy looked up, not sure why Mr. Meevers would include such a grim article in his scrapbook of otherwise lighthearted school memories. Curious, he twisted around and flipped over the next page, and found another article dated a week later: AUTHORITIES STILL HAVE NO CLUES REGARDING HOUSE FIRE. Flipping over another page, he found yet another article on the house fire, this one dated five years later:

STILL NO LEADS ON YOUTHS WHO BURNED
MAN'S HOUSE FIVE YEARS EARLIER

Five years after an eyewitness saw three youths enter the backyard property of a house which later burned to the ground and resulted in the death of the owner still remain unknown, despite public appeals for them to come forward and explain what they were doing there at that time of night. Since then, it has been learned that Mr. Henry Fitchins had had an altercation with several youths tossing trash onto his front lawn several months prior to the torching of his house, and that they had exchanged words. Although the youths refused to pick up their discarded soda cans, authorities have no proof these were the same youths seen entering Henry Fitchins backyard months later, shortly before his house went up in flames. As part of the still active investigation, local police are

315

After finishing, Andy flipped the page once more, but there were no more news articles. Instead, he was looking at an 8 x 10 photo of Meevers, standing among a group of fellow college students outside a Michigan State University building. Seven in all, Meevers stood dead center, tall and tanned, his arm draped around a female college student—*Janelle Pickering*.

Andy swallowed.

Hard.

Something terribly wrong here...

How could Ms Pickering have been a college student at the same time as Budd Meevers—a man at least ten years her senior.

Unless...

Unless she was much older than she appeared—not at all a woman in her early thirties as he and other students had always assumed, but more like her late thirties, if not early forties.

Holy shit, Batman!

A stealth cougar!

And to think she had shoved her middle-aged cunt smack dab into the middle of his face.

Fighting not to retch, the teen's mind relived his last hours at the Halloween party, his mind lost in a fog of alcohol as Lyla helped their Social Studies teacher drug him with the date-rape drug Rohypnol—all while Coach Ortega waited outside preparing to kidnap the two of them as soon as Ms Pickering had had her fun. And then...Budd Meevers—coming down the street, as if by coincidence—when it wasn't that at all.

Coming...

To intercept him.

Yes.

Intercept him.

Meevers, alerted by Schmidt's cellphone call mere seconds after Andy had fled down the street into the night. But what made his heart skip a beat was the face of the male student standing on the opposite side of smiling, bighearted Budd Meevers. It couldn't possibly be, Andy told himself, and yet—if it was—then all along the *three* of them had known each other...

"Hello, Andy," a feminine voice said.

Andy whirled, the sick feeling in the pit of his stomach plummeting even deeper—for there stood Ms Pickering, big, bright piranha smile on her face.

"Oh, Andy, Andy, Andy..." she said, looking at him from across the room, obviously having come in through the same door that Meevers had disappeared through earlier. "You turned me down because you're so enamored of that blonde little tart, Jeena. Oh, that's right. Not so enamored that you couldn't resist fucking Lyla Van der Velden's brains out, now isn't that so?"

Andy saw a strange glint in her eye; sweet and yet deadly poisonous, like some beautiful but toxic jungle flower. He had never seen such a look before in anyone, and it frightened him in a way he could not explain.

"Why didn't you eat me, Andy?" she asked, taking a step closer. "You see, it was supposed to be my going away present to you."

Slowly, Andy backed himself up against the trophy-cluttered credenza, as if his teacher exuded some sort of deadly vapor he could not risk exposure to. As he did, the fingers of his handcuffed hands touched the edge of a trophy.

"Why not, Andy?" she repeated. "You should have, you know. Because you and I will never see each other again."

At that moment, the door opened again, and in stepped Manuel Ortega, wearing a big, greasy mestizo smile on his face. "Did you really think you could get away from me, punk?"

Silently, Andy's fingers fumbled along the surface of the credenza, searching for something he'd seen earlier.

Finally, in stepped Budd Meevers, big smile on his tanned and handsome face, gun in hand. "That's right, Andy. Me too."

"Where's Lyla?" Andy croaked, fighting against the horror of it all.

"Outside in the van being carefully guarded by Schmidt. Where you'll be again, soon enough. That is, after a little chloroform puts you to sleep."

"Like you did to Tina Sawyer and Brett Hinkle four years ago, when you kidnapped them?"

"You see?" Budd Meevers said, with mocking joviality, looking at the other two as if over a point proved. "That's why Andy gets into so much trouble at school. He simply can't keep his nose out of other people's business."

"You mean," Andy said, "like kidnapping, sex trafficking and," he glanced toward Ms Pickering, "murder?"

Meevers regarded him curiously, with that bogus look of fatherly concern he used to great effect at Titanis High. "And what murder is that, Andy? Because I assure you that Brett Hinkle and Tina Sawyer are still alive...in whatever part of the world they've been taken."

It was an ominous admission by Meevers; one that hinted at Andy's own fate.

"Not them," Andy said. "Henry Fitchins."

For a moment Meevers and Ms Pickering stared calculatingly at him, then slowly at each other, the first crack in their otherwise calm façade.

Gradually, Meevers nodded. "Looks like I left you alone a little bit too long, didn't I, Andy? And with trouble-making teens like you that's downright dangerous. Even in handcuffs you were able to snoop around, weren't you? Into things that don't concern you. Like scrapbooks, for instance...and old newspaper clippings."

"And college photographs," Andy softly added, "of you and Ms Pickering and...if the third face in that picture is who I think it is, then so is my–"

"Better come out, Peter..." Budd Meevers suddenly announced, cutting Andy off. Slowly, the side door swung open, and out stepped Andy's father, Peter Hupp.

For a long moment father and son looked at each other, but only one face reflected sadness. "Tell me one thing, dad— *why?*"

Ever so slightly, Peter Hupp's head drooped. "We all make mistakes, son. Some of us outgrow them. But I...I could never escape mine. Or those," he glanced toward Meevers and Pickering, "who knew what I had done. Try to be understanding."

"Understanding? Of what, dad? Murder? Of burning an old man to death?"

"I wanted to tell," Peter Hupp said, his bespectacled eyes pleading for understanding. "Jesus Christ, I wanted to! We— we only meant to burn his house down as revenge for the way he talked to us. That's all. Nothing more. We never meant for him to die! Believe me, Andy! Please! Besides, it was Janelle who carried the gas can and Budd who struck the matches! Please God stop looking at me that way!"

"It's alright, Peter," Budd Meevers soothed. "Let me help you explain it to your son. It's like this, Andy: like the rest of us, your dad is an opportunist. You see, he had the goods on Janelle and I, and likewise Janelle and I had the goods on him. So any one of us could have sent the other two to prison at any time. Maybe even cut himself a deal for a lighter sentence for ratting out the other two. Which, quite honestly, must have been tempting to your dad. So to prevent that from happening, we made a pact, you might say. A pact of guilt and a pact of fear. Mostly the latter. Years later, after coming to Titanis High, I met Coach Ortega, and he promised me lots of easy money, if I ignored certain things he did. Later on, when your dad's landscape firm needed some quick cash to keep it afloat, I got him to help me, Ortega, and Schmidt turn over Tina Sawyer and Brett Hinkle to the cartel. As their principal, they trusted me, and got into the van that night without any fuss, once we waved them over along that lonely country road. As for Peter, he helped me tie them up while Schmidt and Ortega held their guns on them, and for that he got the extra cash he needed." A wry grin momentarily etched Budd Meevers' face. "There were four of us that night, just to make certain Hinkle and Sawyer had no chance of getting away. In retrospect, it seems cutting our team down to two tonight wasn't such a good idea, especially with a slippery joker like you, Andy..."

Silent, Andy's eyes remained fixed on his father, even as Budd Meevers went on: "You see, Andy, your dad isn't nearly as good a businessman as that fancy house of his suggests, so he needed occasional infusions of life-saving cash to keep him from going bankrupt. And that's where Ortega and I and the Sinaloa Cartel came in. In exchange for lucrative odd jobs here and there, my good old college buddy Petey kept his mouth shut about what Ms Pickering and I were involved in, and agreed to help us whenever we needed an extra pair of hands. You know, scratch my back and I'll scratch yours kind of thing. And in exchange, you and your sister Amanda got to live the good life...

"Only problem is, your dad kept needing more and more cash to keep his shaky business afloat, what with all the competition coming into the Austin area and such, and this last time he realized he needed a lot more than his side jobs with us were paying. So when he looked around to see where he might scrape up a hundred grand, the only thing he had left of value was...*you*. That's right. You, Andy. You–the sexy teenage model, good-looking, nicely built, just the kind of young man certain clients in other parts of the world would pay big money to get their hands on..."

Gradually, understanding appeared on Andy's face.

"That's right, Andy. I've known for some time that you were a model in your after school hours. So now it's all starting to make sense, isn't it? You see, after Peter told me he needed to make some big money and make it fast I introduced him to Dr. Adler Rothman, who in turn used his cartel connections to sell you to an Arab sheik. A sheik with...let's just say, peculiar tastes for handsome white teenage boys. In exchange, your dad makes a neat hundred grand plus several lucrative business contracts down in Houston that he otherwise wouldn't have had a chance of getting. Don't look so stunned, Andy. It's the way certain under-the-table businesses operate in our globalized age. Besides, Lyla's parents got nothing for her, because they'll never know what happened to their daughter, other than she vanished from a party one night and was never seen again." A sardonic grin cut across Meevers' face. "Who knows? They might even come to believe she secretly eloped with you and was never heard of again."

From across the room, Peter Hupp saw the devastating hurt in his son's eyes—the son he had resented for so long; for his good-looks, his movie ambitions, and the money he made so easily as a successful teenage magazine model, while he had to scrape, beg, and borrow every inch of the way while working his fingers to the bone—

"Can I leave now?" Peter Hupp abruptly said, in a defeated tone of voice, now avoiding his son's haunted, accusing, hate-filled eyes.

"Of course, Peter. I just wanted to make sure your son understood who really had sold him—and why."

After Andy's father departed, Budd Meevers studied the teenaged youth for a long, thoughtful moment. Then he said, in the same calm tone of voice used many times before from behind his high school office desk: "So you see, Andy, it wasn't me or Janelle who sold you to the cartel. It was your own dad, and part of the deal was being here tonight to let you know. I certainly didn't want you thinking I was the one. Really, I'm just not that type of guy."

"And Lyla?" Andy barely managed to say.

Meevers smiled. "Well, you got me there. Truth be told, I'm getting two hundred and fifty grand for her, since she's choice, just like you. Certainly not a virgin, but then, what modern high school girl is. Then again, she's not a street hooker or a sleazy bimbo, and that makes her prime USDA– in other words: Undeniably Super Delicious Ass. But then, I've got to cut in Ms Pickering and Coach Ortega and our friendly cargo pilot for fifty grand apiece, so it ain't all gravy, son."

"What about the one who left her black panties in your office after you fucked her? You know, the ones stuffed between the sofa cushions? What was her name?"

Janelle Pickering's eyes glittered. "I'm afraid those were mine, Andy." she said, behind a wickedly demure smile. "If I recall, Budd and I got a little cozy on the sofa one rainy afternoon a couple of years ago and...well...we just couldn't help ourselves. Budd must've stuffed them there after ripping them off my ass and in the passion of the moment I forgot where I'd left them. Didn't matter, since I always carry an extra pair in my purse."

"I thought you fucked only teenage boys."

"They're my caviar, Andy. On the other hand, men like Budd are merely an occasional in-between snack I permit myself whenever a boy like you isn't available..."

As Ms Pickering talked, Andy carefully slipped the Boy Scout knife into the back of his pants, slithering it underneath the waistband of his dark-green pair of Mann Hunt underwear, wedging it between his buttocks.

Just in time, because he saw Meevers give a telling glance to Ortega, and the mestizo circled off to the side as the high school principal moved the other way, his gun steady on Andy.

"Janelle, it's time to get the chloroform."

"When I arrived," she said, "I checked the supply out in the workshop and the bottle's nearly empty."

"Then try the main house. You'll find some in the refrigerator."

And with that she quietly crossed the room and disappeared

out the front door, closing it gently behind.

"Don't worry, Andy," Meevers consoled, turning his attention back to the youth. "It's quite painless. And when you awake again you'll be far south from here, in sunny Central America. Then, after a few fun-filled weeks of exciting activities, you'll be on your way to an undisclosed location in North Africa–and a whole new life."

Glancing sideways, Andy noted the picture window, beige drapes on either side. A dash of only twelve feet and he just might be able to crash through–

"I wouldn't try it, Andy," Budd Meevers calmly warned, his hand tightening on the semi-automatic. "Not unless you want a bullet in the back of your head and a shallow grave somewhere on my thirty acre property, next to three others who wouldn't cooperate."

Realizing he had no chance, Andy dropped the idea. Then, looking back toward Budd Meevers, his green eyes haunted, he suddenly muttered two words, more to himself than to the man holding the gun: "Dr. Adler..."

"He really liked you, Andy. He told me so himself."

"Then why would such a man–?"

"Become involved in sex trafficking? But why not, Andy? Greed doesn't distinguish between the lower and upper classes. And Dr. Adler is very much on the upper part of the equation. After all, with his high-level connections he's met a lot of interesting, powerful people from all over the world. Rich people, Andy. Ones that have certain...hungers. And you and Lyla just happen to be two of them."

"Right from the start he gave me a strange feeling," Andy recalled. "Something about him...just wasn't right."

"Yes... Occasionally, some people can sense what he is."

"You're not saying–?"

"Saying what, Andy?"

"That Adler... That he's–" Andy struggled to say, his mind squeezed tight against the horror. "That he's a pedophile?"

"Part of a network of them, to be exact. They bring in a lot of business for the cartel."

Andy Hupp wanted to vomit.

The world, he realized, was a lot filthier than he'd ever imagined.

After a long moment, he grimly asked, "What's going to happen to me?" He didn't really want to know, but maybe by finding out he might be able to develop a plan of escape.

"Depends if you want to go on living, Andy. Cooperate, and you will. I recommend cooperation. If you do, you'll be flown down to Mexico to a secluded airfield. After your plane is refueled it's on to festive Central America. We get a lot of immigrants from down there, as you know. In fact, our very own Coach Ortega was born in Guatemala. So it's kind of heart-warming to know I'm sending one of our own back there. You, Andy. Just like we sent a dozen others back over the last few years, from various high schools in the region. And no, none of them were victims of a serial killer, unlike what that laughable book Rodney Crutchley stumbled upon in the school library. That is, excluding the three buried out back. But if the public wants to believe some sort of Ted Bundy or John Wayne Gacy is responsible for the disappearances, then that's just fine and dandy with the cartel. It helps to cover our tracks."

"What about Mrs. Meevers?" Andy queried. "She must know what you've been doing."

"Oh, yes. I almost forgot: there is no Mrs. Meevers. You see, we divorced almost seven years ago. Since then, I've lived here alone."

"Then your mother-in-law...?"

"Died years ago, in another state. Never once stepped foot in this house. But then, that was a necessary lie too. To make everything seem more homey. You know, wife cozy and a-sleep in the main house, dearly departed mother-in-law's cabin remade into my private man-cave, that kind of thing. Otherwise you might have become alarmed knowing you were out here—totally alone—except for me."

"And when I get to Guatemala?"

"Well, to say the least, it will be a whole new experience for you. True, Brett and Tina had some trouble adapting, so I'm told, but in time they adjusted. You see, there's a whole group of us down there. All run by the Sinaloa Cartel, reaching all over the world. On a very secluded banana plantation, hidden in the jungle. A banana plantation, I might add, with a lot of six, seven, and eight inch bananas. The hard kind, Andy. The kind that ripen quickly, once they get hold of a Tina Sawyer or a Lyla Van der Velden or...in your case, a good-looking boy. Because that's where you're headed. And if you cooperate, and do as you're told, you might even be allowed to join our operation a few years down the road, once the sheik grows tired of you and trades you in for a younger model. But I won't lie. It will be difficult for you at first. Especially...especially after what they're going to do to you."

"What do you mean?"

"You see, months ago I turned over a dozen magazines featuring your modeling ads to the cartel. They especially liked your Mann Hunt motorcycle ad. In fact, it was that ad that got you sold to a Middle Eastern sheik right off the bat, so I'm duly impressed. And since your dad was a willing seller, a deal was struck. But to answer your question, they're going to use you in sex videos at first, that will eventually be sold on the black market worldwide. You'll be famous, Andy, at least in the underground world of Darknet porn. And once they've finished that little project, you're off to an unspecified Arab country where you'll take up your new life. You see, those swarthy Arabs have this thing for young, handsome white boys like you. Don't ask me why, I don't swing that way. And these particular clients have plenty of money to burn on exotic hobbies. But since I know you're not gay, you'll have to first be repeatedly raped by some of the cartel's specially trained employees down in Guatemala. You know, to prepare you for your new job as a sex slave in the

Middle East. It's necessary to soften you up, you understand. To make you totally pliant and submissive. Until you have lost all memory of fucking cute little white girls like Lyla Van der Velden. By the end of it all they'll have made a woman out of you, Andy, and by the time three or four years have passed and the sheik is bored with you he'll either kill you or sell you back to the cartel, minus a hefty discount fee since by then you'll be used goods. By that time, you'll either join us like Brett Hinkle and Tina Sawyer—or die."

At that moment, Janelle Pickering returned.

"Had to use the ladies room while I was back at the house," Janelle Pickering explained. "Sorry for the delay."

"No problem, Janelle. I was married once and know how you women are." He glanced over at the handcuffed teen. "Well, looks like we're ready now, Andy," Budd Meevers said. "So make it easy on yourself and just lie down on the sofa. Janelle has done this before so she'll be quick."

Andy looked at each one in turn: Budd Meevers, Janelle Pickering, Manuel Ortega. Sighing with resignation, he calmly approached the sofa. But at the last instant he dashed sideways straight for the window, reaching it just as a muscular brown arm whipped around his throat and pulled him to the floor.

"Let me go!" Andy screamed, twisting violently as Janelle Pickering stepped into his field of vision, standing above him with bottle of chloroform and rag in hand, prim smile on her lips.

"Since you didn't want to eat my pussy," she said, pouring chloroform into the cloth before leaning down and mashing it into his face, "you'll just have to eat this."

An instant later, spinning down a bottomless whirlpool into darkness, the last thing he heard was the sound of three people laughing, laughing, laughing...

Until his mind winked out.

CHAPTER 25

Drifting weightlessly through an endless void, Andy Hupp kept swatting at a fly. An enormous black fly. Yet no matter how often he shooed it away it persistently returned, buzzing and buzzing and buzzing as it maddeningly droned on and on and on.

Then.

Suddenly.

He awoke.

Looked around uncertainly.

And realized the fly was still buzzing.

I must still be dreaming, he thought, even as a harsh ray of sunlight stabbed deep into his left eye, turning the iris a luminescent greenish-yellow. The other eye, still cleaved by shadow, remained a darker green, the color of deep woods.

But the fly...

Buzzing.

Was it real?

Then his mind cleared further, finally realizing what the source of the sound was: the steady drone of twin airplane engines.

Suddenly, everything came rushing back: the Halloween party and Lyla, his kidnapping, Meevers, Ms Pickering, Manuel Ortega, the chloroform-soaked cloth, the mocking laughter, fading consciousness...

Now here he lay, on the floor of a small, twin-engined aircraft, his arms handcuffed behind his back. What's more, his ankles were now duct-taped. After a long time of just lying there, in stunned silence, trying to gather his wits as he fought to keep his fear under control, he gradually became aware of a radiant warmth from behind. Rolling partly over, he came up against Lyla. She too was handcuffed and duct-taped, and now fully dressed, lying there as she softly moaned and writhed in her sleep, as if she too were trapped in a dream. But whether she was still under the soporific effect of some drug or simply asleep from fear and exhaustion, he couldn't say. Still, he made no attempt to wake her. Because whatever he might be forced to do in the next few minutes, it was best if she remained unaware.

Focusing again on where he lay, he took stock of his surroundings: floor sheathed in metal, with walls the same, curved and riveted. No windows, just a solid cocoon of anodized aluminum. Normally, such a small aircraft would have featured eight to ten passenger seats bolted to the floor, Andy reasoned, having flown in similar airplanes before on his way to various photo shoots. But in this aircraft the passenger seats had been stripped, along with every other amenity, obviously to make room for several metal crates–of unknown content–as well as two bound and kidnapped teens. The crates partially obscured Andy's view down the length of the aircraft, where he glimpsed a sky-filled windshield and a lone man with shaggy blond hair, headphones clamped to the side of his head. The van driver, by the looks of it—now behind the wheel of a plane, headed deep into southern skies. Toward a place Brett Hinkle and Tina Sawyer vanished four years earlier, Andy knew. A nightmare place of captive sex slaves imprisoned by a ruthless Mexican crime syndicate. To do with what they willed; to sell them or kill them, rape them or torture them, with no one the wiser. The kind of people who were invading all of Western civilization, with the help of millions of Janelle Pickerings and SJW robots like Lyla Van der Velden.

The very thought made Andy sick to his stomach.

That Budd Meevers and his own father were also involved

made him angry. And anger was the one thing he needed right that second–a burning anger that told him he would somehow find a way out, and get back home.

For revenge.

But most of all–for Jeena Kirtland...

With that in mind, he carefully tugged at his handcuffs.

As expected, they weren't coming off.

Then he remembered.

Was Budd Meevers' Boy Scout knife still stuffed in the back of his pants, where he'd shoved it the night before? Eager to find out, he rolled over onto his butt and felt a hard lump of metal press into his flesh. So Ortega hadn't searched him; or, if he had, hadn't done so carefully.

With effort, Andy dug his handcuffed hands beneath his pants and wriggled them about beneath the waistband of his briefs, probing deftly. Snagging the knife with his thumb and index finger, he slowly pulled it free. As he did, the engines droned on, a steady thrum that masked his movement. That, and the pair of headphones Schmidt had clamped over his ears. Was he listening to some crucial flight report? Andy wondered. But he doubted it, since the pilot's right hand was rhythmically tapping out a beat on the control console as his shoulders swayed from side to side, apparently jamming to whatever kind of music sex traffickers dug.

With the Boy Scout knife clutched between his two handcuffed hands, he pried open the blade. Now to cut the duct tape so he would have freedom of movement. But after trying as many contorted positions as possible, he still could not reach his ankles. Resting a bit, he tried again a few minutes later, but once more gave up, since he could not stretch far enough to reach the duct tape with his blade. For a moment he just lay there, drifting away, as if to close his mind to what was happening–and the fate that awaited him: violent and repeated homosexual rape, then forced participation in lurid sex videos for the Darknet.

That–or die.

Then he thought of Jink.

What had happened to her?

And then he remembered Rodney's final text, mentioning the sudden arrival of three Mexicans up at Klimmen's Point. Grimly, he realized who they must have been: MS-13.

Sent by the cartel.

To–

A sick feeling suddenly came over him.

They must be dead: Rodney, TJ, and Jeena.

Like him, they knew the truth about Ortega–that he was a thug and a criminal who used his day job as a gym teacher as a front for what he did at night–run drugs and stolen goods for the cartel, with an occasional detour into sex trafficking and murder. As such, he must have had some of the cartel's hired killers follow Jeena, TJ, and Rodney out to Klimmen's Point and–

Slumping back against the metal floor of the airplane hold, Andy became overwhelmed by an all-consuming depression, knowing Ortega, Meevers, Ms Pickering, and his dad were sitting smug right now, content with the knowledge that he was long gone, that they had literally gotten away with kidnapping and murder–with him headed far away, to join with the unexplained disappearances of Brett Hinkle, Tina Sawyer, and all the others. But if he were lucky, he grimly considered, he just might end up as a followup chapter in the next edition of *Shot, Stabbed, Strangled, and Snuffed: Unsolved Murders & Unexplained Disappearances In America's Heartland.*

Yeah, maybe.

Then again...

"When Andy puts his mind to it, he can do anything..."

Long ago words from his mother, resonating across the years, when he was but a small boy just beginning to open his eyes to life's possibilities; possibilities he had always wanted to make real.

Slowly, his expression changed from hopelessness and defeat to one that was uncharacteristically hard and cold. Carefully looking around as he assessed the situation, he divided up his problem into smaller, more manageable goals. Accomplish that first goal, he told himself, and then worry about the next. As this strategy formed in his mind, his eye caught sight of the cargo crates, noting several perforations in the metal sides. Scooting closer, he peered inside—and saw facing racks of M4A1automatic rifles—the US Army's main combat weapon.

Holy shit, Andy thought—gun runners too.

Stolen or bought on the black market didn't matter, he knew—just as illegal as the rest of the operation. But the perforations gave him an idea, which he quickly acted upon by lodging the handle of the knife into one. Done, he spun around on his hips and raised his duct-taped ankles toward the protruding knife blade. In seconds his bound ankles were free.

Now the second goal.

Rocking backward while simultaneously folding his legs inward, Andy swung his handcuffed arms up and around his ankles until his arms were repositioned in front.

Then, pulling the knife free of the armaments shipping crate, his eyes hardened as he set his mind on his third and final goal: taking out the pilot.

With that in mind, he clenched Principal Meevers' Boy Scout knife and began to incrementally make his way forward, slithering between two metal armament containers and several indeterminate canvas bundles as silently as possible, even as the Aero Commander 500S Shrike flew on, its twin Lycoming six cylinder engines churning out 600 horsepower of combined thrust.

Ahead, seated at the controls, sat a man for whom violence had been a way of life for years. Were it not for the fact that his mind was distracted by piloting the plane, the music-blaring headphones, the background drone of two powerful airplane engines—all topped off by a brain swimming in a psychedelic haze of hallucinogenic smoke, Andy knew he would never have attempted such a risky assault.

Carefully, sweat pouring down his face and throat, eyes ablaze, he came up behind the pilot almost before he knew it, knife clutched in right hand, and brought his handcuffed arms up, over, and down Schmidt's head, as if slipping an execution hood over the condemned.

And in a way he was.

Schmidt, stoned on weed, his head screeching with head-banging electric guitar music and shrieking voices desperate to pass for singing, had only a sluggish instant to see the chain-linked handcuffs pass suddenly in front of his eyes.

"What the—!"

Andy had seen plenty of throats slit in countless movies, but in real life it was not so easy. He got the blade into the pilot's meaty throat well enough, and ripped it from left to right with commendable zeal, causing a big gout of blood to spurt out. But fuck if the pilot didn't go all limp like they did in the movies, a fact Andy would have to remember next time he filmed a script with a throat-slitting scene.

On the other hand, Schmidt's performance was Academy Award worthy, bellowing as he did as Andy's knife gouged his throat again and again—almost as if Schmidt, for some odd reason, didn't want to die. Even so, his cool looking Hawaiian shirt quickly turned a bright crimson where a gorgeous scene of Waikiki Beach used to be. And for a whole minute teen and pilot struggled like this, as the plane tilted sideways then crazily rolled back the opposite way, its twin engines groaning angrily as it drilled through the air at 200 mph.

Finally pushing free of the bleeding man, Andy decided throat-slashing wasn't as effective as those damn TV shows made it out to be. Desperate now, he instead rammed the blade into Schmidt's right eye, and the scream was positively ungodly—also Academy Award worthy. Schmidt again yanked Andy's arm free, and again tried to turn the knife back on him. What's more, Andy knew if the pilot ever struggled free of his seat he'd kill him in an instant with his bare arms. So

Andy stabbed him in the other eye, twisting the blade round and round like he was coring an apple. Understandably, the pilot went insane with rage, bucking like a Brahma bull trying to break free of its stall at a Texas rodeo, even as Andy went to town on him, going full Jack the Ripper.

Incredibly, Schmidt still refused to die.

Then Andy saw the seatbelt release and darted his hand-cuffed hands downward and yanked the clasp. At the same instant he leant forward and unlocked the pilot's side door while shoving Schmidt hard against it. But Christ and fuck if this pot-smoking, drug running, sex-trafficking scumbag wouldn't cooperate! For once again Schmidt struggled and grappled and tore blindly at Andy's face with his free hand as he fought to hold on to the steering wheel with the other. Redirecting his attack, Andy turned his knife blade toward Schmidt's crotch and jack-hammered it half a dozen times— which was quite a feat when your hands were handcuffed.

But it did the trick.

Ululating like a Bantu, Schmidt vomited blood as Andy raked what was left of his face with the chain links of his handcuffs, splintering two front teeth before smashing the cartilage in his nose with a double-fisted blow.

Now halfway hanging out of the aircraft as he fought to hold on, hair whipping wildly in the 200 mph slipstream and bleeding like a sieve from fifty-odd stab wounds, Andy had to wonder if Schmidt wasn't at that very instant reconsidering drug-running and sex-trafficking as a long-term career plan.

"Please—" the pilot begged, his eye-sockets red pits in his wind-torn face, hanging on now by only three fingers to the door frame. "Let's...let's make a deal! You...you can't fly this plane and—"

"Maybe I can't," Andy shouted above the roar of the wind, "but then, you can't grow wings!" as he shoved him through the doorway into open air, sending him tumbling backward, twisting, end over end, shrieking in horror and rage as he plunged toward the hungry earth below.

Gasping, exhausted, covered in blood, Andy Hupp barely tugged the door shut before collapsing into the pilot's seat, even as the twin engines relentlessly bore the plane on. He had just sent a man to his death, he realized, feeling both proud and sick at one and the same time; proud that he had stopped this one-way express down to a Central American ass-fucking factory, but sick that killing was too often the only solution to a bad situation. Then again, Schmidt was right about now smashing face first into the hard earth below...

So—

That cured his stomach problems right up.

Turning, he stumbled back to where Lyla lay, making sure she was alright. Better let her sleep, he thought, safe in whatever subconscious sanctuary her mind had taken refuge. Because they still had one minor problem: they were streaking along at 200 mph with no pilot aboard.

Retreating toward the front again, Andy plopped down in the recently vacated pilot's seat, a brooding look clouding his youthful face. Slowly, his green eyes wandered over the complicated array of gauges, dials, buttons, switches, and glowing indicator lights that made up the control console of the Aero Commander. He thought: if car dashboards looked like this, ninety-five percent of America's high school students would never graduate driver's training.

Finally locating the fuel gauge, which was one of the easier ones to understand, he read the grim news: less than half a tank left. Still, even that told him little, since he had no idea how quickly the plane drank fuel. Drifting his eyes over the rest of the control panel, he knew one thing with cold certainty: his chances of landing this plane were next to nil. True, he might have escaped involuntary membership in the Sinaloa cartel's Club Butt Fuck, but the trade-off would be a long plummet to earth once the fuel ran out.

Then he noticed a nylon bag sitting on the seat beside him. Curious, he pulled it over and unzipped it. What he saw took his breath away—a sackful of shrink-wrapped cash packets, each about an inch thick, comprised of hundred dollar bills. He estimated the total amount to be around three hundred thousand dollars.

Holy Jesus, he thought.

Looks like crime *does* pay.

That is, unless you get shoved out an airplane without a parachute...

But there were other items in the bag, Andy noticed. A roast beef sandwich, for one thing, which he immediately tore out of the sandwich bag and scarfed down. As he did, he rummaged a bit deeper and pulled out a cell phone. Turning it on, the screen flashed:

No Signal

Glancing out the side window to the world far below, he saw why: a sea of green for as far as eye could see. But whether he was over Mexico's southern jungle or Guatemala's northern one, he had no idea. Yet jungle it was and all that mattered now was that the cell phone was worthless in a region where few, if any, cell towers existed. Tossing it aside, his eye caught sight of what appeared to be second cell phone inside the bag, this one black with a bright-yellow rim, of a brand he was not familiar with: Iridium.

Puzzled, he took it out and closely examined it, then flipped it over. On the back side, a computer-printed label the pilot must have taped there had instructions on how to make a call to the US, perhaps needed when his mind was so fucked-up on marijuana he couldn't think straight. Andy read the instructions aloud: "To call the US, dial '00' then country code '1'. Then dial the US area code and phone number."

Was it possible? he wondered, realizing this was not a cell phone at all, but instead a satellite phone. He'd never used one, nor even held one before, but he knew it didn't rely on land-based cell towers to transmit a phone call, but instead communicated directly with the nearest Low Earth Orbit satellite, then beamed it back down to a ground station before transmitting it directly to the party being called.

Hardly believing his serendipitous fortune, Andy carefully followed the instructions on the back of the Iridium 9555, slowly and meticulously imputing a number, as if going too quickly might somehow cause the satellite phone to evaporate into thin air. Afterward he waited, as the phone went through all the necessary satellite connections, first bouncing a signal into space and, far away, back down to Earth.

Andy caught his breath.

For somewhere far away...somebody answered.

CHAPTER 26

Fighting to keep his emotions under control, Andy Hupp quietly said: "When you told me you loved me, Jink, I never said I loved you back. But only because...because I–"

Far, far, away, at the other end, a teenage girl broke down in sobs, tearful, joyous sobs, her voice filled with wonder: "Andy! *Oh, Andy!* You're...you're alive! We thought–" And for a moment neither could say another word, each overcome by all that hadn't been said in those first halting moments. Then the girl found her voice again, "Oh, Andy! You're a *boy!* And boys always find it hard to say they love a girl for the first time! But even so I saw it in your eyes! So I knew it anyway! I always knew it! Right from the beginning! No way you're gonna hide that from me, buster!"

Andy swallowed, knowing he had loved Jink too–right from the beginning. But for guys, well... They just couldn't always admit to those kinds of things. Not right away, at least. And then, there had been those last vestiges of longing lust for the elusive, red-haired Lyla Van der Velden–a terrible mistake and something he would have to explain to Jinky when the time came, and humbly ask her forgiveness.

But for now–

"I love you, Jeena Kirtland."

As Andy Hupp's solemnly spoken words reached out across the vast distances to Jinky, she broke down crying again, then laughing, then let go all manner of little sighs and murmured endearments a teenage girl expresses once she realizes the boy of her dreams is finally hers.

After a long pleasant silence between them, almost as if they had been holding each other close, Jinky suddenly said: "Andy–what's that noise I hear in the background? It almost sounds like–"

"An Aero Commander 550S?"

"An Aero Commander *whatzit?*"

"My plane," he explained. "The one I'm flying."

"The one...*you're flying?* But you don't know how!"

Andy chuckled. "Well, I've got the first lesson down; I'm sitting in the pilot's seat."

"In the...? But Andy–where *is* the pilot!"

"You might say he stepped out for a moment. Anyway, that's why I called." He puffed out a sigh. "Because now there isn't one."

"But–!"

"So listen carefully, Jink. Because there isn't much time. Okay? Got a pen and paper handy? Good. Now take down this name, address, and phone number..." he instructed, giving her the information necessary to contact a man named Ed Hartmann, as well as providing his own call-back number. As she took down the information, Andy went on, "After we disconnect, call Ed right away and tell him you're coming over because Andy Hupp is trapped aboard an Aero Commander 550S without a pilot–got it? Hartmann's a retired airline pilot so if anyone can talk me down, he can. Oh, yeah–tell him not to call the police or he may be putting my life in danger. I'll explain later, promise. In the meantime I need him to help me turn this thing around and land it. I know, I know, I love you too, Jink, but there's no other way. Now get over to Ed Hartmann's house at Warp 9 and tell him to call me back at this phone number soon as possible. And hurry, Jink! Because I have less than half a tank of fuel left. Now go!"

Life is good, Principal Budd Meevers thought, leaning back in his high-backed chair as he tossed his feet atop his desk.

Here I am, secure in my position, respected, with a good income. Yep, got a lot to be thankful for... True, I made some mistakes in my younger days. But heck, who doesn't? Since then, the dullards running the Michigan police department had all but given up ever solving the Henry Fitchins case.

Yep, old Fitchins is long dead...

Rotting away in his grave these past twenty years.

Wouldn't have happened had that grumpy old bastard kept to himself and not gotten huffy with us.

But then, we taught him...

But good.

And now here he was, years later, raking in a tidy sum every month from Coach Ortega and the cartel just for minding his own business while the Guatemalan spread good cheer among the region's drug addicts and high school kids with all the crack and crystal meth he and his MS-13 thugs could deal.

And why be concerned about that? he thought.

After all, pot was already legal out in California, wasn't it? Elsewhere too?

Likewise, street drugs of all sorts were just an everyday fact of life now, he told himself, so why not do what so many others were doing and cash in? Sure, most were still illegal, but hey, that would change over time. And then, every once in a while the cartel would let Ortega know they had a buyer from a foreign part of the world looking for a hot young teen for an in-house sex companion, and whenever that happened he'd get another lucrative 'finder's fee'.

All nice and neat.

Respectable.

The American Way.

Well, actually more like the Mexican cartel way, but then, Mexicans were everywhere nowadays, weren't they? And gosh darn if there just wasn't any way of stopping 'em. After all, they were swarming like roaches over the border and literally changing Central Texas into Northern Mexico. Spanish spoken everywhere. Black-haired, brown-faced heads bobbing up and down the streets everywhere you went. Gangs. Knifings. Shootings. Drugs. Rundown, shit-hole neighborhoods whenever their sheer presence pushed out whites. What had Janelle told Andy Hupp? *"...imagine it's a new computer program called America 3.0, Andy. You know, like a fantastic new video game we all get to play."*

Yes, poor, poor Andy...

Truth be told, he'd really liked that kid.

Smart.

Talented.

Good-looking.

Yes, very good-looking...

Ironic, that.

How those good-looks had been his downfall.

All because there were certain men who could never merit the company of such photogenic youth as Andy Hupp, but instead were forced to pay for it–or simply take it by force. And such men usually wanted more than a one-night stand with someone who looked as good as Andy Hupp–much more. They wanted him under their complete and utter control, to ravish and rape in any manner they chose, whenever they pleased; to commit the most vile sexual depravities imaginable, up to and including torture and murder. Such men were invariably wealthy, Meevers knew, and lived in countries where no one looked too closely at what they did behind the high security walls of their private palaces and estates. Such buyers often came from the Middle East, and one particular buyer from Saudi Arabia had been eager to buy Andy Hupp soon after seeing his photo in a magazine ad for Mann Hunt underwear. And with Lyla Van der Velden thrown in to sweeten the pot, Meevers had gotten a nice chunk of change for making it all go down, just as he had with Brett Hinkle and Tina Sawyer and a dozen other kids over the years.

Just business.

Nothing more.

Nothing to get upset about.

After all, people wanted sex, didn't they? And some were willing to pay anything to get it, or take any risk, provided it was something they could not otherwise have–precisely the commodity that made them want two gorgeous teens like Andy Hupp and Lyla Van der Velden–albeit at a premium price.

Meevers sighed, wistfully.

Right about now Andy was probably strapped to a table, face down, legs spread, beads of sweat pouring down his forehead, getting his ass fucked harder than a jackhammer going into concrete. And Lyla was likely in the next room, swallowing six hard inches of Guatemalan sausage while handcuffed and buckled to a chair. But then, sex slaves were a commodity, and like any commodity had to be properly prepared and conditioned to be obedient, Meevers knew, before final delivery to their proud new owners. A commodity specially produced in a factory dedicated to savage lust–one churning out high quality but obedient cocks and cunts to be sold to the highest bidder. And he was simply a middleman in this long chain of supply and demand, merely helping the consumer public get what they wanted...

His desk phone rang, shaking him from his reverie.

He glanced at the caller ID screen:

JANELLE PICKERING

Languidly, he reached forward and picked up the handset. "Are you alone?"

"At the moment," he lazily answered. "But in fifteen minutes I've a meeting with a cute little student reporter from the school newspaper. Wants to interview the big handsome principal for an article."

"Peter's dead," she abruptly said.

For a moment his mind went blank.

"Peter?... *Who's Pe–?*" Then he jerked forward: "You don't mean Peter Hupp?"

"I do."

"But how?"

"Suicide," Janelle Pickering informed. "Shot himself."

"When?"

"Twenty minutes ago. His wife just called. The police are there now and she's hysterical, Budd. She told me she thought Peter was despondent over their son's disappearance and—"

Meevers broke out chuckling. "Despondent? Whatever he was, he sure wasn't that. Remember, he got fifty grand for selling him."

"Even so, something's not right," Ms Pickering went on, her voice edgy. "I don't know why but I feel it. Even for Peter it's just not like him to suddenly kill himself."

"Did his wife say anything else?"

"No... Wait. She said Peter received a phone call a few minutes before he shot himself. He had left the office early and had only been home a few minutes when he got the call on his cell. She was standing in the kitchen and briefly saw him listening to someone on the other end when his face suddenly went white."

"Went white?"

"Those were her words. Like someone had just told him something disturbing."

"And then—?"

"And then he turned and wandered down the hallway to his office and quietly closed the door. She thought nothing more of it until a minute or two later, when she heard a gunshot."

Meevers fell silent for a moment, thinking. Janelle was right; something didn't feel right about this. Abruptly, he said: "I'll call you back in a few minutes."

Five minutes later he had her on the phone again: "Where are you now?"

"In my classroom, of course. Grading papers. My next class is not for another ten minutes."

"Come to my office."

"But–"

"Do it."

Seven minutes later Janelle Pickering walked into his office. Budd Meevers was standing behind his desk, hastily shoving papers and other items into a briefcase.

"What are you doing?" Ms Pickering asked.

"Shut up and listen," Meevers barked, "we've got to get out of here."

"What are you talking about?"

"I just got off the phone with Coach Ortega. He says Andy Hupp and Lyla Van der Velden never made it to Guatemala."

"You can't be serious," Ms Pickering said, aghast.

"Dead serious. Ortega told me that Mexican authorities found Schmidt's plane only a couple of hours ago, but have reason to believe it crashed at least two days earlier. Somewhere outside a town called Tamazunchale."

Janelle stared at him, uncomprehending.

"Don't you get it, Janelle? Or is a cold-hearted bitch like you too self-absorbed to understand? They never *got* to Guatemala! For whatever reason Schmidt turned the fucking plane around! Then he ran out of fuel and crash landed."

"But...why would he turn the plane around?"

"How the fuck should I know! Maybe the plane was hijacked when he landed in central Mexico to refuel. There's bandits crawling all over the place in that shit stain of a country. Or maybe Andy Hupp somehow got hold of his gun and forced him to return. None of that matters now!"

"But surely they must have died in the crash," Janelle said, her eyes wide with disbelief.

"Apparently not, since Mexican authorities found no bodies. Get it? No bodies, Janelle! Not Andy's or Lyla's or the pilot's. Just the fucking plane."

"Then Ortega–"

"Called Peter first. Asked him if he had heard from Andy, right after the cartel informed Ortega that Schmidt's plane never reached Guatemala. When Peter said no, Ortega told him the same story I just gave you. And according to Ortega, Peter was scared shitless. The filthy coward would be. That's why I regret not killing him long ago. But he did us a favor by doing the job himself. Now we've got to run. I told Ortega we would meet him at his office and then together drive our cars out to the airstrip where he's got a plane and a cartel pilot waiting to take us down to Guatemala."

Janelle collapsed onto Meevers' sofa, limp with shock and confusion. "Budd, I just can't pick up and leave. I've got a life and a job here. My own condo. A nice car. I can't leave all that behind and run off to Guatemala. Not now. Not ever."

Meevers came over and yanked her to her feet. "Listen up you stubborn, boy-raping bitch! If you're worried about your supply of teenage boy lovers being cut off there's plenty of horny Guatemalans you can pick and choose from once we get down there! Besides, if you think I'll risk leaving you behind so you can plea bargain yourself out of a life sentence for the Fitchins murder and everything else at my expense you've got another thing coming!"

Janelle looked at him, her eyes full of suppressed fury; it went against her grain for any man to dominate her. But there were some situations a woman's pussy couldn't control or influence, and this was one of them. Reluctantly, she nodded.

"I'll need to pick up some things back at my condo."

"No time," Meevers said. "Now let's get moving."

She made a move toward Meevers' side exit, the one he used whenever he wanted to make a discreet exit without anyone knowing.

"Not that way," Meevers said, pulling her instead toward the main door. "I want Mrs. Rath to see us leaving. I'll tell her you're not feeling well and that I've recommended you go home for the rest of the day. She can send one of her office assistants over to post a notice cancelling your classes. That way she won't get suspicious."

"What about you?"

"Easy. I'll mention I'm leaving for a meeting and won't be

back for the rest of the day. Then we'll follow Ortega to where the plane's waiting."

With briefcase in hand and a quick straightening of his tie, Budd Meevers, Titanis High principal, escorted Janelle Pickering out the door into the reception area. After informing Mrs. Rath that he and Ms Pickering wouldn't be returning for the day, they hustled on into the main corridor as students just leaving their last period class flowed past.

"I'll miss my students," Janelle said, her voice remote and sad, wondering if she had even made a positive difference in any of their lives, or had merely come and gone, like a small ripple across water, only to subside once more into stillness.

"You mean your fuck-buddy boy-toys, more like it."

She turned a venomous eye toward him. "Why you ever joined the teaching profession is beyond me," she bitterly said, as they moved into the thick crowd of rushing students, several of which called out in greeting. "But I will miss this place." For a moment she thought fleetingly of Andy Hupp, and for the first time felt a twinge of guilt for having lured him to the Halloween party–and his fate.

"Well, I won't," Meevers said, his jaw hard. "The paycheck, yes. The teen pussy, definitely. But nothing else. High school kids are mostly assholes, judging from professional experience. But then, so is the rest of society."

"You really must hate people, Budd. How do you live with yourself?"

"And how do you live with your own self, Janelle? You had a hand in burning Fitchins to death, or have you forgotten? Now you prey on teenage boys, then sell them into sex slavery the next day without batting an eyelash. Helped buy that nice Jaguar too, didn't it? What's more, how can you stomach your own lies, standing in front of your class five days a week preaching your social justice bilge. Lies about equality and brotherly love. All that tripe about the coming world of racial harmony? Did I ever tell you that your multicultural bullshit made me want to puke every time I happened to hear it? But that I let you do it because there was always the fear in the back of my mind that a feminist bitch like you just might turn on me if I didn't, and expose our involvement in the Fitchins murder."

"Maybe I should have," she shot back. "Gotten a plea bargain, served five or six years while you got life." She looked straight ahead, wishing now she had done exactly that. "After I got out, I could have moved on with my life forgetting that I had ever known anyone like you."

Turning down a side corridor leading to Ortega's gymnasium office, Budd Meevers made a decision then and there that somewhere along the way, as they flew over the vast, empty, vulture-haunted deserts of Mexico, Janelle was going to get "accidentally" shoved out the airplane on the way south to Guatemala. It would be days, weeks, months, or even years before her remains were found.

Then again, maybe never...

Ahead, they saw Ortega.

Standing just outside his office.

Stock still.

Not even noticing them.

Odd, Meevers thought.

Something.

Not.

Right.

In the next instant Ortega came into full view, and Meevers saw the handcuffs. Simultaneously, six dark-suited men sprang forth from concealment.

"FBI!" one of them yelled, flashing a badge. "Up against the wall!"

Janelle shrieked, turned, and ran helter-skelter down the corridor, even as several agents rushed up and seized Budd Meevers, slamming him against a bank of school lockers. As they did, Janelle Pickering frantically pushed her way through a wall of students, knocking three of them down as she twisted and squirmed like a cornered rat in her desperation to get away. But she too was seized, hysterical, shrieking, kicking and screaming like a wild animal as she struggled to break free, her hair flying, until she finally broke down in helpless sobs as handcuffs slapped cold steel across her wrists, her face crushed into the cold tile floor.

Nearby, face mashed sideways against a lime green locker, Principal Budd Meevers caught sight of a teenage boy out of the corner of his eye, looking straight at him. A boy with his arm in a sling, red scratches and purple bruises evident on his face, standing among a group of other students. A good-looking boy, Meevers distantly thought, with a fierce intelligence, a mop of golden-brown hair, and two all-seeing forest green eyes; a boy that reminded him of himself, long ago, before things took a different, darker turn, that night, sneaking through the backyard of Henry Fitchins house with matches and gasoline in hand.

And beside him, amid all the pandemonium, stood a beautiful blonde-haired girl, with eyes as clear and blue as a summer sky. Seeing them, Meevers felt the last bittersweet moments of his academic career fade into shades of gray–the gray of a coming life behind cold steel bars, set amid a twilight world of gibbering negro inmates, sudden shower stall rapes, and savage prison yard knifings.

A moment later, as Budd Meevers was ushered past the awestruck students of Titanis High by two FBI agents, he stared in newfound awe at Andy Hupp, knowing he would meet him one last time inside a courtroom. As he did, he finally realized, for the first time, just what kind of indomitable spirit he had always been up against.

Following after Budd Meevers, Janelle Pickering glanced one last time at Andy Hupp, stunned that he was still alive. As she gazed with almost fearful wonder upon him, her piranha teeth no longer flashed out their Social Justice Warrior superiority, but instead were hidden behind lips pinched tight in bitter lament, knowing in that instant that her former student knew she was headed for a place where the only sex she would ever know again would come from repulsive negro vaginas shoved endlessly into her horrified face, in one long, screaming nightmare of lesbian prison rape. Until, perhaps–like her brother before her–she met the same fate as he.

And finally came José Manuel Ortega, alone among the three holding his head high, proud of his criminal ascendancy. For there was a certain glory in it for him, Andy could see, which ultimately exposed the utter worthlessness of the mestizo race.

"One day, punk..." Ortega menacingly whispered, as he was led past Andy Hupp and on down the hallway. "One day..."

And then Meevers, Pickering, and Ortega were gone.

Beside Andy, Jinky turned and looked into his eye. "You've got a lot to be forgiven for," she solemnly said. "For Lyla... and everything you did with her."

Andy slowly nodded, and lowered his eyes.

"Well, I know one thing, buster," Jeena Kirtland assured, "that was the last fling you'll ever have. You got me, Andy Hupp? From this point on I'm the only naked girl you'll ever see again."

Raising his eyes again, Andy humbly smiled.

Properly chastised.

Oh boy, was he ever!

"I promise I'll never look at another girl, Jink," he said, taking her into his arms. And he meant it too, with all his heart–as they held each other, there in the hallway, in their last year of high school, standing on the threshold of the great wide world beyond, before it forever swallowed up these bittersweet times of their lives.

"I love you, Andy," she whispered, a sheen in her eyes threatening to become tears.

"I don't think you ever had a choice, Jeena," he tenderly said. "And neither did I. Because sometimes life just points us in the right direction and then steps back and let's us find our way."

"So what's this about us going down to Mexico next summer? After what happened to you down there?"

"I'll tell you later," he promised, thinking again of the satchel of cartel money he had taken from the crashed airplane and buried nearby, while Lyla huddled near the wreckage, banged up and in shock, but somehow alive after Andy crash landed the plane. Good ol' Ed Hartmann, he thought. Without his professional piloting skills instructing him how to bring the Aero Commander down–even though Andy did end up smashing the plane into an outcropping of rock and cacti, tearing off one wing before somersaulting end over end followed by an ear-shattering crash–he and Lyla would surely have died.

Now he might have enough money to launch his own independent film company after he and Jeena graduated from college, got married, and started a home, once he went back down and retrieved it. Maybe he'd take TJ along, and make him a partner in his new film company, along with the new Mrs. Hupp. Call it JAT Film Productions–after their three first names. But then Andy remembered: there would always be a fourth partner, even though that fourth partner had given his life that night the carload of MS-13 thugs had come up to Klimmen's Point and got out, guns in hand. Had it not been for that big, clumsy, but powerfully built kid that nobody liked and nobody understood pushing Jeena and TJ stumbling down the night-darkened hillside toward safety while he turned and faced them alone, none of them would've survived.

What's more, the mystery of Rodney's parents had finally been solved, according to Jeena, that night up on Klimmen's Point. As the three of them drank beer and brandy, Rodney came to tell them of a time years earlier, back in Mississippi, when he had gone out on his first date ever with a girl, riding in the back seat of his parents' car as the four of them headed for a movie–a movie from which they never returned–all save for Rodney. Carjacked by three negroes at an empty intersection while stopped at a red light, Rodney, his parents, and his thirteen year old girlfriend were taken at gunpoint to an abandoned farm house, where Rodney's parents were immediately shot to death. Terrified, Rodney was forced to watch as the first and only girl he had ever kissed was stripped naked and savagely raped, then stabbed to death in front of his eyes. When they finally came for him, he found some inner will to live and ran blindly into the night, even as gunshots cracked from behind.

When he was found the next morning by a truck driver, curled up in a ball by the side of the road, trembling uncontrollably, he was sent to live with his grandparents out in Texas—where his elderly grandfather Gibb Galloway, a former attack helicopter pilot during the Vietnam War, worked as a high school janitor. Himself emotionally damaged from the horrors he'd seen, he took thirteen year old Rodney under his wing; but sensitive to the viciousness of teenagers, had never let it be known of their kinship.

So now, Andy sadly thought, it all made sense...

In the most tragic of ways.

But then, life was often like that, he realized.

And perhaps, always would be.

People that should've lived a long and productive life suddenly flicker out like a wind-blown candle flame—and are gone. Rodney Crutchley had been such a candle flame, flickering brightly for a brief time in Andy's life. At least, that would be how he always remembered him—as someone who had a lot to give, far more than the cartel thugs who shot him in the chest then hacked him to death with machetes.

They would likely never be caught, Andy realized.

And the world, for better or worse, would simply go on.

All in all, it was a hard thing to accept for a seventeen year boy on the threshold of manhood. Even so, Andy Hupp knew he would never forget Rodney Crutchley. So, with that in mind, he made a decision then and there to christen their new independent movie company JART Film Productions.

"Andy?"

"Yeah, Jink?"

"You went all silent and brainiac on me just now."

"Lot on my mind," he said.

"Like what?"

"Like you."

And with those words, and those bittersweet but happy thoughts in mind, Andy Hupp took hold of Jeena Kirtland's hand and led her away through a cheering crowd of students. As he did, some anonymous voice yelled out, "There he goes, boys and girls! The kid who single-handedly took out two teachers and one principal in one fell swoop! So say it loud and say it proud: One Buck For A Suck Hupp does it...

Again!!!

THE END

If you enjoyed *Fast Times At Cultural Marxist High*, please leave a book review at www.amazon.com. Each one is very much appreciated. Such reviews also help in the positive promotion of white nationalist fiction, something this and other writers need if we are to remain motivated in this difficult and often vilified field.

And be sure to look for upcoming novels.

Sincerely,

Ward Kendall

**BE SURE TO ORDER ALL MY
NOVELS ON AMAZON.COM**

Made in the
USA
Middletown, DE